CW00449987

Yael Politis

THE LONELY TREE

Holland Park Press London

Published by Holland Park Press 2010

First Edition

A CIP catalogue record for this book is available from The British Library.

ISBN 978-1-907320-08-8

Cover designed by Reactive Graphics

Printed and bound in Great Britain by
CPI Antony Rowe, Chippenham and Eastbourne

www.hollandparkpress.co.uk

The real Lonely Tree was given its name by the first settlers in the Etzion Bloc and has since become a symbol for this area.

'She marched up the path, opened the lock on the front gate of the kibbutz to let herself out, and half-ran along the feeder road until she came to the fork where a majestic oak stood, the one that the settlers called the Lonely Tree.'

Tonia moves with her family from Poland to British Mandate Palestine, first to her uncle's small apartment in Tel Aviv and later to the kibbutz that her father Josef helped to establish.

Due to the hardships of life in the kibbutz and against the backdrop of what is happening in Nazi-occupied Europe, she longs for security and comfort.

Then she meets Amos, tall with ever so long legs and dark complexion, her 'Italian boy'. Both have their hearts set on different ideals, yet they are unmistakably drawn to each other.

They make an interesting pair. Amos is a handsome and exotic Yemenite who fights in the Jewish underground, to which Tonia's father is vehemently opposed. Despite their different backgrounds Tonia and Amos fall in love.

This budding romance is interrupted by the siege of Tonia's home, Kfar Etzion. The desperate fight is described very movingly in this fictionalized account of the siege and fall of the Etzion Bloc.

Afterward Tonia makes a great sacrifice in order to realize her dream. She moves to Grand Rapids, Michigan in the US, hoping her family will follow her. But is this where she belongs?

CHAPTER ONE

May 1946, Jerusalem, British Mandate Palestine

The day that Tonia Shulman first noticed Amos had begun as an ordinary one. When her tenth-grade Civics class – and the school day – finally ended she stretched and looked at her watch.

'Feel like going to Café Atara for coffee and cake?' Ilana Rozmann swiveled in her seat to face Tonia.

Tonia shook her head. 'Can't. No time.' She had heard that the gooey chocolate cake they served was delicious, but she had to catch her bus back to the kibbutz. Besides, she had no money.

Ilana shook her wavy blonde hair and ran the fingers of her right hand through it. 'My treat,' she offered.

Tonia felt her face flush as she stood up. 'No. Thanks, but I can't. Have to work today.' The last thing she wanted, today of all days, was Ilana Rozmann, or any of the Rozmann family, paying for anything else for her.

Ilana slid sideways from beneath the battered, ink-stained wooden desk. 'More fields to clear?' She raised her eyebrows and stared at the scrapes and cuts on Tonia's hands.

Tonia held her hands out, palms up, as if to ask, what can I do? Then she busied herself gathering books while Ilana swayed toward the door to join her friends. Bunch of spoiled rich kids, Tonia thought. Let them choke on it. She shrugged into the straps of her backpack and tied the sleeves of her frayed navy blue cardigan around her waist. She could see Ilana giggling with two other girls out in the hall. They all wore brightly colored shirtwaist dresses and white patent leather pumps. Tonia watched them for a moment and her resentment faded. What did she care? She was not ashamed of her faded blue skirt and scuffed work shoes. She wouldn't want to get a permanent wave or wear stupid nylon stockings if she had all the money in the world. That much she had inherited from her parents – a disdain

9

for fashion and the accumulation of material goods for their own sake.

Though Tonia had little in common with her classmates, she loved her new school. Thank God her father had agreed to allow her to switch from Miss Landau's school for religious girls to the prestigious Hebrew Gymnasium of Jerusalem. At Miss Landau's they still taught deportment; at the secular and co-ed Gymnasium Tonia was learning philosophy, economics, and physics. A diploma from Jerusalem's first modern high school would get her into a good university. That it was located in the snooty Rehavia neighborhood and mainly attended by the children of professors, doctors, and government officials was a minor annoyance.

Ilana stuck her head in the door and waved goodbye. Tonia smiled and waved back. Ilana was nice enough, Tonia reminded herself. Anyway, it wasn't her fault that Tonia had no choice but to accept her parents' charity.

Tonia descended the wide stone steps and strolled through the shady neighborhood with its elegant dress shops and flower vendors. As usual, downtown Jerusalem was deserted. Few cars passed, and the owners of many of the hole-in-the-wall shops had closed up for their afternoon nap. She window-shopped toward the Pillar Building on Jaffa Road to wait for the battered bus that would take her home to kibbutz Kfar Etzion, about a forty-minute drive south of Jerusalem. The long black bonnet of the bus soon nosed around the corner. It had high fenders and pop-eyed headlights on either side of its tall grill, and its side was covered with deep scratches and dents. Since yesterday, six of the seven windows on either side of it had been fitted with squares of plywood.

'Hey there, Tonia, how are you today?' The stocky driver – dressed in khaki shorts, sleeveless blue T-shirt, and sandals – left the engine running and the door open. 'Don't go anywhere without me,' he called over his shoulder and raced up the street. Tonia knew he would soon be back with a large bottle of seltzer.

She rapped her knuckles against one of the wooden shields before climbing onto the bus. With the windows covered, the empty bus was dark and airless. Tonia chose the seat halfway back, next to the still-uncovered window on the right side, where she would have enough light to read.

By now Ilana and her friends would be lounging around a table at the café. That's what they did after school, threw away their families' money. It never occurred to any of them to get a job. To work for anything. Tonia did not envy them their wealthy lifestyle, but was determined to one day attain the security that money could provide. She was prepared to work hard for it; no one would ever have to offer to pay her way again. She was going to be rich enough for her children to eat whatever they wanted, whenever they wanted it. For years, she had dreamed of boarding an airplane for New York and escaping this wretched not-even-a-country. Now she was fifteen and would soon be old enough to do just that, once she saved up some money. Her children were going to grow up somewhere they could feel safe.

'That's only so we don't suffocate,' the driver said when he came back and saw Tonia next to the unprotected window. 'No one's supposed to sit there.'

'At least until Bethlehem,' she begged.

The driver shrugged, took his seat, and put his head back to pour half the contents of the bottle of seltzer down his throat. Five more passengers boarded. Three women, members of Tonia's kibbutz, to whom she nodded, and two young men she did not recognize. She presumed they were Palmach boys, stationed in the kibbutz by the Haganah, the unofficial Jewish army. A bivouac of tents in Kfar Etzion housed a contingent of them, the isolation of the kibbutz allowing the Haganah to conduct illegal military training on its hillsides, far from the eyes of the British Mandate authorities.

'Is there anyone I should wait for?' the driver asked, turning around.

The passengers shook their heads, and he pulled out onto Jaffa Road. The thick pale walls of Jerusalem's Old City soon appeared on their left, majestic under their battlements. A chaos of pushcarts, donkeys, and camels mobbed the clearing outside the Jaffa Gate. Tonia craned her neck to watch the driver of a red delivery van try to maneuver past them, but the single bare window allowed her only a glimpse.

At least the sky was clear, and she wouldn't get drenched and muddy again. She was assigned to work in the orchards and had three hours of work ahead of her when she got back to the kibbutz. If only she could skip work, get in bed, and read, without having to squint in the flickering light of the old kerosene lantern or take her book to the dining hall. Of all the luxuries Ilana Rozmann took for granted, Tonia did envy that one – the electric light next to her bed.

When Tonia got her dream house in America, she would fill it with bright lights and never turn them off. And it would be some place where they had too much water. Some place where you could take a hot bath every evening. You could leave the faucet running all day if you wanted. She would have a room full of books with an enormous desk and a thick rug on the floor. And a huge wooden table in the kitchen, where friends and family would gather for uncomplicated, delicious food. Mrs. Rozmann's recipe for honey and garlic chicken. Grilled eggplant salad. Roasted potatoes. Almonds with tea after the meal. She would set the table simply, with white plates. Maybe a silver rim around the edge, but no fussy flower patterns. Tonia would sit at one end of that long table, the man who loved her at the other. The shadows of her fantasies cloaked his face, but she knew he was tall, slim, and had a warm smile. He would entertain the guests with his wit, but his eyes would always linger on Tonia.

She sighed and took out her copy of *Anna Karenina* in English. The bus soon jolted to a halt at the roadblock on the outskirts of Bethlehem, and an unfamiliar British police officer boarded. The regular policeman was friendly and usually waved them through. When he did stop the bus, it was to ask how things were or warn the driver about something he had heard. But this

12

one was a stranger to them, young and arrogant-looking, brandishing a nightstick, square jaw jutting high.

'Open that,' he ordered Tonia and poked the stick at her backpack, which lay on the seat beside her.

His rudeness angered her and she ignored him, looking down at *Anna Karenina* and pretending to read.

'This bus isn't going anywhere, Miss.' He almost smacked his lips on the 'M' of 'Miss' and bent down to bring his face closer to hers. 'Not until I've checked that none of you Jews are carrying illegal arms. So open the bag.'

She unzipped the bag and pushed it toward him.

He turned the backpack upside down and shook it, spilling everything out. Her schoolbooks, notebooks, and the books she had bought for her father, still wrapped in newspaper, fell on the seat and floor. 'Oops. So sorry about that. Now you can unwrap those packages.' He tapped her father's books.

Tonia rolled her eyes, did as she was told, and then gathered up her things while he searched the other passengers.

'Get those wooden panels off the windows,' the policeman barked at the driver. 'Against traffic regulations.'

'I didn't put them on, and I can't take them off,' the driver said. 'You'll have to lodge a complaint with the bus company.'

The policeman wrote a citation, muttering about bloody hooligans and terrorist thugs. He handed it to the driver and gave Tonia a nasty look before getting off the bus. Then they pulled away, going south toward Hebron.

'Tonia, get away from that open window now,' the driver said, eyes flitting between the road in front of him and the rearview mirror. 'Be a good girl and don't make me have to explain to your mother that I let you sit there.'

'I'll tell her it wasn't your fault.' She picked up *Anna Karenina*. At least the time she spent riding the bus should be hers, to do as she pleased.

The road ran over the crest of a range of hills that formed a watershed. To the east lay the Judean Desert – naked peaks of earth and rock, glorious in their desolation. On Tonia's right, the

13

rocky hillsides glistened green, and tangles of yellow wildflowers clung to them. These straggly flowers could not rival the brilliant patches of pink and white cyclamen and red, white, and purple anemones that had sprung up after the first winter rains and just as quickly disappeared again, but they still afforded a better view than plywood.

They were approaching Solomon's Pools, a water reservoir two miles south of Bethlehem, believed to have been dug during King Solomon's reign. The area looked like a picture book. Cultivated plots near the pools surrounded small homes. Vineyards spilled down the hillside.

They had just passed the large rectangular stone building called Nebi Daniel and the driver had to slow for a curve. Tonia glanced up and saw three figures – three young men with *kaffiyahs* wrapped around their faces – rise from behind the acacias that hugged the roadside. She watched in paralyzed fascination as they raised their arms and threw the rocks they gripped at the bus. In the same motion they bent to scoop up a second round.

The first barrage crashed into the bus with frightening force, making the vehicle seem to shake. One of the women in the back screamed, and the engine roared as the driver tried to accelerate, but then hit the brake. Tonia could not take her eyes off one of the Arabs. He seemed to be staring right at her as he let loose the large jagged rock that came flying through the unprotected window.

It missed her head but grazed the end of her nose, and she felt blinding pain. The rock smashed into the opposite side of the bus and fell to the floor. Tonia instinctively moved her hands toward her nose, but was afraid to touch it. It felt as if the rock had torn it from her face, but she looked down and saw only a small trickle of blood dripping onto her lap. It couldn't be that bad. She placed a finger on each side and, reassured that she still had both nostrils, let out a deep breath. The tip of her nose was bleeding, but she did not seem to be badly hurt.

The driver kept glancing at her in the mirror as he maneuvered on the tortuous road. 'Are you all right? Can you talk?'

14

'Yes. I'm okay. It's not so bad,' she said, resolved not to reveal how shaken she was. She wiped the blood on her sleeve.

He did not slow down until they had gone a few more miles, past the dilapidated village that stood high on a hill overlooking the highway and past the summer residence of the Mukhtar of Bethlehem. Meanwhile, the other passengers huddled around her and subjected her to a thorough inspection, clutching the overhead rack, as they were tossed from side to side by the motion of the bus.

'God in heaven, look how you're bleeding,' one of the women said.

'It's not so bad, I don't think, really,' Tonia said. Her body had begun to relax, fear replaced by exhaustion. She wished they would leave her alone. She would be home soon, and her mother would take care of her. 'Just tell me – what does it look like?'

The woman took Tonia's chin in one hand. 'It scraped off quite a chunk.'

One of the Palmach boys bent to pick up the heavy rock and fingered its sharp edges. 'Could have killed you,' he said and shook his head. 'Easily. No wonder that bloody copper wanted the plywood off the windows. Bet the bastard knew. Good thing you opened the window. Broken glass could have blinded you.' He set the rock down on the seat beside her. 'Hang on to that. Good story for your grandchildren. You can see your blood on it.'

When the driver stopped, the Palmach boy went to the front for the first aid kit and cleaned the wound for her. She winced as he doused it in purple iodine and felt ridiculous when he taped a piece of gauze to the end of her nose. 'Looks like it might leave a scar,' he said, 'but only a small one.'

The driver started up again.

'Come, lie down in the back.' One of the women tried to take hold of Tonia's arm. 'Until you can collect yourself.'

'I'm all right,' Tonia said.

'The shock of these things sometimes takes a few minutes to set in,' the woman said. 'That thing almost hit you in the head.'

'But it didn't. It only scraped my nose.' Tonia shrugged her shoulders and shook her head. She could not stand people fussing over close calls. Didn't they know that life was one long narrow escape?

The other passengers finally retreated to their seats.

'One more centimeter and she'd have been a goner,' Tonia heard the woman say.

'That girl has nerves of steel,' the Palmach boy added, shaking his head.

'Of course,' one of the other women pronounced, 'a person should have better sense than to sit there in the first place, especially after the driver asked them not to. Some people always have to do things their own way. There's no talking to them.'

The driver caught Tonia's eye in the mirror and winked. She raised her hands in surrender, tossed the rock out the window, and held tightly onto the seat in front of her while she moved around to sit there. She opened her book again and squinted, but could not read in the dark. It occurred to her that now she probably wouldn't have to go to work. That was almost worth a few millimeters of nose. Finally, they turned off the Jerusalem-Hebron road, up the feeder road, and arrived at the kibbutz.

That was the first time she saw him – when she got off the bus by the gate of Kfar Etzion. He was working with the group of Palmach boys who seemed to spend every waking hour digging new outposts along the perimeter fence. He swung a pickaxe with steady strokes, and, though the air was cool, sweat poured off the taut brown muscles of his bare back. He straightened, stretched, turned to take a cigarette from the boy beside him, and grinned at something he said.

Tonia ignored the pain and tore the gauze from her face. How ridiculous she must look, her nose all purple. She stuffed the bloody bandage in her pocket and pretended to fuss with her backpack, but she couldn't take her eyes off him. He was tall and lean. Long brown legs stretched from khaki shorts to thick blue socks rolled down over work boots. She flushed, her gaze drawn

16

to the backside of those shorts and down those legs. No suntan was that even, and his complexion was so dark that she would later lie in bed and think of him as 'that Italian boy'. The yarmulke that clung to his thick black hair seemed out of place. How could a religious person exude such a physical presence? Maybe he wore it to be polite, since Kfar Etzion was a religious kibbutz. In profile, she could see his strong jaw line. No need for him to grow a pious beard. Tonia always suspected that most of the men who had them were camouflaging the lack of a proper chin.

Then he turned and noticed her. He was not handsome but striking, large heavily lashed green eyes above hollow cheeks. He stared straight at her, and his face spread into an easy smile, both friendly and challenging. Her eyes caught his for a long moment, and she felt something inside her turn warm and liquid. Then he threw down his cigarette, ground it out, and wiped his hands on his shorts. He bent to pick his shirt off the ground and started walking toward her. He was going to come and talk to her. She felt her face turn red, as she clutched her packages and fled. So much for her nerves of steel.

CHAPTER TWO

Tonia's parents, Leah and Josef Shulman, sat at a small table
under the oak tree outside their room, having afternoon tea and
a slice of Leah's famous apple strudel. Their three children had
joined them, as they did most afternoons. They sat on wooden
folding chairs that partly blocked the path, balancing their teacups and cake plates on their laps. Tonia had already assured her
mother that she had been to see the doctor, and the missing tip
of her nose was no cause for concern. Now Josef rose and paced
as he fretted over the precarious finances of the kibbutz. He was
a tall man with a mop of sandy hair and a beard that was already
graying. Tonia got her dark hair and eyes from her mother.

'Leah'le,' he began. His intonation was pleading, but his
stance and gestures said he had already made up his mind. 'We
still have your mother's jewelry and the gold watch and chain.
And that pouch of gold coins. They must be worth something.'

Leah's usually soft eyes blazed. 'What are you getting at,
Josef?'

'Leah'le ...' He knelt at her side, a humble supplicant.
'How can we, how could anyone who understands the significance of Jewish settlement in Palestine, let personal greed stand
between—'

'You can't be serious.'

Tonia exchanged glances with her brother and sister. They
had heard their mother fume behind closed doors, but their parents did not argue in front of them. Certainly not outside like
this, where anyone who passed by would hear.

'But Leah—'

'No, I won't hear of it. Those things are all we have left.
I won't hear of it. Think of your own children for once.'

'Think of the children?' Josef said and got to his feet. 'Who
do you think I am thinking of? Whose future are we building here?' He turned and looked at them all. 'What do you

think a few grubby coins can buy them of greater value than a homeland? A place to live without fear?'

'The homeland will rise or fall without my mother's jewelry. Next thing I know, you'll be after my wedding ring or Bubeh's candlesticks.'

'The candlesticks! I forgot about them. They must be worth a small fortune.'

'Josef ...' Leah paled. Her husband knelt back down and took her hand in both of his.

'All right, Leah, all right,' he said softly. 'Not the candlesticks. I understand. But tomorrow the rest of it goes to the kibbutz secretariat.'

Leah attempted another feeble protest, but he sat down and launched into a lecture on Jewish history, socialism, Zionism, and the role of the individual in the course of human endeavor. Leah leaned back, and Tonia watched her mother's resolve drain away. Stand up to him, she wanted to shout, why can't you just stand up to him for once?

Tonia could not bear it. What she had discovered about Mrs. Rozmann in school that morning had been bad enough. Now, after the attack on the bus, she couldn't stand any more. She sat still, lips a tight line, digging her fingernails into the arms of the chair. Then she rose and uttered a loud, 'No!'

Too late, she realized that her timing could not have been worse – at just that moment, a group of young men came around the curve of the path, and her outburst drew their curious stares. The Italian boy was one of them, and there she stood, with her nose still purple, shouting at her father. No wonder she hated this place – they lived on top of one another, everyone heard everything, saw everything, knew everything.

'Abba, you can't do that,' Tonia said. 'You have no right. Those things belong to all of us, not just you. And not to your kibbutz.'

Tonia looked around at her family, waiting for someone to back her up. Her sister Rina was a lost cause, as big a fanatic as their father. But she was sure her mother and her brother Natan felt as she did. She was painfully aware that the Italian boy had paused at the fork in the path and was standing there, watching her performance. She lowered her voice, but could not stop. This was too important.

Josef stared at her, mouth open. Leah watched the two of them with an impassive expression, but Tonia thought she saw a glimmer of satisfaction in her mother's eyes. Natan turned his face away in sad consternation. Rina stared wide-eyed at her.

'No right?' Josef leaned forward in his chair. 'I have no right? Am I no longer the head of this family? Responsible for its future? I have not only the right, but a duty–'

'You don't even care if we want to be here. You never asked any of us. Not even Ima. We should have a choice, and that money–'

'Enough!' His face turned from white to red. 'When you are old enough you can–'

'When you were my age–'

'I said enough! This discussion is over. First thing tomorrow morning, I'm taking the jewelry and the coins to the secretariat. I will decide what is in the best interests of this family.'

'You always do. Decide, at least. I don't know about best interests,' Tonia said and stomped off, relieved to see that the Italian boy had disappeared.

She marched up the path, opened the lock on the front gate of the kibbutz to let herself out, and half-ran along the feeder road until she came to the fork where a majestic oak stood, the one that the settlers called the Lonely Tree. She knew it was not safe to be outside the fence alone, but sometimes she had to get away from her father, escape the barbed-wire confines of the prison to which he had sentenced them. At least out here she didn't have to stifle her sobs. She sat with her back pressed into a fold of the tree trunk, elbows on knees, fists pressed into her eyes. She was trapped here, no way out. They were all going to die. Why couldn't he see that? He would be furious if he found out she had gone outside the fence again. So if he knew how dangerous that was, how did he think they could live in this place? And her mother. What kind of a mother agreed to bring her children to a place like this?

After a while, she looked up at the orange sun hanging low in the sky and let the cool breeze calm her. They would never understand. They were stuck in a way of thinking that would never change – not until it was too late for all of them. She would turn sixteen in eight months. Old enough to get a job without his permission. Then there was no way he could make her stay here. She'd have to swallow her pride and move in with the fancy-pants Rozmanns. After she finished high school she could get a real job, typing or something, until she saved enough money for an airplane ticket. This was not her life. Not this kibbutz and not this not-even-a-country. She would leave first, but her family would follow, eventually. They'd see that she had been right all along and thank her, once Abba got it into his head that there was never going to be a Jewish state.

The sun sank lower, and she reminded herself that she had to get back before dark.

Suddenly she heard footfalls crunch in the unpaved road behind her. She started to rise, was already on her knees turning around, and then looked up and froze. She saw a gray-haired Arab man standing not five meters from her. He wore baggy white pants, a white shirt, a long gray vest, and a white *kaffiyah*. Her heart pounded, and she had to struggle to catch her breath. She looked around, but there was no one else in sight. He remained still, made no move toward her. Tonia got to her feet and wiped her hands on her pants. Her panic subsided enough for her to look at his face. Wasn't this Tabet, or was his name Tahel, from Beit Umar? Hadn't he been a guest at the party to celebrate the dedication of Kfar Etzion's new dining hall?

They continued to stare at one another for what seemed a long time.

'*Es salaam aleikum.*' Tonia stumbled through the only words in Arabic she knew.

'*Wa aleikum es salaam,*' he responded and then asked in Hebrew, 'Are you not the daughter of Youseff?'

21

Tonia nodded.

'Not good that you are out here.' He raised his hands, palms up, and looked around. 'If the *shabab* see you ...'

'I know. I'm going home.'

'I take you.'

'That's all right. I'll be fine.'

He held up a hand. 'Yousseff is my friend. You are in my protection. No one will harm you.'

They walked in silence. Tonia could think of nothing to say to him. What kind of conversation was she going to start? Please don't tell my father you saw me out here? Thank you for not killing me?

When they reached the gate of the kibbutz, she said, 'Thank you very much. Tabet, is it?'

'Yes, I am Tabet. Your father is a very good man. Don't go outside the fence again,' he said and continued toward his village.

When it was dark and she knew her parents would be in the dining hall having their evening meal, Tonia stole into their room, knelt down on the floor by the large wicker basket in the far corner, and lifted its lid. She had not lit the kerosene lamp, and her hands searched in the dark through worn linens and clothing. Finally, she found the two black velvet bags her mother had jealously guarded for years. Tonia slipped them into the potato sacking she had taken from the kitchen and got to her feet.

Her grandmother's ornate silver candlesticks stood on the table by the window, and the glint of moonlight on them caught her eye. No. That would be going too far. Anyway, her father had promised. But Tonia hesitated for only a moment before adding them to her collection of treasures, just in case.

There was no place to hide anything in the room she shared with her nosy sister, so she went to the tool-shed for a shovel.

The night air was cold, but she pulled off her raggedy blue sweater and tossed it aside. She was perspiring, both from the physical exertion of carving a hole into the rocky hillside and from the anxiety of defying her father. She wiped her hands on her khaki pants and reached back to tug two handfuls of hair in opposite directions, tightening the rubber band around her ponytail. Then she picked up the shovel and continued digging, a few meters inside the perimeter fence, not far from the front gate.

The small wooden crate at her feet held the potato sack of valuables. She hated doing this, but what choice did she have? Her mother would always succumb to the onslaught of charm and energy with which Josef Shulman overwhelmed anyone or anything that stood in his path. Someone had to stand up to him. If he had his way this time, he would leave them destitute.

The shovel clanked against a rock, and Tonia peered into the black of the moonless night, half-expecting the men on guard duty to come running, weapons raised. She had heard stories about members of other kibbutzim who had wandered too far from the living compound – their comrades had mistaken them for intruders and shot them.

She set the shovel down and attempted to put the box into the ground, but removed it from the hole again with a sigh. She would have to dig deeper. She wondered if she had wrapped the precious items well enough to protect them from the damp earth, but dismissed that concern – they wouldn't be underground that long. When she left Kfar Etzion, she would dig them up and take them with her, save them for her mother.

How could he consider selling it all to buy more saplings, more feed for the animals, and more illegal weapons for the British to confiscate? No one – not even the nutcase Communists who ran this place, who thought Moses had forgotten to chisel in the Eleventh Commandment, 'Thou shalt have no private property' – had ever suggested that members donate their families' Shabbat candlesticks to the common treasury. Only her father was that big a fanatic.

Everyone knew that five Arab armies were getting ready to invade the minute the British pulled out. Why should they die on this barren hillside, defending an indefensible position, in a war they could not win? One day, when it was all over, he would thank her for salvaging this pittance. Her foresight would provide her family with some means of support.

She squeezed her eyes shut for a moment, dreading the confrontation that must come when her father discovered what she had done. Her thoughts wandered to the story from the Book of Genesis – Rachel on her camel, sitting on the household gods with which she was absconding and lying to her father, Laban, claiming that she did not know where they were. Had the commentators approved of her actions? No. Rachel may have had lofty intentions – preventing the perpetuation of Laban's idolatry – but she had been punished for defying her father.

Beads of sweat formed on Tonia's forehead, and she wiped them away. Nonsense. 'Honor thy father' can't mean that a child is supposed to stand aside and do nothing while a parent destroys himself and his family. And Abba had been defying *his* father when he dragged them from Poland to this place.

She stopped digging and tried again. At last, the hole gaped deep enough. Tonia pressed the crate down into the ground, shoveled the displaced earth over it, stomped it down, and kicked the excess soil and rocks away.

Then a loud scraping sound pierced the silence, and she froze. A few meters from where she stood a tiny burst of fire appeared and quickly receded into the flame of a match. Someone seated on a large, flat boulder lit a cigarette. In the fleeting halo of light, she recognized the features of the Italian boy. He flicked the match away, and took a long drag on his cigarette. Though his features were no longer illuminated, she knew he was grinning.

'I guess you're always going to get your own way,' he said. 'When you want it bad enough.'

Tonia dropped the shovel and fled from him again.

The dreaded confrontation with her father never came. Neither Leah nor Josef asked Tonia about the missing items. The next day was Friday, and Rina, Natan, and Tonia gathered in their parents' room for Sabbath Eve candle-lighting. A pair of squat brass candlesticks stood on the table, two small bright beacons that they all pretended not to notice. Leah placed candles in them, pulled her blue silk scarf over her hair, held a match to the wicks, and covered her eyes to say the blessing.

Tonia imagined she could hear the grinding of her father's teeth, but he said nothing. Natan and Rina exchanged questioning looks, but neither asked what had happened to the silver candlesticks. Leah always embraced her children after welcoming the Sabbath and wished them each 'Gut Shabbes'. Tonia thought the hug she received from her mother that week was especially warm.

When Tonia returned to her room after dinner, she found something hanging from the door handle – the old blue sweater she had left lying on the ground by the gate. Whoever had put it there had woven a sprig of jasmine through the holes in its front.

CHAPTER THREE

Tonia was barely four years old in 1934 when her parents packed up wooden boxes and wicker baskets and traveled from Poland to Vienna, to Trieste, to Alexandria. From there they took the train to Cantara. She remembered clutching a cloth doll with black buttons for eyes and long thick strands of orange yarn for hair. The rest of her memories of that time were a confusion of actual recollections, contents of letters she had read, and frequently retold family stories.

The Shulmans bounced in the back of a donkey cart that delivered them to a sun-baked street in the seaside town of Tel Aviv. It stopped in front of a three-story block of flats built on stilts and encased in dingy gray stucco. Josef helped the driver pile their belongings in the street.

'Leah, you take the children up. I'll stay and watch our things,' Josef said. 'Send Natan back down after he's had something to drink.'

The three exhausted and quarrelsome children straggled up three flights of stairs behind their mother. A short, bearded man in a sleeveless white undershirt, gray pants, and red suspenders opened the door. An even shorter woman with patches of scalp showing through her thinning hair looked over his shoulder.

'Hello, I'm Leah–'

'Come in, come in.' The woman nudged her husband aside and pulled Leah through the door into the small entry hall. 'You must be so tired, after such a trip. Come, come, sit, I'll get you something to drink.'

'Rina, Natan, Tonia ...' Leah turned and lightly tapped each of their heads. 'This is Uncle Shmuel and Aunt Rivka. They've been kind enough to invite us to stay with them for a while.'

'Kind, *shmind*,' Aunt Rivka said as she herded them inside. 'You're family. Where is your Josef?'

'Downstairs, waiting for Natan to come back down and keep an eye on our things while he starts carrying them up.'

Uncle Shmuel moved toward the stairs. 'No need for that, I'll give him a hand.'

The tiny flat reflected white from every surface. White-tiled floors. Whitewashed walls. Windows bare of curtains. They could barely fit into the small entry hall, which was already crowded with a table and chairs.

Aunt Rivka maneuvered them into the living room. It held a simple wood-frame sofa and two matching chairs, their flat cushions covered in dull brown fabric. A low coffee table stood before the couch and an enormous bookcase covered the wall next to it. Aunt Rivka left them there while she went to the kitchen. She returned with a tray of not-quite-warm bourrekas, sliced tomatoes sprinkled with chopped parsley, and a bottle of seltzer water.

'We'll have a real dinner later,' she said as she moved chairs from the hallway into the living room to accommodate all of them. She pulled her own chair close to where Leah sat on the couch, anxious to hear about her relatives in Poland.

Tonia backed out of the living room to peek through the other doorways. There was only one bedroom, so where were they supposed to sleep? Wasn't there a little bed, like the one she had at home? Where was she going to put her special pillow with the flowers? She didn't want to stay with these old people. Aunt Rivka was scary, with her sparse red-tinted hair and the big bump growing on her forehead, and Uncle Shmuel smelled funny. When she heard Uncle Shmuel coming up the stairs she fled back to the living room and climbed into her Ima's lap.

'When are we going home?' she asked, interrupting Aunt Rivka.

Ima gave Tonia a hug while she explained that this was their home now, but she sounded so tired and strained, as if she was making an enormous effort not to lose her temper, that Tonia didn't dare to ask any more questions.

Abba and Uncle Shmuel each made several trips up the stairs. By the time they finished, they had buried the table and every centimeter of floor space in the front hall.

'It won't all be staying here,' Ima said. 'A lot of that is for the kibbutz, and we brought some things to sell.'

'Yes, we're sorry about the mess,' Abba apologized. 'And to be putting you out like this.'

Aunt Rivka leaned forward to glance through the doorway, looking a bit dismayed, but put a brave hand on Ima's arm. 'Don't worry, don't worry. Once you've unpacked, it won't look like so much. We didn't think three children came in a pillbox. Maybe we don't have so much room, but we'll manage,' she said. 'What's important is that you're here. With these beautiful girls of yours.' Aunt Rivka managed to reach out and pinch Rina's cheek, but Tonia hid her face in Ima's lap. 'And this handsome young man.' She beamed at Natan, who leaned back in his chair, avoiding her touch.

Then the room grew silent and Aunt Rivka rose. 'I'll start getting supper. You must be famished. Oh, but first let me show you where you can freshen up. We have indoor plumbing,' she said proudly.

Ima offered to help with the meal, but Aunt Rivka wouldn't hear of it. 'You need a good rest after such a long trip.'

Abba and Ima sat side by side on the couch, hands in their laps, too exhausted to speak. Tonia sank to the floor and lay face down on the cool tiles, resting her forehead on the backs of her hands, trying not to cry. She had never seen her bossy father so quiet. Maybe that was good, she thought. Maybe he was busy figuring out how to take them back home. She peeked at her brother and sister. Rina and Natan had left their chairs and sat cross-legged on the floor, patiently waiting for the grown-ups to tell them what to do. Why were they so quiet? she wondered. Why weren't they crying? Didn't they see how awful it was here?

Uncle Shmuel wiped his brow, crumpled his large white handkerchief back into his pocket, and stood in front of Natan, making funny faces and snapping his red suspenders.

'I don't want to stay here,' Tonia complained later, while Ima was putting them to sleep on two layers of quilts on the living-room floor.

'It won't be for long. Some of our friends from the Community of Abraham are already here and more will come soon, and then we'll go live on a new kibbutz.' Ima stroked Tonia's hair and kissed her forehead.

'Abraham from the Torah?' Tonia asked, imagining a bearded man in flowing white robes, leading his flocks from Poland to the Promised Land. In her mind Abba's strange friends skipped along behind the goats, singing and carrying hoes over their shoulders.

'No, I've told you before, we named our group of pioneers after Rabbi Kook. Rabbi Abraham Itzhak Hacohen Kook. He's a great Rabbi and believes that all the Jews from all over the world will come to live here in Eretz Israel.'

'What's pioneers?'

Ima thought for a moment. 'People who are the first to do something. Who clear the way for others.'

'What're we gonna clean up?'

'Not clean ... I meant make a new way. We'll get some land and grow things on it. Build houses on it. And make a new kind of community, where everyone is equal. Where no one is poor or rich.'

'Then how can we ever get rich?' Natan asked.

Tonia later heard Ima repeat this question to Abba, and they both laughed. She didn't understand why. She thought her brother had asked a perfectly good question.

By the time Tonia woke the next morning, Abba was standing by the door with his backpack on, ready to go out looking for work.

'No,' Tonia protested loudly. She clutched his leg, shouting, 'No, no,' and began crying.

Abba bent to pick her up. 'Don't worry, I'm not going far. Just to a work camp where they'll give me a job. Maybe picking oranges or helping build a road. Wouldn't you like me to bring you some nice juicy oranges?'

'No. No oranges. Home. I want Baffy.' She had never cared much for Baffy, the small fluffy dog Rina had adopted in Poland, but now she claimed to miss her terribly. Tears ran down her cheeks, but she didn't resist when Ima pulled her from Abba's arms.

Leah was left behind to manage with the children on her own. During the months and years to come, she never complained, never blamed Josef for the hardships of her life. As she grew older Tonia thought her mother looked at her father the way a mother contemplates an adored, gifted child with whom she cannot cope. Only Tonia blamed him. Seldom out loud, but in her heart constantly. Why aren't you ever home? Why does Ima have to work so hard, up on the roof doing other people's disgusting laundry? Can't you see how tired she is? Why can't you be like other fathers? They don't go away.

On the rare nights that her father came back to share a roof with his family, he was wrapped up in the kibbutz they would establish, the new social order they would help create, the new Jew about to be born. Late at night Tonia often heard him declare that he worshipped the ground beneath Leah's delicate feet. So why, she wondered, did he lose interest in his wife and children after about five minutes?

When more members of the Community of Abraham arrived in Palestine, they gathered in a camp farther south, outside the city of Rehovot. They shared it with another group of young people who were preparing themselves for their new lives, learning how to farm. Later that year more of the group came from Poland, and Josef went to live with them in the training camp. After that, his family saw even less of him – Leah and the children remained with Uncle Shmuel and Aunt Rivka in Tel Aviv.

'Why don't we go live with Abba?' Tonia constantly asked Ima.

'I told you. It's not a place for children. They're living in tents.'

Tonia's eyes lit up. 'I want to live in a tent.'

'Anyway, we couldn't go now, even if we wanted to. Some of the other people in the community don't think that we belong with them. They are all much younger and don't have children yet,' Ima answered while she brushed Tonia's hair.

'So what?'

'So there's no place for children to live where they are now. And a brand new kibbutz might not be able to cope with children. Not at first anyway. There will be only simple rooms to live in, and no children's houses. And there won't be a school, or any of the other things that children need.'

'So why is Abba there?'

'He's trying to convince them. He says that no matter where the kibbutz ends up, there will have to be a school somewhere nearby. So then there won't be any reason that we can't go with them.'

Tonia frowned, considering everything Ima had said. 'What're children's houses?' she asked.

'Special houses where all the children live together.'

'Without their Ima?' Tonia asked, horrified.

'Don't worry,' Ima gave her a hug. 'The children go see their parents every day, after the grown-ups are done working. They have a few special hours just to be together. No one's busy with cooking or cleaning or laundry - all that time is just for their children. Then the children go back to the children's houses to sleep. It will be great fun, you'll see. Like having a sleepover with your friends every night.'

Silent tears ran down Tonia's face as she contemplated the prospect of the horrible life her Ima was describing.

Only once did Ima take her and Rina and Natan to visit the temporary lodgings of the Community of Abraham, and that was on a day when it was pouring rain. Suddenly Uncle Shmuel's tiny flat didn't look so bad, compared to the sea of mud that swamped the tents in Rehovot. At least in Tel Aviv she could make pee-pee without having to pick her way to the disgusting latrines in freezing rain, over a trail of slippery rocks and slats of wood. She was on her way there late that night when she overheard the voices of two men in one of the tents. They were talking about Abba. She had never been so wet and cold, but stopped to listen.

'That Shulman won't give up. I don't see why the man refuses to face simple facts. There's no way we can take three kids that age.'

'What's he going to do? What would you do in his shoes? Because the man has a family, he's going to give up his ideals?'

'So what, you think we should accept them?'

'I think we should wait and see. Let the Jewish Agency offer us a location. Maybe some kind of an arrangement can be worked out. You have to admit, he contributes more than his share.'

'He puts in a good day's work. We all do that.'

'And then give a Torah lesson every week? And volunteer for extra duty in the dining hall? And be the first to fill in whenever someone else is sick? You have to admit, the man is a phenomenon.'

'And what about that middle-class wife of his? She'll never fit in.'

The other man sighed. 'Yes, I think you can count on her to solve the problem. I can't quite see her fitting in. Not much of a kibbutznik.'

You're mean ... you can't talk about my Ima like that, Tonia wanted to shout. My Ima would be a better kibbutznik than any of you stupid people. At the same time, however, she was praying with all her heart that Abba and Ima would never, ever, ever take her to live in a terrible place like this.

Shortly afterward the Community of Abraham – and Josef – moved north to Kfar Pines. They settled into yet another training camp, more tents, still temporary, but more permanently temporary. It was even farther away than Rehovot, and letters remained their main form of contact. Leah read many of his aloud at the dinner table. 'The bigger the obstacles in our path, the stronger our determination and devotion to our cause.' The letters all sounded the same to Tonia, and she barely listened. But Leah had no friends to talk to and discussed their contents at length with her young children. She was visibly distressed that the Jewish Agency seemed to have abandoned the small group of pioneers to cope on their own. Using their own resources, they had cleared a plot of land, put up a small building, and planted a vegetable garden. But they received no financial help and depended on whatever they earned as day laborers in the neighboring orange groves and construction sites. Finally, Josef wrote that the Jewish Agency had granted them their first loan, enough to put up a building.

Leah smiled widely when she read that letter to them. 'You see, children, it will be all right. They take us seriously. Official agencies don't throw good money away.'

Josef returned to Tel Aviv only when there was no work available near Kfar Pines. Then he'd turn up on Uncle Shmuel's doorstep bearing a basket of vegetables or eggs or brandishing a scrawny chicken by its feet.

The 'little while' that they were supposed to stay with Uncle Shmuel and Aunt Rivka stretched into several years. The Jewish Agency was in no hurry to allocate land to the Community of Abraham. Sleeping on blankets on the living-room floor came to seem normal to Tonia. Their clothes remained in the stack of boxes beside the couch. Tonia didn't mind. She liked school and spent her afternoons jumping rope and playing Five Stones with the girls who lived downstairs. She had stopped worrying that one day her father might come and whisk them off to a kibbutz. That was a fairy tale her parents enjoyed telling.

Tonia was in the second grade in the fall of 1938 when news from Europe began to overshadow their lives. The grown-ups huddled around the radio every evening, speaking in hushed tones. The announcer droned on. Jews can't do this. Jews can't do that.

Leah always turned the volume down when the children were in the apartment, but when Josef was home he insisted they listen. The strange names and places had nothing to do

33

with Tonia. The news did not frighten her; but she resented the amount of attention the grown-ups lavished on the radio. She often felt like taking a hammer and smashing it to bits.

Then one chilly afternoon Uncle Shmuel came up to the roof where Ima was stirring a tub of laundry. Tonia sprawled nearby doing her homework, but sat up when she saw the letter in his hand. The arrival of mail was always cause for excitement, so why was Uncle Shmuel chewing on his bottom lip like that?

'Leah, this came for you.' He held out the thin envelope. 'It's from Over There.'

Ima set down her long wooden paddle, dried her hands on her apron, took the letter, and opened it. The color left her face as she read.

'Tonia, go downstairs with Uncle Shmuel,' she said. 'I have to go to the chemist's and phone Abba.'

Ima seemed too upset to notice that Tonia hadn't obeyed her. She doused the fire under the tub of laundry and hurried down the stairs, without bothering to duck into the flat to arrange her disheveled hair and take off her apron. Tonia had never seen Ima go out in public looking so untidy and followed her down the stairs.

'I'm coming with you,' Tonia said, running to keep up. 'What's wrong? What happened?'

'My Aunt Celia. The Germans, may their name and memory be blotted out, deported her and my Uncle Stephan. Threw them over the border like trash.'

'What's deported?' she asked, but Ima wasn't paying any attention to her.

When they reached the chemist's, Ima asked to break in front of the three other people waiting in line to use the telephone. That was very strange, Ima had never done that, it wasn't polite. People often quarreled about such requests, but Ima looked so frantic that all three stepped aside and the man using the phone cut his conversation short. Ima gave the operator the number for Kfar Pines and tapped her foot.

34

'I need to leave an urgent message for Josef Shulman,' Ima said. 'What? He's there in the office? Oh, thank God, please call him to the phone.' Ima's foot stopped tapping, and Tonia saw a familiar expression of relief wash over Ima's face. She knew what her mother was thinking. Josef knows people. Josef will make everything all right.

Ima's eyes lit up when Abba came to the phone. 'Josef, a letter arrived from my Aunt Celia ... Yes, the one who moved to Hanover when I was a child. They must have lived there twenty years, she and her husband have German citizenship, perfectly legal, but the filthy Nazis have expelled them, just dumped them on the Polish border. You have to go to those people you know at the Jewish Agency, find out how we can contact the Red Cross, how we can send them–' Ima stopped to listen for a moment, then held up the envelope to study the postmark and reread the contents of the letter.

'She didn't mail the letter until October 21st, but it happened before, on the 18th. Men from the Gestapo pounded on their door, said they had to leave early the next morning. One suitcase, nothing else. They couldn't even get to the bank to take out money. The next morning the men came back with dogs and bayonets.' Ima's voice sounded strange, and she began mumbling, 'Good Lord, they must be in their seventies by now, dogs and bayonets–' Ima paused again to listen to Abba.

'They're at a Polish border station called Zbaszyn. They have nothing, no money, no food, nowhere to go. They are sleeping in a stable.' Ima glanced up at the calendar on the chemist's wall, squares of paper to be ripped off, day by day. 'It's been almost three weeks, we have to–' Ima paused again. 'Yes, Josef, all right.'

Ima hung up, thanked the people for allowing her to make the call, and asked the chemist for quantities of aspirin, iodine, and cough syrup. Then Tonia traipsed along with her to the grocer's, where Ima asked the man behind the counter for bars of chocolate, packages of dried milk and eggs, and tins of sardines, beans, vegetables, and peaches. When they turned to leave, Ima asked the owner if she could take one of the empty cartons stacked out on the sidewalk.

'Thank you for coming with me, Tonia,' Ima said, calm and determined. 'I couldn't have carried it all alone. You can help me pack a box to send them.'

Tonia couldn't believe her ears. Ima had bought all those things to send Over There, after she was always saying they didn't have any money for toys or new clothes. She never bought them chocolate or tins of sweet peaches. But Tonia watched Ima nervously and didn't dare complain.

When they got home, Ima began going through their belongings, looking for warm socks, sweaters, hats, and gloves to pack with the food and medicine. The sad-looking box with nowhere to go stood in the living room for days. Ima went to the chemist's every few hours to ask if there had been a message from Abba. On the fourth day, Abba appeared at the door, cap in hand, looking sad and very tired. He tossed a newspaper onto the end table, then put a hand on Ima's shoulder and gently guided her to the couch.

'They're both dead,' he said in Yiddish. Her parents spoke only Hebrew at home and thought of Yiddish as their secret language, but Tonia understood what Abba said. 'A man from the Jewish Agency found them on a list of the dead that he got from a Red Cross representative. The Red Cross got their names from one of their neighbors, who was expelled together with them. The neighbor found them in the morning, lying in some hay. There was an empty chemist's vial in her purse. He thinks that perhaps ...'

Ima clutched his forearm, but she didn't cry. She looked more angry than sad.

'There's an article in there about the Polish Jews being expelled.' Abba nodded at the newspaper he had brought with him. 'Says that the Germans dumped about 12,000 people at that station. Nobody knows how many of them have already died.'

'And the bodies?'

Abba lifted both hands, palms up. 'Presumably the Poles took them away. The paper doesn't say anything about that. And

36

we won't be getting any more newspapers. It was on the radio – the Germans have closed down the Jewish press.'

'I used to spend my summer vacations with Aunt Celia and Uncle Stephan,' Ima said softly. 'Aunt Celia made me paper dolls. She drew them herself, on the sheets of cardboard that the laundry put in Uncle Stephan's shirts–'

The door to the flat opened and slammed. Uncle Shmuel came in, pale and out of breath. 'Turn on the radio!' No one asked why.

'… but we are getting similar reports from all over Germany,' the announcer said. 'Mobs breaking into the synagogues, hacking the furniture to kindling, dousing everything with petrol, and burning them to the ground. The police stand by watching, do nothing to prevent even the beating of Jewish men. If the police do take any action, it's to arrest Jews and load them onto trucks.'

Uncle Shmuel switched to another station – that announcer was describing a mob that had pulled the terrified children in a Jewish orphanage out of their beds and taken axes to the furniture.

Ima let out a short cry and put her hands to her cheeks. She looked at her three children, and Tonia knew she was going to tell them to go into the bedroom and shut the door. But Abba batted his hand in the air. 'No. Let them listen,' he said. 'This is the world we live in.'

Every radio station in the world seemed to be broadcasting from Berlin.

'They aren't even ashamed of what they're doing.' Abba shook his head. 'All the newspapers have sent reporters to watch and write about it, and they don't care.'

On another station, a foreign diplomat told a reporter in English, 'Early this morning we found a young woman wandering in the street outside our home. She was in a daze, still in her nightgown. We brought her inside and managed to calm her down, so she could tell us what happened. She and her husband were in bed – it was still dark – when they heard their front door being smashed open. A gang of men burst in, swinging axes at everything in sight. They threw the china out of the cupboards, broke the piano to splinters, ripped pages out of books, and poured wine and jams on the carpets. When her husband went down and tried to save their wedding album, they dragged him back upstairs and threw him off the porch. She called for an ambulance, but when the driver saw it was a Jewish home, he turned around. She ran up the street to get their doctor, but they had broken into his house too and thrown him onto a truck. By the time she stumbled back home, her husband was dead.'

'Thank God neither of us has any more family in Germany,' Ima whispered.

Abba stood up and switched the radio off. 'At least, they've finally hit bottom. It can't get any worse than this. There will be an outcry. The German people won't stand for what these criminals are making of their country.'

Tonia didn't understand why they were so upset. They didn't know anyone else in Germany. When they listened to the radio Tonia always felt a vague sense of guilt, as if she may have done something wrong. She hated the stories on the radio, the way they described the Jews. They said the Jews were frightened, scurrying, terrified, helpless, hopeless, begging. It was nothing to do with Tonia. Her family wasn't anything like that.

CHAPTER FOUR

Josef had again been gone for a long while, and then there was a knock on the door late one evening. Rina went to open the latch and shouted, 'It's Abba.'

Tonia and Natan had been on their knees for hours, laboring over the 'more than 1000 pieces' of the new jigsaw puzzle Aunt Rivka had bought for them. All afternoon and evening, they had squealed in protest if anyone dared step on a single piece, but now they jumped up and stampeded over it, racing one another to the door. They had to wait for their father to finish swinging Rina around before they could clamp their arms around him, one on each side.

'What a wonderful surprise!' Leah came out to the front hall, hands arranging her hair. Her eyes lingered on the suitcase that stood behind him.

'I'll be here for a while.' He put his arms around his wife and kissed her. 'Lord, you smell good.' He took an exaggeratedly deep breath and smiled before he turned solemn. 'Most of the men have had to leave Kfar Pines.'

'Why? What's wrong?' Tonia asked, but was ignored as Uncle Shmuel and Aunt Rivka emerged from their room to greet him.

'I'm afraid it's going to be even more crowded for a while,' Josef said to them.

'Does a sardine notice if you shove one more in the can?' Uncle Shmuel shook Josef's hand and slapped his shoulder.

Josef picked up his bag and moved toward the living room, but had to stop to pry Tonia from his leg.

'Let him go,' Rina scolded her. 'He can't even walk. What a big baby you are.'

Josef bent to pick Tonia up, and she stuck her tongue out at Rina over his shoulder. 'Heaviest baby I've ever lugged around.' He threw her over his shoulder like a sack of flour. 'How old are you now? Five? Six? Seven?' he teased.

'Nine. I'm nine,' Tonia shouted.

Aunt Rivka made tea, and after they settled themselves in the living room, Leah asked him what had happened.

'Hitler happened. Since he invaded Poland, no one can get any supplies, everything's shutting down. There are no jobs at all.'

'Well, at least we'll have you here with us.'

Abba went out early the next morning to look for work, but returned in the late afternoon. Tonia followed him up to the roof where Ima was stirring a pot of laundry.

'Let me do that.' Abba tried to take the wooden paddle from her.

'No, this is my job. You'll find something, Josef, don't worry, you always do.'

'You might as well let me help while I can.'

'No, I'm used to it. You'll get me spoiled and then disappear again.' Ima's tone was light, not critical, and she was smiling.

'Then I guess there's nothing for me to do,' Abba said and turned, eyes wide, 'but eat one of these good-for-nothing children you keep around here.' He growled and stomped, raised his hands like bear paws, and Tonia squealed as he chased her around the roof.

But that evening when her parents announced that they were going out for a walk, Tonia was surprised to find herself wishing that her Abba hadn't come home.

Ima usually spent half an hour with each of them at bedtime. Tonia loved the peace of that quiet time, while Ima brushed her hair and listened to everything she said, as if there were only the two of them in the room. She had been waiting all day to read Ima the story she had written for school, but that night they had to put themselves to bed, and the next morning Ima didn't even get up when she was supposed to. By the time she did drag herself out of bed, they had made their own sandwiches and were ready to leave.

'Have a good day at school,' Ima murmured, barely looking at them.

One Sabbath morning Abba returned from the synagogue and lay on the couch, his head in Ima's lap. Rina was in the chair, reading a book. Tonia and Natan sat on the floor, playing Concentration. Aunt Rivka and Uncle Shmuel had gone to visit friends.

'I've made your life miserable, haven't I, Leah'le?' Abba asked softly.

The children froze and exchanged glances, not wanting to miss a single word of Ima's response.

'Don't talk nonsense.' Ima stroked his forehead.

'Believe me, I know how you've suffered. I know it's you who has the worst of it, holding the family together on your own.' Abba sat up. 'But things will get better. The British aren't monsters; they have to open the doors to Jewish immigration now. Our families will come to join us soon.'

'And if the British still don't let them in, Josef?'

'Don't be ridiculous. The world won't stand for it. Millions will come.' Abba rose and paced the few meters of the room not taken up by his three children, his eyes brilliant.

Ima's anxious eyes followed him, and Tonia recognized the look on her face, frightened to hear more bad news.

'I'm going to go back to Kfar Pines, Leah. We have to keep some men there to keep things going. You understand, don't you?'

'Yes, Josef, I understand.' Ima exhaled with relief. 'Thank God. I thought you were going to tell me that you've enlisted in the British army and are off to single-handedly defeat Hitler's armies.'

'British army, me? I'm no soldier. I'll settle for fighting to keep the plough behind the mule.'

Why don't you demand more? Tonia wanted to shout at Ima. Maybe if he stayed here, we could get a flat of our own, live like a normal family. And what was wrong with Abba? Now that he had been there with them for a while, he had seen how hard Ima worked. Three days a week up on the roof, sweating over boiling pots of the neighbors' laundry. Every night, squinting in the lamplight, mending other people's clothes and knitting sweaters for them. Don't you care? Have you ever wondered how she must feel, having to live with your relatives? And what about me? Your own daughter doesn't even have a bed.

Abba interrupted her thoughts, suddenly turning and clapping his hands. '*Kinder*! Listen. Tomorrow you're getting up early. We have places to see before I go back. Tonight as soon as the Sabbath ends we'll get packed and Rina, you'll be in charge of checking the schedule for the earliest bus to Beer Sheva. You'll all need your good walking shoes. We'll get off part way there and hike to the Ela Valley. They say the hills are smothered with wild flowers since it rained. Natan, you're–'

'But Josef, what about school?' Ima objected.

'Priorities, my dear wife, priorities. This is more important. Natan, bring that book you have, the one that shows the different kinds of trees and wildflowers. And your Scriptures. We'll find the exact place where David let Goliath have it.' Abba smacked the heel of his hand against the center of his forehead.

Tonia was excited, already planning what to put in her small backpack. The hikes Abba took them on were exhausting, but exhilarating. There would be a campfire and stories. A pancake breakfast at sunrise. When Abba made time for them, he didn't give his usual boring lectures. He actually let them talk.

'I'll pack up the pup tents–'

'You plan to stay overnight?' Ima asked.

'Sure, if we're already there, we might as well go see the caves in Beit Guvrin the next day. But first the Ela Valley.' He rose and plucked a volume of the Scriptures off the shelf.

'Josef–'

'I promise, Leah'le, trust me, the sun will continue to rise in the morning, even if they miss two days of school.'

'That's not what I was going to say … I think … I think that perhaps this time I would like to come along with you.'

Four heads turned to Ima in stunned silence. It took a moment for them to begin clapping their hands and for Abba's face to break into a grin.

'That's wonderful, Leah'le. You know you'll have to wear some decent shoes, no high heels.'

'I have the ones I work in, with rubber soles.'

'And trousers. We might do a bit of climbing.'

'Uncle Shmuel's would fit you,' Rina said, jumping up. 'He's small.'

'All right, that's settled then.' Abba lightly slapped Ima's thigh, beaming like a child who has received a long-coveted gift. 'Now which one of you brilliant scholars knows anything about Goliath?' He returned his attention to the book in his lap.

'I do,' Natan said. 'He wanted to have a fight – him against one of the Children of Israel.'

'Why did he want to do that?'

'Instead of having a whole big war,' Rina said. 'If Goliath won, the Children of Israel would be slaves of the Philistines, and if Israel won, the Philistines would be their slaves.'

'Sounds like a sensible fellow, this Goliath,' Abba said. 'But I've always wondered, it says here that after Goliath lost all the Philistines ran away, and David had to go chasing after them. So what about their agreement? All those Philistines were supposed to come over and say, "Okay, we lost, here we are, slaves at your service".'

'I'd run away too,' Tonia said, 'if it was me.'

'Yeah, you would. You'd start a whole 'nother war,' Rina said and stuck her tongue out.

'Okay, we'll get back to the wisdom of trusting your enemies later,' Abba said. 'Let's talk about David. If he was the one that went out to fight Goliath, he must have been the biggest, toughest guy the Children of Israel had on their side.'

'No, he was little,' Rina said. 'Really young and little, with curly hair and pink cheeks. Goliath made fun of David when he said he was the one who was going to fight.'

'So how did he win?' Abba raised his eyebrows.

'Because God was on his side,' Rina said.

Abba nodded and looked thoughtful. 'Okay, *kinder*, it's time we all had a good *schlafstunde*. We'll need all the energy we can get tomorrow.' He closed the book. 'But while you're falling asleep, I want you to think about two things. First is a question.' He held up a finger. 'Do you think that whenever someone wins a fight, it means that God is on their side? Second, there is an important lesson for us to learn from David. Remember how King Saul took off his armor and tried to put it on David, but David wasn't having any part of it?'

They all nodded.

'That was because David was a clever chap. He might not have been a righteous man, but he was usually right. Smart. He knew how to take a disadvantage and turn it into an advantage. He thought, "Look at that Goliath, the way he can hardly budge with all that heavy stuff all over him. Maybe he's bigger and stronger than me, but I'm light on my feet, and I'm going to stay that way, be able to move around, get wherever I need to take aim."' Abba rose and mimicked David with a few quick feints, before he started moving furniture aside so they could all lie down for a nap. 'And that's the second thing I want you to think about. Nowadays, we Jews have a lot of problems – no money, no weapons, almost no experience in fighting, surrounded by a sea of Arabs. I bet you can think of a lot more. But,' Abba said, wagging his forefinger at them, 'I bet if you put your minds to it, you can think of a way to turn at least one of those weaknesses to our advantage.'

They spent two wonderful days together before he left them again. Abba carried the tents, food, and water in a huge pack. Ima tramped along at his side, looking young again, wildflowers woven through her hair. They all sang at the top of their lungs. Tonia and Rina did not quarrel, even collapsed in giggles when their tent caved in on them in the middle of the night.

So Tonia got over being angry with her father for a while, not sure that she would really want him to be more like her friends' boring fathers. But she was still certain that their lives were abnormal – even by the abnormal standards of life in Palestine under the British Mandate.

CHAPTER FIVE

Tonia came in from playing and found her mother slumped on the couch in gathering darkness, staring at the silent radio, her face gray.

'What's the matter, Ima?' Don't go away, Tonia wanted to shout. Lately her mother often withdrew into herself, hiding behind a blank face. Tonia could not bear being shut out, but neither did she want to crawl into that dark space with Ima. What she wanted was to have Ima back, the way she used to be. Why does she have to listen to that stupid radio all the time? Those things are all so far away, what's the point of worrying about them? Anyway, what's the big deal? So they are sending Jews to work camps. Abba goes to work camps all the time.

'It's nothing, sweetie.' Ima shook herself. 'Did you have a good time?'

'Why do you look so sad?'

'Grown-up stuff.' Ima rose and went to the window. 'Did you see Natan and Rina outside? It's time for them to come in and wash up.'

'Abba says we should know the truth, that we live in the world too,' Tonia insisted, though she couldn't have said why. She did not really want to know, did not care about the world. Abba had always brought too much of the world barging into their home, until there hardly seemed to be space left for them. Still, something made her keep pressing her mother.

Ima sighed, sat back down, and pulled her onto her lap. 'I'm worried about my family. And Abba's.'

'In Poland?' Tonia managed to keep the resentment out of her voice.

I should feel sad too, Tonia scolded herself. She's so worried about her family. Her parents. I should feel just as bad. They are my grandparents. No wonder Ima doesn't love me so much any more. There must be something wrong with me. But why should I care about people I don't even know?

'Yes. Except they said on the radio that it's not even called Poland any more. Germany has taken over all the towns where my parents and my brothers and sisters live.'

'Kolo?' Tonia was showing off. See, I am not such a bad daughter, I remember the strange name of the town where you grew up. Where we were born.

'Yes. They live in Kolo and some other towns near it.'

'Abba's parents live in Kolo too.'

'Yes, that's right, they do. And his brother Daniel. That's where I met Abba.' Ima hugged her and continued. 'Our families went to the same synagogue. The first time I ever saw Abba was on his Shabbat Bar Mitzvah. His voice had already changed, and he read the Torah portion so beautifully. I told my sister Chava that I was going to marry him someday, and that was before I had seen anything but the back of his head. After he turned around, I told her I was going to marry him right away.'

Tonia giggled, glad to be back in the sunlight of their own lives, and waited for more details of her parents' courtship and marriage.

'But now all of those towns are in Nazi Germany, and the Germans, may their name and memory be blotted out, are going to Germanize them.'

Tonia looked up blankly.

'That means they are going to make all the Poles and Jews move away, so they can give their houses to Germans. Just like they did to Aunt Celia and Uncle Stephan.'

'Where will they move to?'

'I don't know. I suppose somewhere else in Poland.'

'Maybe they'll come here,' Tonia suggested. That was the one thing that could put an end to all the fuss. If those people came to Palestine, then Ima wouldn't spend so much time sitting around looking sad and waiting for letters. Tonia frowned, imagining dozens of strange relatives crowded into the apartment, speaking Yiddish and dressed in funny clothes, like the pictures in the newspapers.

46

'I wish they could, sweetheart,' Ima said. 'But the British aren't giving out many Certificates and won't give any to Jews from Germany.'

'But you said they're the ones who need them the most.'

'I know, but according to British laws, anyone who lives in Germany is an enemy alien.' Ima sighed again. 'It's been so long since I've had word from anyone. Not since Aunt Celia and Uncle Stephan died. No one answers any of my letters.'

Leah devoted most of the next few weeks to chasing after scraps of news. She phoned and wrote to organizations that still kept offices in Poland, begging for help. She mailed stacks of letters, not only to each of their relatives, but also to the addresses adjacent to theirs, in hope that the neighbors might know something. In each, she clearly printed Uncle Shmuel's address and the phone number of the chemist. She sent off large boxes of food and medicines, with no way of knowing if any of them reached their intended destinations. She haunted the post office, waiting for a reply from Over There. None came.

Tonia tagged along with her, offering whatever help she could, growing accustomed to having a mother who was permanently distraught. She began to dread her father's visits, hating the way her parents shut themselves up in Aunt Rivka and Uncle Shmuel's bedroom and came out looking ill. Even on the brightest, sunniest day their lives were cloaked in gloom. She could not remember the last time she had heard Ima laugh, and she was sick of hearing about the big black hole Over There.

One day she let it out. Ima was in the kitchen, speaking with Aunt Rivka in the familiar low tones. Tonia stood in the doorway, trying to get her mother's attention. Finally, she shouted, '*We're* right here. We're your family. Don't you care about us any more, just because we're not in a ghetto or a work camp?'

Ima froze. Aunt Rivka shook her head and mumbled something, but Ima seemed incapable of responding. She stood and stared until Tonia turned and went back to the living room, where she angrily threw herself down on the couch. Natan and

Rina were on the floor doing homework and pretended not to have heard her outburst. Living in such close quarters, selective deafness was an art they had all mastered. After what seemed like a long time, Ima sat down next to her and pulled her into her arms. 'Of course, I love you,' she said. 'You are the most precious things in the world to me. And don't you ever talk like that – about you being in a ghetto or a work camp. Never, ever say those words.'

Late that afternoon Leah came out of the shower smelling of bath powder, the one luxury she allowed herself, and announced that it had been far too long since they had all gone for a nice walk together. She pinned her hair up, put on her best blouse – shiny pink with white buttons – chose one of her plain dark skirts, and pulled on high-laced shoes.

'Shouldn't you save a nice blouse like that for a special occasion?' Aunt Rivka asked.

'Any time I have to spend with my children is an occasion,' Leah replied with her old warm smile. 'Who is more special to me than them?'

She led them along Hayarkon Street, on the seaside. A fiery sunset blazed over the steel-gray Mediterranean. Rina had their father's energy and ran rings around them, her mane of strawberry blonde hair wild in the wind. Natan stayed at their mother's side. He was a beautiful boy, with his father's height and sandy hair and Leah's reserve. All the looks in the family wasted on the boy, Josef liked to tease. Tonia lagged behind.

Ima chatted, repeating stories her mother had told her when she was a little girl, about Polish princes and thieves. But when she stopped to gaze out over the horizon of sky and sea, her face dissolved. Tonia had never seen anyone look so sad.

When they returned home, Ima sat with them on their bed of quilts and told stories of parents and children having adventures together.

Tonia imagined all those happy families living in houses like the one in the picture she had stuck to the wall above the couch. She had cut it out of a glossy magazine that morning, a white

Cape Cod nestled under shade trees, its front windows spilling red and blue flowers. She knew how it looked inside. Lots of soft furniture and carpets, walls lined with bookcases, a fireplace in every room, nooks and crannies where children played hide and seek. That was what a home was supposed to be like. Not this cold, white apartment, with nothing but hard surfaces.

While Ima was brushing Rina's hair before they went to bed that night, Aunt Rivka shuffled into the living room, armed with her dust rag. Aunt Rivka leaned over, hand out, as if intending to rip the picture from the wall, and Tonia shrieked. 'No! That's mine. That's my house. Just like the one I'm going to have. You leave it alone.'

Ima stared at her for moment, and then raised her eyebrows at Aunt Rivka in silent appeal. Aunt Rivka retreated, mumbling that it was a big fuss about nothing.

'What are you making such a big deal about a stupid picture for?' Rina asked.

'It's my picture. And don't you touch it either.'

'All right, Tonia, that's enough commotion,' Ima said and reassured her, 'No one is going to take your picture.'

She didn't care how silly they thought she was being, she wasn't going to give up her daydreams about that house. A mother who lived in a house like that would not lie alone on somebody else's couch at night, stifling sobs, the way Ima did almost every night.

The war dragged on, and the insidious Over There was no longer so far away. It crept relentlessly toward them. One afternoon, during Tonia's first week in fifth grade, a series of blasts rocked Tel Aviv. When the noise stopped, teachers and pupils ran outside and saw columns of black smoke rising over the white buildings of the Nordiya neighborhood.

Tonia sighed with relief. The sky over their neighborhood was clear. She frowned, thinking for a moment of all the places her mother could be – the grocer, the post office, the chemist. None was in the direction of the dark billows of destruction.

The teachers assumed that Arab terrorists had set off the explosions and herded the children back inside. Hours later, the principal came into Tonia's classroom and gave them permission to go home.

'It wasn't Arabs; it was airplanes. Bombs dropped by Italian planes. There are more than a hundred dead and God knows how many wounded,' the principal said to the teacher and turned to leave.

'Italians? What did we do to the Italians?' Tonia asked, but received no reply.

Tonia went to the sixth-grade room and found Natan at his desk reading, though his class had also been dismissed. 'Come on, let's go see.' She tugged at his arm.

'Go see what?'

'Where the bombs fell.'

'Ima won't let us.'

'I didn't say let's go ask her. We'll go see on the way home. She doesn't know we got let out early.'

He hesitated a moment. 'Should we go get Rina?'

'Rina? Forget it. She'll tell.'

She pulled him along toward the residential area that had been hit, where they joined the large crowd of people that stood outside the police cordon. Three agitated men were arguing with a group of uniformed police officers, demanding to be allowed near their building.

'The bodies are being taken away for identification,' the youngest of the police officers told them. 'See that man over there by the ambulance, the one in the red sweater. He'll take your names and the names of people you think might have been in the buildings. He can give you more information. He has a list of the injured taken to hospital.' He turned and waved his arm at Tonia and Natan. 'You kids get out of here.'

The modest one-story homes had been demolished. The guts of the taller buildings spilled to the ground, meeting in a pile of rubble in the middle of the street. Rescue teams worked feverishly, maneuvering around the damaged cars and wagons that blocked the road. A few meters from Tonia and Natan lay a dead horse, reddish brown, with a white throat and dark brown mane. It was still hitched to an upended cart, its hind legs missing. A glassy eye stared up at Tonia.

She stood there for a long while, frowning, her mind refusing to digest the fact that children were going to come home that day and find their parents gone, bodies to be identified. She looked up at the clear skies and understood that the airplanes could come back any time they felt like it. Adults behind her were complaining. It was bad enough that there were no anti-aircraft guns; at least the air-raid sirens should have worked. But there had been no warning. No warning at all.

'I mean it. You kids get out of here.' The police officer shooed them again. 'This is no place for you.'

This time Tonia let Natan drag her home. She stayed at her mother's side for the rest of that day.

The following summer Tonia saw the Vichy French planes that showered Tel Aviv with bombs. She and Rina were playing in the sand on the beach when they heard the drone of the engines and looked up.

'There!' Rina pointed and then slapped both hands to her cheeks.

They watched in silent dread. The bombs seemed to come sailing down; it took them so long to hit. The sisters grabbed one another's hands and raced for home. They had left their sandals behind, but were oblivious to the searing hot asphalt and the pebbles that cut into their bare feet. They could see from a distance that their block was untouched. The nearest fire was at least half a kilometer away. When they turned the corner, they saw Ima out in the street, shrieking, 'Rina, Tonia! Tonia, Rina!'

'Ima, Ima, we're here,' Tonia shouted as they ran up to her.

They clung to one another, all of them crying.

'Is Natan home?' Rina asked.

'Yes, he's upstairs. So are Aunt Rivka and Uncle Shmuel.'

Later Tonia learned that one of her playmates from down-stairs had been out shopping with her mother when they were struck and killed in the street. Tonia refused to go down to their apartment to pay a *shiva* call and did not play with the dead girl's sister any more after that. She didn't bother asking what they had ever done to the French. She had begun to wonder the opposite – if there was anyone left in the world who didn't want to kill them.

Not long after the bombing, the mailman delivered a clean white envelope addressed to Josef, postmarked Geneva. Inside was another envelope, tattered and dirty, from a return address in Bugaj, Poland. Leah left the second envelope sealed, as she expected Josef home the next day. She glanced nervously at it each time she passed the table where it lay, a viper coiled to strike. Josef arrived late the next morning and opened it with great care, having heard that sometimes people Over There had no paper and wrote on the inside of the envelope. It held two stained invoices for shipments to a textile factory. The backs of both were black with cramped writing, in Yiddish. Josef squinted and haltingly read each word aloud.

> Dear Mr. Josef Shulman, I write to you believing you to be the son of Sonia (Kaplinsky) and Berl Shulman of Kolo. This letter is from Fania Brodsky, born in Babiak –

Leah gasped. 'I think I know her. They lived next door to Chava.' Josef continued reading.

> – born in Babiak, August 25, 1875 to Isaac and Freda (Solchek) Ginsburg and married to Henryk Brodsky, also of Babiak. Your letter miraculously followed your parents here to the ghetto in Bugaj, so maybe a second miracle will bring mine back to you. A man here named Yaschke Hafetz (of Kowak) works outside of the ghetto and one of his German guards says he knows a businessman who travels to Switzerland and promises to take letters

and mail them. Of course, this Nazi saint wants much money, but I can buy nothing better with my last worthless zlotys than the hope that my message reaches you. It is a terrible letter, and I beg your forgiveness for each word I must write, but I believe one of the few comforts left to us is to know the truth. In October 1940, your parents and your brother Daniel and his wife were driven from their homes in Kolo to this ghetto in Bugaj. The same happened to Henryk and me and every other Jew left in Babiak and to those in many other towns. We were the lucky ones. Before this, many hundreds of Jews were taken away and disappeared. No one knows what happened to them. In the ghetto, me and my Henryk shared a two-room flat with your parents. Your father of blessed memory was beaten to death by an S.S. devil while on a work detail. Yaschke was working next to him and saw this with his own eyes. The reason for his murder was that he coughed. Dear Berl suffered terribly with pneumonia. Yaschke said the first blow was very hard, so your father's death was quick. Your mother of pure soul succumbed to typhus within weeks. I believe she left this life with desire for nothing but to be reunited with your father. After this, your brother Daniel told me that he and his wife had decided to leave the ghetto. I don't know how they planned to do this. He said they were going to escape with six friends. I heard rumors that a group of young Jews trying to escape were all shot, but I know of no eyewitness to this. Your parents were wonderful people and spoke proudly of you every day. It was their one consolation, knowing that you and your family are safe in Palestine. We were not blessed with children and I beg you to preserve the memory of my beloved husband (the son of Otto and Ida Brodsky). My dear Henryk suffered from a heart condition. In this place there is no medicine and he died in the night. I could not bury him, only ask the neighbors to take him down to the street where I sat with him until the men with the pushcart came to collect bodies. There are always bodies. They shoot people every day. I don't know why. In this place there is no why. They kill us as you swat a fly. My prayer is to join my Henryk quickly. I believe it was a mercy that your parents left this world when they did. It becomes worse here every day. You will live and tell the truth of this place. God bless you.

Josef put the letter down and said nothing for a long time. Leah wiped tears away and put her arms about him.

'I was always jealous,' he said in a monotone, staring out the window, 'that I didn't have a big family like yours, so many brothers and sisters and all those cousins that are like more brothers and sisters. Now I am grateful.' He gently removed Leah's arms and rose. 'I am going out,' he said softly.

After the door closed behind him, Leah picked up the letter and read it again. Then she put it down and sobbed. Rina stood by her side and patted her shoulder.

'My parents lived in Kolo, too,' Leah said and hugged Rina. 'So did my brothers and sisters. Except for Chava and Alexander. Chava moved to Babiak when she got married, and Alexander got a job not far away, in a town called Dabic.'

It was late that night when Tonia heard her father come back in.

The next day Josef went to the morning service at the synagogue to say the Mourner's Kaddish for his parents and Henryk Brodsky. When he came back, he and Leah each drank several cups of coffee while they sat at the table writing out several copies of Fania's letter, so it would never be lost. Then they spent hours composing a reply to her. They made and mailed three copies of it, one to the address in Geneva, one care of the Red Cross, and one care of the Judenrat, Bugaj Ghetto. They never received a reply, but every week until the end of the war, Leah mailed a package to the Red Cross, addressed to Fania Brodsky in the Bugaj Ghetto.

The following days Josef sat on a cushion on the floor. Leah covered the mirrors, and men from the neighborhood came in to make a *minyan* for prayers. He had consulted with the Rabbi. Since a great deal of time had passed since the death of his parents, he would sit *shiva* for three days, rather than the customary seven.

CHAPTER SIX

At the beginning of the sixth grade, Tonia's teacher hung up a large paper map of the Middle East. Thick black lines marked borders, against a white background. Little green dots shaded the tiny Jewish *yishuv*. A sea of red dots – Arab territory – engulfed it. By the end of the school year, the teacher had cut out pieces of colored cardboard to paste over it, blue showing the Vichy French in Syria and purple for the Germans in Libya. Ominous thick black cardboard arrows showed them progressing toward Tel Aviv.

Tonia started having nightmares about a fierce-looking giant named Rommel, roaring across the desert toward them, at the head of a column of invincible German tanks.

When Tonia went down to throw out the trash one evening, she saw Rina standing on the other side of the street, whispering with Shai, one of the older neighborhood boys. She had just opened her mouth to shout 'Rina has a boyfriend!' when Shai pointed at her. She tossed the garbage in the bin and skipped over to join them.

'She's too little,' Rina said. 'My mother would kill me if we got caught.'

'So we won't get caught.'

'Won't get caught doing what?' Tonia asked.

'Putting–'

'Shut up, Shai.' Rina poked his arm. 'I told you, she's too young. They think *I'm* too young.'

'She can go last; all she has to do is smooth them out. Even if they catch her, she won't be carrying anything, so what's the big deal?'

'If who catches me?' Tonia asked loudly.

'Shhh,' Rina hushed her. 'You're going to get us in trouble.'

'If you don't tell me, I'll go tell that there's something to tell.'

'I told you, she's a little brat,' Rina said.

'You wouldn't really tell, would you?' Shai said. 'You don't look like a *shtinker* to me.'

'I'm not a *shtinker*, I was just saying that. You can ask Rina. I've never told on her for anything,' Tonia said. Not that she cared what Shai thought about her. The other young girls seemed to think he was good-looking with his wavy blond hair, but Tonia thought he was stuck-up and in love with himself.

Rina conceded that she had never been a tattletale.

'We've got to get somebody,' Shai said. 'Elboim is sick, and the stuff is already waiting.'

That evening Tonia went to work for the Haganah, the underground Jewish army, something she found very exciting. She was going to help Shai and Rina plaster the surrounding neighborhoods with the notices they put up in lieu of a newspaper. Once a week someone left a note underneath a rock outside Shai's building. It told him where he would find a can, a brush, a list of locations, and a roll of posters. This time they had been hidden behind the garbage bin.

'Any car on the street at night is most likely British,' Rina warned her. 'So if you see headlights, duck into the nearest building. Go up two flights. If anyone comes in after you, turn around and pretend to be on your way down.'

'What do they do to you if they catch you?' Tonia asked.

'Nothing too terrible. Sometimes they hit the guys – you know, slap them – trying to make them tell who gave them the posters. That's why Shai gets a note like that, so we won't *know* where the posters came from. But I never heard of them hitting a girl. And they're not going to hit someone like you, only eleven years old, so don't worry.'

'Is that all?'

'Well, sometimes they drive kids far away and let them out of the car in the middle of nowhere.'

'Together?'

'Yeah.'

'Okay. I can do that,' she said and hugged her sister. This was exciting. Once in a while Rina turned out to be all right.

As soon as it grew dark, the three of them set out. Shai went first. He carried the brush and the can, in which he had mixed up a paste of flour and water. He stopped, slopped a large circle of paste on the telephone pole at the corner of Allenby and Pinsker, and ran off. Rina was close enough behind him to be able to see where he had put the paste, but far enough away to be able to flee in a different direction if she had to. She had the most dangerous job, carrying the roll of incriminating posters under her arm. She ran ahead, peeled one off the roll, slapped it onto the wet circle of paste, and then continued running. Tonia's job was to follow behind Rina and smooth the paper out, making sure it stuck. She was supposed to look like an innocent passerby who had done nothing but stop to read it.

When Tonia saw where Shai had slapped the paste for the next one, she got angry. She put her thumb and forefinger in either side of her mouth and let out a blast, imitating what Rina thought was her secret whistle. Shai ducked into a building, and Tonia did exactly what they had warned her not to do – she followed him. When she caught up with him, she began to scold.

'You put it right on top of an Irgun poster,' she said, out of breath, referring to another underground Jewish organization that was more militant than the Haganah.

'That's what we're supposed to do, stupid,' he said.

'What's the matter?' Rina came up behind them.

'Your bratty little sister has to learn to do as she's told.'

'He covered up the Irgun poster,' she said, turning toward Rina. 'That's not right.'

'You know what Abba says about them. They're a bunch of criminals.'

'Don't you think they cover up our posters?' Shai sneered.

'Well, it's not right. Everyone in the whole world is ganging up on us. We should at least stick together.'

'Look, stupid–'

'Stop calling my sister stupid,' Rina shouted, and Tonia looked at her sister, surprised to have Rina stand up for her.

'Put ours beside theirs,' Tonia said. 'I bet a lot of people want to read both.'

'And we don't want them reading Irgun trash,' Shai said.

'It's supposed to be like a newspaper. People have a right to read whatever newspaper they want.'

'Why do you care so much?' Rina asked her quietly.

'Don't you remember how sad Ima got when Hitler closed all the Jewish newspapers? She said that's the real end of freedom. And I don't know why Abba hates the Irgun so much. Don't they bring boats full of Jews here?'

'Yes, but–'

'So how do you know it won't be an Irgun boat that brings Ima's family to Palestine?'

Rina smiled and smoothed Tonia's hair the way Ima often did, and Shai conceded. Tonia enjoyed the rest of that clandestine evening, her one disappointment being that no British soldiers turned up to chase after them.

One evening Abba arrived home for a visit looking haggard. He barely mumbled hello to them.

'Leah, come.' He nodded toward the bedroom.

He shut the door behind them, and Tonia pressed her ear against it. Rina did not scold herwas not reproachful, as she normally would have been; she watched Tonia, keeping very still, anxious to find out what was so wrong.

'Leah,' Abba began, his voice breaking. 'I … I don't know how to tell … there have been reports …'

'Just say it, Josef. Please.'

He took a deep breath. 'It's not … I don't know anything specific about any of your family. But the rumors – about death camps – they've been confirmed.'

'How?' Ima's voice was steady.

'After the British arrested the Templars for hanging up Nazi flags,' Abba said, referring to a sect of German Christians who had settled in Palestine, 'negotiations began, to trade them for our community leaders, people who were sent to Poland before the war. Some of them arrived home a few weeks ago. They were in Poland for years. In the ghettoes. And they've spoken to eyewitnesses.'

'Eyewitnesses?'

'People who escaped – from the trains and the camps. People who saw. I read one of the reports. Last February a man escaped from a place called Chelmno. Not far from Kolo. About six kilometers.' Abba paused.

'Go on. Tell me.'

'All right. But I will say these words only once, and then I will not speak of this again. Not ever.' Abba stopped to take a deep breath. 'At first they took people out into the woods and shot them. Sometimes with machine guns, sometimes they made them lie down and shot them in the back of the head. Everyone. Old people. Children. Hundreds, maybe thousands of people from Kolo and the towns around it were murdered that way.'

He paused again. 'Then they built this place called Chelmno. I don't know why they call it a camp. It has no tents or barracks to live in. No one lives there. The only reason people are brought there is to be killed.'

He continued, his voice a monotone. 'There was an old manor house in the woods. The Nazis put a fence around it and started bringing groups of Jews there. An SS man in a white coat greets them in the courtyard and tells them they are being taken farther east, to work camps, but first they have to be disin‐ fected. They give them each a piece of soap and take them into a large room, say they all have to undress. Everyone. All in the same room. Men and women together. Completely naked.'

Tonia was used to her father pacing about and speaking with great animation, but there was no sound behind the door other than Abba's dull voice. An image formed in her mind – her own family, terrified, crowded together with neighbors and strangers, and forced to undress. To stand in front of everyone without any clothes on, even Ima! She pushed the image away and grew an‐ gry with her father. Why was he saying these horrible things?

59

'Then they make them go down to the cellar,' Abba continued, 'to a long corridor that leads outside. At the end of it, there's a steep ramp. It slopes down, right into the back of a truck. Things usually go quietly up to that point, but when the people see the ramp and the truck and that there is no shower, they panic, they don't want to go. But by that time, it's too late, the ramp is too steep, and the SS come behind them shouting, with dogs, and beating them, and they fall down into the truck. Fifty or seventy at a time. Then the doors slam, and the driver turns on the engine. He connects a pipe that pumps gas into the back of the truck. When everyone stops screaming, the truck drives to the woods. They bury them all together, in large pits.'

There was a long silence.

'This man who wrote the report, he saw this with his own eyes?' Ima asked in a choked voice.

'Yes.'

'And it is still happening?'

'Every day.'

There was another long silence, and Tonia took her ear away from the door.

'What are they talking about?' Rina whispered.

'I couldn't understand,' she lied. 'They are speaking Yiddish and I can hardly hear.'

'You must have heard something.'

'No, I didn't.' She moved away from the door and raised her voice, wanting her parents to come out.

Rina tiptoed over to listen.

'Stop that, leave them alone.'

She tried to pull her sister away and then pounded her fist on the door. 'Ima, can I come in?'

A few moments passed before the door opened and they came out. Abba hugged each of them, and Ima said she would make tea.

Tonia watched them warily until she decided they weren't going to repeat those terrible things that her father had made up. They weren't true. She hadn't really heard them. That had been

60

her imagination, like a bad dream. She had to forget about it. It didn't make any sense. How could people get killed in the back of a truck? It was just a crazy story. People hated the Nazis so much that they made up crazy stories. Even if they wanted to kill people, why would they make them take their clothes off? No. Nothing like that could be true.

'I need to talk to you about something else, Leah'le,' Abba said when Ima came to sit beside him on the sofa. 'Don't you have an old friend from school who lives in Haifa?'

'Yes. Esther Sofer.'

'I want you to stay in contact with her.'

'We exchange notes before the holidays. That's all.'

'But you know her address? How to get in touch with her?'

'Yes. Why the sudden interest in Esther Sofer?'

'It would be good to know that all of you could go and stay with her, if you had to.'

'Why on earth would we want to go to Haifa?'

He took a deep breath. 'If Rommel takes Egypt, the British will leave Palestine, pull back to Iraq.'

Ima paled. Tonia frowned, watching her parents. For years, all she had heard the adults talk about was how to get the cursed British out of Palestine. Now all of a sudden the thought of them leaving was a catastrophe?

'If they do, the Haganah has decided to concentrate all its forces in Haifa.' Abba looked at the three of them, all sitting cross-legged on the floor, listening. 'You children, I want you all to keep a bag packed. If your mother or I tell you we have to leave in a hurry, you are ready in five minutes. No questions.'

'Would they really abandon the rest of the country?' Ima asked.

'There's no way we could defend ourselves against Rommel's tanks and the Vichy French coming from Syria. At least in Haifa, we'd be on high ground, good defensive positions. And possibly retain control of the port. Perhaps people could be evacuated.'

'Surely this is only talk?'

'Who can know?' He shrugged. 'All we can do is pray for the Allies. But if the Germans come, we won't surrender. There can be no question of that. That's the reason I told you ... those things. So you'd understand. The Nazis have an *Einsatzkommando* in North Africa, waiting to follow along behind their army, to take care of the Jews, the same way they did in Poland. I have spoken to the Haganah men who are drawing up the plans for pulling back to Haifa. They're calling it "Masada on the Carmel". So you see why we must go to Haifa, even if we have no place to stay. And why I have brought you this.' He went to the bag he had brought with him, removed a pistol, and laid it on the table. 'Tomorrow we will go to the beach, and I will teach you and Rina how to use it.'

'She's only fourteen years old!'

'The Germans don't care.'

'I can learn, Ima,' Rina said. 'I'm the oldest, and I know it's not a toy.'

'Teach me, too,' Natan said. 'I am Bar Mitzvah'

'Yes, so you are.' He looked at Tonia, as if expecting her to demand to be taught how to use the pistol too.

'Show me what to do,' Tonia said, 'but I don't want to shoot it.'

CHAPTER SEVEN

At the end of the summer of 1942, the Community of Abraham was still living in the camp in Kfar Pines, a temporary arrangement that had lasted nearly seven years. Their numbers had grown, many couples had married, and there were a dozen babies in the nursery. When representatives of the Religious Kibbutz Federation asked if they would be willing to settle in the rocky hills about ten miles south of Jerusalem, midway to Hebron, most members of the group were vehemently opposed to the idea. There was little water in the area, the topography was difficult and unsuited to traditional farming, and the Arab population was hostile.

A representative of the Jewish National Fund did his best to convince them to accept the offer. A secular Jew himself, he argued that a religious group should settle in Kfar Etzion – they would have the fortitude to settle such a difficult area and they would appreciate its significance, halfway between the holy city of Jerusalem and Hebron, the City of the Fathers. A member of the community was taken on a tour of the area and returned with little to say, apparently unenthusiastic, but reluctant to denigrate any part of Eretz Israel.

Josef was in favor. The Judean Hills were the heart of the ancient homeland. He spent hours in the community reading room, combing history books and religious tomes for references to the area, often glassy-eyed with tears. Though many members of the group considered the question of Kfar Etzion closed, Josef had a strong ally in the representative of the Jewish National Fund.

One Friday after work, Josef gathered up soap and towel and marched off to the common showers, one of the main hubs of his lobbying activities.

'Hey, what are you doing in here so early?' he asked Eli, a member of the secretariat who opposed the plan. 'I thought you follow that donkey of yours around right up to candle-lighting time.' Josef hung his towel on a peg.

'Sometimes I follow a stubborn donkey around the fields, sometimes one follows me into the shower.' Eli put his face under the showerhead, turning his back to Josef.

'Is that any way to greet a comrade?' Josef stripped off his clothes and stepped into the next stall.

'A mule-headed one, yes.'

'Aha, so I am mule-headed.' Josef turned on the shower only long enough to wet himself and then shut it off. 'Some people won't even listen to a new idea, and they call other people mule-headed,' he said as he soaped himself.

'Don't start, Shulman. I have no patience for your speeches today.'

Josef paid no attention to the protest. 'You insist that a settlement in the hills will never be able to support itself.' He continued lathering himself while he lectured. 'But you ignore the simple fact that our forefathers lived mainly in the hill regions. Before the destruction of the Second Temple there were three or four million Jews in Eretz Israel, most of them in the Judean Hills, Samaria, and the hills of Galilee.'

'Shulman, we all know how to read. May I remind you that a few centuries have passed since then? Living conditions have changed.' Eli stepped out of the shower and toweled himself. 'The land has lain fallow for hundreds of years. The rain has washed away whatever topsoil there once was, right down to the rocks–'

'Ah, those rocks you so malign. They protect the rich earth beneath them, conserve the moisture. They have been patiently waiting for us to gather them up and turn them into restraining walls, so we can make terraces for our orchards and vineyards.' Josef turned the water back on, letting it pour over his upturned face. 'Those rocks are not our enemies.' He shut the water off and shook his head like a dog. 'They have been holding onto the land for us. Mountain produce is far superior to that of the coast. Our grapes will make theirs look like raisins. And don't forget, we'll have a longer growing season. Thanks to the cooler climate, our fruit will still be coming to market when everyone else's is gone.'

'Where do you think you're going to get the water for all those vines and orchards? You know there are no subterranean water sources in the area. If you think we have a water shortage here–'

'No water sources? Says who? Maybe there aren't so many natural wells, but the rainfall is plentiful. There are already some cisterns there, and we'll dig more.'

'Look, Shulman, I never said the area can't be settled. I hope it will be. Just not by us.'

'And why not?'

'We're not kids any more. You're the last one I should have to remind of that. We have children now. Kfar Etzion will be an experiment. Let a group of youngsters who can afford to fail go there. Not us.'

'You think a few years make such a difference? A few more summers and winters and a man loses his purpose, his vision, his faith in himself?'

'Shulman, for once face reality – which is that the majority of us, for whatever reason, don't want to go there. We'll wait for a location that's better for farming.'

'Non-agricultural enterprises may turn out to be the most profitable. We could open a guesthouse, for example–'

'I have been training for nine years. I'm an expert in field crops. Field crops, Shulman, field crops. My personal vision involves tractors and broad waves of grain, not crawling around on rocky terraces, or waiting table on a bunch of city parasites on vacation.'

'A true pioneer sets his personal preferences aside and does whatever is necessary, what the Movement asks of him. If that land isn't settled, it will be lost to us.'

'But why by us?' a woman's voice demanded from the other side of the thin wall that divided the men's and women's showers.

Josef shouted back at her. 'Why not by us? Who are we to pick and choose while the Jews of Europe are burning?'

'That's pure demagoguery.' Eli stomped out.

'Judea is the heart of Eretz Israel,' Josef called after him. 'Lucky for us there are no Philistines around. They'd have a stronger claim to the coastal plain than we do. I don't believe David and Solomon ever had the pleasure of a visit to Tel Aviv.'

Josef lay in bed, palms behind his head, feeling weary, heavy, and old. He was still dressed, too tired and uncaring to remove his only good white shirt. He had remained in the dining hall, arguing the merits of Kfar Etzion, until his comrades began drifting off to their families or girlfriends.

What are Leah and the children doing now? he wondered. Children. They are no longer children. Natan is already Bar Mitzvah, and what have I given them? Hardship. He sighed and shook his head. But we are not living in normal times. What do our insignificant problems matter? Only one thing matters now – building a refuge for those who survive the catastrophe in Europe.

The British had shattered his expectations of what one could expect of the civilized world. They kept the doors to Palestine slammed shut, even after undeniable evidence of Hitler's Final Solution had reached the Allies. People complained that Josef was obsessed with the creation of an independent Jewish state. He did not see how one could be otherwise.

He knew he should spend more time with his family, but begrudged every missed day of work. He would have seen even less of them, had his comrades not raised their eyebrows and asked, 'How is Leah, Shulman? How does she manage there all by herself, when you don't even bother to visit?'

But there was one visit home he made eagerly, in fact he could have run all the way.

'Did you hear, kids?' He burst into the apartment. 'Montgomery's army has the Germans running back across

Africa, all the way to Tripoli.' He picked Tonia up and swung her around.

Uncle Shmuel opened a bottle of wine and poured glasses for all, including the children.

'To Life!' they all called. Tonia looked up at her mother, who was smiling for the first time in a great while.

Josef drained his glass and then said, 'Let's offer a prayer of thanks for the welfare of those who still suffer.' In his prayer, he included 'the brave English soldiers who spilled their blood to defeat our enemies'.

Tonia had not paid much attention to the British soldiers in the streets when she was a little girl. They were part of the landscape, young men in creased uniforms, usually friendly and smiling. The Australians were famous for passing out candy or money to the children. The only effect these strangers had on her life was a welcome one – whenever there were 'troubles', they imposed a curfew, and there was no school.

Later she learned from Uncle Shmuel that they were a band of thieves. 'You want a driving license?' he grumbled. 'Pay a bribe to the British official. You want a permit to breathe? Pay a bribe to the British official in charge of air.'

Then the Haganah posters she helped paste up painted them as enemies, betrayers of their mandate. Instead of helping to create a Jewish homeland, they refused immigration certificates to desperate Jewish refugees and allowed the Arabs to stockpile weapons.

Now they were heroes. Saviors.

'So are the English good or bad?' she asked her father.

'When they turn ships full of Jews back to Germany, they are bad. But today they are wonderful. Today we love them.' He drank what was left in Leah and Rivka's wine glasses and got up to dance around. 'Tomorrow I am going to take you all to the cinema. Maybe they will have a newsreel. We can watch the great Aryan master race fleeing through the sand, like rats. And maybe they'll even be showing something with Humphrey Bogart.'

Through the fall and winter, the Community of Abraham debated whether to settle in Kfar Etzion. The only other site that had been suggested for them was near Gaza, an area that could boast broad fields but had little rainfall and a brackish water table. They took several votes, sometimes by a show of hands, sometimes by secret ballot. The majority was always against, but the number of votes in favor increased with each count, and the representative from the Jewish National Fund continued to lobby for Kfar Etzion. This was despite the fact that the offer to settle there was not yet concrete. They were still engaged in exhaustive legal battles to regain title to Jewish lands that had been lost when Jews were twice in the past forced to evacuate the area. They were also negotiating to purchase more land from Arabs willing to sell.

'We would like to send a delegation to visit the area,' the man from the Jewish National Fund said. 'This time five or six of you. On the way, we'll stop by Kiryat Anavim and Maaleh Hahamisha. Both these kibbutzim have a similar topography, and you will be able to see how well they are managing.'

Josef got himself included in the delegation. He listened impatiently while the farmers at the two other kibbutzim explained how they dealt with their water problems. He needed no convincing and was anxious to see what he was sure would become their new home.

Finally, they were on the Jerusalem–Hebron road, Josef traveling in the first of the two cars. The sky was clear, but the ground was still wet with last night's rain. The sun reflected off the rocks on the hillsides, and scattered groves of peaches, plums, and apricots glistened. The damp earth was a deep red-brown; grape vines and berries grew wild by the roadside.

When they turned off the main road, they bumped over unpaved dirt, rutted and strewn with rocks. It did not take long for the car to get stuck. They got out, put stones and heaps of weeds under the tires, and pushed.

'Of course, the road will be graded and paved. We'll see to that,' the Jewish National Fund man said as he struggled, his shoulder against a back fender.

When the car was free, Josef straightened and shaded his eyes. On a high hill to his left, the red-tiled roof of a stone building peeked through a thick grove of oak, pine, and cypress. Closer to the road, slender leaves glittered silver over the gnarled trunks of ancient olive trees.

'That's the Russian Monastery,' their guide told him as they got back in the car. 'Unfortunately, it's not for sale. But, look, up ahead here on the left is Wadi Shahat.' He stopped the car and they got out again to view the only area they had seen that was plowed and cultivated. 'It is for sale, and we're working on it.'

They pushed the car out of the mud again and continued west.

'Up there is the German Monastery,' the guide said over his shoulder and pointed out another lovely stone building on a hill-top. 'It's not ours yet, but it will be. It's a complicated negotiation, so we're not going to go in there today. No point in getting the Arabs and British all riled up.'

They passed terrain so steep and rocky that not even Josef could imagine growing anything on it. Then they stopped near the western slopes of the area. The few hundred acres of land there were almost completely white, hidden beneath a blanket of boulders and stones. The guide assured them that forty to fifty acres could be cleared and planted with orchards and vineyards. The rest could be made into narrow terraces, though access to them might be difficult.

Josef put his hand to his forehead, shielding his eyes from the sun. Far to the west, he could see the white buildings of Tel Aviv. Closer, the southern agricultural settlements were spread out at their feet. Jews must have control of this hilltop, he thought. From up here, the width of the entire country was in the palm of his hand. So tiny, and yet the international negotiators wanted to cut the area of the proposed Jewish state by half.

The next day was the Sabbath, and members of the delegation sat in the dining hall in Kfar Pines, answering questions about what they had seen. Josef had a new argument.

'Jews have to settle in all the high areas. We must cover every hill and mountain range with kibbutzim and moshavim. You can forget about having a state, if you don't control the hills. To neglect Judaea is a negation of the Zionist ideal, of returning to the land of our fathers. But now that I have stood on those hills and seen with my own eyes, I know that a presence on them is also a military necessity.'

The 'Yeses' were becoming more sure of their position and, therefore, more persuasive. The 'Nos' grew less so. While they still held the majority, the 'Nos' passed a resolution. A simple majority in favor of Kfar Etzion would not suffice. Such a crucial decision, with such grave consequences, would require a majority of at least two-thirds.

While the debates continued, the community received an urgent message from the Jewish National Fund. They had completed the purchase of the German Monastery and must take possession of it, in order to establish de facto ownership. The members of the Community of Abraham did not have to make a final decision, but were asked to send a unit of five or six men to establish a Jewish presence in the monastery.

This request aroused another round of arguments. The 'Nos' claimed it was a trick to force them to settle in Kfar Etzion. To avoid conflict, the Religious Kibbutz Federation asked another group, intended for settlement in the Beit Shean Valley, to take this obligation upon themselves temporarily. They agreed, but Josef and a few others from the Community of Abraham declared that they felt a personal responsibility to see this task fulfilled and insisted upon joining them.

A few days later, Josef and five other Jews slipped into the German Monastery. Abu Tzadek, a Christian Arab from Beit Umar who had been leasing the monastery, accompanied them. They were at first embarrassed by the warm hospitality Abu Tzadek extended to them, since they were in the process of claiming their rights to this property and thus displacing him. But he acted as a gracious host and began preparing a meal for them, while they scrubbed the black walls of one of the rooms.

Shortly after their arrival, there was a knock on the door. The Mukhtar of a nearby village stood outside with two companions. Abu Tzadek went out to welcome the Mukhtar, and they conversed in Arabic for a few moments. The six Jews came out and stood to one side.

'I told him,' Abu Tzadek turned and explained to them in Hebrew, 'that you have rented rooms from us.' They all nodded.

At that moment, a rider appeared on an impressive white horse, a rifle slung over one shoulder. He wore a long heavy brown coat and a wide-brimmed hat, both sides of the brim folded up and pinned to the crown.

'This is Yigal, their watchman,' the Arab informed the Mukhtar, again translating for the Jews. 'The Jews have asked him here to protect them and their property.'

Everyone, including the Mukhtar, had heard of Yigal. One of the founders of the Jewish Watchmen organization, famous for his successful tactics against Bedouin thieves in Galilee, Yigal had been living in the monastery for a while. A second rider appeared and Abu Tzadek introduced him as Yigal's servant. The Mukhtar nodded respectfully and left.

'He certainly is an accommodating fellow,' Josef nodded at Abu Tzadek's back.

'Yes, they thought the lease he held might prevent the sale, but he negotiated for compensation and seems satisfied with the deal.'

'Who did this land belong to before?' Josef asked.

'An Arab from Beit Umar built that smaller house out back and then sold it to some Benedictine Monks. They built the monastery.'

'What made the monks decide to sell it to us?'

'The British put them under arrest when the war broke out. Enemy aliens. So they were anxious to sell, but before we got around to making an offer, they had already given Abu Tzadek a lease on the place. That's why it took so long to get title.'

Josef entered the dark and dank interior, oblivious to the unpleasant odor left by its current furry residents. He walked up and down the corridor, peeking into the rooms. It was a mansion. He smiled widely and ran his hands over the stone, so wonderfully substantial. What more could they ask for? There were small groves of pine, olive, figs, and other fruit trees, as well as some small vineyards. Besides the monastery and the small house, there were a few outbuildings and a cistern. True, they would still have to truck in their water. The cistern could hold only 1,200 cubic meters of rainwater, and they estimated that their needs would be at least 3,000 a year. But it would make a good beginning. An excellent beginning.

One of the other men saw him looking uncertainly at the crucifixes and religious pictures that still hung on the walls. 'Don't worry. The British are letting the monks come back to get their property some day next week.'

Josef stepped back outside and gazed at the surrounding hills, greedily breathing in the crisp air. Abraham, Isaac, and Jacob had walked this ground. David had herded his flocks and hidden from King Saul on these slopes. Traces of stone terraces were still visible, remnants of long-abandoned Jewish villages. His connection to that past had never seemed more important to him. His people had survived so much, and here he was. The Community of Abraham must settle here.

A few weeks later Josef returned to Kfar Pines. Everyone gathered in the dining hall for what they hoped would be their last vote. They were all fed up with the constant bickering and wanted it settled, one way or the other. One of the members came around with a box, gathering the small slips of paper with everyone's votes. Then he and another man went to the office to count them.

They were soon back. The man who had collected the slips of paper said, 'We have counted the votes. Twice. We are one vote short of a two-thirds majority in favor … However, I did not yet cast a vote.' He paused and surveyed the silent dining hall. 'You all know I have been against this plan from the beginning. But in these circumstances, I feel compelled to vote in favor.'

No one objected to the unusual, and probably illegal, practice of casting the final vote after the others had been counted. Josef looked around, glad to see that even the leaders of the weary opposition appeared relieved to have it over. He strode to where they sat, plucked one man out of his chair, and began dancing an enthusiastic *hora* with him. 'You won't be sorry,' he said and stopped to hug the man. 'We will make a paradise of the place.'

CHAPTER EIGHT

The day after the vote, on his way back to the German Monastery in Kfar Etzion, Josef stopped in Jerusalem. He did not know the Jewish Quarter in the Old City well and was soon lost in its maze of alleyways, shivering in a cold drizzle. He finally found the address he had been given, knocked on the heavy wooden door, heard a mumbled answer, and pushed it open. Inside a dark-skinned man with long side locks and a colorful embroidered yarmulke crouched on the floor, rolling up a large topographical map. The walls of the room were covered with unevenly hung maps and charts. A desk piled with papers stood in one corner and a battered file cabinet in another. A radio on top of the file cabinet, turned down low, spit mostly static.

'Shalom,' Josef said. 'I'm Shulman, from Kfar Pines, on my way to Kfar Etzion. I was told you have something for me.'

The man sat back on his heels and slipped a rubber band around the rolled map. He remained squatting and took a long look at Josef before he got to his feet, turned to open the top drawer of the file cabinet, and withdrew two ancient-looking pistols. Josef set his suitcase on the desk, opened its latches, and slipped the guns beneath its thick lining. Looking at the man more closely, Josef saw that he was hardly more than a boy. He did not seem to have begun shaving yet.

'Those are all we have,' the young man said. 'And these are all the bullets I can give you for now.' He reached back into the drawer and handed Josef a small white box. 'Maybe come back in a few weeks.'

'Do I owe you?'

'It's been taken care of. Oh, God in heaven, listen.' The young man turned up the volume of the radio. 'The bastards have brought in flame-throwers.'

They could barely hear the voice of the BBC correspondent through the static. 'Since yesterday they have been systemically burning every building, block by block, to the ground. People on the Aryan side have reported seeing women with small children in their arms jumping out of windows and off roofs, their clothes on fire.'

'The Warsaw Ghetto,' the man said.

'I know,' Josef said tonelessly. 'I heard some people have escaped through the sewers.'

'Maybe. Some. Until the Nazis pumped them full of gas. That was on the radio last night.' The young man shook his head.

Josef wished he would turn it off. He didn't want to hear.

'They managed to get a message to the Haganah,' the young man continued. 'Begging us for arms.'

'I have to hurry,' Josef interrupted. 'Thank you.'

In truth, Josef had time to kill, but he could no longer stand listening to the steady voices of correspondents describing such things. He entered an Arab café in the Christian Quarter and asked for black coffee with cardamom. He was careful to keep the suitcase wedged between his ankles, while he pressed his fists into his eyes. He felt tired. And angry. Children were being burned alive while he sat in a coffee house. The radio was more a curse than a blessing. What was the point of knowing things you could do nothing to stop?

The owner of the café brought his coffee, and Josef looked up at him. My enemy, he thought. This soft-spoken old man with large brown eyes. Do I need a weapon to protect myself from him? From his son? Well, wasn't the Mufti of Jerusalem still in Berlin, extracting promises from Hitler that he wouldn't neglect to exterminate the Jews of Palestine?

'*Shukrun*,' Josef thanked the Arab.

He leaned back and looked out the window. The sun had come out, and the world looked bright and clean. Two teen-aged girls stopped to finger the merchandise piled outside the shop across the street. One had deep auburn hair and the other was blonde. They were both pretty. Such lovely young bodies, wrapped in bright-colored skirts of some supple material that clung to their legs. Their skin must be so soft.

75

The blonde picked up a colorfully embroidered Bedouin dress and held it up to the front of her body. Her friend noticed Josef watching and smiled at him. He felt his body respond and lifted three fingers in a half-hearted salute. What would it be like to spend an afternoon with a strange young girl? To forget about everything. To let the world begin and end with the wonders of her body.

Men did such things. He had heard of people who walked out of their lives. Husbands went out for a pack of cigarettes and kept on going. He could understand the impulse. Erase everything. No past. No ties. No responsibilities. Nothing you had to care about.

The auburn-haired girl said something to the blonde, and she giggled the way young girls do, covering her mouth with her hand. Then both of them smiled boldly at Josef and waved before they continued up the street, arm in arm. He knew they were aware of his eyes following them. Here's to youth and beauty, he thought. He picked up his glass of coffee and toasted the sway of their backsides over the cobblestones. Then he pushed the glass of dregs away.

Not that he had ever wanted to leave Leah. No. He loved her and always would. It wasn't her he sometimes wanted to escape. It was his own skin he wanted to crawl out of. He was sick of being Josef Shulman. Sick of caring. Sick of feeling helpless. Sick of trying to show them all that anything was possible. On days like today, nothing seemed possible.

He was suddenly aware of an enormous pit in his stomach and asked the Arab to bring him a plate of hummus, some warm pita, and a tomato and cucumber salad. He ate ravenously, feeling only the slightest tinge of guilt for satisfying his hunger in a non-kosher establishment and neglecting to perform the obligatory washing of hands before eating bread. Could God really come complaining to a Jew today? When he finished his meal, he asked for another cup of coffee and felt much better.

The body always wins. He could not decide if that was a blessing or a curse.

76

He paid the bill and walked to the Jaffa Gate. The two friends from the Community of Abraham that he was to meet there soon arrived, and the three of them walked to the corner where the Arab bus to Hebron stopped. There was a pair of empty seats behind the driver, and Josef motioned for his friends to take them. He set his suitcase at their feet and clung to the overhead rail, grateful not to have to converse with anyone. When they reached the turn-off to the feeder road, Josef bent down and asked the driver to stop.

It had not rained there, and the sun had baked the deep ruts in the mud. They plodded along in silence. Josef felt as if he were watching himself and his two companions from a distance – three stateless Jews with two antiquated pistols, on a barren hill, surrounded by God knows how many Arabs. He felt fear. Worse than that, he felt doubt. Could he really bring his family to this isolated place? How could he consider such a thing? The Arab Legion would sweep down on them, with tanks and artillery. The unthinkable was happening all over the world. Who was Josef Shulman to think he could make one small patch of it safe for his children? Maybe Tonia was right – maybe they should run away. But where? The world had been divided into countries in which Jews could not live and countries to which Jews could not go.

When they reached the monastery, he waved the others inside and remained outside alone, watching the sun set over the hills in peaceful silence. He stood there a long while, waiting for renewed strength to infuse his body. He closed his eyes. When he opened them, he did not see the jagged pavement of boulders and rocks that covered the hillsides. Nor did he see the Arab villages in the distance. He refused to think about how far they were from the nearest Jewish settlement. He looked up at the sky.

All right, it's true. I am a pathetic little ant, dragging crumbs from place to place. I cannot stop the world being what it is, any more than an ant could topple that boulder down the hill. I control next to nothing.

And there you have it – the most well-worn excuse for doing nothing at all. No. He clenched his fists. I refuse to do nothing. I refuse to raise children to do nothing. There is one thing I do control – my own actions.

'Shulman, you want to come give us a hand?' someone called.

'I'll be right there,' Josef shouted back and turned for a last look at the darkening hills.

He saw the orchards and vineyards that would soon cover them. He saw the future. He saw life.

A small group of men from Kfar Pines arrived in Kfar Etzion the following Friday. A few cars spilled out the Jewish officials who had come to mark the occasion. One of them gave a short speech, produced a bottle of wine for a toast, and warned them not to speak with any journalists or do anything else liable to draw the attention of the British.

Josef and another man set about preparing simple dishes of chicken and rice, while the others cleaned rooms and dug guard posts. After sundown, they gathered to receive the Sabbath. They were only seven, three short of the required *minyan*, and recited the *Maariv* prayers individually. Saturday was a quiet and lonely day of rest. After sundown on Saturday night, they lit a campfire and sat around it, singing and telling stories to drive away the darkness.

On Monday they awaited the arrival of the next contingent from Kfar Pines. The truck finally arrived, carrying ten men, three women, and a load of beds, mattresses, and cooking utensils. They were joined by a dozen Palmachniks, who would help guard the new kibbutz. A few days later, their very own tender drove up. The driver honked its horn loud and long and received a great round of applause. They were no longer stuck there alone, cut off from the world.

Josef's misgivings evaporated. All was going well, and Kfar Etzion began to feel like home. A dozen young Arab men from the surrounding villages had come to the new kibbutz asking for work. They toiled side by side with their new Jewish neighbors, helping to weed the orchards and put in a vegetable garden.

The rest of the men moved from Kfar Pines to Kfar Etzion, and more trucks arrived, loaded to twice their height with stacks of thick wooden slats. The settlers quickly unloaded them and hammered them into simple structures that stood over slabs of poured concrete. Heaps of cement blocks became living quarters with red tiled roofs.

Two dairy barns and six chicken runs would soon begin operating, along with a quarry, a machine shop, and a carpentry shop. They had their own generator and a small clinic. In the spring of 1944, after the Passover holiday, the women and children came from Kfar Pines. Kfar Etzion now had a population of 120.

Josef stopped to admire the main path, along which he had helped to set neat borders of whitewashed curbstones. Children shouted and laughed nearby. Can a man feel deeper satisfaction that this? Too bad, he thought, that we have to mar the countryside with those ugly strings of barbed wire, but they seem to be necessary, for now. He sat down on one of the stone benches he had built and surveyed the dream that was coming true. It was time.

He went to Tel Aviv and maintained an expectant silence for a few days, waiting for his wife to broach the subject of moving to Kfar Etzion. After the Friday evening meal, he could wait no longer.

'Well, Leah?'

'Well what?'

'After all these long years, we have a home of our own, yet we continue to dine at someone else's table.'

'Oh, Josef, what would the children do there? There are no other children their ages, no school. I always thought our kibbutz would be near other settlements, that there would be a school nearby. But if we go there, they will have to travel to Jerusalem every day for school, on that horrible road.'

'The secretariat will see that there is transportation to school, and arrangements can be made for them to sleep over in Jerusalem a few nights each week. Either we overcome these difficulties, or we give up everything.'

Leah began packing.

'Most people accumulate belongings as they get older,' she said aloud to herself as she folded bedding. 'I seem to shed them.'

'So why are you going? Why are you making us go?' Tonia shouted at her mother.

Leah let the sheet she was holding fall to the couch and stared at her youngest daughter. 'Don't start, Tonia,' she said wearily.

'It's my life too. I don't want to go there. I won't. You can't make me.'

Leah turned on her. 'You will do as you are told. And you will stop behaving like a spoiled brat. I don't need you acting up now.'

Tonia's eyes grew wide. Her mother often yelled at her, but never in the tone she was using now. Never in a voice that sounded like she hated Tonia.

'I'm not acting—'

'I don't want to hear it. Just be quiet,' Leah said. She picked up an armful of clothing and shoved it in a jumble into the open carton on the floor. 'And if you don't want to come with us, fine. Don't. Stay right here in Tel Aviv. Then we won't have to listen to your constant whining about going to America.'

Tonia waited for her mother to turn around and apologize, but she continued throwing things into the carton, her back stiff and unrelenting. Tonia went outside and managed to make it down the stairs and around to the side of the building, where no one could see her, before she burst into tears.

CHAPTER NINE

The Shulmans traveled by Egged bus from Tel Aviv to Jerusalem, where they heaped their belongings into two Arab taxis. Tonia and Natan rode with Leah in the taxi that led the way, Rina and Josef in the other that followed behind. The taxis stopped outside the front gate of Kfar Etzion, and thirteen-year-old Tonia opened the door for her first look at her new home. It was worse than she had imagined. She knew her father always exaggerated with his lyrical descriptions, but still, this was his fairy-tale village? One pretty building of cut stone tried to lend a feeling of permanence, but the rest was all too familiar, flimsy wooden structures and white tents. And the road they had to travel to get there. Narrow, winding, the last part not even paved, the few villages they passed all Arab.

Rina skipped up the path and turned around to smile at her father. Natan helped the drivers remove their cases from the trunks and the roof racks. Tonia held onto the open door of the taxi, one foot still inside.

'Leah'le, you must come see the dining hall.' Josef tugged at his wife's elbow.

'Abba, maybe Ima would like to get settled,' Natan suggested.

It had taken less than two hours to get from Uncle Shmuel's to Jerusalem. Two more hours passed while they stopped for lemonade, looked for two taxis willing to take them to Kfar Etzion, and made the trip to the kibbutz. By the time they got there, Leah looked pale and worn.

'Oh.' Josef's expression was puzzled. 'Are you not feeling well? How about a nice cup of tea? I bet you don't remember the last time I made you one, do you? I do. You came to visit me right after the move to Kfar Pines, when we were still in tents. I came off guard duty and tripped over your bed, and we both fell into the mud.'

'Shulmans! Welcome!' Three men came up the path to help them carry their belongings to their accommodations.

The living quarters consisted of narrow wooden structures, each shared by a number of couples. Their long front walls had no windows, but four doors that opened onto a narrow covered porch created by the overhang of the red-tiled roof. Muddy work shoes stood outside most of the doors. A long-handled squeegee, broom, and a bucket with a floor rag spread over it to dry stood at the end of each. Josef showed them to a room at the end of one of these structures.

'Here, Leah'le, this is ours.' He opened the door and smiled, watching his wife's face.

A tiny window on the back wall let in some light. A small table stood under it, a pair of slatted wooden chairs on either side. Two metal-frame twin beds took up one wall, a tiny wardrobe another. There were no other furnishings. Josef piled some of their boxes and the large wicker basket in a corner and thanked the men for their help. It was mid-August and hot, and the room was stifling.

'It's lovely, Josef,' Leah said. 'How wonderful that we finally have a room of our own.'

'You know we're the only family with children your ages,' Josef said, turning to Rina, Natan, and Tonia. 'The next oldest are only seven. So there is no children's house for you. You'll share a room like this. Come, leave everything here, and I'll show you.'

He led them down a path to another, similar structure. Their room had no table. Three beds and two small wardrobes took up every centimeter of wall space. A single light bulb hung from the ceiling. Tonia noted with dismay how dark it was. She would never be able to read in there, except maybe in the middle of the afternoon – if the sun was shining and she sat right under the window.

And it looked so dirty. She knew her father must have swept and mopped the floor in preparation for their arrival, but they had already tracked in enough dirt to cause Aunt Rivka serious palpitations. All you had to do was open the door, and the whole world blew in. Tonia looked around with narrow eyes, wondering about snakes, mice, and spiders. Leah came to stand beside her and put an arm around her shoulders. Tonia tried not to cry.

'Come, I'll show you where the toilets and showers are.' Josef went out and strode up the path.

They were on their way to have a look at the dining hall when someone asked Josef to come help unload a truck of supplies that had arrived from Jerusalem. Leah never got her cup of tea.

Tonia went back to the room she was to share with Rina and Natan and lay on one of the beds. It was an awful place. How could he bring them here? She wasn't yet fourteen. So long to go before she could graduate from high school and get a job. How could she stand to live here for that long? She felt like she was suffocating. When Rina and Natan finished exploring and came back, she pretended to be asleep. Natan sat beside her on the bed and poked her shoulder.

'I know you're awake,' he said. 'It's not so bad, Tonia. It'll just take you a while to get used to it.'

'It's awful.' She turned over. 'It's horrible. I hate it, and I hate him. You can't tell me you want to live here.'

'Isn't it better than sleeping on the living-room floor?'

'No. At least there we had Ima with us. At least there you could go outside and find friends. There were stores and playgrounds. There's nothing to do here. Nowhere to go. It's the worst place I've ever seen. And we'll have to go to school in Jerusalem, all that way, so even if we make any friends, we'll never be able to see them after school.'

Rina was quiet, sitting on one of the other beds. Tonia glanced over at her, expecting to be scolded.

'It won't be easy,' Rina said softly. 'It won't be easy at all. But it's important, Tonia. He wouldn't have brought us here if he didn't think it was really important.'

'You and Rina can have the room to yourselves,' Natan said. 'While I was looking around I saw the tents for the Palmach guys. They found an empty bed for me in one of them. I can sleep there.'

'You can't sleep in a tent!'

'Sure I can. They're good tents. I'll be joining the Palmach soon anyway. Might as well get used to it.'

Tonia never got used to the kibbutz. She felt constantly surrounded by dozens of staring eyes. In Kfar Etzion there was even less privacy than there had been at Uncle Shmuel's. She could not decide what was worse, eating in the communal dining hall with everyone looking at what you put on your plate, or using the common showers, where they had not even bothered to put up curtains. And that was when you were lucky and they let you take a shower at all. Everyone was always kvetching about saving water, and you were only allowed to take one shower a week. There was only one thing to be grateful for – that they had not come here when she was little. She could not imagine herself five years old, being put to bed in a room full of other children, far from her mother.

'There have been incidents on the road,' the kibbutz secretary told the Shulmans. 'I would advise you to send your children to boarding schools. Or we could make arrangements for them to sleep in Jerusalem, come home for the weekends.'

Leah refused to consider it. 'No. I won't send them away.'

She enrolled Tonia and Rina at Miss Landau's school for girls in Jerusalem, where they would learn Hebrew, English, French, German, arithmetic, and geography. Natan would be at a boys' school not far from Miss Landau's. Twice a week they would be able to get a ride back with the kibbutz tender. The other days, they would take an Arab taxi home.

'There are still a few weeks before school starts,' Josef told them after dinner, on the day they arrived. 'So you'll be scheduled to work.'

'Work where?' Tonia asked.

'Work assignments are posted every evening on the board in the dining hall. As far as I know, you and Rina will help clear the fields. I think the electrician wants Natan to help him for a few days.'

'What about me?' Leah asked.

'Probably one of the children's houses. We can ask. Is there a particular job you would prefer?'

'No.' Leah shrugged. 'So as long as it isn't laundry.'

The next morning they rose in the dark, and Tonia donned the work clothes her father had brought for her – a dark blue work shirt and puffy shorts with elastic around the legs that made them balloon and left red marks on her thighs. She burst out laughing, and even Rina had to agree that they looked ridiculous. Then Josef came in with so-called 'dummy' hats, bowls of thick khaki that he overturned on their heads.

'Now you are official kibbutzniks!' he beamed.

They trudged behind him, up to the dining hall for coffee and then out to their jobs. Tonia and Rina had indeed been assigned to helping clear the fields of rocks. The workers picked up the smaller stones and tossed them into shallow iron sledges that stood on the slope. The larger rocks that had become tightly embedded in the soil tore at their hands. Some were so big that it took two men with crowbars to pry them from the earth. When a sledge was full, it was hitched to a horse or mule and dragged to the side, where the stones were unloaded. They would eventually be used to build retaining walls for terraces.

Tonia stood and stared at the endless sea of stones. The slope was white with them. Had they lost their collective minds? It seemed an impossible task. After an hour she was filthy, her arms and back ached, and her hands were scraped bloody. What a waste of human energy. How had anyone, even these lunatics, looked out on a rocky hill like this and thought, that looks like just the place to plant an orchard?

At eight, they trudged back to the dining hall for breakfast. More coffee or tea, dark bread, olives, white cheese, and slices of tomato and cucumber. Then back to work. By ten, the sun was beating down relentlessly. The men and women working nearby also looked tired, but seemed determined not to show it.

Rina was intolerable, saying things like, 'We'll strike roots here, just like the trees we plant.' When she added, 'And like the trees, we'll always strive for greater heights,' Tonia rolled her eyes and sat down to rest in silent protest.

'Already?' Rina raised an eyebrow.

Tonia ignored her, and Rina stepped up her own pace of work, heaving rocks into the sledge faster and faster. The more pointed the sound they made crashing into the sledge, the better Tonia felt about remaining seated. She stretched her legs out in front of her and leaned back on her elbows. Rina pitched one last rock and stood over Tonia, hands on her hips.

'Tonia, do you think it's right that others do your share?'

'Well, since you started working twice as fast the minute I sat down, there's no loss. I get to rest, you get to feel like a saint, and everyone's happy.'

Eventually Tonia rose with a sigh, picked up the rock at her feet, and flung it into the sledge. It was so hot. She started calculating how many more days, hours, and minutes of this she would have to endure. How would she ever get away? The way these Socialists ran things, you couldn't even save up by working overtime. All you would get for working longer hours was a pat on the back from comrade Rina.

After long days of backbreaking work, the slope was cleared and terraced. Then another. By the end of the summer Tonia could not deny a sense of accomplishment as she gazed at them, but she had never been so eager for school to start. Not that it would rescue her entirely; they would still be expected to work on days that they got back from school early or had vacations.

On her first day at Miss Landau's school, Tonia heard some of her classmates talking about the 'modern' high school in Jerusalem, where boys and girls learned together and the teachers all had university degrees.

'What school are you talking about?' she asked.

'The Gymnasium in Rehavia. It's for rich kids,' one of the girls answered. 'You have to know someone to get in, and anyway, it costs a lot of money.'

Tonia had no clear idea of what was meant by a 'modern' school, but she made up her mind that when she started high school next year, it was going to be at the Gymnasium.

CHAPTER TEN

Tonia opened the door of the children's house where her mother helped take care of the four- and five-year-olds.

'Here you are, Ima. How come you're still at work?'

'It's a whole lot easier to clean up after they've gone to their parents.'

'Need any help?' Tonia went in, smiling at the neat row of tiny rubber boots by the door.

Although Tonia hated the idea of small children living apart from their parents, she could not resist the charm of this parallel, child-sized universe – small brightly colored tables and chairs, tiny beds, miniature sinks and toilets, hives of cubbyholes for their toys and drawings. The accommodations were spacious, compared to those of the adults, and had windows that let in the light. Still, how could they do it? If a little boy or girl woke up from a bad dream, they wanted their mother, not the comrade who happened to be on night duty. They even left tiny babies in the nursery, with one woman sleeping there to look after them.

'There are a few plates in the sink you could do up.'

Tonia finished the dishes and hoped she sounded casual when she asked, 'Ima, don't you have some cousin who lives in Jerusalem?'

'Cousin?' Leah had finished mopping the floor and she and Tonia stepped outside onto the porch. 'No. I don't have any family in Palestine. You know that.'

'But I remember you talking about her. It was a long time ago, but I remember. You said that you should go visit her, ask about her mother. I think you said she lives in Rehavia.'

'Oh, you must mean Eva Kutzky's daughter. They're not really family. Eva lived across the street from us in Kolo. She and my mother were close, so I used to call her Aunt Eva, but there's no blood relation. They only had the one little girl. Nella, I think her name was. That must be who you mean.'

'So did you ever go to Rehavia to see Nella?' Tonia asked.

'No. That was all so long ago. Another world. And even though we were the same age, I was never friends with Nella. Wouldn't know her if I saw her. You can go and tack those up on the bulletin board.'

Tonia had gathered up the finger paintings the children had left out on the porch to dry. She found a box of thumbtacks in one of the kitchen drawers and began pinning them up.

'But she was your neighbor,' she said over her shoulder. 'They lived right across the street.'

Leah stared at Tonia for a long moment. 'I told you, I never played with her. And then her parents sent her away, to some fancy boarding school in Germany. She met her husband there, someone older. I think he was one of her teachers or something. She was only fifteen when she got married.' Leah stacked red and blue plastic cups in the cupboard over the sink.

'Fifteen? Like me'

'Yes.' Leah smiled. 'Of course, that wasn't uncommon back then. Aunt Eva was so proud of her rich *Yeki* son-in-law,' Leah said, using the Yiddish term for referring to a German Jew. 'She went around bragging to anyone who would listen. Of course, all of Kolo was talking – thinking Nella must have gotten, you know, in trouble. And the magnificent *Yeki* was not observant. They were married in a Reform Synagogue in Berlin, and I can't tell you what a big scandal that was for all the religious Jews in Kolo. It all worked out for the best though.' Leah sighed and went back to arranging dishes. 'He brought Nella here, to Palestine, even before Hitler. Lord knows what became of Aunt Eva and Uncle Simon. That's probably the real reason I never looked Nella up. Didn't want to have to ask her. Didn't want her to have to ask about my family.'

'So is she rich?'

'Nella? How would I know? Now, Tonia Shulman ...' Leah paused, folded a dishtowel, and turned to face her daughter, '... I want you to tell me why all this sudden interest in Nella Kutzky. And I want the truth.'

'There's a high school I want to go to next year. It's in Rehavia.'

'The Gymnasium?'

'Yes.' Tonia was somehow surprised that her mother had heard of it.

'But it's not a religious school, Tonia.' Leah pulled out one of the small wooden chairs and sat down on it.

'I know,' Tonia said as she seated herself next to her mother. 'But that's not so important, Ima. Really it isn't. I can say prayers on my own. It's a good school. Better than Miss Landau's. They learn more things.'

Leah pursed her lips and frowned.

Encouraged that her mother had not said no, Tonia persisted. 'Please, Ima, I want to go there. It's not fair. I didn't want to come live here. I should at least get to go to the school that I want.'

'What in the world does all this have to do with Nella Kutzky?'

'I'm sure my marks are good enough, but everyone says you need *protekzia*, you have to know someone to get in. I thought that if this Nella is rich and lives in Rehavia ... maybe she could help get them to accept me.'

Tonia did not mention that everyone also said that the school cost a lot of money. First, she had to get herself accepted. Then she would worry about that. Maybe there were scholarships she could apply for.

Leah took Tonia's hand and patted it. 'I'll talk to your father, if it means so much to you. But before I do, you think hard about it, make sure that's really what you want. You won't have much in common with your classmates.'

'I don't care. I don't need to think about it. I want to go to a good school, so I can go to university.'

To Tonia's amazement, though she was still frowning, Leah nodded her head.

'I get out of school early tomorrow,' Tonia said. 'I want to go and try to find Nella.'

'You want to talk to her yourself?' Leah looked surprised and relieved.

Tonia had not meant that. She meant she would try to find out where Nella lived, and then Leah could go see her. 'I could, if you don't want to.'

'Maybe that would be best.'

'So how do you spell Kutzky?'

'Oh, Kutzky was her maiden name. I'm not sure I remember her married name. The *Yeki*'s name was Viktor, that I do remember. But what was his last name? ... Rozen, Rozenfeld, Rozenberg, Rozenblatt ... No, Rozmann. I'm pretty sure that was it. Viktor Rozmann. But I don't have their address. How do you think you're going to find them?'

'If they're so rich, they must have a telephone.'

'I suppose. All right, I'll discuss it with your father tonight after dinner.' Leah patted Tonia's hand again. 'He's not going to like it, but he'll have the rest of this school year to get used to the idea.'

After dinner, Tonia walked up and down the path past her parents' room a few times. Only with great difficulty did she resist the urge to move closer and crouch beneath the window, to listen to what they were saying. She did hear her father grumble loudly about rabbit-eaters and Sabbath desecrators, but he was not shouting. Early the next morning Leah came to look for her before she left for school.

'It will be all right,' she said, and Tonia hugged her mother.

As soon as school got out, Tonia started walking toward Rehavia. She stopped into some of the stores on the way and asked to see their telephone directory, but they either had no phone or had misplaced the directory. She was not as disappointed as she might have been; she had never used a telephone and had been nervous about trying to place a call for the first time. By the time she reached the quiet, shady streets where all the *Yekis* lived, the shops had closed for the afternoon *schlafstunde*. Tonia looked at her watch – she had only two hours before the kibbutz tender would depart for Kfar Etzion. If she missed it, she would have to ride on an Arab bus all by herself or spend the night in Jerusalem, with no way to get a message to her parents. Either way, her father would be furious.

Tonia sat down to rest on the stone steps of one of the homes, chin in hands, then got back up and brushed herself off. She spent the next hour and a half walking up and down streets and looking at the names on mailboxes, before running to catch the tender. She wasn't discouraged. She would go back and keep looking every time she got out of school early, until she found Nella Rozmann. It might take a long time, but she had all year and might get lucky. There were not that many streets in Rehavia. Tonia took a piece of paper out of her book bag and wrote down where she had begun and which street numbers she had already looked at. The sun looked brighter, now that she had a plan.

Two days later, she resumed her quest. Her book bag was heavy and her back ached, but Tonia plodded along. She crossed the street to approach a couple walking arm in arm.

'Excuse me, I'm looking for the Rozmann family and seem to have lost their address. I think it's on this street. Viktor and Nella. Do you happen to know them?'

'Sorry.' They shook their heads and walked on.

Tonia took a few more steps, and suddenly there it was – the Hebrew Gymnasium. Wide steps led up to the stately building of Jerusalem stone. She was tempted to go up and peek in the door, but knew that would only make her feel foolish. A trespasser. Anyway, who cared what it looked like? She continued up the street, until it was time to hurry to catch her ride home. It became a twice-weekly routine, and she refused to give up.

Working in the orchards under the hot sun had been unbearable, but there was worse to come. The day the winter rains began, Tonia found herself longing for the scorching sun. Drenched, she worked her way up the rows that had been marked off and stopped every two meters to carve a hole into the unforgiving earth. Another girl came along behind her, set a sapling in each hole, and shoveled the displaced dirt back over it. Tonia wore knitted gloves, but they quickly became soaking wet. She peeled them off and tried blowing warm air into her cupped hands, which were covered with blisters. The wind was almost worse than the rain. It chilled them to the bone and nearly blew them down the hillside.

They planted hundreds of fruit and forest trees. Rina remained a constant annoyance, singing while she labored. Tonia crawled back to their room after work, peeled off her cold soggy clothes, and shivered under a pile of blankets. She dreaded having to go back out into the cloud of cold mist that seemed to have settled over the kibbutz and walk all the way to the dining hall for her dinner. She could not remember how it felt to be dry and warm. She stared at the picture of 'her' house – brought with them from Tel Aviv and tacked to the wall over her bed – and mentally stocked its closets with great piles of quilts and satin comforters, imagining herself sipping hot chocolate in front of a blazing fire.

She continued her search for the legendary Rozmanns, week after frustrating week. One day she was caught in a sudden rainstorm. It passed quickly, but left her soaked and freezing. The shops were closed, and there was no place to warm up. She sank down on the nearest steps, the cold stone sending an even greater chill up her body. She was so tired, her backpack was so heavy. She looked down at her hands, calloused and blistered, nails jagged and dirty, and burst into tears.

Then she noticed a woman walking up the street toward her, and wiped her eyes. The woman held a gold umbrella, but stopped, looked up, decided it was no longer necessary, and closed it. Tonia stared – she was the most elegant woman Tonia had ever seen. Her soft light brown coat was unbuttoned, and under it she wore a tailored suit the color of her umbrella. Light brown shoes and handbag matched her coat. Her wavy blonde hair was swept back in a complicated arrangement, and a tiny hat perched on the side of her head. Tonia had never understood how women managed to walk in high heels without breaking their necks. This slim, long-legged woman glided along in hers. Tonia waited for her to pass by, wishing she could make herself invisible. The golden vision stopped in front of Tonia.

'Are you all right, dear?'

Tonia nodded.

'Are you lost?'

'No.' Tonia got to her feet, painfully aware of her muddy shoes, wet, wrinkled clothes, and uncombed hair. She knew she looked a mess even compared to ordinary mortals, but faced with this stylish goddess, she felt like a freak. 'I know where I am, but there's a family I'm trying to find. Maybe you know them. Mr. and Mrs. Rozmann.'

The woman let out a short laugh. 'Well, what do you know, here I am. I am Mrs. Rozmann.'

'Mrs. Nella Rozmann?' Tonia froze.

'Yes.'

'Nella and Viktor Rozmann?'

'Yes, dear, that's me. Now do you plan on telling me why you are so eager to make our acquaintance?'

'My mother ...' Tonia could not think how to begin.

'Listen, it's awfully cold out here. You must be freezing. Our house is right around the next corner. Why don't you come in and let me give you a cup of tea?'

Tonia was amazed to find herself on the verge of tears once again. She almost never cried. She glanced at her watch – she had a little more than an hour.

'That's kind of you. But I wouldn't want to impose.'

'Nonsense. No imposition. You can't imagine how curious I am to know why anyone would go to such lengths to find me. And I could use a nice cup of tea myself. Come along. What's your name?'

'Tonia.'

Tonia picked up her backpack, horrified to discover that she had set it down in the mud. She trudged along behind Mrs. Rozmann, who turned up the walk to a single family home. It had a small garden, hidden from the street by a low wall of stone and a stand of cypress trees. The door was unlocked. Mrs. Rozmann pushed it open and called, 'Yaffa!'

A heavy-set young woman came running, black woolen skirt and red sweater under her apron. Four hair clips on either side of her head failed to contain a halo of frizzy black hair.

'Oh my, did you get caught in the rain, Mrs. Rozmann?'

'I didn't, but our guest did. Yaffa, this is Tonia. Can you please bring her a pair of slippers and a towel?' Mrs. Rozmann turned and saw Tonia setting her book bag down on the porch. 'Oh, I don't think you want to leave that out there. Yaffa, see what you can do about that too, will you dear?'

'Oh my, yes, let me have that.'

Tonia handed the bag to Yaffa with an apologetic shrug. Yaffa held it up like a dead rat, tssking and shaking her head. 'I'll get that cleaned right up for you, such a shame, a nice bag like that, but don't you worry, I'll see right to it.'

Tonia bent down to remove her shoes. Her socks were damp, and as she stepped through the entry into the spacious living room, she feared tracking up the gleaming white tile floor. The decor was not to Tonia's taste – hard-looking couches covered with a brocade of blue, green, and gold and several dark paintings in heavy frames. It looked more a museum than a home. Definitely not a place to curl up with a book.

'Come on.' Mrs. Rozmann wiped her own feet on the mat and led the way to the kitchen, which, though small, was more welcoming. She hung her coat on a rack, reached for Tonia's, lit the fire under the kettle, and pulled out chairs for them at a round wooden table.

Yaffa appeared with the towel and slippers and clucked around Tonia for a moment.

'Thank you very much.' Tonia smiled meekly at her and then at Mrs. Rozmann. She felt like a cyclone of muck and debris that they had managed to contain in this tidy house But some of her energy was returning.

Yaffa brought a plate of chocolate cookies and set glasses of sweet mint tea in front of them.

'All right,' Mrs. Rozmann said. 'Let's hear what makes a pretty young girl sit down in the street and cry.'

CHAPTER ELEVEN

'I was just tired. Tired and cold and wet,' Tonia explained, head hanging.

'So why didn't you go home?' Mrs. Rozmann asked.

'There's still an hour until my ride leaves.'

'Don't you live in Jerusalem?'

'No. In Kfar Etzion.'

Mrs. Rozmann raised an eyebrow. 'That new kibbutz on the way to Hebron?'

'Yes. But I go to school in Jerusalem. At Miss Landau's.'

Mrs. Rozmann remained silent for a few seconds, frowning and picking at a cookie. Then she said, 'And you were looking for me because ...'

'I ... I want to go to the Gymnasium next year. I thought that since you live in Rehavia–'

'A lot of people live in Rehavia,' she said. 'Did you think that I am the principal there, or a teacher or something? Because I'm not. And where did you get my name?'

'No, I didn't think that,' Tonia said, feeling foolish. 'I got your name from my mother ... I mean, I remembered her talking about you and your family. She is from Kolo. She used to live across the street from you.'

Mrs. Rozmann froze and studied Tonia for a long moment before raising her hand, finger pointing, and opening her eyes wide. 'You must be Leah Mendel's daughter. Aunt Vivi's granddaughter,' she almost whispered, as if confronted by a ghost.

'Yes. That's the way my mother refers to your mother too – Aunt Eva. Is she ... are your parents all right? Have you heard from them?'

'Not a word. What about Leah, has she heard ...'

Tonia shook her head. She lifted her glass, fingertips at the top, above the steaming tea, and took a sip.

'I didn't think there was anyone left from Kolo. We've heard such ...' Mrs. Rozmann blinked and looked out the window.

'We left before. In 1934.'

There was a long silence.

'Good Lord, look at your hands.' Mrs. Rozmann touched Tonia's arm. 'What on earth have you done to yourself?'

'Oh, that's from work. On the kibbutz.' Tonia put her hands in her lap, wishing she hadn't been too exhausted to clean her nails after work yesterday.

'What kind of work do you do?'

'Clear rocks from the fields. And plant trees.'

Mrs. Rozmann pursed her lips and shook her head. She looked at her own manicured nails and then back at Tonia. She smiled again. 'Well, good for you. As you can see, I'm quite useless myself.'

Tonia had no idea how to respond to that and distracted herself by taking a cookie.

'I have a daughter your age. Ilana. She'll be going to the Gymnasium next year. You could be in her class.'

Tonia smiled and nodded.

'Are you hungry? Can I fix you a sandwich?'

'No, thank you.' Tonia shook her head and looked at her watch again. 'I should go pretty soon.'

'You have to get back to the kibbutz?'

'Yes.'

'But you come to school in Jerusalem every day?'

'Yes.'

'Over that awful road to Hebron?'

'Yes.'

Mrs. Rozmann sniffed, thought for a moment, and rose to consult the calendar hanging on the wall next to the coats. 'Can you come back to see me again in a week? Next Monday?'

'Yes.' Tonia nodded her head.

'Well, you do that. I'll have a talk with some people. Not that it's true, what you seem to think about needing *protekzia*. The Gymnasium isn't just for rich kids from Rehavia, like I suppose everyone says. They take students from all over, as long as their grades are high enough. But I'll find out how you should go about applying.' She took a brown paper bag out of a drawer, shook it open, picked two shiny red apples from the bowl on the counter, and put them into the bag. Then she stepped back to the table and added a handful of cookies. 'Here, take this with you. For the way home. Please give your mother my regards. My warmest regards. Does she work on the kibbutz too?'

Tonia rose and shrugged into her coat. 'Yes. In one of the children's houses.'

Mrs. Rozmann shook her head again. For a moment, Tonia thought she was going to hug her or perhaps burst into tears.

'Do you have brothers and sisters?' Mrs. Rozmann asked.

'One brother and one sister.'

'Did Leah marry someone from Kolo?'

'Yes. Josef Shulman.'

Mrs. Rozmann screwed up her face, one eye closed, and then grinned. 'Yes, I remember him. Big handsome fellow. All the girls were after him. Including me. Good for Leah.' She put her hand on Tonia's shoulder, and Tonia again sensed that the woman wanted to embrace her.

'I'm glad you found me, Tonia. Please come back next week. Here, wait.' She turned to the countertop for a piece of paper and wrote something on it. 'This is our phone number. I'll be waiting for you. It would be lovely if your mother came too. Any time she's in Jerusalem. Any time at all. I would love to see her again.'

Tonia did not mind work that day. She had so much to think about, the hours flew by. She felt silly, as if she had fallen in love with Mrs. Rozmann. She could not stop thinking about her. Her hair, her clothes, her long slender fingers. Tonia felt more relaxed than she had in a long time, confident she would go to the Gymnasium next year. Mrs. Rozmann would see to it. That would be the first step of Tonia's journey to a different life. The kibbutz might balk at paying the higher fees, but Tonia would get a job in Jerusalem if she had to.

After work, she went to her parents' room and was pleased to find Leah alone. 'I found Nella Rozmann,' she told her mother. 'She remembered you right away. She even remembered Abba. Said he was really handsome, all the girls were chasing after him.'

97

'Well, that's true.' Leah smiled. 'How is Nella?'

'She's beautiful. And rich,' Tonia said. She told her mother all about her visit to the Rozmann home, Mrs. Rozmann's offer to inquire about applying to the school, and her invitation to Leah.

'Yes, I'll have to go, the next time I'm in Jerusalem. It would be wonderful to talk with someone from Kolo. Someone who remembers everyone. Wonderful, but in another way horrible.' She sighed.

'Are you going to come with me next week?'

'Oh no, you know I have to work. But invite her to visit us. It might be interesting for her, to see a kibbutz.'

'Sure.' Tonia could not quite picture Nella Rozmann crammed among the passengers in a crowded Arab bus or taxi, or perched on a stack of concrete blocks in the back of the tender, the wind whipping her hair and clothes.

When Tonia arrived at the Rozmann home the following week, Mrs. Rozmann opened the door as if she had been standing behind it waiting. The smell of roasting meat pervaded the house, and Tonia's stomach growled.

'Tonia, come in. You're looking dryer and happier today. Let me take your coat.'

She tossed it over a chair and called, 'Ilana, Tonia is here.'

At first, Tonia thought Rina had followed her. Ilana had the same strawberry blonde curls as her sister, though a bit less unruly. The two girls awkwardly shook hands.

'Come on, let's go into the kitchen. I hope you're hungry, Tonia, at least for a little something. Don't worry, it's kosher.' Mrs. Rozmann turned back to smile at her guest. 'We are not religious, but the kitchen is kosher.'

'It smells wonderful,' Tonia said.

Yaffa was bustling about, setting out roast beef, mashed potatoes, green beans, hummus and eggplant salads, sauerkraut, and warm pita bread. Mrs. Rozmann held out a hand, motioning for Tonia to seat herself. Tonia first went to the sink and used an empty cup to pour water over each hand, the ritual washing before eating bread. Mrs. Rozmann and Ilana politely waited for her to sit down, eat a small bite of bread, and murmur the blessing. Yaffa said a loud 'Amen', put a bottle of water on the table, and sat down to join them.

'Please, help yourself before it gets cold,' Mrs. Rozmann said to both the girls.

'So you live in a kibbutz?' Ilana asked as she reached for the green beans. 'What's that like?'

'Everything belongs to everybody–' Tonia began.

'I heard about this girl on a kibbutz,' Ilana interrupted her, 'who got a new dress. A present from her grandmother in Tel Aviv. The next day she saw some other girl wearing it.'

'I've never heard about anything like that happening on Kfar Etzion. Except for work clothes. Those aren't personal. They get washed and put in a pile by size, and you take the one on the top of the pile. But our own clothes all have our number on them. We get them back from the laundry.'

'And another guy told me how he used to run away from the children's house at night. He was scared and wanted to get in bed with his parents, but they locked the door. Left him out there crying and wouldn't let him in.'

'Well, some people do believe strongly in the ideology.' Tonia concentrated on her plate.

She was grateful she had to catch her ride and wouldn't have to stay long, but the food was delicious. She wondered who she was supposed to compliment, Mrs. Rozmann or Yaffa? She looked at the air between the two of them when she declared it the best meal she had had in ages.

Mrs. Rozmann rose and set a folded piece of paper on the table next to Tonia. 'That's the name of the principal. There's a phone number too, in case you have any questions. You'll have to bring them your report cards for the last two years and take a test.'

'What kind of test?'

'English and maths. I'm not sure what else.'

'I already took it,' Ilana offered. 'There was some history and some, you know, what is the next number in the series type of questions. It wasn't hard, except for the English. That part was really hard.'

Tonia smiled. Her best subject.

'If you'd like, you can do that next Monday. I told them you seem to be free on Monday afternoons, and they said that would be fine. Come have lunch with us, and then go take the test. Of course, you don't have to. There's no hurry, if you want more time to prepare.'

'No, Monday is all right.'

'You'll miss your ride, I suppose, if you do that. But you're welcome to sleep over here. Ilana, while Yaffa's getting the dessert, why don't you show Tonia the guest room?'

Tonia followed Ilana, somewhat apprehensive. Were they coming to the part of the story where, once out of her mother's earshot, the wicked daughter turns on the unwelcome rival and hisses a nasty warning for her to go away and never come back. But Ilana continued to be cordial, if awkward, and showed Tonia a small room with a double bed and a set of shelves.

'This is where you could sleep,' she said.

Tonia looked at the soft bed, its head piled high with pillows, a reading lamp on the wall above it. Had she ever, in her entire life, spent a night alone in a room, with a door that she could close? Not that she remembered.

'It's very nice,' Tonia said. 'Your mother is being so kind to me. I don't know how I can ever thank her.'

'It's not like she went to a lot of trouble. All she had to do was walk over to the school and talk to someone. It took her about ten minutes.'

'Still, she didn't have to do that. And lunch and everything. Offering to let me sleep here.'

'Yaffa does the cooking.' Ilana shrugged. 'And washes the sheets. I don't mean it isn't nice of my mother. I just mean that you don't have to feel so bad about it.'

Tonia looked Ilana full in the face and felt her smile broaden. In this fairy tale, even the potentially wicked stepsister character was turning out to be nice.

100

Tonia returned the following Monday to take the test. After another comforting lunch at the Rozmann's, Ilana offered to walk with her to the school.

'Is it true that you don't live in the same apartment with your parents?' she asked.

'My parents don't have an apartment. Just one room. To sleep in. They don't need a kitchen, because there's a dining hall where everyone eats. And communal bathrooms and showers.'

'So where do you sleep?'

'In another room, like theirs, with my sister. But that's because we're the only children our ages. Usually each age group of children has its own house where they sleep together.'

'Yeah, that's what I thought. Only it's hard to imagine. Well, here we are. Good luck on the test.'

The secretary directed Tonia down the hall to a stern-looking man in a suit.

'Yes, please, be seated.' He pointed at a desk on which a pale blue test booklet and two sharpened pencils awaited her. 'You have ninety minutes.' He looked at his watch and wrote the time on the front of the booklet.

She handed it back to him in less than an hour. 'How long will it be until I know how I did?' she asked.

'I can check it for you right now.' He surprised her by smiling. 'Wait here, and the principal will be in to tell you your score.'

He turned to leave, and Tonia shook her head and bit her top lip. Mrs. Rozmann must be a force to be reckoned with. She sat and picked at her cuticles while she waited. Twenty minutes later, another man in a dark suit approached her. He walked ramrod straight, and Tonia felt like a small bug when he looked down at her.

'Miss Shulman?'

'Yes.' She got to her feet, feeling as if she should salute.

'I am the principal of the Hebrew Gymnasium of Rehavia. Dr. Goldshmidt.'

Tonia nodded.

'I have the pleasure of informing you that you have passed the acceptance test, and we are able to offer you a place here for the next school year.'

'Oh, thank you!'

'Thank only yourself. Your hard work has led you to its rightful reward. I am also happy to inform you that your test score and grades are high enough for us to be able to offer you a special scholarship. So you needn't trouble yourself about the fees.' He turned and marched off.

Tonia drifted back to the Rozmanns' on a cloud.

But the part of this wonderful day that she remembered best all winter long had nothing to do with the school. It was the luxury of the incredibly soft, incredibly warm bed in the Rozmanns' guest room. A whole room, all to herself. A bright light she could turn on and off whenever she felt like it. And there was a toilet right down the hall, no rushing up the path in the rain. She almost hated to fall asleep and miss any of that night.

That winter they planted acres of fruit trees and vineyards and thousands of forest trees. The saplings looked pathetic, shivering in the wind. Tonia could not believe they would survive, but they stubbornly clung to the soil, and winter finally ended. The air turned cool and crisp, the wildflowers glowed in the sun, and she was surprised to find herself beaming with pride when she looked at 'her' trees, imagining the orchards and forests into which they would grow. She had to admit, the lunatics had been right. And she had helped do that, with her own two hands.

In May, Hitler's armies surrendered to the Allies, but there were no effusive celebrations in the Shulman household. Their relief that the carnage had ended was accompanied by two conflicting thoughts: the hope that now they might learn what had become of their families, and the dread of having their worst fears confirmed.

CHAPTER TWELVE

When spring came Tonia again assumed that the hard work was over. What remained to do in this clement weather, but stroll up and down the rows of trees and watch them grow, bend down here and there to pull a weed? She soon learned the answer to that question – irrigation. She trudged behind a donkey cart that carried a tank of water. When it stopped, she filled a tin and emptied it around the base of the next tree. Then on to the next. And the next. Why on earth had they planted so many? Spring turned to summer and she labored long days under the blazing sun.

Finally, school started. The night before her first day at the Gymnasium, Tonia went to the communal laundry and ironed her threadbare navy blue skirt and white blouse. She cleaned and mended her book bag, sharpened her pencils, and made sure she had her dog-eared English dictionary.

The principal had told her to come to his office on the first day. She had hoped this was for something simple, like filling in some forms, but was appalled to discover that he intended to accompany her to the classroom and introduce her. He kept her in his office until after the bell had rung and the corridors were empty.

'Come, Miss Shulman, I'll show you the way.'

The room grew silent when he opened the door. The students scrambled to their feet and stood stiffly at the sides of their desks. He went to the front of the class and motioned for them to be seated. Tonia hung back in the doorway, but he turned and waved her to him, then swung an arm around her and clamped onto her shoulder.

'Class, I want to ask you to please extend a warm welcome to Miss Tonia Shulman.' He let go and turned to face her, clapping his hands. The students exchanged amused glances and applauded along with him. A few low whistles came from the back of the room. Tonia wished she could crawl under the teacher's desk.

'Miss Shulman brings with her more than impressive scholastic achievements,' he said, his iron grip back on her shoulder.

Had he not been holding on so tight, Tonia might have fled. Her eyes flitted around and focused on Ilana, sitting at a desk in the second row. Ilana had a broad grin on her face, but when she winked, Tonia knew she was not laughing at her. Tonia rolled her eyes in response and someone in the back row guffawed.

'Now I know it's everyone's first day, but most of you already know one another. Miss Shulman, however, is not from Jerusalem. She will be commuting quite a distance in order to attend our school. She and her family are among our nation's brave and intrepid pioneers.' His voice rose dramatically. 'They have helped establish a new kibbutz – Kfar Etzion – courageously shoring up Jerusalem's southern defenses. I'm sure I needn't remind you that the Hebron Hills are a desolate and difficult part of Eretz Israel, and that Arabs in that area have twice in recent history employed violence to force Jews to abandon their homes.'

He launched into a tedious lecture about these events, and Tonia stood through it expressionless, a rare specimen on display, conscious of her faded clothing and scuffed shoes. She felt like a terrible hypocrite for allowing her silence to affirm his description of her courageous dedication and sacrifice. Well, she could not very well say, 'Excuse me, Sir, but no one asked me. And if they had, Kfar Etzion would have been about the last place on earth I would have chosen to live.' He fluttered on about the unimaginable perils the brave settlers faced every day, and Tonia imagined the black cloud of doom her classmates must see gathering over her head.

At last he left, and Tonia took an empty seat, keeping her eyes glued to her book or the teacher. Ilana came over to her at the break.

'Hi, brave pioneer girl.'

Tonia cringed.

'Oh, don't pay any attention to him. Come on, let's go outside,' Ilana said, and Tonia sighed with relief that Mrs. Rozmann's daughter had apparently decided to take her under her wing.

When they went down the stairs to the courtyard she learned what a tremendous asset Ilana's patronage was. Tonia expected teasing, if not outright ridicule and insults, but Ilana stayed at her side, and her friends came over to introduce themselves to Tonia and welcome her. And that was that. Tonia was accepted. She would never fit in with them or feel truly at ease, but no one picked on her. No one made fun of her clothing. No one sneered 'brave pioneer girl'. No one sniggered when she found a quiet corner to say her afternoon prayers or murmured the Grace after Meals when she finished her lunch.

Tonia knew her classmates vacillated between admiration, pity, and resentment. The fact that Tonia never had any money, that she always had to rush home to work, and that her hands were rough and calloused aroused some unwanted sympathy, but they also had the unfortunate effect of making the other students feel like spoiled brats.

'My mother said to tell you,' Ilana said one morning, 'that you're more than welcome to sleep in the guest room whenever you want. If you did, you wouldn't have to travel back and forth every day. She said she'd give you your own key to the house, and the guest room could be your room.'

'Don't you need it for guests?'

Ilana shrugged and looked at the ceiling. 'I can't remember the last time we had guests. I mean, we have a lot of company. But no one ever sleeps over.'

'What did your father say?' What Tonia really wanted to ask was, 'How do *you* feel about it?', but she didn't hear any resentment in Ilana's voice.

Ilana let out a little laugh. 'The basketball team could move in and he wouldn't notice. He goes to a lot of conferences, and when he is around, he comes home late.'

'What does he do?'

'Professor. Mathematics.'

'I'll have to ask,' Tonia said, though she knew the kibbutz secretariat would be glad to be relieved of having to provide daily transportation, and her mother would not object.

A few days later Tonia packed a bag with her toothbrush, nightgown, and a clean blouse and went home with Ilana after school. Tonia was luxuriating in the wonderful bed when she heard the front door open and close. A few minutes later Mrs. Rozmann tapped on her door.

'Tonia, are you sleeping?'

'No. Reading.'

'Could you come out for a moment, dear?'

Tonia pulled her coat on over her nightgown and followed her out to the living room.

An extremely tall man stood up and held out a hand. A dark three-piece suit perfectly fitted his slim body, and he had striking deep blue eyes. His most prominent feature, however, was his bullet-shaped head. His completely bald head. Not a hair on it. It shone brilliantly even in the dim light, and Tonia thought it must be terribly cold.

'I'd like you to meet my husband, Mr. Rozmann. Viktor, this is Tonia.'

Tonia took the hand of the famous *Yeki*. 'It's nice to meet you, Mr. Rozmann. And I'd like to thank you for letting me stay here.'

The giant shook his head. 'No need for that. Well, I hope you're all settled in.'

He sat back down and opened a newspaper. Tonia looked over at Mrs. Rozmann, who nodded, granting her permission to return to her room.

Mrs. Rozmann soon tapped on her door again and sat on the edge of the bed. Tonia could smell the wine that she drank every evening on her breath.

'Are you comfortable, dear? Do you have everything you need?'

Tonia nodded.

'What's that you're reading?'

'*The Scarlet Letter.*' Tonia held up the book, which was in English. 'I have to write a book report about it for school.'

'How are you enjoying it?'

'Not much.'

Mrs. Rozmann was wearing a blue silk dress and had blue shadow on her eyes. She seemed to want to say something else, and Tonia waited.

Then Tonia was horrified to hear herself blurt out, 'You look really pretty.'

Mrs. Rozmann smiled and pulled Tonia into a hug. 'Aren't you the sweetest thing? You did extend my invitation to your parents, didn't you? Your mother and your father too?'

'Yes, Ma'am, I did. They said they would love to see you and to meet your husband, but it's hard for them to take a day off work, and it's hard to get into Jerusalem and back.'

'Well, get a good night's sleep.' She patted Tonia's leg and rose. In the doorway, she turned back. 'Your mother could run faster than anyone else at school. She even beat all the boys.'

'My mother ran races?'

'Oh yes. I don't mean official or anything … just on the playground, you know.'

Tonia fell asleep wondering what other amazing things Nella Kutzky might know about her mother.

It was hard to believe that the Rozmanns' house was less than a twenty-mile drive from Kfar Etzion. To Tonia it seemed like a foreign country. They held dinner parties with special china and silverware. British officers, university professors, foreign diplomats, and big shots from the Jewish Agency sat on their couch sipping expensive wines and imported whiskey. Ilana was usually out with her friends on these nights. Tonia stayed home and offered to help Yaffa serve and clean up.

'You don't have to do that.' Mrs. Rozmann pulled her aside the first time she appeared carrying a tray. 'You are a guest in our home.'

'I don't mind. Honest.'

Mrs. Rozmann studied her. 'Oh well, I suppose you enjoy watching the goings-on, don't you? I would have, at your age. Just don't feel like you're turning into some little Cinderella or something. And be careful what you overhear.' She winked.

Mrs. Rozmann drew the line, however, when one of her guests asked Tonia if she could hire her to serve at a party. Tonia said she would be delighted, but Mrs. Rozmann took her by the elbow and said she needed her in the kitchen.

'I will not have you working for that woman.'

'But why? I've been trying to think of a way to make some pocket money.'

'I won't hear of it. I'd rather pay you *not* to do it. She's only asking so she can go around telling everyone I don't take care of you. "Poor thing has to go out and work". Maybe we should start giving you some kind of allowance.'

'No, I couldn't take money from you,' Tonia said, chin out. 'And what's wrong with working? Hasn't Ilana ever had a job?'

'Heavens, no.'

Tonia stopped feeling angry and almost laughed. The difference between her two worlds was even greater than she had imagined.

One night the Rozmanns announced they would be home late – they were going out dancing at the Café Vienna. Tonia waited until they had been gone an hour and Ilana and Yaffa were both upstairs in their rooms. Then she pulled on her clothes, slipped into a light coat, and let herself out. She walked quickly and could soon hear the music lying softly on the cool night air. A waltz. She lurked in the shadows for a long while, hugging her coat to her as she swayed and hummed. Then she ventured closer to the foggy window to spy on the dazzling vision that was Nella Rozmann, gliding through the air with one partner after another. The *Yeki* had one elbow on the bar, watching. He kept his expression blank, but Tonia squinted hard at him and thought she saw a tinge of distaste.

Tonia grew tired and walked back to the house. She lay in bed with her hands behind her head for a long while before she fell asleep. There were so many ways to live a life.

The next day she went home to the kibbutz, found Leah in the children's house, and paused in the doorway to watch her. A dozen curly-headed children were seated around two tables, having afternoon tea. Leah looked end-of-the-day worn out in her faded blue work pants and gray shirt, her hair carelessly pinned up. She moved about easily, taking a spoon from one child who was using it to beat another over the head, spreading white cheese on bread for another, sponging up spilt milk. Tonia went in to help her mother wash tiny hands and wipe faces. Tonia's favorite, Eran, a tow-headed little boy with red-apple cheeks and a mischievous smile, climbed into her lap and asked her to help him put on his 'outside' shoes.

When they had all gone off with their parents, Tonia hugged her mother and said, 'You're way prettier than Nella Kutzky.' Leah laughed and put her hands on Tonia's cheeks.

It was true. Leah did not need silk dresses and high-heeled shoes, and Mrs. Rozmann would have been quite plain without the props. But it was not that difference between the two women that was on Tonia's mind. What she would have liked to say to her mother – but did not know how – was that, for all her complaints, Tonia knew that Leah was living a better life. Albeit difficult, but focused, purposeful. Tonia was not indifferent to what her parents and the rest of the Community of Abraham were accomplishing. She was aware of the desperate need for her people to shape a future. Mrs. Rozmann might be kind-hearted and generous and laugh the way they did in the movies, but most of her concerns were frivolous. Tonia would never admire her the way she did her mother.

But when Tonia imagined the life she wanted for herself, there was no escaping the truth. As long as it was not with Viktor Rozmann, she would rather go dancing.

CHAPTER THIRTEEN

Tonia was home in Kfar Etzion for the first night of Hanukah. Everyone gathered in the dining hall to light candles and sing songs about the few and weak vanquishing the strong and many.

'Elon, this is my sister Tonia.' Rina introduced her new boy-friend, an earnest-looking fellow with square glasses and a pronounced cowlick. Tonia took an immediate liking to him. 'He lives on Massuot Yitzchak.' Rina referred to the new kibbutz that had been founded near Kfar Etzion a few months earlier. A group of settlements was planned for the area; they would become the Etzion Bloc.

Rina had made a valiant attempt to control her wild cloud of hair, and the radiance of her smile made it obvious that this Elon fellow was making her happy in a way Tonia envied. She was wearing her old gray sweater and a faded blue skirt, but Rina the tomboy suddenly looked feminine. In a natural way, from the inside. In fact, all of the kibbutz women looked good to Tonia that night, their faces scrubbed, none of the elaborate make-up and hairstyles of Mrs. Rozmann and her friends.

After releasing Elon's hand, Tonia stepped over and gave her sister a hug. 'You look beautiful,' she whispered.

Rina blinked with surprise, but her puzzled expression settled into a smile, and she returned the hug. 'That's how he makes me feel,' she whispered. 'I'm so happy, Tonia.'

Tonia gave her sister's arm a gentle squeeze as she pulled away. She found Natan standing next to her, offering her a tiny glass of wine to toast the holiday.

'So how's your adopted family?' he asked, as he raised his own glass to her.

'I wouldn't exactly call them that. I think they need to adopt each other first. They hardly ever see each other.'

'And your friend?'

'Ilana?'

Natan nodded. He had met Ilana once, when he came to the Gymnasium to bring Tonia a book she had forgotten at home.

'She's all right. We don't do much together. I help her with her English homework, and she invites me to come along when she goes places – and is glad when I say "no thanks". It's better that way, I think. Not much opportunity for us to quarrel about anything.'

'Do you have any friends there?'

'Not really. I spend more time with the Rozmanns' maid than anyone else. But that's not because they're a bunch of snobs. They are friendly enough, and it's not like I'm the only poor kid there.'

'We're not poor.'

'I never have any money, and my clothes are all falling apart. What would you call that?'

'I suppose. I just never thought of our family that way.'

Tonia thought for a moment. 'That's because most poor people don't have any choice. They're in a big pit that they can't climb out of. But Abba and Ima aren't like that. They have high-school educations, they're smart, they know languages,' she said. 'But they made a choice – they volunteered to be poor. By the way, Ilana asked about you the other day.' Tonia cocked her head and looked at her brother sideways. 'You two like each other, don't you?'

He shrugged. 'I only saw her that one time.'

Tonia took a step back and looked her brother up and down. Tall and slim, lush sandy curls, eyelashes Mrs. Rozmann would kill for. 'I never noticed how good-looking you are.' She punched him in the arm. 'I bet Ilana does like you. That wasn't the first time she's asked about you, come to think of it. You certainly would make a gorgeous couple. But she's … I don't know … she's nice enough, but that family is pretty strange.'

Her eyes strayed to Josef and Leah, who were standing together, holding hands. 'I used to think our family was weird, but the Rozmanns … it's like they never even talk to each other.'

111

The next day she went to the Rozmanns' after school. On her bed, she found a large pale pink box, tied with a shiny red ribbon. Embossed silver letters on a thick white card wished the world at large a Happy Hanukah. Tonia went out to the living room and listened at the foot of the stairs for a sign of life, but the house was empty. Not even Yaffa seemed to be home.

She propped herself up in bed and tried to read her book, but could not keep her eyes off the box lying at her side. Maybe they would not mind if she opened it before they came home. That did not seem very polite, but who knew when they would turn up? Finally, she could stand it no longer. She went to the front door and looked out, but no one was in sight.

Tonia carefully slipped the wide red ribbon off and opened the box. In it, swathed in tissue paper, lay an astonishing, entirely white creation of silk, lace, and beads. The most beautiful dress she had ever seen. It must be a mistake. A package for Mrs. Rozmann had been accidentally left on her bed. She looked at the card again, turned it over, but there was no name, no writing on it at all. Only the commercially printed holiday greetings.

She went to the bathroom to wash her hands before she dared touch it. Then she lifted it out of the box, as if it were gossamer, and held it up against her body. This had to be a mistake. Who would buy such a dress for a fifteen-year-old girl? She could not imagine what it must have cost. She returned it to the box, trying to fold the tissue paper exactly as it had been before, and slipped the ribbon back in place.

Tonia longed to try it on. She had never owned a new dress, even a plain one. She wore her sister's hand-me-downs and whatever was available in the kibbutz storeroom. A dress like the one in the box was beyond the realm of her dreams. What if it *was* intended for her? She got up and looked out the front door again. No one was coming. What could it hurt to try it on? After all, the box had been on her bed, a reasonable mistake for her to make.

She tore her clothes off and slipped the cool, smooth fabric over her head. There was a full-length mirror at the end of the corridor, and she stood mesmerized in front of it. The silk clung to her body, beaded lace draped over her shoulders. She pulled her hair back and held it up and thought, I am pretty. I am really pretty. She was tempted to go upstairs and get Mrs. Rozmann's silver high-heeled shoes to try on with the dress, but did not dare. The footsteps on the front porch took her by surprise.

'Tonia,' Mrs. Rozmann called out. 'Are you home?'

Tonia ducked back into her room. There was no time to take the dress off. She considered shutting the door and pretending to be asleep, but instead decided to step out to meet her fate.

'I knew it,' Mrs. Rozmann clapped her hands, 'I knew it would be fabulous on you, with your dark hair. And I even got the size right. How clever of me.'

Ilana was behind her mother. 'I helped her pick it out,' she said.

Tonia looked from one to the other and burst into tears.

Mrs. Rozmann fished a handkerchief out of her handbag. 'Here, watch out, you'll stain the silk. What's the matter, don't you like it?'

Unable to speak, Tonia held the handkerchief to her eyes. If ever there was an occasion when she felt like the poor cousin, a beggar, this was it, but she didn't care. She would be a charity case. She would accept handouts. She wanted the dress. 'I ... I love it. It's the most beautiful thing I've ever had. It's the most beautiful thing I've ever *seen*. I can't believe you bought it for me.'

Mrs. Rozmann blinked and smiled, looking both nonplussed and pleased by the intensity of Tonia's outburst. 'Don't you worry, you'll have lots of nice things when you grow up. Let me have a better look at you.' She spun Tonia around. 'You really are lovely,' she declared, an artist proud of her creation.

'I told you it would look great on her,' Ilana said.

'Thank you so much,' Tonia repeated several times, and put a hand on the arm of each.

Tonia thought she could understand Mrs. Rozmann enjoying the role of bountiful savior, but Ilana was a puzzle to her. Why wasn't she jealous and resentful? What made her so generous to this intruder in her home? Ilana was watching her with an expression she could not read. Pity? Probably, but then her face spread into a warm smile, and she gave Tonia a hug. Tonia might have been a poor little thing, but she was their poor little thing.

Ilana announced that she was going out to meet some friends and ran upstairs to change. A light bulb went on for Tonia. Of course. Obviously. How stupid of her to think that Miss Queen Bee of the Rehavia Gymnasium could ever be jealous of the pathetic pioneer girl. Ilana could afford to be munificent to their live-in mouse in her frayed clothes, no friends, nose in her books, rushing home to bloody her hands. Tonia felt deflated, but only for a moment. She would not allow herself to care what they thought. It didn't matter. She could settle for Ilana behaving well toward her. No matter that she was probably rushing off to tell her friends how the poor thing had actually burst into tears over a silly dress. It didn't matter. None of this was important. All Tonia had to do was get through high school. This was not real life. Not yet. In real life, Tonia would show them all.

Mrs. Rozmann went to the kitchen, calling for Yaffa. Tonia admired herself in the mirror again. Now all she needed was a ball to attend. Then she went back to her room, took the dress off, wrapped it back up, and slipped the box under the bed. Yaffa discovered it there, the next time she cleaned.

'What's wrong, Tonia, don't you like it any more, why didn't you take it home with you?' Mrs. Rozmann asked.

Tonia was reluctant to answer. Mrs. Rozmann would never understand how laughable was the notion that she might have occasion to wear a dress like that at Kfar Etzion. Besides, Tonia was not sure they would let her keep it. There was no telling what the fanatics on the kibbutz secretariat would do. They might even decide to put 'that Shulman girl's decadent bourgeois dress' on the agenda of the weekly meeting. It was just the type of thing people could get themselves all worked up about. They passed enormous budgets and major security measures brought up by the secretariat with little discussion and a perfunctory show of hands. But when it came to personal property and perceived slights and inequalities, the arguments could drag on into the night. And if they did let her keep it, where would she put it? She had only five shelves in the wardrobe for all her belongings, and the roof above it often leaked.

'If you don't mind, I'd rather keep it here.'

Mrs. Rozmann patted her arm. 'No, I don't mind. I guess we'll just have to find someplace here in Jerusalem for you to wear it.'

That never happened, and the dress stayed in its box under the bed, but Tonia was happy just knowing it was there. Every so often, when no one else was home, she got it out and put it on. A reminder that another Tonia was possible.

Tonia often arrived home at the kibbutz to find it seemingly abandoned, everyone having dropped whatever they were doing and gone to gather around one of the radios – it was time for the broadcast of the Search Bureau for Missing Relatives. The Jewish Agency had begun broadcasts in Yiddish and Hebrew, reading out the names of people who had survived, their home town, and where they could be contacted. Leah listened with her eyes closed, but none of the names she prayed for were ever on the lists. She never heard of anyone at all from Kolo. Chelmno, where Leah assumed her family had been murdered, was seldom mentioned. Almost no one taken there had survived.

Tonia skipped school one spring morning. Looking over her shoulder to make sure no one was watching, she slipped into the already crowded yard of the American Consulate and took a number. She stood outside in the sun with no place to sit and no place to get a drink of water for three hours. After she was let into the building, she waited in another long line and was exhausted by the time it was her turn to step up to the counter. At least the young Arab woman behind it was surprisingly kind. Tonia had expected hostility, but the woman patiently answered her questions about how she could apply for a student visa to the United States and admittance to an American university. She also gave Tonia information about scholarships for foreign students. Well, on second thought, why wouldn't she be helpful? Tonia thought on her way out. One less Jew in Palestine.

She stuck her head out to survey the street before she left, wary of being seen there. People talked about others who left the country as if they were criminals, traitors, a lower form of life. She could not imagine the scene her father would make, if he knew. She went back to the Rozmanns' and hid the stack of forms and brochures from the Consulate in the box, beneath the white dress. It was discouragingly large, but she had two years to figure it out.

Then she went out again and spent the afternoon looking for a part-time job, inquiring at every store she passed. No one could afford to take on help. She thought of hiring herself out as a cleaner, but she could imagine how Mrs. Rozmann would react to that. She had sniffed loudly the one time Tonia babysat for one of the neighbors. Work isn't something to be ashamed of, Tonia felt like shouting at her, but, of course, did not.

The next morning the homeroom teacher informed them that they would be going on their annual class trip at the end of the month. She passed out permission slips and told them they must bring in the payment by the end of the next week.

After the bell rang, Tonia approached the teacher. 'Is there some way I can earn the money for the trip?' she asked.

'Oh, Tonia, you don't have to worry about it. When Mrs. Rozmann paid your tuition for the year, she took care of all the other fees too.'

'Mrs. Rozmann? She didn't pay my tuition. I have a scholarship.'

The teacher paled. 'Oh, I must be confused. In any case, all your fees have been taken care of. By your scholarship.'

So, she was even more of a charity case than she had imagined. For the first time in her life, she felt ashamed of her father, who could not – or would not – provide for her education. All he cared about was his stupid kibbutz, while his daughter had to beg from strangers. No wonder her parents had never accepted the Rozmanns' invitation.

Even more disturbing to Tonia was the discovery that she was dependent on Mrs. Rozmann's continued good will. Up until now she had considered it simply good manners when she deferred to Mrs. Rozmann's wishes. Now she could not help but see herself as groveling.

That was the day they had been dismissed early, the day of the attack that had taken off the tip of her nose. Her father had chosen the worst possible day to announce that he intended to donate the last of her own family's valuables to the kibbutz.

So Tonia had marked off a spot four paces from a flat boulder and five paces from the perimeter fence, and her grandmother's candlesticks had gone into the ground.

CHAPTER FOURTEEN

A few days later, Tonia was at her parents' room for afternoon tea. Josef strode up the path, carrying a batch of papers. 'Take a look at this.' He placed a sketch of a building on the table. 'That's what Neveh Ovadiah will look like,' he said, referring to the new cultural center that was being built. 'Real cut stone.'

'It will be lovely, Josef,' Leah said and poured his tea.

'It's wonderful,' Rina said.

'You,' he said, pointing at Tonia, 'could show a little interest for a change.'

'Marvelous,' she replied.

'Tonia isn't interested in anything but her English dictionary,' Rina said.

'I wouldn't be so proud of neglecting my own studies, Rina.' Leah raised an eyebrow.

'What they're doing here is more of an education than they'll get out of any book.' Josef sat down and picked up his glass of tea.

'Josef, I'm surprised at you. Why I can remember all the poetry you knew by heart, the philosophy books you pored over–'

'Those were different times,' he replied. 'What the Jewish people needs now are not farmers who can quote verse to their donkeys or argue about Spinoza with their cows. We need farmers who know how to grow a decent piece of fruit.'

'The two don't necessarily negate one another,' Natan said.

Josef ignored him and poked his finger toward Tonia again. 'Another thing,' he said. 'I hear you aren't being very helpful with the Youth Aliyah kids. Aren't very friendly.'

'Sorry, Abba. I guess we've been in this wasteland for so long, I've lost my social skills. You brought me to this place with no one to be friends with, and now you expect me to know how to be friendly.'

'You could make an effort,' Rina said.

'Rina, please, must you always quibble?' Leah sighed and passed a plate of cookies.

'Why shouldn't she quibble? Because she's right?' Josef demanded. 'You always take Tonia's side. I'm sure you even approve of ... everything she does. And says.'

This was his first oblique reference to Tonia's theft of the Shulman family crown jewels. Tonia flushed and wondered what he thought she had done with them. And what did Rina and Natan think had happened to the candlesticks? Did they assume their father had sold them? Neither of them had mentioned their disappearance to her.

'She is entitled to her own opinion,' Leah said.

'That's your liberal education,' Josef complained. 'You'll let her grow up to be an individualist, an egotistical ingrate with no sense of responsibility to her family, let alone her people.'

'You're a great one to preach family responsibilities,' Tonia said.

'Is that so?'

'Yes, Abba, that is so. You were never there when we needed you, when we were little.' She felt the shame of her words as she spoke them and rose to flee up the path.

'Are these arguments necessary, Josef?' Tonia heard her mother ask.

Tonia slowed her step, wanting to hear her father's reply.

'Yes. It's time she learned that God put us on this earth for more than– Where are *you* going?' he demanded.

'To talk to Tonia.' Tonia heard her brother reply, no challenge in his voice.

Natan caught up with her, and they walked in silence to the room Tonia shared with Rina. She stretched out, and he managed to squeeze beside her on the narrow cot.

'Feel better?'

'Sometimes I hate him,' Tonia said.

'You don't want to talk like that.'

'Don't you ever feel that way?'

'No. Why would I hate him?'

'For making us come here.'

119

'I guess I don't think it's so bad. And I'm different from you, more of a fatalist. Haven't you ever wondered – suppose you do make it to America, and then you get run over by the first fancy car that goes by?'

'No, Natan,' Tonia answered wearily. 'I have never wondered about that.'

'Take it easy.' He patted her leg and rose. 'Everything will be all right. He can't stay mad at his favorite for long.'

'Favorite?'

'You must know you are. Everyone else does.'

The Shulmans did not always sit together in the dining hall for their evening meal, but that night, by unspoken agreement, they presented themselves as one big happy family. Tonia and Josef both made a special effort to be polite. Would you like more potatoes? Can I pass you the fried eggplant? When they rose to leave following the Grace after Meals, Josef lightly squeezed Tonia's elbow.

Tonia gradually stopped resenting the fact that Mrs. Rozmann was paying for her schooling. How else could she have gone to the Gymnasium? All right, she didn't like having to feel so grateful, but then Ilana didn't like being made to feel less patriotic than Tonia. What did it all matter? All that mattered was that she was getting an education.

Tonia continued to spend two or three nights a week at the Rozmanns', and the next time Ilana offered to treat her to coffee and cake, she accepted. Life is short. If someone offers you something, take it, enjoy it, and say thank you.

One night her father came to her room in Kfar Etzion.

'It's tomorrow,' he said. 'Ein Tsurim. The trucks are coming tomorrow.' He was referring to the third kibbutz that would become part of the Etzion Bloc.

'Yes, I know.'

'Stay home from school tomorrow. I want you to be here. You and I will both take a day off and watch it together.'

'Watch what? People unloading trucks?'

120

'People creating the future. Please, Tonia.'

'All right, Abba.'

He knocked on her door early the next morning. 'Come, Tonia, get dressed.'

He led her to the dark and deserted kitchen. She shivered with cold and rubbed sleep from her eyes, watching him cook an omelet with onions and tomatoes for her. While she ate, he prepared cheese and tomato sandwiches and a thermos of Turkish coffee that he put into a small backpack. The sun was coming up as he led her out the front gate of Kfar Etzion, down the feeder road past the Lonely Tree, and over the next hill.

'Is there anything more beautiful than a new day?' Without warning, he turned, picked her up, and swung her around the way he used to when she was a little girl.

He put her down and hugged her so hard to his chest she had trouble breathing. But she did not protest, savoring the moment. She tried to remember the last time she had been so close to him, the last time they had touched one another. She wished his strength could envelop her forever. When he let her go, she saw that his eyes were rimmed with red.

'Here, let's sit here.' He nodded at a pair of boulders and they settled themselves, shifting from side to side until their backsides accommodated themselves to the hard irregular surface. The heavy dew seeped into the seat of her khaki pants.

'There's a reason I got you up so early. It's important for you to see that.' He pointed at the hill slightly north of where they sat. 'Tell me what you see.'

She squinted and shrugged. 'A bunch of tents.'

The sharply pointed white cones, as tall as they were wide, were stark against the gray-brown hills.

'You see basically nothing, correct?'

She nodded.

He reached for his pack. 'I think it's time for coffee,' he said, and poured two cups.

They drank in silence, and then he took out his prayer shawl, *tefillin*, and two prayer books, one of which he handed to Tonia. He rose to say the *Shaharit* prayers, and when he came to the

121

Shmoneh-Esreh, she stood a few meters from his side and murmured it along with him.

When he had finished, he closed the prayer book, kissed it, and smiled at Tonia. His eyes remained on her for a long while, and she swore to herself that she would never quarrel with this extraordinary man again. Before either of them could speak, they heard the distant rumble of trucks.

A convoy of vehicles snaked along the road from Jerusalem, up the hill that would become Ein Tsurim. Flatbed trucks were piled to the sky with stacks of wooden slats. Men and women rode on top of them and clung to their sides. They jumped down almost before the trucks came to a halt, and, together with the people who had materialized out of the tents, began unloading.

'What do you think you will see over there by this afternoon?'

'More tents, a few huts.' She shrugged. 'There aren't very many bushes. They'd better put up the toilets first.'

In fact, she was amazed by the speed at which they worked. The first structure was taking shape as they spoke. She remembered the day they had founded Massuot Yitzhak. When she left for school that morning there had been nothing there; by the time she returned at dusk people were arranging chairs outside their rooms.

'In eight hours, ten hours, those people will have turned nothing into a home.'

'How come you aren't over there helping them?'

'Because it's more important for me to be here with you. To try and turn the switch in your head.' He made a motion with his hand, as if starting a car. 'You are like my father and my grandfather. A pessimist. You see the difficulties, the reason that something cannot be done. When someone overcomes an obstacle, instead of cheering him on, you point out the next one, the reason he should give up. Today I want you to see, really see, the power of optimism. People can do anything, Tonia.' He turned and put his hands on her shoulders. 'Anything. Their capacity for evil seems to be without limit, but so is their ability to create, to do good.' He removed his hands and stared over the horizon. 'Of course, most people do neither. They pass through life doing nothing.' He turned his gaze back to her. 'Don't be one of them, Tonia. You are meant to be so much better than that.'

She gave him a weak smile, and they sat in silence for a while.

'In fifty years these hills will be covered with cities. Tens of thousands of Jews will live here.'

'I hope so,' she said.

She was not going to argue with him today, had no intention of pointing at the Arab villages in the distance and asking, what about them, Abba? Their optimists believe it is possible to slit all our throats.

He seemed to read her mind and recited his standard speech about the friendly relations they had with the Arabs in Beit Umar, Saffa and Hirbet Zakaria, and with the two monks and one Christian family who lived in the nearby Russian Monastery.

She smiled at her father. She did not ask, 'But what about the other 85,000 Arabs out there. What are you going to do about them, Abba?'

CHAPTER FIFTEEN

Leah stretched back in her chair, pleasantly tired. A gentle breeze cooled her as she listened to the sounds of late afternoon – husbands, wives, and children greeting one another, shouts of laughter, and the faint drone from the machine shop. She smiled, grateful for the long-elusive peace of mind that she seemed to have achieved. She could not look in the mirror without noting a new wrinkle, but her face seemed to have lost some of its pinched look. Josef came up the path and pulled a chair next to hers.

He clasped her hand. 'You look happy, my wife.'

'I suppose I am.' She smiled at him. 'Today has been good to me.'

'Leah'le,' he began and paused. 'Natan and Rina went to Jerusalem this morning. They're both enlisting in the Palmach.'

She shut her eyes. 'So soon? They're children. Couldn't they finish their studies first?'

She knew it was a feeble protest. Natan was sixteen and Rina seventeen. All the youngsters their ages were enlisting. She sighed. Natan and Rina must be thrilled. Neither was much of a student; their textbooks gathered dust under their beds. Of her three children, only Tonia showed any interest in school. Her English textbooks were always worn, the bindings coming apart. Leah fretted that the older two were not receiving a proper education, but Josef shrugged off her concern, muttering, to school they go, what more do you want? They are intelligent, they read, they have more important things to do than scramble after a meaningless scrap of paper.

Josef stroked her hand. 'Perhaps it can be arranged so that Rina, maybe both of them, will receive basic training here in Kfar Etzion.'

She closed her eyes again. 'It's all right. I knew this was coming.'

'I joined the Palmach this morning. Rina too,' Natan told Tonia. They were working side by side, clearing rocks from a section of hillside.

'You thought you had to, for Abba.' She heaved a rock onto the sledge, and it landed with a loud thud. Then she got down on her knees and struggled with a larger one that was embedded in the earth.

'No. Abba's never mentioned it.'

'Abba doesn't have to mention things like that.'

'No, I didn't enlist for him. Really. I did it for me.' He took a step toward Tonia and squatted on his haunches in front of her, so he could look into her eyes. 'For all of us. Every time I look at them,' he said, voice lowered, and nodded at a group of young Czechoslovakian Jews working nearby, who had managed to escape the Nazis and had been smuggled into Palestine, 'I know Abba is right. We have to stand our ground here. Fight.'

'How can you all be so blind? What happened to the Jews in Europe should tell you the opposite. We sit around asking why they didn't see it coming, didn't have enough sense to get out in time. Hitler said it all, wrote it down, black and white, exactly what he was going to do, but they sat there, thinking it could never happen to them. And now here we sit, surrounded by a hundred million Arabs, who make no secret that they are waiting for the British to pull out so—'

'Would you run away?'

'Yes. Anyone in his right mind would run away from a place like this.'

Natan's eyes searched her face. 'They didn't stay in Europe because they wanted to.' He nodded again at the Czechs, who had taken a break and sat in a circle laughing. 'There was no place on earth willing to let them in. And what makes you think anyone wants us? Your wonderful America didn't take Jewish refugees either. Abba goes a bit overboard, I'll grant you that, but he's right. This is where we belong. Where we'll stand and fight for ourselves, without begging anyone else for help that isn't going to come. Look, you're bleeding.' He nodded at her

125

hands where the jagged rocks had torn the skin away. 'You should wear gloves.'

She wiped the blood on her pants. 'So if you enlisted, what are you doing here?'

'We'll get our orders soon.'

She sighed and put out a hand to touch his cheek. 'I can't quite see you as a soldier,' she said.

'Me neither.' He laughed and stood up. 'Let's go get a drink of water.'

'There's a dark-skinned guy who's always hanging around,' she said and extended a hand for him to help her up. 'Tall, wears a yarmulke.'

'Yeah. I've never met him, but I know who you mean. Why?'

'What's he doing here? Does he belong to the Palmach?' she asked as they walked toward the barrel of water.

'I don't think so. He comes when he can. Helps out. There are rumors about him, that he belongs to the Irgun.'

'Is he religious?'

'Why else would he wear a yarmulke? What's your big interest in him? Oohh, I don't believe it. Heartless Tonia has a crush on someone.' He reached out to pinch her cheek, and she slapped his hand away.

'I do not. I was just wondering, that's all. He doesn't look religious.' She took a tin cup from a nail, dipped it into the barrel, and drank.

'So what do religious guys look like?'

'Never mind, forget I asked. How come Rina didn't come back with you?'

'She had something to do in Jerusalem.' He filled his own cup.

'Now her I can see as a soldier. Great at taking orders. Even better at giving them.'

'Why do you and Rina have to be in a fight all the time?'

'We're not in a fight. We just can't stand each other.'

He sighed. 'Let's get back to work.'

126

'Poor Natan. You should have been born into some nice reserved English family, not a bunch of bickering Jews.'

'I'll ask around about that guy for you.'

'Don't you dare. I mean it, Natan, don't you dare.'

He lowered his voice and nodded at one of the Czech girls who was walking toward them. 'Do you know her?' She was baby-doll pretty, with a face of porcelain and lips that protruded into a kiss. A wisp of light blonde hair had escaped the rubber band that held her ponytail. 'I think her name is Malina or something like that.'

'No, I don't know her. I don't know any of them. I ... I don't feel comfortable around them. But she's looking right at you.' Tonia nudged him. 'You go for blondes, don't you? Why don't you go talk to her?'

'Maybe I will, after we're done filling that last sledge. And you're gone.'

Tonia grinned at him.

He bent over to pick up a rock and looked back at his sister. 'You won't really leave, will you?'

'The minute I can.'

'Well, I suppose now that the war's over, you could always go back to Poland,' he sneered and threw the rock into the sledge.

CHAPTER SIXTEEN

Kfar Etzion had turned its living quarters into a guesthouse. Kibbutz members moved into white-peaked tents for the summer months, allowing tourists to occupy their rooms. This summer Tonia had been given a new job as welcome committee, housemother, and chambermaid to these guests. She loved it. No more crawling around in the dirt. She was surprised to discover how much she enjoyed meeting new people, having tended to think of herself as shy or anti-social, or both.

One afternoon she took the bus back from Jerusalem, lugging packages of new sheets and towels that she had bought for the guest rooms. Natan met her on one of the paths, and she handed him some of the parcels.

'You got a new customer a little while ago.' He grinned as they walked toward the guesthouse office. 'Caused quite a stir.'

'Why?'

'This rusted-out jalopy pulls up, and this tiny lady gets out, goes into the office alone, no suitcase, all her stuff tied up in a sheet.' Natan mimicked carrying a bundle over one shoulder.

'Sounds colorful,' Tonia said, balancing the packages she was carrying against the door of the guesthouse storeroom while she searched for her keys.

'Colorful is the word. She was dark-skinned and wearing a long black dress, up to her chin and down to her wrists and ankles. The front had fancy red and orange embroidery all over it, and she had her head covered with a scarf full of blue and gold beads.'

'Who was working reception?'

'Dorit. And I guess she about fainted on the spot. Thought the lady was an Arab. Went rushing off to the kitchen to get Edna. Edna told her it was okay – she must be Yemenite. I guess they dress like that.'

'I'll have to go meet this lady. See if I can help her settle in, after that wonderful greeting. Thanks for helping me with this stuff.'

Tonia finished arranging her purchases, prepared some tea, and headed up the path to the room for which this intriguing lady was registered. She had two new towels for the guest under one arm and carried a tray of pastries and tea, so she tapped the scuffed toe of her work boot against the door.

'Yes?'

'Mrs. Amrani?'

'Come.'

Tonia bent her knees to push the handle down with her elbow and nudged the door open. 'Shalom. I'm Tonia Shulman. I'm the one to tell if you need anything. How are you?'

'Blessed be God, I am well,' Mrs. Amrani answered.

The tiny brown woman was sitting on a cushion on the floor, knees bent, back against the wall, holding a piece of embroidery a few inches from her nose. She lowered her handiwork and looked Tonia over.

The unconcealed appraisal made Tonia nervous. What was it she saw in the woman's face? Disapproval? Curiosity?

'I've brought you some tea. For myself too, if you don't mind me joining you.'

'Thank you. Please. Sit.'

Tonia set the tray on the table and laid the towels on the bed. She handed one of the cups of tea to Mrs. Amrani and put the plate of pastries on the floor next to her. Then she took another cushion off a chair, placed it on the floor facing Mrs. Amrani, picked up her own tea, and sank down onto the cushion.

'If you'd like, I could show you around the kibbutz.'

'What is it you want to show me?' Mrs. Amrani's guttural Hebrew was slow and precise.

'If nothing else, at least where the dining room is.' Tonia offered her friendliest smile. Then she noticed a framed photograph on the nightstand and said, 'What lovely children! Are they yours?'

'Yes. That's an old picture from many years ago. The only one I have. That is my oldest boy, Amos. He brought me here.'

Mrs. Amrani leaned forward and pointed at a tall, gangly boy who stood apart from the others. Tonia counted six boys and

129

one girl, all with enormous eyes. Amos wore an ankle-length white *galibiyah* and had long side curls. His head was shaven, and he was barefoot. He stared defiantly into the camera.

'This vacation was his idea ...' Mrs. Amrani sighed. 'I told him it was a waste of money.' She leaned back and resumed embroidering.

Tonia tried to guess Mrs. Amrani's age. She had all those children, but her skin was smooth, and no gray showed in the hair that escaped the scarf. 'You must have married when you were very young.'

'Fourteen.'

Tonia hoped her face did not reveal how appalled she felt. 'Will your husband be joining you later?' Tonia asked. Many women arrived ahead of their husbands, who joined them for the weekend.

'I am a widow. Since I was twenty-three.'

'Oh, I'm sorry. You mean you raised seven children on your own?' She calculated that since the age of fourteen Mrs. Amrani must have given birth to a child almost every year and was even more appalled.

'I had some help.' Mrs. Amrani squinted at one of the stitches in her embroidery. 'My husband's sister never married, and she lives with us. We sell our embroidery and weaving and the cakes we bake. And we work as cleaners.'

Tonia looked at the photograph again. 'How old is your daughter now? About my age?'

Rachel lowered her handiwork and gazed up at Tonia. 'My Sarit is dead, murdered during the riots in '39.'

Tonia flinched. 'I'm so sorry. I seem to have a talent for asking–'

'Pshaw. How could you know?' Mrs. Amrani waved a hand and resumed working. 'Don't feel bad. And you can call me Rachel.'

Tonia knew she was asking too many questions, invading the privacy of a stranger, but she was fascinated.

'You must have a big house.'

'Two rooms. In Jerusalem, near the Mahane Yehuda market.'

Tonia knew the area and imagined a dark, damp flat, almost bare of furnishings and smelling of kerosene lamps and heaters. The buildings of thick Jerusalem stone in those neighborhoods were picturesque, with their high ceilings and arched windows, but she knew that they were cold and clammy through Jerusalem's rainy winter. She pictured Rachel making her way out to the cistern to haul up endless tins of water. How would one do the laundry for eight people under such conditions? How could eight people sleep together in two rooms? Tonia suddenly felt wealthy.

Rachel Amrani smiled as they talked, wondering what this deer-like girl with almond-shaped eyes wanted of her. Can it be that she wants to learn to embroider, but is too shy to ask? No. Young people have no appreciation for that kind of work, nor the patience to do it. Especially these kibbutz creatures, brash Ashkenazim, always in a hurry, running on schedules, no time for anything. So what does she want? What is she doing here? Rachel was glad enough of her company, and she seemed like a sweet child, but Rachel knew how these Polish and German Jews looked down their noses at the Yemenites. The snobs in Rehavia treated their dogs with greater kindness than they did their Yemenite cleaning woman.

'So, would you like me to show you around the kibbutz?' Tonia asked.

Rachel nodded and, accepting Tonia's outstretched hand, got to her feet with an effort. Tonia led her to a large area of level ground shaded by tall oak trees, under which the kibbutzniks had set out dozens of lawn chairs for the vacationers. Many of the chairs were occupied, and Tonia called greetings to some of the guests, who waved back to her.

'This is a lovely place to sit and read in the morning.' Tonia turned to Rachel. 'And there would be plenty of light for you to do your needlework while you chat with the other women.'

131

Rachel nodded and said nothing.

Tonia led her up another path to a second resting place for the guests – a large stone gazebo filled with comfortable chairs. Four women sat there; Tonia smiled and nodded to them, and they nodded back, but they all seemed to be staring at Rachel. Tonia suppressed a sigh, thinking that Rachel was probably going to be spending a lot of time alone on the floor of her room. Tonia's grand tour of the kitchen, dining room, children's houses, chicken runs, and workshops turned out to be short. Rachel listened politely to the unsolicited explanations that she offered.

'You see, this way, with the communal kitchen, laundry, and all, the women are freed from housework and child care and can put in a full day's work, just like the men. In the kibbutz we believe in complete equality between men and women.'

'I have heard that. Where does your mother work?'

'In one of the children's houses.'

'Caring for other women's children, instead of her own?'

'We don't look at it that way.'

'And do some of the completely equal men also work in these children's houses?'

'Well … no,' Tonia replied.

'Tell me, is it true that you are paid nothing for your work?'

'Yes. But it's not like … I mean, we don't receive salaries, but we don't pay for anything either. The kibbutz takes care of all our needs.'

'But you receive no pay? You don't get more money if you work harder than another one who is lazy?'

Tonia started to explain about mutual responsibility, but broke off mid-sentence. She stopped and turned toward Rachel, shaking her head with a wry smile. Rachel watched her face with an inquiring look.

'I … It's funny … Talking to you, I sound like my father. He always says those things. But the truth is, I never wanted to live on a kibbutz. And as soon as I can, I will leave.'

'Where will you go?'

'To America, I hope.'

'Leave Eretz Israel?'

Tonia heard the criticism in Rachel's question. 'It's not that I don't think it would be a wonderful thing for the Jews to have a country of their own. I just don't believe it's going to happen.' She started walking again, looking out at the sun setting behind the newly planted orchards, and Rachel matched her pace. 'I appreciate what the people here on the kibbutz have accomplished.' She continued speaking, more to herself than to Rachel. 'Sometimes I can almost cry, when I think of the sacrifices they have made, the way they believe they can create a better world. But I don't believe that can be done either.'

They walked on.

Rachel broke the silence. 'So many people together, sharing money, not even relatives. And you, do you like your job?'

'Yes, I do. Very much. I didn't think I would, but I get to meet all kinds of people. Like you. I mean, most people on the kibbutz think pretty much alike about everything. Not that you'd know it, if you heard the way they argue at meetings. But that's always about little things. It's nice to talk to people with different ways of life. Different ways of thinking.'

They arrived back at Rachel's room and stopped outside the door.

'Would you mind if I came back for you later? It's almost time for dinner, and I could go to the dining hall with you.'

Rachel smiled. 'Why don't you come in and wait with me?' She took hold of Tonia's elbow and led her inside.

It was growing dark, but Rachel did not bother to light the lamp before she settled herself on her cushion. Tonia could not take her eyes off her face, the dark skin stretched tautly across delicate cheekbones. Rachel could have been beautiful, in the hands of a Mrs. Rozmann.

'So, you came here from Yemen?' Tonia asked.

'No. I was born here. My grandparents brought my father when he was a boy.'

'Oh. So you don't know what it was like, back there in Yemen.'

133

'Like every exile. Very bad.' Rachel sighed.

'What do you mean?'

'Goyim are goyim. When it pleases them, they allow the Jews to serve them. When it pleases them, they slaughter the Jews.'

Goyim are goyim. One of her father's favorite expressions.

'Do you know how they got here? I ... I'm sorry. Do you mind me asking you all these questions?'

'No.' Rachel smiled. 'It's all right. It's nice that someone is interested. There was a war – a civil war. They left their home and wandered for some years, until they heard there was a prince named Rothschild who was buying Eretz Israel and giving it back to the Jews. So they came here.'

'How did they get here?'

'They walked for many days to a place where they could get a caravan. They bought camels and things they would be able to sell when they got to Eretz Israel, but the Bedouin stole everything.'

'And when they got here, what did they do?'

'They managed.'

'Where did they live?' Tonia asked.

'With the Silwanim, by the Mount of Olives. What you Ashkenazim call Kfar Hashiloach.'

'I thought Arabs live there.'

'Yemenite Jews lived with them in the same village. The same way they lived together with the Muslims in Yemen.'

'I don't think any Jews live there now.'

'No.' Rachel sighed. 'The Arabs started killing Jews in '26. They all had to leave. But long before that my parents left me with my grandparents and went to look for work.'

'Where did they go?'

'To Rehovot.' Rachel stiffened and seemed reluctant to elaborate. 'But they didn't like it there, so my father went back to Jerusalem – to the flat where I live now.'

'What a coincidence. My father spent a few months at a work camp in Rehovot when we first came here. What didn't they like about Rehovot?' Tonia asked. What she really wanted to ask was why Rachel had said that 'her father' and not 'her parents' went back to Jerusalem.

Rachel offered no reply. She shook her head, leaned back, and closed her eyes, and they sat in silence for a few minutes.

'I think I'll stop bothering you and let you get some rest. I'll come back for you when they start serving dinner.'

Rachel nodded, eyes still closed, and Tonia picked up the tray and slipped out the door.

'Where are those from?' one of the women who worked in the kitchen asked, when Tonia returned the teacups.

'I took some tea to Mrs. Amrani and showed her around the kibbutz,' Tonia replied, ignoring the woman's bossy tone. It was one of the few advantages of living on a kibbutz with no desire to be there. You could choose not to care. What were they going to do, fire you?

'I was trying to make her feel more comfortable,' Tonia continued. 'Public relations, you know.'

'That's all we need – you drumming up the Yemenite trade. It will cost more to fumigate the rooms after they leave than they pay in rent.'

Tonia glared at her for a moment before saying, 'You are a stupid pig.' She stomped out.

For the next three days, Tonia shared afternoon tea with Rachel. On the morning that Rachel was leaving, Tonia went to say goodbye.

'Can I help you with anything, Rachel?'

'No, I'm all ready to go, just waiting for my Amos to come get me.'

'I hope we'll see you here again.'

'Perhaps,' Rachel said with an obvious lack of enthusiasm. 'You must visit me in Jerusalem.'

There were footsteps on the path and a rap on the door, which opened before Rachel had time to say, 'Come in.'

'Ready, Ima?'

Tonia paled. It was the 'Italian' boy. The long-legged young man who had seen her quarrel with her father and then caught her in the act of burying her stolen treasures.

'Well, hello.' He nodded to Tonia.

'You're Rachel's son?' she blurted out, good manners abandoning her, along with the color she felt draining from her face.

'Oh, do you know Tonia?' Rachel asked.

'Old friends. Done some work on the trenches together,' he teased, and Tonia's cheeks burned.

'I have to get back to work. Goodbye, Rachel. It was lovely having you here,' Tonia said and fled.

She hurried back to her tent and collapsed on the mattress feeling nauseated. Once her stomach had settled, she whispered the name a few times. Amos Amrani. So exotic. So unlike the Horowitzes, Katzes, and Silberschmidts she was used to. So he was the tall skinny boy in the picture, with the stubbly head and long side curls. She saw the resemblance, but found it difficult to make the connection between the boy in the photograph and the muscular bare back, easy grin, and deep voice.

He had been wearing shorts again, and Tonia flushed. Those long brown legs. Why had she behaved like such a fool? Every time she saw him, she ran away. Why couldn't she have behaved like a normal person? Offered him a cup of tea? At least said something polite, like it was nice to see him again? She cringed, imagining what he must think of her. Worse was her conviction that there was no reason for him to think of her at all. She was nothing but a clumsy child to him.

In fact, Amos Amrani had spent a great deal of time thinking about Tonia Shulman, since the first time he set eyes on her as she climbed off the bus from Jerusalem. Lying in bed on Sabbath afternoons, he thought about the way she moved as she cleared tables in the dining hall. He had once caught a glimpse of her rushing home from work in the orchards, maintaining her grace of movement even in the pouring rain.

She was a pretty girl who would grow into a handsome woman. How he had enjoyed watching her stand up to her father, Josef Shulman the great, the boss of everyone, the most patriotic Jew on earth. Amos smiled to himself when he recalled that display of spirit. But her defiance of her father also gave him pause – what kind of wife could such a girl make? And then he wished he could put her out of his mind.

CHAPTER SEVENTEEN

Rachel's husband, Benjamin Amrani, was the son of a silver-smith and the grandson of a scholar, but grew up in Eretz Israel in humble circumstances. He tried to maintain his independence by working as a skilled day laborer, but after he married and had children to support, he accepted steady employment as a poorly paid janitor at an elementary school. The children loved Beni. They often begged him to intervene for them with the teachers, who heard him out with patronizing smiles.

When Benjamin died of influenza, nine-year-old Amos did not cry. He sat silently on a mattress on the floor, barely moving. People who came to pay *shiva* calls patted his arm and assured him that time would heal the pain, but the passage of time made it worse. Not only was his father gone, but the blurred memory of him seemed to fade by the hour. They did not have a single photograph. A man had been in the world, and then he was gone, nothing left behind, not a trace, no way to keep his face in your memory. Amos did remember his father coming home in the evening, stretching out on a mat on the floor while he waited for his dinner, accepting a small glass of *arak* from Rachel, and solemnly asking each of his children if they had behaved in a manner befitting a Jew that day. But it was growing difficult to recall the sound of his voice.

Amos's most vivid memory was of the Friday afternoon his father had taken him to a bathhouse in the Old City. Amos had been excited that morning, anxious for his father to come home so he could tell him about the two goals he had scored in the soccer game. He was also eager to talk to him about the counselor, the young man from the Labor Movement, who had begun appearing in the neighborhood every afternoon and was organizing the children into team sports. Amos spouted a steady stream of enthusiasm for the Movement that this young man – who wore a Russian peasant blouse and no yarmulke – wanted the children to join. Benjamin listened without comment as they walked to the bathhouse.

Father and son bathed and wrapped themselves in thick white towels. Afterwards they sat on slabs of marble in a dark steamy room and ate dried fruits and nuts. After a few minutes, Benjamin rose and left the room. He returned and presented his eldest son with a gift wrapped in newspaper. Amos waited for his father to nod permission and removed the paper. His face broke into a grin as he proudly held up his first pair of long pants. That day Amos's father spoke to him with a special gravity that he would never forget.

'Listen to me, my son. This young man and the games he teaches you, the Russian songs, I know that he means well. All of his kind think they mean well. But look around you with keen eyes. These Ashkenazim talk about brotherhood and equality, but who does their laundry, cleans their houses, carries their water, and picks the grapes in their vineyards? The Yemenites. The Poles and Russians speak beautiful words of national unity, but you can't trust them. Never depend upon them. If you want to work for them, all right, but make sure you have a profession, so that your family will always eat, even when they turn you away. Keep your independence, and learn to make do with little. That is our equality. Don't ever beg them for favors.'

Amos nodded, and his father put his hands on his shoulders.

'There's something your mother and I have never told you, but you are old enough now, it's time for you to understand such things. It's about your grandmother. Ima's mother.'

'I know,' Amos said. 'She died having a baby.'

'Yes. She died trying to have a baby. She went with her husband to Rehovot, to look for work in the orange groves there, even though she was pregnant, and even though she had to leave her little girl – your mother – in Silwan with her parents.'

'Yes, I remember you telling me about that,' Amos said.

A young Arab boy came and served cups of hot mint tea, and Benjamin waited for him to move away before he continued his story.

'They did find work, but there were no houses. They had no place to live. So your grandfather did as the other Yemenite workers did – he patched together a hut of tin and old wooden crates. The farmer they worked for never asked them where they lived. Why should he care?

'It wasn't so bad in the summer, but when the rains came your grandmother was sick all the time and feared losing the child. One day there was a big storm.' Benjamin swirled his arms about. 'And their little hut blew to pieces. They had nowhere to go. They needed a place to sleep for that one night, until your grandfather could build a new hut. It was late, and there were no more buses back to Silwan.'

Benjamin stopped and took a sip of tea. Amos sat still, waiting for him to continue.

'Your grandmother decided to go talk to the wife of the farmer. Surely, she would understand. Who could turn away a pregnant woman? She walked up the steps to their house and knocked on the door. She wasn't going to ask to stay in their house, God forbid. She wanted permission to sleep in their barn. In the *barn*. For just one night.' He held up one finger. 'But the farmer's wife opened the door, saw a Yemenite woman standing on her front steps, and didn't even listen. She was busy, on her way out. This enlightened European had no time to bother with the troubles of a primitive Yemenite worker, standing in the rain with a swollen belly. She opened her umbrella and brushed past. Your grandmother tried to make her listen, put her hand out like this.' Benjamin's touch was light on Amos's forearm.

'She was begging to be heard, but the farmer's wife pulled her arm away.' Benjamin jerked his bent elbow back with a sudden movement, as if he had been seared by fire.

'She hit your grandmother and knocked her down the steps. It was an accident, she didn't mean to hurt her, but your grandmother lost the baby, and she died the next day. All because she went to beg a great favor – to sleep in their barn.'

Benjamin paused and sipped more tea. 'So do you see what I am trying to tell you?'

Amos nodded.

'Learn from this counselor what you can, but never forget the differences between them and us. They despise us, they teach disrespect for parents, and they are godless. So never trust them, and make certain that when you are grown, you never have to go begging for a roof over your woman's head.'

1939 was a year of anti-Zionist demonstrations and violent riots, but eleven-year-old Amos Amrani was not concerned with politics. He was too busy quarrelling with his mother. Lately he had missed more days of school than he had attended, and she was furious.

When she got back from her morning job and saw that Amos was home, she glared at him before she went into the kitchen, a tiny structure out in the yard with a battered tin roof, where she began chopping vegetables for the soup pot while lecturing him. Amos sat on the edge of the cistern, listening to her complaints. She paused every few moments to step outside and jab the air in his direction with the knife or large wooden spoon in her hand.

He hated fighting with her. He knew how hard she worked to keep her children clothed and fed and how much she wanted him to remain in school. But she should understand. He was the eldest son and could not let her bear the burden alone. School would have to give way. He had to make money, not read books. His father would have expected it of him.

Rachel's long harangue began to wear itself out. 'So you will go to school every day,' she pronounced.

'No, Ima, I will find more jobs,' he said. 'And soon you will stop cleaning up after other people.'

She wiped her hands on her burlap apron and came to sit next to him. 'Why, my son,' she asked him, 'do you not see it as a loss of dignity when Haim Elharizi kneels down to measure out kerosene for me, but feel humiliated because I wash the floor in someone else's house? Each of us does a necessary job. You don't mind that I bake cakes for you to take to school and sell to your classmates, so why are you angry when I bake the same cake in some other woman's oven?'

He did not know how to answer, but he knew that it was different. And that his father had known it was different. His father had always said there were some things women did not understand.

'It will be all right, Ima. Don't worry.' He patted her arm and made a tactical retreat.

He crossed the narrow street and climbed the makeshift ladder he had nailed together, up to the flat roof of the synagogue. It was a hot day, but Amos was comfortable in his shady alcove under the eaves, lying on the remains of an old mattress. With nine people in two rooms, there was little privacy at home, and he spent many hours up on the roof, mostly concocting money-making schemes. Someday there would be enough money. They would throw away bread that had burned and would no longer eat food that was 'not quite spoiled'.

Nothing went to waste in the Amrani household. Rachel did not peel vegetables before they went into the big aluminum pot. Soup was made from boiled chickens' feet. The rinse water from the first batch of laundry was saved for the wash water for the second and then used to wash the floor. The water they bathed in was poured over the irregular paving stones in the courtyard. Their tiny flat held little furniture. At night, its floor was a sea of straw-filled mattresses.

Since his father's death, Amos had constantly sought ways to make money. He told his mother that he sold her cakes in the schoolyard during recess, but in fact he took them to the Schneller Barracks, or sometimes all the way to the Allenby Encampment, where the British soldiers paid a few pennies more for the syrupy baked goods. He had also ingratiated himself with some of the officers, and they tipped him well for running errands for them.

If he could save enough for a used bicycle, he would be able to get around faster and earn more. That morning someone had offered him a bicycle – all he had to do to get it was betray his people.

CHAPTER EIGHTEEN

James Dougan was a quiet-spoken, middle-aged, pipe-smoking British officer. He had expected his posting to the Holy Land to be a great adventure and an inspiration. After a year of it, he would have preferred to be almost anywhere but hot, dusty Palestine. All he did here was referee between excitable Arabs with lively imaginations and no qualms about wielding a knife and earnest, long-suffering Jews who were often too clever for their own good.

Dougan sometimes sent Amos to run errands for him. That morning when Amos brought him a few of Rachel's yeast cakes, Dougan had asked him to step into his office.

'Close the door, Amos,' he said in English, 'and sit down.' Dougan indicated the chair on the other side of his broad desk, but Amos remained standing, chin up.

'You're quite the enterprising chap,' he began, but stopped. The boy had an uncanny knack for picking up English, but one had to keep it simple. 'I like you, Amos,' he said.

It was true. Amos was bright, proud, and ambitious. He was straightforward and did not go sneaking around, the way most of these locals did. He never fawned and always kept his part of a bargain. The first time Dougan had sent the boy for hot drinks, he happened to be watching out the window and saw another British officer bump into Amos and spill the coffee. Amos did not come whining to Dougan for more money, as his other errand boys would have done. He accepted his losses and went back for more. He set the tiny white cups down in front of Dougan and his guests without a word. Dougan had suppressed a smile and slipped the skinny young boy a large tip.

Dougan also suspected that under certain circumstances Amos might prove to be of a ruthless nature. He certainly knew things no eleven-year-old had any business knowing. Which was why Dougan had the boy standing in his office.

Dougan shifted in his chair and began plodding through his unsavory task.

143

'Amos, there has been a bit of trouble between Arabs and Jews lately, and there will be more. Do you follow?'

Amos nodded.

'We would like you to help us stop that kind of trouble. Too many people have weapons. Jews and Arabs. And when Arabs see Jews with guns, then they want more guns.' He paused and Amos nodded again.

'So we think it best that no one should have guns.' He fiddled with his empty pipe. 'We know that you know a lot of people. You get around, all over the city. All we want you to do is keep your eyes open, and if you see anyone making trouble or anyone with guns, come and tell me about it.'

Amos stared at him, unblinking.

'We would pay you, of course.' Dougan coughed and watched the boy's eyes narrow. 'But you wouldn't be doing it for the money. You would be sort of a police officer, keeping people from getting hurt. Would you fancy that?'

He was making a right cock-up of what had been a bad idea to begin with. Becoming part of His Majesty's Forces was the last thing on earth this boy would ever fancy.

'We know that you would be a better policeman if you could get around quickly. I heard you talking to one of the other boys about wanting a bicycle. I could help you out with that.'

Amos stared at the floor. 'How much?' he asked.

'Well, I say, that would rather depend on the information you provide. But I'm sure it would be enough to be a help to your mother. You needn't give me an answer now. Go home and think about it.'

As the day came to an end, Amos sat up on the roof of the synagogue thinking. The idea of spying on Jews was sickening, but he turned Dougan's offer over in his mind, trying to find a way to turn it to his advantage. He could try feeding the British useless information, but he would only be able to do that once or twice before Dougan caught on and got angry with him. That would mean no more tips. He could contact the Haganah and ask them what information they would like him to pass on, but there would be nothing in it for him. Anyway, Dougan was too smart to buy it for long.

Amos needed money. He rose at 4:30 each morning and delivered bread and rolls until 7:00. Then he walked to Rehavia, where the housewives paid him a few pennies for each wooden-handled can of water he hauled from the cisterns, to fill the large clay jars that stood in their kitchens. The British had installed new public faucets after opening a pipeline from Rosh Ha'ayin, but even the housewives who lived closest to the taps were willing to pay Amos to take their place in the long queues that formed, waiting for the city supervisor to come and turn on the water.

Rehavia was a five-minute walk from his home, but Amos moved through it like a foreign country. The women kept a careful eye on him, as if afraid he might steal something. Their children followed him down the street calling 'Black! Black Sambo!' and making fun of his patched clothes, shaven head, and bare feet.

The sun was setting behind the rooftops, and Amos rose, stretched, and looked down at his little sister, playing in the courtyard below.

'Sarit,' he called down. 'It's time for you to go in.'

'Just a little while longer,' she pleaded, as if Amos were her father, rather than a sibling two years her senior.

She was small and frail and often in bed with fever. Their mother sat up many nights with Sarit, and Amos took special care of her.

'It's time for him to come. Please,' Sarit begged, jumping up and down, almost tripping over her long black skirt.

The children liked to linger outside at dusk, waiting for Mustafa the milkman to herd his flock of goats into the courtyard. Each morning and evening, he made his rounds, calling out in Yiddish, Hebrew, Ladino, and Arabic. The older children ran out with tin containers into which he milked the goats. Their mothers stood about haggling with the good-natured Mustafa over how much he was charging them for foam, while the smaller children timidly petted the goats.

145

A deep voice called out in Hebrew, and a tall man in red, brown, and orange-striped robes entered the courtyard. It was not Mustafa, however, but the fierce-looking Afghan who came around once a year to sharpen knives. Well aware of his ferocious appearance, he called out a dare to the children, and the bravest of them gathered around to tug on the enormous moustache that drooped past his chin. The neighborhood women came outside and organized the queue for his services, and he followed Mrs. Levin toward her kitchen.

'Now, Sarit. It's late,' Amos called.

'Just one more minute, here comes the lamplighter.'

The children crowded around the man from the city, hoping this would be the night the glass exploded after he lit the light. Amos watched impatiently. An hour ago, when Rachel left for the market, she had called up to him that he was in charge, and Rachel did not allow her children, least of all Sarit, to remain outside after dark. There were too many troubles these days, too many attacks on Jews. The man finished lighting the lamp, which remained intact, and children began drifting home.

'Okay, Sarit, that's it,' Amos shouted. 'Inside.'

She waved a skinny arm at him and stooped to gather the buttons she had been playing with. Amos heard a distant commotion, then footsteps, people running from the direction of Jaffa Road. Amos glanced at Sarit and started descending the ladder. He was halfway down when two young Arabs raced into the courtyard. Amos froze when he saw the weapons in their hands. One swung a tire chain. The other, who wore a bright orange shirt, wielded a thick wooden bat with rusty nails protruding from its end.

Sarit straightened up and watched them, eyes open wide. The one holding the chain shouted something to the other and pointed toward the arched opening at the far end of the courtyard. The second youth nodded back to him and ran in that direction, toward Sarit. She stood and stared, without moving.

'Get inside!' Amos found his voice and screamed, but she was rooted to the cobblestones. Amos's foot missed a rung, and he fell to the ground.

As the Arab passed Sarit, almost as an afterthought, he raised the bat and brought it down on her tiny head, breaking her skull apart with a loud crunch. By the time Amos got to his feet, the attacker was out of sight.

He half-stumbled, half-crawled to where Sarit lay next to the cistern and tried to rouse her, one hand over the horrible wound that gaped in her head. Sarit was a lifeless heap in a small pool of blood, her paralyzed brother on his knees at her side, silently screaming, wishing to die before his mother returned from the market.

That same day Amos accompanied Rachel to the police station. The British officer said they were sorry for her loss, but were helpless to pursue such cases. A week after Sarit's funeral, the day the family got up from sitting *shiva*, Amos went to Dougan's office and struck a bargain with him.

'I will not spy on Jews for you,' Amos said. 'And I will not ask you for money. You give me a bicycle, and I will tell you what we know about the Arabs.'

'That sounds fair enough.' Dougan offered his hand. 'I ... I wanted to say before ... I heard what happened to your sister. Awfully sorry. Please. Let me.' He held onto Amos's hand, while he lifted a bank note from his desktop and pressed it into Amos's palm, curling his fingers around it. 'Please.'

Amos looked at the money. 'Thank you,' he said stiffly. He turned to leave, but paused. 'It didn't "happen" to her,' he said, his voice steady. 'She was murdered because your policemen don't do their job. The reason they sent you here was to make a Jewish homeland, but you are afraid of the Arabs. Or maybe you hate Jews. But you're not doing what you were supposed to do, and you have no right to be here.'

Amos left without giving Dougan a chance to respond.

Amos began his search of the city. He had gotten a good look at Sarit's murderer. Dark hair, wide forehead, broad nose, protruding ears. Amos would never forget that particular face. Each day he pedaled through the Jewish neighborhoods of new Jerusalem toward the Old City. He left his bicycle at the Jaffa Gate, securing it with the lock Dougan had given him, and continued on foot. Many of the narrow alleyways inside the walled Old City consisted of steps, and the bicycle would have been no use inside the walls. Amos hated the markets – the crowds, the stench of beef hanging in the open air amidst clouds of flies – but he loitered in them, studying each Arab who passed. He did not sleep well at night; the face leered in his dreams.

It took two months, but late one autumn afternoon Amos found him, sitting in a coffee house in the Old City. It was the orange shirt that first caught Amos's eye. The same orange shirt he had been wearing on the day he shattered Sarit's head. Amos could see the remnant of a stain on its front and glared at what he thought must be his sister's blood. He scrutinized the face for long moments, assuring himself it was him, not some cousin who had borrowed the shirt.

Amos fingered merchandise and haggled with shopkeepers as he waited for the Arab to get up and leave. When he did, Amos followed him and made careful note of which door he entered. Then Amos walked on, looking for a suitable location. His enemy was stocky and a head taller than him, and Amos did not intend to risk a contest of strength. He had to take him by surprise, somewhere no one would see them.

Two days later, Amos returned to the Old City, with a slender dagger taped to his arm beneath the sleeve of his long white *galibiyah*. He made his way to the coffee house and sat there until dusk. The Arab never showed up, and Amos went home cursing. That night he didn't sleep at all.

When he returned the next day, he found his prey. The Arab, wearing a shiny red and black striped shirt, was playing backgammon with a friend, laughing as he shook the dice. Amos passed by without staring at him, sat down in a nearby coffee house, ordered a glass of orange juice, and hoped that the *galibiyah* concealed the sweat pouring from his body. He took small sips of his juice and fingered the concealed knife. His head was pounding. An eternity passed before the game ended, and the Arab rose to leave.

Amos forced himself to remain seated; he did not want to be seen following his target. Once the Arab was out of sight, Amos rose and went after him. He stayed a safe distance behind, the bright stripes of the Arab's shirt making him easy to track. When the Arab turned into a deserted street, Amos caught up with him and hissed.

The Arab turned and glanced at Amos, but continued on his way.

Amos hissed again, anxious to catch his attention while they were on that particular street, which was not overlooked by any windows. 'Mister, you like girls?'

The Arab stopped.

'Jewish girls,' Amos said softly, almost a whisper.

'What girls?'

'My sister.' Amos lowered his eyes. 'She is thirteen. A virgin. You can have her now.'

'How much?'

Amos hesitated. 'Half a pound.'

'Where?'

'The Jewish Quarter. Not far. But you have to come now, before the landlady comes home. Please, Mister,' Amos whined. 'We're orphans. We haven't eaten for days.'

Amos walked toward the Jewish Quarter, with the Arab following close behind him, and turned up the alley he had selected. It had a single wooden door at its dead end and no windows facing onto it. Amos stopped near the door and nodded at it.

'She's in there.'

The Arab reached for the doorknob, and Amos moved behind him. He tore away the tape, slipped the knife out of his sleeve, and held it behind his back.

'Hey, Mister,' he said, 'Wait a minute, there's something I forgot to tell you.'

The Arab turned.

Amos plunged the dagger into his soft belly, up to the handle. He pulled up hard, surprised at how easily it cut through the flesh. Blood began to spurt, and he jerked his hand away, leaving the dagger. The Arab did not cry out. He stared at Amos and dropped to his knees, his throat emitting a gurgling sound.

'What I forgot to tell you is that my sister isn't in there,' Amos whispered into his ear. 'You killed her.'

The Arab fell to the ground and lay on the cobblestones of the alley.

Then Amos heard footsteps and voices speaking Arabic coming up the street. He stepped back and pressed his body against the cold stones of the wall. How stupid of him to choose this alley, no place to hide, nowhere to run. Clop, clop, clop. The footfalls turned up a different street and faded away. Amos nearly fainted with relief.

His *galibiyah* was splashed with bright red stains, and he stripped it off. This he had planned for – he wore shorts and a shirt underneath. He wiped his hands on its hem, rolled it up so that no stains showed on the outside, tucked it under his arm, and stepped out onto the street. He forced himself not to run. Once he was outside the walls, he shoved the bloody garment into the first trash bin he passed. Then he vomited on it.

'Where have you been? Do you know what time it is?' Rachel demanded when he arrived home.

'I had some things to do,' he answered.

He went to the clay jar in the corner and filled an enamel basin with water to rinse out his mouth and wash his hands with soap. Instead of emptying the basin into the jar of sullied water that his mother would find a use for, he went outside and poured it on the lemon tree in the yard.

Rachel grunted her general disapproval and returned her attention to her embroidery.

'I'll get you some rice and lentils,' she offered when he came back in.

'I'm not hungry, Ima,' Amos said and was thankful that she was too tired to argue with him.

He unrolled his mattress in his corner of the room and fell asleep. He awoke before the sun was up and lay motionless in the dark, hearing the sleeping forms around him breathing and sighing.

He felt no remorse or fear, but did wish he could know what his father would have said.

CHAPTER NINETEEN

Natan was standing near the bus stop by the front gate of Kfar Etzion when a stocky construction worker in a sweat-stained shirt approached. 'Hey you, kid, you waiting for the bus to Jerusalem?'

'Yes.'

'Can I get you to deliver a message for me? I'll give you money for the cab ride out of your way.'

'What message? Who to?'

'You know Amrani, tall Yemenite guy, spends a lot of time here?'

'Yes, I know who you mean.'

'Take this to him, all right?' The man held out a sealed envelope. 'Address is on it. You got to deliver it personally, all right? Don't go giving it to some cab driver or delivery boy.'

'All right.'

'Here.' The man took some money out of his pocket and put it into Natan's hand.

'Who should I say it's from?' Natan asked.

'He'll know.'

The man turned and waddled away without a word of thanks.

Natan did not mind, in fact he was happy to be asked. It would give him the chance to talk to the mysterious Amrani, who came and went as he pleased and was rumored to be involved with the Irgun, the Jewish underground. That cryptic 'He'll know' had made Natan feel part of something clandestine and exciting, brightening his otherwise boring day.

He spent the ride to Jerusalem rehearsing how he would introduce himself. He wanted to sound serious, but nonchalant, to hide how childishly excited he was about being asked to deliver a piece of paper. He got off the bus in Jerusalem, hurried through his own errands, and then took the envelope out of his pocket to look at the address. It was in the Beit Israel neighborhood, near ultra-orthodox Mea Shearim. He looked about for a taxi, but had never hailed one before and feared looking foolish. He threw the strap of his pack over one shoulder and began walking.

The neighborhood became increasingly orthodox. The long-bearded men he passed wore almost identical black suits, white shirts, and wide-brimmed black hats. They turned and eyed with distaste his kibbutz-issue blue work shirt and khaki shorts, so short that the bottom two inches of the front pockets stuck out beneath the pant legs. He walked quickly, eyes on the pavement, and located the address, a flat-roofed, three-story building. It looked neglected, the Jerusalem stone marred by streaks of black and rust. He climbed the front steps and studied the names on a row of battered mailboxes. Beneath them, someone had stuck a scrap of paper that read 'A. A. on the roof'.

Natan climbed three flights of stairs to a door that opened onto the white-tiled rooftop. To his right were a forest of water tanks, rusted iron bars, and assorted junk. To his left stood a small structure of concrete blocks, of the kind originally intended for use as a communal laundry. A larger room occupied the far side of the roof, and he pushed two hardback chairs out of his way to walk toward it. He hesitated before approaching the door on which A. A. was scribbled in black ink. No one answered his knock. He squinted at the narrow window in the door, but it was covered with a dark gray curtain. He removed the envelope from his pack and bent to shove it under the door, reasoning that even if he didn't put it into Amos's hands, this still had to count as delivering it 'personally'. No one could expect him to wait all day for Amrani to show up.

He heard a soft noise inside and straightened up to knock once more. Again, no answer. He looked at the envelope in his hand. That noise might have been made by British police officers, waiting inside in ambush. No, he couldn't leave the message and risk letting it fall into their hands. He would go downstairs, sit on the front steps until Amrani came home, and warn him there was someone waiting for him upstairs. He started toward the stairs, but after a few steps turned back. He tucked the envelope inside his shirt before pounding on the door.

'Amrani? It's Natan Shulman, from Kfar Etzion. I'm sorry if I'm disturbing you, but I've brought you some ... grapes from the kibbutz. The guy that gave them to me wanted them delivered to you personally.'

'Come in.' A deadbolt scraped.

Natan opened the door halfway and slipped into the dark interior. Then the door flew out of his hand and someone grabbed his arm, yanked him into the room, and put a gun to his temple.

'Sorry.' The person released his grip and lowered the gun. 'Just being careful.'

Natan turned to see it was Amos Amrani. His eyes were bright and his hair lank with sweat.

'You're Josef Shulman's son,' Amos said.

Natan nodded.

'You brought something for me?'

Natan nodded again.

'From a big heavy guy?'

Another nod.

'I told him to ask you,' Amos said as he moved stiffly toward an army cot shoved up against one wall. 'Gave him a few names, people I thought could be trusted, if he ever needed to get a message to me.'

Natan looked around the tiny, narrow room. A faded green and pink flowered sheet lay rumpled on the thin mattress of the cot. The three pillows piled at its head all bore dark brown stains. A second mattress lay on the floor beneath it. On the wicker nightstand, a glass held the gritty dregs of Turkish coffee and the butts of several cigarettes. A battered wooden chair completed the decor. The flickering kerosene lamp on the wall provided the only light, other than what came in through the open door. There were no windows, and the room smelled of blood, garbage, and sweat. To the right of the door, a small kitchen niche jutted. A white enamel sink, overflowing with dirty plates and battered aluminum pans, rested in a rusty frame. Next to the sink, a slab of marble rested on a stand of metal shelves, forming a makeshift countertop. More dirty dishes and a primus burner stood on it.

Natan closed the door and drew the envelope out of the waistband of his shorts. 'He gave me this. Oh, you're hurt.' Natan stared at the bloodstained cloth wrapped around Amos's shoulder.

'Let's see it,' Amos said and lowered himself to the cot, wincing in obvious pain.

Natan handed him the envelope, and he tore it open. Amos studied the paper, then crumpled it and shoved it under the pillow.

'Is it important?' Natan could not resist asking.

'Yes,' Amos answered. 'Addresses. Where people can be found, including a doctor. You have great timing. I could use your help, if you can go get someone for me.'

'Sure.' Natan nodded.

'Go to the Bukharian Quarter, corner of Rabenu Gershom and Fishel, house with the red gate, second floor, and ask for Mr. Cohen. Bring him back here with you.' He settled back against the pillows and closed his eyes. 'There's a motorbike downstairs you can take. Key's there on the counter.'

Natan repeated the instructions and turned to leave.

'Wait, before you go.' Amos pulled the crumpled paper from under the pillow and held it out to him. 'Burn that in the sink over there. There are matches on one of the shelves.'

Natan held a match to the paper and washed the blackened remains of it down the drain. Then he ran down the stairs and out onto the street, a man with a mission. He had not bothered taking the key to the motorbike, as he had not the slightest idea how to operate one. He ran all the way to the house with the red gate and arrived gasping for breath. Mr. Cohen turned out to be a pudgy balding man. Natan carried his black bag for him and urged him to hurry.

'He's hurt really bad,' he kept repeating as they climbed the stairs to the roof.

'It's us,' Natan called and waited a moment before he shoved the door open. Amos lay on the cot, looking pale and exhausted.

Another moment passed before the doctor finished wheezing up the stairs and appeared in the doorway.

'Hi, Dr. Livni.' Amos opened his eyes and grinned. 'How nice to see you.'

'Again, Amos?' The doctor sighed. 'A sieve has fewer holes in it.'

The doctor set his bag on the chair and went to rummage through the shelves under the kitchen counter. He found a half-empty bottle of whiskey, which he handed to Amos.

'You'll become a drunk just from what you use for medicinal purposes.' The doctor sighed again.

Amos poured some of the liquid down his throat and made a face. 'I don't know what's worse, drinking this poison, or having to trust an old quack like you.'

Natan stepped back onto the roof to stay out of the way until the doctor finished. He propped the door open with a chair and paced back and forth, peeping in to watch the doctor pull a bullet out of Amos's shoulder and dress the wound. The last time he looked in Amos had lost consciousness.

'Can you stay with him?' the doctor asked as he packed up his bag.

Natan nodded.

'He'll sleep for a long while.' He set a bottle of pills on the nightstand. 'Give him these when he wakes up. He knows how many to take. Come and get me, if you need me. I'll be where you found me.' He patted Natan's shoulder and left.

Natan sat on the chair and stared at Amos for half an hour. Then he glanced at his watch and hurried down the stairs to the street, feeling guilty for leaving Amos alone, even for a few minutes. He ran all the way to Jaffa Road, where the bus to Kfar Etzion stopped. A group of people was waiting, and he asked one of them to tell his parents he would not be home that night. Then he raced back to Amos's building, where the dark, deserted rooftop made him uneasy. He let himself back into the room and sat on the edge of the chair, like an uninvited guest unsure of his welcome.

He stared at Amos for a while longer, wondering how he had gotten shot, then took a closer look at the depressing room. Paint flaked off the walls and black and green mold grew in the corners. Cigarette butts littered the floor. The air was heavy with a mixture of unpleasant smells, and Natan rose to prop the door open.

It must be true, Amos must be in the underground. If an Arab had shot him, he would have reported it and gone to a hospital. But not if it had been a British police officer. Though he was opposed to terrorism, Natan could not help admiring men capable of ruthless, daring acts. He envied them their single-mindedness. Natan could always see the other side's point of view. Even the Arabs'.

He rose, took the dirty glass to the sink, and washed it and the other dishes. The plates at the bottom looked as if they had been there for weeks. Amos might be brave, but he was a brave slob. Natan hated to think how long the washing-up sponge had probably been lying there, wet, growing germs, but found nothing else to use and overcame his disgust. While he was washing the dishes, he wondered what had made Amos think he could trust him. They had never spoken to one another before today.

After he finished washing up, Natan took the foul-smelling bag of trash down to the bin, and then came back up to the roof, raised his arms over his head, and stretched. To the left of the room was another makeshift structure he had not noticed before. He nudged the door open, and a rust-stained toilet with no seat stared at him. An improvised showerhead dangled from the ceiling over it.

He went back inside. The room still stunk, but not quite as badly. He found no broom, so picked the cigarette butts off the floor before reaching under the bed to pull out the second mattress. It fit between the bed and the wall, leaving no extra space. If Amos needed to get up in the night, he would have to walk over Natan.

He found a kettle and put it on the primus to boil for tea. He poked around looking for edible substances, but found only a tin

157

of tea, another of coffee, a bag of sugar, and a saltshaker. Before he settled himself on the bare mattress, he stood studying Amos, who had not moved. Natan put a timid hand to his forehead.

Then he settled on the mattress, back against the wall, and sipped his tea, his thoughts alternating between the sweet-faced Malina and Ilana Rozmann of the unruly strawberry blonde hair. He had not yet had the courage to speak to Malina, but made up his mind to do so the next time he saw her. Too bad he wouldn't be able to tell her about today. Maybe he could, if he didn't mention Amos's name.

The room was soon stifling, and he rose to open the door again. He did not like the idea of the rats, much less the humans, who might swarm over them in the night, but did not see how they would survive until morning without fresh air. A low moon threw a strong beam of light through the open doorway, and he fished a small anthology of Israeli poets out of his backpack and tried, unsuccessfully, to read for a few minutes before he lay down and fell asleep.

When he awoke the next morning, Amos was sitting up in bed smoking a cigarette. 'Good morning,' he said.

'The doctor said I should stay. So I could call him if you needed him.'

'Thanks. Natan, isn't it?'

'Yes.'

'You turning up and going for Doc Livni probably saved my life. I didn't think it was so bad, thought I could wait until my brother comes around this morning. One can't be too careful these days.' He watched Natan steadily. 'You never know how rumors of gunshot wounds might reach the ears of our British guests.'

'You don't have to worry about that, I would never say anything to anyone,' Natan said. 'Not even in the kibbutz. I know there are Jews who ... who believe ...'

'Who believe that they are justified in betraying other Jews? Turning them over to the British?' Amos finished for him and stubbed out his cigarette.

'Yeah.'

'But you don't.'

'No. Why did you tell that man he could trust me? You don't know me.'

'You're Josef Shulman's son.'

'My father hates the underground.'

'Maybe so, but if he were in it, the British would have been trampling one another to get out of Palestine years ago.' Amos grinned.

'Do you know my father?'

'No, but you can't spend ten minutes in Kfar Etzion without knowing who he is. And a man like him would never betray another Jew.'

'It was a test, wasn't it? There wasn't anything important in that envelope. You wanted to see if you could trust me. But you didn't plan on getting shot.' It was Natan's turn to watch Amos's face.

'So, I was right. Not only trustworthy, but smart.'

'So what, you want to recruit me into the underground?' Natan shook his head.

Amos said nothing.

Footsteps sounded outside, and Amos pulled his open shirt closed to hide the dressing.

'It's Ya'acov,' a voice called out.

'Come in. I have company.'

A younger, shorter, somewhat less impressive version of Amos entered the room.

'My brother, Ya'acov. This is Natan Shulman. From Kfar Etzion. He's all right.'

'What happened to you?' Ya'acov demanded as he nodded a greeting to Natan.

'Had an accident. Livni's already been here. Natan went and got him for me.'

'Why didn't you go straight there?' Ya'acov raised his voice. 'You shouldn't have come back here alone like that.'

'I didn't think it was bad. Thought it went through.'

Ya'acov shook his head and sighed. 'Did you pick up any dry goods?'

159

'Kirshstein has them.'

'You sure Livni fixed you up all right?'

'I'm sure.'

'Okay, I'm going for food. I'll be back in a while.'

'Get something cold to drink,' Amos called after him.

'I guess I'd better be going,' Natan said, though he did not want to leave.

'Wait. Stay and have something to eat. He won't be long. You play backgammon?'

'No.'

'Poker?'

Natan shook his head.

'No games?'

'Chess.' Natan shrugged. 'Do you want some tea?'

'Sure. Why not?'

Natan lit the primus, then collected his things, shoved the mattress back under the bed, and put the chair back in its place.

'What was that book?' Amos asked when Natan passed him his tea.

'Just something I brought to read on the bus.'

Amos held out a hand, and Natan took the book out of his pack and handed it to him, prepared to be made fun of.

'Poetry?' Amos asked, but he seemed to be requesting clarification, not mocking him.

Natan nodded.

Amos opened the book at random and read aloud a few lines from one of the poems, his voice deep and resonant. *'I have never done heroic battle, have but conquered fields with my feet.* That's very beautiful.' He closed the book.

'Do you like poetry?' Natan asked.

'Never read any. Only what is in the Siddur and the Scriptures. I left school when I was ten.'

'But you don't need schooling.' Natan leaned forward. 'When people try to teach poetry they ruin it.'

Ya'acov's returning footsteps cut him off. He had brought orange juice, fresh warm rolls, white cheese, and large ripe tomatoes. The three of them took chairs out onto the roof and used an old water tank for a table. Natan ate ravenously.

'You see the new girl working in the shop up the street?' Ya'acov asked Amos, holding his hands cupped in front of his chest.

'In five years she'll be playing football with them,' Amos said.

'No one's good enough for him,' Ya'acov said to Natan, jerking a thumb at his brother. 'You're not getting any younger, you know. All the good ones are getting married.'

'I'll take my chances.' Amos glanced at Natan, and Natan thought he looked embarrassed for some reason.

'Why won't you meet Aliza? That day you got a look at her she wasn't done up right.'

'You can put a silk dress on a camel,' Amos quoted the Talmud, 'and neither will benefit.'

'Yeah, yeah. A philosopher. I gotta go. I'll come back later with lunch.'

'Bring a newspaper.'

'Okay, okay. See you around.' He nodded to Natan, who rose and picked up his pack, preparing to leave.

'You in a big hurry to get somewhere?' Amos asked Natan.

'No, not really,' Natan lied. He was scheduled to work, but he hated to lose what would probably be his only chance to spend time with someone like Amos.

'So keep an invalid company. Feel like reading me some poetry?'

A few hours later Ya'acov returned with a pot of Rachel's spicy turkey neck soup and fresh pita bread. He had also brought an afternoon paper, and Natan glanced through it while he ate. He found the item he was looking for on one of the back pages – yesterday morning, unknown assailants had stolen the rifles of two British soldiers. One of the soldiers had gotten off a shot from his pistol and thought he might have wounded one of the perpetrators as they fled.

Ya'acov rose.

'Do me one more favor before you go,' Amos said to his brother. 'Take that big plastic tub down off the roof of the shower and fill it with water. I've got to clean myself up.'

'Don't you have to keep the bandage dry?' Natan asked.

'I can tell you how to do up a new one for me,' Amos said. 'If I don't wash, my skin is going to crawl away.'

Natan put on water to heat and told Ya'acov he would fill the tub. While Amos washed outside on the roof, Natan reread the article in the newspaper several times. Amos came back into the room, hair dripping, bandage damp, wearing a pair of tight shorts. He opened the tin of Turkish coffee and prepared two cups. He handed one to Natan and slumped back down on the cot with his.

'This tastes different,' Natan said as he sipped the coffee. 'What was that you put in it?'

Amos tossed him a small packet of ground cardamom. 'Take that with you. Next time I'm in Kfar Etzion, I'll know where to get a decent cup of coffee, not that instant poison you Ashkenazim drink.'

Natan put a new dressing on Amos's wound, then handed him the newspaper. 'How do you suppose they did that?' His fingers tapped the article. 'Took guns away from armed soldiers?'

Amos read while he drank his coffee. 'You planning on obtaining some weapons?' He looked up at Natan with a grin.

'No. But I'm curious. Really curious. How can they do something like that, without killing them?'

'They can't – not from just any soldiers. They have to be patient, wait. Soldiers have to carry those things around with them from the minute they get up in the morning until they go to bed at night. They're bound to get careless.'

'But they have them strapped over their arms.' Natan stood to put his glass in the sink.

'You think they don't get fed up with that weight hanging on them?' Amos asked. 'Never set them down when they stop at a kiosk to look at the headlines in the evening paper, or while they're making a phone call? Don't you think that two young soldiers enjoying some delicious chocolate cake at Café Atara might lean their rifles against the corner wall behind them? Without noticing that the window is open?'

Natan shook his head. 'That easy?'

'Like I say, you have to be patient. Careless soldiers aren't enough,' Amos said. He tried moving his shoulder, but bit his lower lip and stopped. 'You also need a nice, quiet street with no other Brits around and a good place to stash the guns right on the spot – say a large trash bin, some thick bushes, or a loose manhole cover.'

'But they'd still catch *you*.' Natan sat back down and nervously eyed Amos's dressing. A small red circle was forming in the center of it.

'Hand me my cigarettes, will you?' Amos nodded at the table. 'By the time the Brits come running, you can be sitting on the street with your hand out, a poor beggar. Transparent to them. After all, they're looking for a vicious terrorist running away with two rifles.'

Natan leaned over and tossed the packet to him. 'How would this imaginary guy get the guns home in broad daylight?'

'He wouldn't.' Amos took out a cigarette and lit it, and Natan resisted the inclination to lean away to avoid the smoke.

'He'd tell someone else where they were,' Amos continued, 'and that someone else would send another someone else to get them. Someone with a donkey cart or a car. A delivery boy with a dolly and a big box. High school students with cello cases.'

Natan frowned for a while, thinking. 'Seems like they might notice a beggar with a bullet in him, bleeding all over the place.'

Amos grinned. 'Yes, that could present a problem, but I bet a criminal mastermind keeps a *galibiyah* in his backpack. Can pull it on over his clothes and be a tired beggar sleeping in the street.'

Natan grinned in obvious admiration. Then Amos grew serious.

'If you are ever tempted to try something like that, Shulman, the first thing is to make sure you know how you're going to get away. That's the most important thing. You *always* have to have a way out. At least one. Never, ever follow anyone up a dead-end alley.' Amos rose and stretched his good arm over his head. 'Now let's talk about something else. You got any brothers or sisters?'

CHAPTER TWENTY

Leah had set a table and some folding chairs out on the small clearing in front of their tent. Tonia came up the stony path carrying the mail. She bent over to kiss her mother on the cheek and set the letters down on the table before taking her own chair. Josef emerged through the canvas flaps of the tent, shaking the newspaper he held in front of him and grumbling about the damned underground.

He whacked the back of his fingers against the paper and complained vehemently about the Irgun attacking British installations. 'Idiots! They are nothing but common criminals. Totally irresponsible. They will send years of diplomatic efforts down the drain.'

'You're going to have to fight back, if you want to stay here. Why can't you admit that?' Tonia said dully. They had recited this argument dozens of times. 'Even the Haganah has figured that out. Whatever the Irgun has done this time, I'll bet the Haganah was in on it.'

'There will be a war, and we will fight,' Josef interrupted. 'When there is a purpose to it. You don't go around blowing people up to make a point.'

'They don't, Abba. The Irgun gives the British plenty of warning, plenty of time to get people out, before they blow up one of their buildings.'

'Who told them to go around blowing up buildings? We have to make the British our allies. Now that the war against Hitler is over, they will go back to supporting us.'

'Is it not possible to pass a pleasant afternoon without being joined by Mr. Begin?' Leah asked with a sigh.

'For you, Mrs. Shulman, anything is possible.' He turned to Tonia. 'And how is the young Miss Shulman this afternoon? Keeping the tourists happy?'

'Trying my best.' Tonia picked a cookie off the plate and nibbled at it. 'Though why anyone spends good money to stay here is a mystery to me.'

Leah nodded toward the path behind Tonia's back. 'Looks like Natan is bringing a guest.'

Tonia turned and flushed when she saw Amos Amrani walking up the path with her brother. She brushed cookie crumbs from her lap, asked her father for the newspaper, and turned the pages.

'Ima, Abba, I want you to meet a friend of mine,' Natan announced from behind Tonia, and she could feel Amos's presence.

'These are my parents, Mr. and Mrs. Shulman. This is my friend, Amos Amrani.'

Leah nodded and welcomed him with a pleasant smile, but Josef barely acknowledged the introduction. Tonia was surprised. Normally her father overflowed with hospitality.

'And this is my sister, Tonia.'

'Yes, we've met. Tonia took good care of my mother while she was staying here.'

'Please join us, Amos. I'll get tea.' Leah disappeared into the tent.

With no newspaper to hide behind, Josef sat staring at the reddening sky. Rina's voice broke the awkward silence as she came up the path, calling out a general hello.

'Are you in the Palmach?' she asked Amos after Natan introduced her.

'No, but I have friends here who are, and I come to help out when I can.'

'You undoubtedly have other friends, elsewhere,' Josef muttered. 'The kind who think we'll win a war with a freelance army that murders British soldiers.'

Leah returned carrying a tray of teacups and scowled her husband into silence.

'Have some cookies, Amos.' Leah held the plate out to him.

'What do you do, Amos?' Rina asked.

'I'm self-employed. Sort of a handyman.'

'And you live in Jerusalem?'

'Yes. I come here to spell friends who want a day off.'

'Oh, does the Haganah allow that?' Leah raised an eyebrow.

'I don't know what the rule book says. So far no one has complained.'

Josef glared at him.

'Can I get you another cup of tea, Abba?' Tonia offered. Josef's cup was always the first to be empty, drained in a few impatient gulps.

'Fine, fine.' He shifted uncomfortably in his chair.

Tonia rose and squeezed past Amos's jutting knees. She stood inside the flap of her parents' dark little tent, waiting for the water to boil over the primus burner, observing the scene outside. Leah had managed to engage Josef in the sort of conversation he had least patience for – small talk about the day's events. Rina was trying her best to be fascinating to Amos, and Natan sat back in his chair, seeming lost in thought.

Tonia clenched her teeth as she watched Rina flirt, but then turned away. What do I care? She can have him. I have better things to do with my life than wait hand and foot on someone who will want fifteen kids. I don't care how long his legs are. She prepared her father's tea and poured juice into glasses.

'It must get lonely here,' Amos said to Tonia when she returned, 'with hardly anyone else your own age.'

'I don't have time to feel lonely.'

'Do you go into Jerusalem often?'

'During the school year. I go to the Gymnasium, and I sleep over with friends two or three nights a week.'

'My mother asks about you all the time. She would love for you to come over for a meal, if you're ever in Jerusalem and have time.' He took a slip of paper and a pencil stub out of his pocket and scribbled something. 'Here's her address.'

'Tonia doesn't have time for socializing,' Josef snapped. 'Too much to be done here.' Then he rose, picked up the pile of letters Tonia had brought, and went back into the tent.

Tonia slipped the scrap of paper into her pocket, her attention riveted on the fact that if she were to turn ever so slightly in her chair, her knee would touch Amos's.

167

'You'd better show me that hole in the fence before dark,' Natan said to Amos, as he rose. 'You feel like going for a walk?' he asked Tonia.

'No, I, uh, have a lot to do,' Tonia stammered.

'I'll come,' Rina volunteered.

'Bye, Ima.' Natan bent to kiss Leah. 'Bye, Abba,' he called in the direction of the tent flap, but there was no answer.

'Thank you, Mrs. Shulman.' Amos took her hand. 'Delicious cookies. It was nice meeting you.'

'It was a pleasure meeting you too. I hope we'll see more of you, Amos. Please drop by whenever you're here.'

'Goodbye, Mr. Shulman,' Amos spoke to the tent flap, but received no reply.

Leah smiled at their departing backs, then scolded her husband through the canvas. 'You certainly were rude, Josef. Whatever got into you?'

'Irgun filth,' Josef said, emerging from the tent. 'Involved with them up to his ear lobes.'

'How can you know that?'

'I have my sources. I hear things. I can't prove it, but I know it.'

Tonia stared at her father, wondering why he looked so pale.

'Well, Josef, just because you've heard some unpleasant rumors is no reason to be rude to a guest. He seemed like a nice young man to me. He's here helping us, isn't he?'

'Spying on us is probably more like it. He'll help the Haganah all right, as long as the price is right.'

'What's that supposed to mean?' Tonia asked.

'He sells guns. Both to us and to the Irgun. Seems to be quite resourceful about getting his hands on them,' Josef conceded, 'but any decent Jew with an ounce of patriotism would give–'

'How are his prices?' Tonia interrupted, teasing.

'He sells cheap, actually, but that's hardly the point. What kind of Jew sells arms at a time like this? For personal profit?'

'I suppose a Jew with a widowed mother and five younger brothers and sisters to support,' Tonia replied. 'And you don't seem to mind Kfar Etzion paying the Haganah for guns.'

Josef ignored that comment. 'I bet he sells or gives most of them to the Irgun. Probably has about thirty-five cousins on active duty with them.'

'Really, Josef ...' Leah objected.

'Everyone knows the Irgun is lousy with Yemenites.'

'Josef! What kind of Jew speaks that way of other Jews?'

'All right. All right. Far be it from me to malign the character of our desert cousins. I know they're good honest workers. But nine out of ten of them think Begin is the Messiah.'

'There are plenty of Ashkenazim who are fed up with your self-restraint,' Tonia commented, but the argument held no interest for her. She noticed that her father kept glancing at her mother out of the corner of his eye. There was something close to fear in the way he was looking at her.

'Since when did you become a political scientist?' he grumbled.

'Tonia, Josef, please ...' Leah interceded wearily.

'It's okay, Ima, I have to be going anyway.'

'No, Tonia ...' her father said, suddenly sounding helpless. 'Sit. Please. I don't know why we're having this stupid argument ... when ...'

'What is it, Josef?' Leah asked warily.

Josef closed his eyes for a moment, then went to stand at her side. 'I didn't know how ... One of those letters that came today ... It's from the Jewish Agency ... that department you wrote to – the one that helps try to find out ...'

Leah's face went white, and she grasped his hand. 'What ... what does it say?'

'I didn't open it, Leah'le,' he replied. 'I think you should go inside first. Lie down.'

'All right.' She rose and reached out for Tonia, pulled her close to her, and the three of them made their shaky way into the tent. Leah sat on one of the cots. Josef picked up the letter and held it out to her, but Leah shook her head.

'Tonia, you read it. Please,' she whispered.

Josef lit the kerosene lantern. Tonia set a chair near it and then carefully tore the envelope open. The letter was three pages long, beginning with a long explanation of the source of the information and how it had been obtained.

'In response to your request for information regarding the members of the Mendel family ...' she read aloud.

Leah held up a hand. 'Tonia, please, you read it and then tell me, without the official language.' Josef sat next to his wife and put his arms around her.

Tonia took a deep breath and scanned the lines of the letter, feeling as if she might throw up. 'Your Abba was taken away by German soldiers soon after the invasion. They said for a work detail, but he never came back. They assume he was among those taken into the woods ...'

'And shot,' Leah finished for her, her voice hard.

'Yes. Shot. So were your brothers, Roman and Alexander. They were with him. There is an eyewitness who saw the Nazis take them all on their way home from the synagogue.' Tonia's throat was tight, and she could barely speak.

'Chava and her husband and two children were taken to Chelmno,' Tonia continued quickly, wanting it over with. 'There are no witnesses, but the street they lived on was surrounded early one morning. They took everyone.' Tonia paused for a moment, reading again, though she knew what the letter said. 'Your Ima died in her own bed. They don't know from what, but a neighbor put her name on a list of the known dead. They don't have any information about Edita and Gilead, but their names are not on any of the lists of survivors.'

Leah lay down and was silent for a few minutes before she burst into loud sobs. Josef held her close, tears streaming down his face.

Tonia left the letter on the chair and went outside. So she would never know what it was like to have grandparents, aunts, uncles, cousins. For a moment, she tried to imagine her mother's pain, tried to imagine receiving such news about her own parents and brother and sister, but she shivered and shook such thoughts from her mind. She and her family were going to live. Her children were going to live. Somewhere safe, far away from here.

A week later, the Irgun blew up British military headquarters in the King David hotel in Jerusalem. Josef flew into a rage and forbade his children to associate with Amos Amrani or anyone else remotely connected to the underground. 'Betrayers of Israel!' he roared.

CHAPTER TWENTY-ONE

One afternoon, as Tonia was finishing her turn clearing tables in the dining hall, she looked up and saw Amos Amrani lounging in the doorway, watching her.

'Hello, Tonia.'

'Hello, Amos. What brings you to Kfar Etzion?' She scrubbed the tabletop, feeling her face turn red.

He said nothing, just stood staring at her, wearing the expression she was familiar with – at once amused, challenging, and expectant.

When he reached to his hip pocket and took out his cigarettes, she looked up and said, 'You smoke a lot.'

'Do you want me to quit?'

She resumed scrubbing, not about to answer either way. He grinned and lit a cigarette.

'I like being here, in Kfar Etzion,' he said, exhaling his first drag. 'I had an uncle who lived here a long time ago, when it was called Migdal Eder. My father used to bring us to visit. Wanted us to see that we had a relative with his own land. It was a *moshav* then. Ashkenazim and Yemenites lived here together and managed to get along with one another quite well.' He stared at the tip of his cigarette and sighed. 'I hope it will work out better for your parents and their friends than it did for them.'

'They had to leave in '27?' Tonia stopped working to listen.

He nodded. 'When the Arabs started rioting, the Jews hid in the Russian Monastery. I don't know how they got from there to Beit Umar, but the Christian Arabs in Beit Umar protected them. They made it safely to Jerusalem, but lost all their property – the Arabs destroyed everything in the *moshav*.'

What made her father think this place was any better for Jews than Europe had been? She looked up at Amos, and their eyes met for a long moment.

'I'm driving into Jerusalem for a few hours, coming back later tonight,' he said. 'Thought you might like to join me for the ride.'

She straightened. 'I can't. My father would never allow it,' she said, trying to keep her tone light. 'He doesn't want us associating with a bad influence like you, who belongs to the Irgun.' She waited for him to confirm or deny it.

His face broke into a wide smile, causing Tonia to wonder how teeth could be so beautiful.

'What's so funny?' she asked.

He held up his right hand and bent thumb to palm, counting. 'One, let's just say that my first impression of you was ... mmm ... not exactly an obedient child.'

She could not help smiling as she threw her dishrag into the bucket of soapy water.

His first finger went down. 'Two, I thought the point of all this collective child-rearing was supposed to be turning out a crop of independent children.' His middle finger joined the others. 'And three, when your father was your age, even younger, I'm sure he was hell-bent on doing the exact opposite of everything *his* father told him to do.'

She shook her head, still smiling, pulled out a chair, and motioned for him to sit down. He did, and she reached to the table behind her for an ashtray for him.

'He's my father, and I'm trying my best to get along with him. You have to understand, Amos, it's not personal. It's not that he dislikes you. But he does believe that you're involved with the Irgun.'

'And?'

'So he thinks ... not that I agree ... or rather, I don't know what I think. I can understand wanting to fight back, but to join an underground movement ...'

'Every Jew in the country is underground. How many caches of illegal weapons do you think there are here on your kibbutz? How many of its members entered the country illegally?'

She could not argue with that. 'Do you belong to the Irgun?' she asked.

'You know that's not a question anyone answers.'

'Oh, what difference does it make?' She rose and began pushing chairs into place. 'You're all crazy. I don't know why

173

you're so anxious to get rid of the British. The minute they leave, the Arabs are going to come and slaughter every last one of us.'

'Ah, but that's where you're wrong, we're going to win. We've got a secret weapon – all the stubborn people like your father that are on our side.'

'These conversations give me a headache,' she said. 'You can all stay here and be heroes if you like.'

'While you go off to America?' He stubbed out his cigarette and stood.

'Yes. While I go off to America.'

'The minute you get permission from your father, of course.'

She wiped her hands on her apron and stared into his green eyes.

'Amos, can you wait here for a few minutes?' she asked.

He nodded, and she walked off toward her parents' tent. She was relieved to find Leah alone.

'Ima, I won't be coming by for tea today. I have a ride into Jerusalem and back. I won't be late, but I have to hurry. Bye.'

She hurried away, not giving Leah the chance to do more than call out, 'Be careful. And have a good time.'

'Okay, I'm coming to Jerusalem,' Tonia said to Amos. 'If I'm still invited.'

'The Zion Theater is showing a film with Frank Sinatra and Gene Kelly, if you feel like going to see it. I'll wait here while you get ready,' he said.

Tonia went back to the tent she shared with Rina, wondering what a girl was supposed to do in order to be considered 'ready'. She skipped up the path to the showers, looking over her shoulder to see who might be watching. She had already taken the one shower she was allowed that week. She washed quickly, feeling like a criminal for using more than her share of precious water, and put on the black skirt and white blouse she wore on Sabbaths. As she braided her hair, she tried to think of a way she could get to the Rozmanns' and change into her fabulous white dress. She knew it was a ridiculous idea – it was way too fancy to wear to the Zion Theater, and people would stare at her. But, still, how she would love for Amos to see her in it.

She found Amos seated on one of the large rocks outside the dining hall.

He rose as she approached. 'I have to go call the others.'

She followed him up the path. He stopped and waved at two men in work clothes, and she traipsed behind the three of them to the parking lot. Amos strode over to a dilapidated brown sedan and opened the door on the passenger side. The seat was tattered, and rusty springs popped through the upholstery. Amos looked from her to the two sweaty men.

'You drive, Cohen,' he said and tossed the keys to one of them.

'Where would you be more comfortable?' he asked Tonia, 'by the window or in the middle?'

'Window.'

One of the back doors was rusted shut, so Amos and the other man climbed in the other side, slid across the seat, and settled themselves. Tonia got in last, beside Amos, and pulled the door shut, anxious to be gone before her father happened by and saw her. The air in the car was stifling, and she tried to roll her window down, but it wouldn't budge.

Amos watched her trying and said, 'Don't bother. They're all stuck. Wait a minute.' He motioned for Tonia to open the door and get out so he could follow her. He picked up a rock and opened the driver's door. He motioned for Cohen to lean over out of the way, and smashed the window, breaking it from the inside out. 'Now well have some air,' he said, tossing the rock aside.

Cohen started up the engine, and they roared away, leaving an enormous cloud of dust and shards of broken glass behind them. Tonia turned to watch the kibbutz disappear and suppressed an eager smile.

She had seen films in the dining hall, but had never been to a movie theater. And she had never been taken anywhere by a young man. She leaned against the door and watched the scenery, too shy to look at Amos. He was wearing his khaki shorts, and his sinewy brown thigh veered toward hers at every curve on the winding Hebron–Jerusalem highway. Despite the stream of air blasting her in the face, she was aware of his musky scent and surprised by how pleasant she found it.

She rested her head against the window, eyes closed, and anticipated the physical contact that must come at the next turn of the road, but Amos somehow managed to maintain perfect equilibrium even on the sharpest curves. He never touched her. Would he take her hand in the movie theater? Yawn and put his arm around the back of her seat?

Bethlehem rushed past, then kibbutz Ramat Rachel. Soon they were in Talpiot, Jerusalem's southernmost neighborhood.

'Where to?' Cohen asked Amos.

Amos turned to Tonia. 'Is there any place special you want to go?'

She shook her head.

'Then drop us at my mother's. Take the car to Moshe. He's going to try and do something about that noise in the engine before we go back.'

'Where do we pick you up?'

'When Moshe finishes with the car, go to my mother's. She'll know where we are.'

'Is it safe to drive back after dark?' Tonia asked.

He grinned. 'Is it safe in broad daylight?'

They turned up Jaffa Road toward the Mahane Yehuda market.

'Right here is fine,' Amos said to Cohen. The car roared off and left them standing alone on the sidewalk.

'Do you want anything from the market?' he asked, and she shook her head. 'My mother lives a few blocks from here, but I feel like walking a bit.'

'Good. So do I.'

The hawkers in the market were closing up for the day. They waved or nodded to Amos as he passed. He put his thumb and forefinger around her elbow and steered her up a long alley to Agrippas Road. His fingertips were light on her skin as he led her through an arched stone entryway that opened into a spacious courtyard. Women dressed like Rachel, in colorful mismatched clothing, sat on the edge of the cistern talking while children played at their feet. They enthusiastically greeted Amos, and it occurred to Tonia that her presence at his side was likely to cause a stir in the neighborhood.

The buildings were low, one or two stories, built around courtyards. They were of thick Jerusalem stone and might have been beautiful, if they had not been marred by haphazard additions of cinder block, weather-beaten wood, corrugated tin, and asbestos. The narrow windows were high and arched, protected by iron grillwork. Amos kept hold of her elbow as they walked over the cobbled paving. Only the main roads of the neighborhood had been covered with asphalt. The narrow alleyways and courtyards remained as they had been built at the turn of the last century.

'Watch your step,' Amos warned. 'I can't tell you how many toes I broke on these stones when I was a kid.'

'This is as bad as a kibbutz,' Tonia observed. 'Everybody knows you.'

'Worse. In the kibbutz they don't necessarily know everything there is to know about your cousins and great-great-uncles.'

It was difficult for Tonia to imagine Amos as a child, the way he looked in the photograph, feet bare, head shaven, and with long side-curls. Amos seemed no different from the other young men she knew; but the women and bent old men they passed on the street were nothing like her parents. It was like visiting a foreign country.

Amos stopped next to three steps that led up to an arched entryway. 'Here.'

'Is this where you grew up?'

'Yes.'

The passage was short, with an entrance at either end. Several flats opened out into the courtyard. The short, chimney-like mouth of a cistern protruded in the center of the little square, rendering it impassable, even to a donkey cart. Tonia stopped and seated herself on it, but Amos remained standing a few meters from her.

'Don't tell me that here in the big city you still have to haul water from a cistern,' Tonia said.

'Only the neighborhoods that were built after they put in the pipeline have running water. You can pay to be hooked up to the water system, but most people, like my mother, think that's too big an expense.'

'I'd think it would be worth a fortune not to have to haul water.'

'I don't know how clever it was to put up all those new buildings without their own cisterns. Not when there's a war coming. There's nothing easier than cutting a pipeline.'

'Do any of your brothers and sisters still live at home?'

'The two youngest, Meir and Benjamin, but they aren't here right now. They spend the summer with my aunt near the beach in Jaffa. Ya'acov has his own room, just over there.' He nodded toward the street. 'Haim and his wife Dina live up the street. He's on active duty in the Haganah. Elazar is married with two kids. Lives on a *moshav* near Hadera.'

'I thought you were the oldest.'

'I am.'

'Elazar is younger than you and already has two kids?'

'We tend to marry young,' he smiled. 'I don't think it used to be so different with your European matchmakers.'

'How nice that some things do change.'

She rose, and he led her toward his mother's flat. Amos had to duck his head under the arched entryway into the yard. A single lemon tree struggled to survive in a patch of dirt left uncovered by cobblestones. It was surrounded by mint, parsley, coriander, dill, and other cooking herbs whose names Tonia did not know. A grapevine covered the outer walls. The yard was spotless; its walls looked recently whitewashed. Two makeshift structures jutted out, each with its own padlocked door and low roof of corrugated tin. Tonia assumed these were the toilet and the kitchen.

Amos knocked on the heavy wooden door. There was no answer; he reached up to the ledge for the key, and they entered a large, high-ceilinged room. An icebox, too tall to fit into the kitchen outside, stood in one corner. A heavy wooden table and chairs took up the center of the room. Crowded around it were a single bed, a small armchair, a large wooden wardrobe with mirrored doors, and a large cabinet. Colorful handiwork covered the patches of wall space that remained. An arched opening with no door led to a second room, which was almost bare. It held two rusty metal frame beds, a pile of mattresses, and a stack of wicker baskets.

This is what dignified poverty looks like, Tonia thought. Crowded. Not much different from the way we lived at Uncle Shmuel and Aunt Rivka's.

One electric bulb burned overhead, and a number of kerosene lanterns hung on the walls. Amos must have been expecting the Arabs to cut off the electricity as well as the water. Amos motioned her toward the armchair and put on the kettle.

She watched his back as he heaped pastries onto a plate. How nice it would be to be a sweet young Yemenite girl, wanting nothing more than to marry a man like Amos. Tonia straightened her back. She had not been able to resist this invitation, but she was not about to fall in love with Amos Amrani. She refused to relive her mother's life, suffering in silence for having chosen the wrong man. Always waiting. Never first. Leah had at least known where her husband was. The unfortunate girl who married Amos would not have that luxury, would live in constant fear for him.

Rachel entered the flat carrying a large bundle, which Amos took from her.

'How are you, child?' She embraced Tonia. 'I'm always telling him to bring you to visit, but I didn't think he'd ever pry you away from your kibbutz.'

'I've wanted to visit you.' Tonia returned her embrace.

Rachel turned and bustled about, setting plates on the table.

'Please, Rachel, don't go to a lot of trouble. Amos is making tea. That's plenty.'

'Ach. Don't insult me.'

Tonia's offer to help was rejected with another 'Ach'. Defeated, Tonia suggested to Amos that they wait outside where the air was cooler. She again perched on the edge of the cistern;

and he again avoided it, setting a battered wooden chair a few meters away.

They sat in silence, watching the stars come out, listening to the banter of the neighbors calling to one another from their porches. A few people poked their heads under the archway to welcome Amos home, and Tonia studied his profile. When their eyes met, they both looked away.

Rachel made several trips to her outdoor kitchen and to her neighbors. Within an hour, the table was laden with more food than ten people could have consumed.

'Amos, can't you do something?' Tonia pleaded in a whisper, worried that Rachel would not eat for a week, her resources depleted by the spread she was putting on for them.

'Don't worry. My brothers will be around. What they don't eat, the neighbors will.'

Soon they were seated around Rachel's table, plates laden with spicy Yemenite food. The conversation revolved around why Tonia was eating so little, when in fact she doubted that she would be able to rise from her chair.

The door opened, and a young man who vaguely resembled Amos burst in. 'Ima, you've got a hero in the family.' He flushed when he saw Tonia, obviously having expected his mother to be alone.

'My brother Ya'acov. This is Tonia, from the kibbutz. So what are you so worked up about?' Amos asked him.

'I was accepted into the Palmach today,' Ya'acov replied.

'Things must be worse than I thought, if they're scraping the bottom of the barrel for the likes of you.' Amos rose, went to the cupboard, and took out a bottle of *arak* and four tiny cups.

'*Le'Haim*,' he toasted his brother.

'Sit, eat.' Rachel brought another plate, apparently unimpressed.

The door to the flat was pushed open again, and an older woman came in.

'You're drinking *Le'Haim* without me?' she said and looked from Amos to Tonia and back again.

'Ya'acov is a new Palmachnik, Aunt Nechama,' Amos informed her. 'We were just congratulating him.'

'*Fech*.' The woman turned away. 'That's something to celebrate? The Arabs don't have enough opportunities to kill us, without us joining armies?'

'Now maybe Amos will be shamed into enlisting,' Ya'acov said.

'What enlisting? He should be getting married. You too.' Aunt Nechama poked Ya'acov in the back.

'At least I've got a girl.' Ya'acov raised both palms in defense. 'Complain to him.'

Two of the neighbors wandered in without knocking, and Tonia felt lost in the ensuing din. She did not understand all of their guttural Hebrew and sometimes thought they must be speaking Arabic. She smiled and nodded like an idiot. Finally, Amos glanced at his watch.

'If we want to see the film, we'd better get going.'

Tonia tried to help clear away the dishes, but was shoved out the door.

'If you want to wash dishes in this house, you have to come much more often,' Rachel said. 'Much more.'

Tonia thanked Rachel for a delicious meal and nodded a general goodbye to the room, while Amos slapped backs.

'When Cohen comes, tell him we're at the Zion Theater and he can pick us up after the show,' he said to his mother.

They threaded their way through the alleyways back to Agrippas Road and started the long walk to Zion Square. Tonia waited for Amos to take her elbow again, skin tingling in anticipation. She was about to pretend to trip over a stone, when a motorbike zoomed up behind them. The rider got off and pulled Amos aside. They spoke for a few minutes in hushed, urgent tones, and the rider sped off.

'I'm afraid the car won't be ready until tomorrow morning,' Amos told her. 'Don't worry, we'll make it back to the Bloc in time for you to get to work. You can stay at my mother's. Is that all right?'

181

'I don't see that I have much choice,' she said. Her father would be furious, but there was nothing she could do about that. Perhaps if they got back early enough in the morning, he would never know she had been gone all night. At least this way they would not have to rush back to the kibbutz tonight. They could sit in one of the cafés after the movie. If they went to Café Atara, Ilana Rozmann might even see her there with Amos.

'Tonia ... there's something else. Something's come up. I can't go to the movie with you. I'll get someone else to take you, and I'll meet you later.'

She was astounded by the depth of her disappointment and anger, appalled that she had to fight tears back, and scolded herself to stop behaving like a child.

'I won't be gone long. An hour or so. If you don't want to see the movie with one of my friends, you can wait at my mother's. Or perhaps there's someone you'd like to visit.'

She could not bear the thought of spending the evening in his mother's flat, with all those people she did not understand staring at her. And why should she believe he would return in an hour? She knew all about the promises of men like Amos. Her father's hours stretched into days and his days into weeks. It was for the best that this happened now, before she started having more of the wrong kind of thoughts about him. Amos could rush off to play his games with the British and feel like a big hero all he wanted. She wasn't going to sit around waiting for him.

'That's all right. I can go to the Rozmanns, the people I stay with in Rehavia.' She squared her shoulders and regained control of her vocal cords.

'I am sorry, Tonia, but I have to meet this guy. It's important. I'll be back as soon as I can.'

'I said it was all right, Amos.' Her voice was ice.

'Don't you want to wait for me, so we can go somewhere later? For coffee at least?'

'No, thank you. I do not want to wait. I'll go spend the night at my friend's.'

'Fine. Have it your way. You go to Rehavia.'

She had turned away and taken a few steps when it occurred to her. He probably didn't have a clue why she was upset. He may have been offended, thinking she didn't want to stay at his mother's home. That it wasn't fancy enough for her – she preferred to stay with her snobby rich friends in Rehavia. Like the people Rachel worked for, scrubbing their floors. Rachel might think the same. How awful to insult them like that.

'No, wait,' she called and turned back. 'I would rather stay at your mother's, if that's all right.'

'Of course, it's all right.' They started walking back toward Rachel's. 'And like I said, when I get back, we can go somewhere.'

'No, I'd rather get to sleep early.'

He stopped and turned to look into her face.

'I'm sorry, Amos, but I'm no good at waiting.'

'Have it your way.'

Rachel made up a bed in the inner room for her. Before he left, Amos hung a blanket over the doorway to give her some privacy. Tonia had a cup of tea with Rachel and then went to bed, claiming to have a headache.

She could not sleep. She lay in the dark, conscious of each footfall on the cobblestones outside, waiting for the sounds of Amos's return. Rachel soon climbed into the other bed, and Tonia almost held her breath, trying not to toss and turn. Rachel, however, seemed to fall asleep instantly. She lay on her back, mouth open, snoring lightly.

Tonia finally heard the door open and close and squinted at her watch in the moonlight. It was 2:00 in the morning. Good thing she hadn't waited up for her cup of coffee. But maybe he would have come earlier, if he had known she was waiting. No, that was wishful thinking. Men like Amos never interrupted what they were doing for anything as trivial as a woman. Let her wait. She can manage.

Tonia punched her pillow and still could not sleep, aware of him lying meters away, on the other side of that blanket. What did he wear to bed?

CHAPTER TWENTY-TWO

The next morning Tonia and Amos exchanged polite conversation over the *malawach* Rachel served them for breakfast and during the ride back to Kfar Etzion. Tonia said goodbye at the front gate, and the car roared off. She glanced at her watch and decided she had time to go to the dining hall for a cup of tea before work. She took it outside to drink, while she stared at the hills.

The future had crept up on her. 'Someday, when I'm old enough' was no longer some distant time to come. If she was to have any hope of changing her life, she needed to start preparing herself now. There was nothing concrete she could do, other than continue to get good grades in school, but she could prepare herself emotionally. She must not let someone like Amos Amrani distract her. She could start reading more about America, thinking about exactly where in that huge country she should go.

She went to her tent to change into her work clothes and found her father sitting on her bed. The initial relief she saw in his eyes gave way to cold, hard anger. To Tonia's surprise, she felt no fear. No guilt.

She set her handbag down. 'Good morning, Abba. Aren't you going to be late for work?'

'Is that all you have to say?'

'Why are you here?' she asked, as she picked her work clothes off the back of the chair next to the bed.

'Why am I here? I have to hear from friends that my daughter – my not yet sixteen-year-old daughter – was seen driving off with a gangster, and she doesn't come back all night, and she wants to know why I am here.'

She pulled the chair aside and sat down. 'I heard there was a car going into Jerusalem,' she said calmly. 'I thought it would do me good to get out of this place for a few hours. I told Ima I was going. But the car ended up needing repairs, and Rachel Amrani was kind enough to let me stay with her.'

Her father stared at her, and she lifted her chin to meet his gaze. It was a matter of survival, being capable of defying this giant of a man.

'I didn't mean to imply ...' he mumbled, looking contrite. 'But I was worried. You know how dangerous the roads are. It's not like you. I came to check that you had gotten back safely. What do you think went through my mind when I saw that your bed hadn't been slept in and no one knew where you were? I had half the local police force checking that there hadn't been any incidents on the road.'

'I'm sorry you were worried, Abba.' Her voice softened. 'But I did tell Ima where I was going, and you know there's no way I could have gotten a message to you after there was trouble with the car.'

He sat staring at his hands, then looked into her eyes and asked a question that took her by surprise. 'Do you still blame me so much, Tonia? Do you think so little of me as a father?'

'I love you, Abba,' she whispered. 'I think the world of you. But I'm not a child any more, and my life is my own.'

The next afternoon Tonia felt lonely and went to look for her brother. Standing outside the Palmach tent, she found nothing to knock on, so she called out timidly, 'Is Natan Shulman in there?'

'Yeah, I'm here.'

Tonia pulled the flap back and stuck her head in. Natan lay on one of the cots, hands behind his head. Amos slouched in the chair next to him, his long bare legs propped on another chair. When she entered, he swung them down and sat up straight.

'Hello, Amos,' she said.

'Hello, Tonia.' Amos bowed his head in formal greeting.

Tonia nodded to the other two Palmach boys in the tent. Amos rose and brought her a chair.

'What's got you thinking so hard, big brother?' she asked, noting Natan's more than usually pensive expression.

'Nothing.'

One of the Palmachniks, a thin young man with a droopy yellow mustache, sneered as he laced up his boots. 'He's suffering from a bad case of bleeding heart.'

Natan rose on one elbow and retorted, 'I seem to vaguely recall that it says somewhere, Thou shalt not kill.'

'And somewhere else it says, He who rises to smite you, you shall rise and smite him first,' droopy mustache replied. 'You'd better remind your brother that we're fighting a war. Just because it hasn't been declared yet doesn't make it any less a war.' Droopy mustache rose and left the tent.

'We were talking about reprisals,' Amos explained to Tonia.

'What kind of reprisals?' Tonia asked, relieved that Amos had chosen to act as if nothing had happened between them.

'Every time the Arabs attack one of our vehicles on the road, we send out a party to attack the next Arab car that goes by,' Amos said.

'So?' It made sense to Tonia.

'That's *random* reprisal.' Natan sat up. 'Against the next poor *shlemiel* that happens down the road.'

Amos kept his voice soft. 'You think a battlefield is so different? The guy you're shooting at is a poor *shlemiel* who happened to get drafted and shoved out in front of the barrel of your gun. Look, I don't like it any better than you do, but right now the road *is* the battlefield. The outcome of the war will depend on who controls it.'

Tonia watched Amos and her brother, not understanding how they had become such good friends. They were so different.

'Just look at what's happening to Kfar Etzion,' Amos continued. 'You can't step two feet outside the compound without an armed guard. You can't send a truck of produce into market without an armed escort. All they have to do is keep this up and they've won. As long as you're closed in here, helpless, while Mohammed over there is free to plough his fields, you've lost.'

'There must be a way to defend ourselves that won't make an enemy out of every peaceful villager.'

'There are no peaceful villagers. What we want, they want. Victory will go to whoever is willing to pay the highest price.

Fighting to regain control of the road is part of that price.' Amos paused and lit a cigarette.

'If you're right,' Natan said, 'we'll never have lasting peace.'

'What idiot told you there's such a thing as lasting peace?' Amos slouched back in his chair. 'Peace is what happens between wars.'

'You think of life as one long battle?' Tonia asked.

'You're the educated one – you know what the history books are full of: wars. Though you will probably be surprised to learn that I did not personally start all of them.'

'So you think the way we live here is normal?' Tonia said with a sigh.

'God kept heaven to himself; all he gave us is the earth. I deal with what's in front of me. At least I know what I'm fighting for. If you go off to America, you'll find yourself sending your sons to fight somebody else's wars.' He rose, picked up a towel and a bar of soap. 'I'm going to take a shower, Shulman.'

'Enjoy.'

Tonia did not manage to keep her eyes off him as he left.

Outside the dining hall after dinner, Amos touched Tonia's arm.

'Walk with me.'

She fell into step with him, and they strolled down the path in silence. He stopped by some trees, where no one could see them, and looked into her face.

'Explain to me why you're so anxious to leave your own country.'

'I have a picture taped up next to my bed. A white house with flowers in the windows.'

'Yeah. So?' Amos asked.

'That's what I want.'

'So you get married, and your husband builds you a house.'

'It's not the house. It's the whole thing, the people who live in that kind of house, the kind of lives they lead. I want to be like them, with nothing more to worry about than what to make for supper. And to go see a movie with my husband without having

187

to check under my seat for bombs. I also wouldn't mind being able to take a shower whenever I feel like it.'

'You want a free ride.'

'What's that supposed to mean?'

'The people who settled America didn't have it any easier than we do.'

'Okay, so I wouldn't have wanted to be a pioneer woman either. I would have sat on my bustle in Philadelphia waiting for someone else to do all the hard work, so that I could catch a train to Los Angeles.' She looked steadily into his eyes. 'I'm sorry, Amos, I have no desire to be a hero. I admit it. I'm selfish. An individualist.' She pronounced the word the way the kibbutzniks did, as if it were accompanied by a bad smell. 'The lowest form of life.'

He put his hands on her shoulders. 'Be careful what you wish for,' he said. He put his arms around her and held her close for a brief moment. She did not pull away; his embrace felt so natural.

'I should pay better attention to my own advice,' he said when he let her go.

CHAPTER TWENTY-THREE

The kibbutzniks crowded around the radio in the dining hall, listening to the UN vote that would decide whether Palestine would be partitioned into two states, one Arab and one Jewish. Members of the secretariat crouched over wrinkled papers, tallying the results. Haiti, expected to oppose, voted in favor, and the kibbutzniks broke into loud cheers, hugging one another.

'Shhhh.' The secretary tried to hush them, ear bent to the radio.

When Liberia – another expected 'No' – also voted 'Yes', the response was louder. They began exchanging glances, afraid to believe. When the representative from Paraguay said 'Yes', they burst into uninhibited cheers. A group of men began singing and formed a *hora* circle. By the time the final count was announced, 33 for and 13 against, someone started playing an accordion. A barrel of wine stood by the door, and they filled paper cups for toasts.

Josef strode outside and rejoiced like a child, hands raised high to the stars overhead, shouting, 'A Jewish state! A Jewish state!'

Tonia followed her father outside and stood with her arms crossed, watching him. She knew she must never forget this night. November 29th, 1947. The beginning of the end. She stood apart from the celebrants, puzzled. She understood their joy, but why did she seem to be the only one who was terrified? In six months, the Mandate would come to an end, and the British would leave them all alone. And how could her father and the others drink to a decision that left the Etzion Bloc in the Arab state? Well, that was for the best. Now there would be no choice but to evacuate Kfar Etzion. The Jewish Agency couldn't possibly leave them there.

Her father came over, swept her up in his arms, and swung her around in a large circle. She whispered, '*Mazal tov*, Abba,' when he set her down, but he did not seem to hear. He was off and running.

Natan appeared at her side and gave her a hug, grinning, mistaking the tears trickling down her cheeks for tears of joy. She did not want to spoil the moment for him and said nothing. More people came outside to dance. How many of them would still be alive this time next year? When Natan went to talk to one of his friends, Tonia slipped away for a lonely walk down the stony path.

She seated herself on a rock – the one Amos had sat on while he watched her bury her family's valuables – and gazed back at the settlement. A bonfire blazed outside the dining hall, flickering against the dark and silent hillsides. The singing and cries of joy sounded pathetic, lost in the surrounding void. From this distance she could see how vulnerable the tiny circle of light was. A dot of flame, flickering in the eye of the coming storm.

No one seemed to be working the next morning. A blue and white flag flew from the roof of Neveh Ovadia. The dining hall was festooned with flowers and banners emblazoned with Biblical passages. The tables were draped with spotless white cloths. Tonia found her father in the radio room, arguing with the dispatcher about the next convoy of supplies expected to arrive from Jerusalem.

'*Mazal tov*, Abba.' She kissed his cheek.

'Child, child.' He hugged the breath out of her. 'You've never had many presents from me. Please accept this one. I did everything I could … my small part to make it happen. For you. For you. Always for you and Ima and Rina and Natan – and for your children and grandchildren.' She did her best to look sincere when she smiled.

That evening the community gathered in Neveh Ovadia to celebrate. They recited the *Hallel* thanksgiving prayer, and one of the members gave a short talk, stressing the suffering that precipitates redemption. Leah sat next to Josef, blinking back tears, clutching his hand.

It did not take long for the road to Jerusalem to become impassable without an armed escort.

190

'Tonia.' Leah came into her room one night. 'I know how much school means to you, and you're missing so many days. If you want to go back to Jerusalem with the next convoy, you could stay with the Rozmanns. That way you'll be able to stay in school and graduate in June. Your father and I think you should. I mean, we think you should do whatever you want, but that would be all right with us.'

Tonia had already considered that possibility and rejected it. 'No, Ima. I'm going to stay here. I'm sure the principal of the Gymnasium will find some way to help the "brave and dedicated pioneer" get her diploma when it's over. I want to stay with my family. I couldn't study now anyway.'

She was assigned to help fortify the guard posts around the perimeter fence and worked hard, her face grim. At night, groups gathered around campfires to sing songs of the ghetto fighters, but Tonia never joined them. Were they all going to forfeit their own lives on this rocky hilltop, so that someday, somewhere, other Jews might sing stirring songs glorifying their sacrifice?

Tonia escaped into frivolous novels and thoughts of Amos, who was stuck in Jerusalem. She was surprised how much she missed knowing he might come up the path any moment. The air seemed different, with no possibility of Amos lingering in it.

On the first day of Hanukkah, a large electric candelabrum was erected on the roof of Neveh Ovadia. The schoolchildren had a party inside, though most of their parents were on guard duty and could not attend.

Later that night Tonia stood at her own post, armed with the ancient pistol she had learned to use, waiting for one of the Palmach boys to relieve her. She heard soft crunches of gravel behind her and then sharp cries that she at first mistook for a cat. She peered into the blackness behind her and a small boy in red and white pajamas emerged, stumbling up the path. He was barefoot and crying.

'Eran?' Tonia said, recognizing one of the children her mother took care of. She set down her pistol, stepped out of the guard post, and picked him up. Wrapping her coat around him, she hugged him to her and rubbed his back. 'What are you doing out here? You must be freezing.'

'Ima,' he said. He stopped crying, but pouted at her. 'I want my Ima.'

'Okay, sweetie,' Tonia said and smoothed his hair. 'I'll take you to your Ima. But you'll have to wait with me here for a little while.' Tonia looked at her watch and stepped back down into the shallow crater that had been dug behind the wall of rocks. 'In five more minutes one of the soldiers will come, and then we can go. Can you wait five minutes?'

He nodded. She sat down on the edge of the crater, pushed the pistol out of his reach, and began rubbing his feet. Some guard I am, she thought.

'Reinforcements?' The Palmach boy had come up behind her.

Tonia got to her feet and held out a hand for him to help her back out of the crater with Eran in her arms. 'He must have had a bad dream, came wandering up the path a few minutes ago. Gun's down there.' She nodded at the pistol.

Tonia hefted Eran to her other hip. 'Okay, big guy. Let's get you to your Ima.' As she walked toward the row of rooms where Eran's parents lived, she prayed that they would open the door and not tell her to take him back to the children's house where he belonged.

Tonia rapped three times and heard stirring inside. Eran's father opened the door and peeked out, then swung it wide open.

'Hey, there, Ranchick, what are you doing here?' He held out his arms for his son, and Tonia gratefully handed him over.

'Thanks, Tonia.'

'No problem.'

She walked back to the main path and glanced toward Neveh Ovadia. The candles were still illuminated – two tiny drops of light in the black. She looked up at them with a sad smile and jumped when the wind rustled through the trees. Every shadow seemed to menace, and she shivered with cold and fear. She swore that if she ever brought children into this world, they would never celebrate a holiday in a place like this.

Amos went to his mother's flat and filled his grandfather's silver menorah with olive oil to light the Hanukkah lights. It was one of their few family possessions that had survived the trip across the desert from Yemen to Palestine.

Afterwards he went out to the truck he had backed up to the arched entrance to the courtyard to finish unloading ten large clay water jars. They were similar to the four that had always stood in his mother's room to hold water drawn from the cistern.

'Why have you brought so many water jars?' Rachel asked him.

'I've got ten more coming after these,' he called back over his shoulder. 'And if you had room for them, I'd get a hundred more. Jerusalem is going to be an easy target. Keep the road to the coast impassable, cut the water line ...'

He stopped to wipe his brow. Despite the cool evening air, his shirt was damp with sweat. He went outside and called to one of the neighbor boys. He gave the boy a few coins and told him to start hauling water from the cistern to fill the jars. Then Amos went back to the truck and unloaded sacks of flour, sugar, rice, beans, bottles of oil, and canned goods.

'Is this necessary?' Rachel asked.

'Ima, I'd never survive a siege without your cakes.' He brushed past her, anxious to be finished.

'But is it right? If everyone starts hoarding–'

'Everyone with half a brain already has,' he said and stopped in front of her. 'In my book "right" is anything that keeps you alive and healthy.'

She smiled sadly. 'Such bad times.' She sighed. 'And such a good son.'

He kissed his mother goodbye and drove to the Jewish Settlement Police Station, where a friend of his was on duty.

'How are things, Haim?'

'Lousy, as usual. You finally come to enlist?'

'Just for one day. I want to ride with the next convoy to Kfar Etzion.'

193

Haim shook his head. 'You nuts? No one's making social calls these days. You know what the roads are like.'

'So who could object to one more armed Jew on a convoy? Just tell me when it's leaving, and I'll worry about getting myself on it.'

Haim shuffled some papers. 'Next one is scheduled for the morning of the 11th.'

'Thanks.'

Haim stood and leaned forward over the desk. 'Listen, I'm telling you, it's really bad out there.'

Amos raised both hands, palms up.

'If you see rocks on the road in front of you,' Haim said, 'it's a safe bet they started building a blockade behind you the minute you went past.'

Amos nodded and left the office. He stood for a moment, staring into the blackness, in the direction of Kfar Etzion. Had he been on higher ground, he might have been able to see the lights on the roof of Neveh Ovadiah.

CHAPTER TWENTY-FOUR

Amos waited on the morning of the 11th, wearing the baggy pants and wide cloth belt of an Arab worker. He had concealed a knife and a pistol beneath his loose white shirt. Shivering, he pulled on a dirty brown corduroy jacket and lit a cigarette. This trip was pointless. Much as Tonia hated living in Kfar Etzion, he doubted she would agree to leave her family. Maybe Leah would be able to talk her into coming back with him. Jerusalem would soon be under siege, but if she came now, he would be able to get her back to her uncle's flat in Tel Aviv.

Four trucks pulled up, and Amos stamped out his cigarette. Light armor covered some parts of the rusty vehicles, and he rapped his knuckles against the side of one of them, unconvinced that plating that thin could stop bullets.

Shimon, the friend who had agreed to take Amos, leaped down from one of the trucks and slapped Amos's back. 'I'm driving the lead truck. You can ride with us. This is Jeremy.' He put his arm around the shoulder of a freckled teenager who had climbed down from the passenger side. The boy was carrying a gun that was almost as tall as he was. 'Jeremy has been in Palestine all of three weeks, but he speaks pretty good Hebrew. Don't you?'

Jeremy nodded and held out his hand to Amos.

'Where are you from?' Amos asked the boy, marveling at his deep blue eyes.

'Vilna.'

'You know how to shoot that thing?'

'Yes, Shimon show me.'

Shimon nodded at the doors of the storehouse that had opened behind them. 'Let's start loading.'

It was afternoon before the convoy was ready to leave Jerusalem. Jeremy climbed in, Amos behind him, while Shimon slammed the doors at the back of the truck.

'I am a soldier in Eretz Israel,' Jeremy said brightly.

'You sure are.' Amos smiled and punched his shoulder.

The windshield was covered with armored plating. Two small squares had been cut out, one in front of the driver and one in front of the passenger. Amos stretched his neck to peer through the small square of light on his side. He opened his door and shouted back to Shimon, 'How do you drive like this? I can hardly see a thing.'

Shimon opened the driver's door and got in. 'You get used to it.'

Amos looked through the tiny window in the door. 'These things aren't much for sightseeing,' he said. 'Better for romance. Nice and dark in here.'

'Yeah, real cozy,' Shimon said, 'until somebody farts.'

Jeremy giggled and looked at Amos out of the corner of his eye.

Shimon started the engine, and they jolted forward. 'Sure you want to take this ride?' he asked Amos, who lifted his left hand, palm up, by way of response.

When they passed Bethlehem, Amos slipped the pistol from his belt and removed the safety. None of them spoke much, their eyes scanning the roadside through the tiny openings. More men were riding in the back of the truck, with the supplies.

They had just passed Solomon's Pools when a machine gun opened fire on them and the deafening racket of bullets smashing against armor filled the cabin.

'I can see where it's coming from,' Amos shouted, flattening himself against the door and peeking out. 'Behind that big boulder up there. But I can't get a shot at the bastard.' He gripped his pistol, then put it down. 'Give me that.' He grabbed Jeremy's rifle and cursed, '*Cus emakh.*' It was going to be difficult to take aim in the cramped cabin, through the tiny hole in the armor.

The truck lurched to a stop. Amos thought they must have hit a blockade of rocks and stretched forward to look through the 'window' in the windshield. But out of the corner of his eye he saw the reason they weren't going anywhere – Shimon was slumped over the wheel, his right eye a gaping hole. Amos turned to stare at him in horror. Jeremy seemed to be paralyzed, gaping wide-eyed at the blood splatter that covered him. Amos reached over Jeremy to shove Shimon's foot off the pedals and grasp the wheel with his left hand. The deafening tak-tak-tak of bullets against the side of the truck continued.

'Fuck.' They had begun moving forward, but Amos was losing control. Shimon's foot had lodged itself on the gas pedal, and Amos let go of the wheel for a moment to bend down and yank it aside.

He straightened and shouted at Jeremy, 'Get down on the floor.' When Jeremy did not react, he shouted again. 'Move! Crawl under my arm.' He tugged at Jeremy with his right hand, trying to watch the road.

Jeremy had wet his pants and stared at him. The truck was idling, nearly at a standstill, automatic fire raining down on it from the hillside on their right. They had come to a curve in the road, and Amos did not dare try to press the gas pedal and drive blindly.

'Kid, get the hell out of the way! Now!' Amos dug his nails into the boy's upper arm, but he still did not budge.

Amos fumbled to retrieve his pistol with his right hand and put it to the boy's temple. 'Listen, if this truck doesn't keep moving, everyone else is stuck behind it. On the floor. Now!'

Jeremy finally obeyed. He ducked under Amos's outstretched arm and got on his knees on the floor, head on the seat, arms over his head, crying. Amos slid over, put a hand on Shimon's neck, and cursed again, the last hope that his friend might still be alive gone. He pushed Shimon's body as tightly up against the driver's door as he could, but still couldn't reach the brake pedal or see through the tiny front window without rising out of his seat and leaning over the body. He let go of the steering wheel for a moment, slid back toward the passenger door, and tugged at the body with both hands, trying to pull it down onto the floor next to Jeremy. He couldn't move it. He looked out the tiny window in the passenger door and saw dozens of figures descending the hill toward them. Desperate, Amos reached over Shimon's body and yanked the handle on the driver's door. The door fell open.

'God forgive me,' he shouted and shoved Shimon's body out of the truck. Even amidst the din of gunfire, he heard the ghastly thud. He begged forgiveness again and swore to come back for him. He knew what the Arabs did to bodies.

He pulled the door shut as he slipped into the driver's seat, put the truck in gear, and stepped on the gas pedal. The truck did not go far. An enormous boulder rolled down the hill and stopped in the middle of the road, a few meters ahead of them. Amos slammed his foot on the brakes, but before the vehicle came to a stop, bullets punctured two of its tires and it swerved into the boulder. The other three trucks in the convoy were now trapped behind them.

Amos opened the door, slipped out of the cabin, and looked back. Men were leaping from the other trucks, crawling beneath them or diving into the ditch on the left side of the road. Crouching, Amos dragged Shimon's body to the ditch and then ran back to the door of the truck.

'Jeremy, get out!'

Jeremy, hands still clamped over his head, peeked up at Amos, a frightened child.

Shimon's pistol had fallen to the floor of the cabin. Amos picked it up and shoved it into his belt. Then he grabbed Jeremy's rifle and slung its strap over his shoulder.

'Come on, kid, you've got to get out of there. The back of this truck is full of gas tanks.' He leaned in and yanked at Jeremy's arm. 'Come on, I've got you covered. You'll be all right.'

Jeremy finally responded, and Amos, choking on dust that smelled of diesel and blood, dragged him over to the ditch and pulled him down into the mud. 'Keep your head down.' He handed Shimon's pistol to the boy.

Amos nodded at Shimon's body. 'If you aren't going to fight, play dead. Hide under him.'

Amos saw motion out of the corner of his eye and looked up in time to see the last truck in the convoy back out of the trap and turn back toward Bethlehem.

'Save your ammunition!' one of the men crouching behind the trucks shouted. 'Don't take anything but a sure shot.'

198

As Amos squatted in the ditch next to Jeremy, the boy lurched and clutched his arm. Amos knew that the boy had taken a bullet and set his rifle down so that he could examine the wound.

'It's not bad,' he said. 'You'll be all right. One of the trucks went back to Bethlehem. The Brits should be here soon.' He slapped the boy's thigh. 'But you've got to snap out of it. Get one of those bastards in your sights and shoot. Remember, you're a soldier in Eretz Israel.'

Jeremy seemed to recover his senses. He lifted the pistol and squinted through its sights. Amos gave him an encouraging nod and crawled over Shimon's body to reach another man who lay moaning. The man's entrails were spilling onto the ground, and Amos had no idea how to help him. He took off his jacket, wiped his hands on his pants, and with cupped hands gathered up the man's intestines and pushed them back into the stomach cavity. He put his jacket over the wound, tucking it under the weight of the man, and placed the man's hands over the heavy garment. 'Hold on,' Amos said. 'There's an ambulance on the way. Just hold on.'

'Watch your backs,' someone called out. 'They're coming around the left, surrounding us.'

Amos put the rifle to his shoulder and picked off two figures creeping up the steep hill behind him. An eternity passed before two British police officers on motorcycles pulled up some distance from the disabled convoy. They cupped their hands around their mouths and shouted, 'Cease fire.'

Bullets continued to rain down on the trapped Jews. A British jeep inched around the bend in the road and stopped. It sat there for a few moments before it backed up, turned around, and drove off. The motorcycles followed. Amos cursed in Arabic. If the British did not intervene, this was going to be a massacre.

The scathing fire continued, killing several men who had dived under the trucks. One scrambled for the ditch, but sprawled in the road, a dark stain spreading over the back of his shirt. Amos turned toward Jeremy; the boy lay motionless in the ditch, his lifeless blue eyes wide open. Only a few Jews were still able to return fire. Amos had five bullets left. A least a hundred Arabs had gathered on the hillside across from him. He scanned the road for other survivors. He saw one man who was still alive, crouching behind the wheel of a truck, but as Amos watched he was shot in the head and fell face first onto the dusty road.

Amos saw a large formation of rocks on the slope below him. He backed out of the ditch and slithered toward it, flat on his belly, thorny underbrush tearing his skin. He hid behind the rocks and from his pants pocket he pulled a piece of black and white checked cloth and the black ring of a *kaffiyah*. As he adjusted the square of cloth on his head, the shooting stopped.

'Search the trucks,' a voice ordered in Arabic, and the throng descended to the road.

Amos rose into a crouch and took a deep breath. Then he stood and walked up to the road.

'Make sure no one is hiding down there in those rocks,' Amos shouted in Arabic, to no one in particular, and waved his arms, the rifle still hanging from his shoulder.

He mingled among the Arabs and made a show of rifling some cartons of food, struggling with the black rage that threatened to overcome him. A wounded Jew moaned, and Amos moved toward him, his mind racing. Where could he hide him? For what reason that would make sense to the Arabs could he pick up a wounded man and carry him away? Before Amos had time to do anything, an Arab stepped in front of him and bent down to stab the wounded man repeatedly in the chest. Amos could do nothing but watch with clenched fists as the Arab pulled the dead man's shoes from his feet.

Amos edged away from the scene. Within minutes, the Arabs had stripped the bodies and trucks of anything that could be carted away. One of them set fire to the truck Amos had ridden in, and the cylinders of cooking gas it carried exploded, dispersing the last remnants of the mob. Amos watched with some other stragglers. He stared wide-eyed at the carnage. He should go back to the road. Someone might still be alive. But he could not move. Could not think.

Then he saw two Arabs walking on the road toward Bethlehem. The rest of them had disappeared as quickly as they had materialized. Anger replaced numbness as Amos followed the two men. He called to them in Arabic, and they waited for him to catch up.

'I have something to sell,' Amos said. 'Something special.'

The men nodded, and Amos put his hand into his pocket. The younger of them bent closer, eager to see what he had to offer. Amos took a step forward, putting himself between him and his friend, and plunged the blade of his knife into the Arab's stomach. The Arab doubled over, choking. Amos pulled the bloody dagger out, pushed the dying man aside, and attacked the other, who barely put up a struggle.

When they both lay dead, Amos stumbled a few steps and fell to his knees, retching. He rested his head against a rock and waited for the world to stop spinning. Then he heard the sound of vehicles on the road and hid behind a rock as three British armored cars appeared around the bend.

'You're a bit late for the party,' he muttered.

He crawled away, past the two dead Arabs. He looked at the one nearest him, who had the grizzled face of a dirt farmer. Amos would have welcomed hatred, but felt nothing. No satisfaction and no remorse. The smell of blood sickened him, always returning him to the old memory of that first man he had killed. On all fours, he closed his eyes and rocked from side to side, wishing he could cry and howl with pain.

You think I don't understand you, Tonia, but I do. You want to live. To live! That's all I want. Never to have to kill another man. Why is that so much to ask?

He rose to his knees and stared at his hands. The Arabs' blood had clotted brown on them. He pulled a handful of scrubby grass from the ground and rubbed at the stains.

He caught sight of something lying on the ground near one of the bodies. A wallet. Amos picked it up and opened it, then closed his eyes again. It belonged to a friend from the Jewish Settlement Police. A small picture of Carmella – his wife, who did not yet know she was his widow – smiled at Amos. He wiped the wallet on his pants and slipped it into his pocket. He would have to mail it to her. He could not return it in person, as he had no intention of telling anyone that he had been on the convoy.

He looked back. The British were moving about the road, gathering the corpses together in one place, too busy to notice him. Amos stood for a while, feeling too drained and tired to move. Eventually he set off through the hills, bypassing Bethlehem. The moon was high when he approached the outskirts of Talpiot and threw his *kaffiyah* into the underbrush.

CHAPTER TWENTY-FIVE

Tonia finished setting the tables for the holiday meal and went up to the roof of Neveh Ovadia to watch for the convoy that was supposed to be on its way with desperately needed supplies. Someone downstairs began playing Hanukkah songs on the piano, and she hummed along. *But now all Israel must as one arise; Redeem itself through deed and sacrifice.* When she heard distant shots, she stopped and froze. The shooting continued for a long while. Then a series of explosions echoed through the hills, and Tonia saw the tips of flames flickering against the sky. She hurried to the dining hall, where people were huddled in small, subdued groups. About half an hour after the shooting stopped, a radio message came through from the Jewish Settlement Police, informing them of the attack on the convoy.

One of the women sobbed. 'Our first widows and orphans.'

'First' was the word that stuck in Tonia's mind. She went to stand near her mother and Natan, and they gripped one another's hands. They stayed in the dining hall, sipping tea and waiting for more news.

A few hours later, Josef came over to the table where they sat, looking tired and broken. 'They have taken the dead to the mortuary of the Bikkur Holim hospital in Jerusalem, but they will bring them here for burial.'

The next day around noon, the funeral procession arrived. It had a British escort and was followed by supply trucks and reinforcements. The kibbutzniks laid the bodies out on the floor of Neveh Ovadia, covered them with plain white cloths, and lit candles beside them. Josef worked shifts with the other men to complete the difficult task of digging graves in the rocky terrain. The dead had to be buried before the Sabbath. Leah gripped Tonia's arm as they filed past the bodies.

The dining hall was quiet during the evening meal. Half the members of the kibbutz were on guard duty. The others ate in gloomy silence.

After dinner, Tonia went to Natan's tent and sat talking with him and two new replacements from the Settlement Police. The conversation was subdued, and it was still early when the one named Haim rose and stretched. 'I've got second watch. I'd better try and grab a few hours' sleep.'

'Yeah, me too.' Natan said. 'You haven't seen Amrani around lately, have you?'

'Few days ago.' Haim looked away, his voice tight. 'He asked me to get him on that convoy. And I did.'

Tonia gasped.

'But he couldn't have been on it,' Natan whispered. 'I saw the casualty list.'

'I don't know,' Haim said. 'I asked someone who was there when they were loading up – he swears he saw a tall Yamani get into the lead truck. But he hasn't been ... I mean, he wasn't among the ... nobody's seen him since then. I've been asking around. Of course, you know Amrani – he has a way of disappearing and then turning up out of nowhere.' The heartiness of his tone rang false.

A wave of nausea swept over Tonia. 'But did you tell anyone that he got on the convoy?' she demanded. 'Did anyone know they should be looking for him? He could be lying out there in the hills somewhere, wounded.'

'Of course – I told everyone who went out there. They all said the same thing – that they made a thorough search of the area, looking for wounded.'

'But he could have crawled away and then passed out. Somewhere where they wouldn't find him,' she cried.

'They looked everywhere. I'm telling you.'

Natan took her hand. 'I'm sure he's all right. He must have changed his mind at the last minute, gotten off the truck. Otherwise, they would have found ...' His voice trailed off.

Tonia could not bring herself to say what her brother was thinking – they would have found his body ... unless he had been in the truck carrying the cylinders of gas that had exploded.

'We have to organize another search party,' Tonia said.

'Forget it, Tonia.' Haim refused to meet her glare. 'No one's going to authorize risking more lives. I'm telling you, they would have found him. We don't leave our wounded behind.'

She looked away, feeling sick. Haim and his friend left, leaving her alone with Natan.

'You know, don't you,' Tonia whispered, 'that if it was the other way around, if it was one of us, Amos would be out there looking. Authorization or no authorization.'

'Not if he thought it was pointless,' Natan said. 'Anyway, he must have gotten off – either before they left or at the station in Bethlehem.'

Tonia rose and paced. 'Maybe we could ask that Tabet from Beit Umar to help us look for him.'

'Don't start thinking about doing anything stupid.' Natan grabbed her arm. 'You can't go out there.'

Tonia spent the Sabbath feeling sick, under a pile of blankets. She did not rise for meals, nor join her family for afternoon tea. Leah brought her a tray of food, but she had no appetite. She felt guilty for lying in bed – the rest of the women were busy filling sandbags, while the men stretched out coils of barbed wire. Chief Rabbi Herzog had granted them a special dispensation to perform defense-related work on the Sabbath.

It was dark when Natan came to her room. 'I'm told some British policemen will be stopping here soon, on their way to Jerusalem. I'm going to try to hitch a ride with them. I'll go to Amos's place, visit his mother.'

Tonia sat up and hugged him.

Late that night Natan managed to get a radio message back to Tonia.

'He is, as I expected, in better health than either of us.'

For the next two weeks, no one came or went from the Bloc. The kibbutzniks spent most of their time on guard duty and shoring up the defenses. Tonia was assigned with some other women to try to prevent the neglect of the vines and trees they had planted. She worked long hours in silence and then collapsed into bed.

The fare in the dining room was meager, but Tonia had no appetite anyway.

'You have to eat,' Leah pleaded with her. 'You are getting so thin.'

Tonia seldom bothered to look in the mirror, but when she did, she saw an old woman staring back at her.

One evening at dinner, Josef told Leah and Tonia, 'They're talking again about evacuating the mothers and children. The money is gone, and with none of our produce going to market, we can't afford to support non-combatants.'

'Why not everyone? Why should the men stay here?' Tonia asked.

'Because this is our home, and we will defend it,' Josef said. 'And without the Etzion Bloc, the Arab Legion will just sail up the road into Jerusalem.'

A few days later, a convoy arrived. It carried food, fuel, barbed wire, and a group of university students who had come to receive rudimentary military training and serve as reinforcements. It also brought a short note from Natan, now posted in Jerusalem, informing his family that he was well. He made no mention of Amos.

Tonia spent long lonely hours at a guard post trying to lock away her feelings for Amos. One Sabbath sick with worry had been more than enough. She was not prepared to live her life like that.

Shivering at her post, Tonia imagined herself curled up with a book by a roaring fire. While she strained her back lifting sandbags, she planned the tiled bathroom she would have in America, the gleaming tub where she would soak in scented water. Her house would have an attic and a cellar for children to poke about in. There would be no snipers and no sleeping in her clothes with a loaded gun next to the bed.

By the beginning of January, the water level in the cisterns was low enough to necessitate rationing. The kibbutzniks again showered just once a week. Fuel was also a scarcity, so the generator was operated only after dark for the security lighting.

That meant that any work that required electric power had to be done in the evenings. There was no kerosene, so there was no way to heat their rooms in the bitter cold. The dining room served meals of boiled potatoes or rice with tinned vegetables. They went for days without seeing a newspaper. When a convoy did arrive, Tonia joined the others around it, hungry for every crumb of information the drivers brought.

The roof over Tonia's bed had started to leak, and Tonia began sleeping in her parents' room, huddling under the covers with Leah. Josef stood at one of the guard posts most nights, and when he came off duty, he put a mattress on the floor for himself.

Late one evening Tonia and Leah were having a cup of tea when Josef came in. He stared at them for a moment and then sank onto a chair, looking defeated.

'What is it, Josef?' Leah paled. 'Are Natan and Rina all right?'

'Yes, they're all right. It's … It's final. They've decided to evacuate the mothers and children to Jerusalem,' he said, his face worn. 'It's not practical to keep non-combatants here, consuming food, water, and fuel.'

'Oh no, Josef.' Leah went to stand behind him and put her arms about him.

'It won't be temporary,' he said dully. 'It's an admission of defeat. Anyway, who's to say you'll be any safer in Jerusalem? They don't have food or water there either. The Arabs shell and bomb the city every day. And who's going to protect you on the way there?' Josef covered his face with his hands, then looked up. 'This is our home,' he whispered. 'But we are to be separated again.' Josef took Leah's hands in his. His face was pale and his eyes rimmed with red.

'I thought they were talking about the mothers of small children,' Leah said.

'True,' Josef said, 'but if there is to be an evacuation, you and Tonia must go with them. Neither of you is a soldier.'

'No. I may not be a soldier, but I won't leave you,' Leah said.

'I do guard duty,' Tonia said. 'I know how to shoot a gun. Other girls my age are in the Palmach.'

'Leah, Tonia.' His voice was quiet, but uncompromising. 'In wartime, families are separated. You know how much I wanted everyone to stay. A man fights so much harder when he knows his family is on the other side of the fence. But if most of the other women are going, you must go with them. I don't want you here. This place is going to turn into an army camp. I beg you not to oppose me. Don't make it more difficult.' He turned to Tonia. 'You'll go with your mother.'

She nodded, feeling numb.

Josef took Leah in his arms and rocked her as she wept. Tonia slipped out of the room and made her way in the darkness to Amos's rock by the fence. She sat in the freezing mist, wiping her tears and her runny nose on her coat sleeve.

She hated this place and longed to leave it, but not like this. When would she ever see her father again? She gazed out at the fields her bloodied hands had helped clear, the orchards she had planted. She knew every stone on every path, every flower, every tree. When the sun came up the next morning, she was still sitting half-frozen on that rock. She rose, wiped her eyes, squared her shoulders, and went to work tending the vines.

Two weeks later, iron-plated vehicles with a British escort arrived to take the women and children to the Ratisbonne Monastery in Jerusalem, in which a hall had been rented to accommodate them. Tonia watched, dry-eyed, as the men loaded their pitiful belongings onto the trucks. One of the women refused to go, and two men had to lift her onto the truck. Tonia's mother and father shared a long embrace before Leah turned and climbed up into the vehicle. The back of the lorry was cramped, full of crying babies, the air stifling, but Leah managed a last serene smile.

Josef turned to Tonia and crushed her to his chest. 'Take good care of Ima. I'm counting on you.' Then he quickly lifted her up onto the truck. Tonia did not look back as they pulled away.

CHAPTER TWENTY-SIX

Though he no longer had small children of his own, Josef was acutely aware of their absence. The paths of the kibbutz were silent and empty, the two newly built children's houses abandoned and forlorn, the dining hall a drab blur of men in khaki. He shuddered, imagining Leah and Tonia in a cold, clammy monastery. Even the name of the place repelled him. Ratisbonne.

So again, Jews had to flee their homes.

One of their Arab neighbors had once remarked to Josef, 'You Jews are just like weeds – we keep pulling you up, and you keep coming back. We pull you up again, you come back again.'

Josef had answered him with a slap on the back. 'Because you can't get at the roots, my friend.'

A group of Palmachniks passed him on the path, looking pathetically young. Did they stand a chance? There were between three and four hundred Jewish fighters in the Bloc. They did not have enough arms to go around. The four settlements together possessed seven machine guns, seven mortars, 165 rifles, and a few pistols. Their grenades and mines were homemade.

That night in the dining hall one of the men at Josef's table said, 'The Arab Legion plans to take the Bloc first. They think we will give them an easy, morale-building victory.'

A few days later, early in the morning, hundreds of Arabs took up positions on the hills surrounding the Bloc, occupying even the nearby hill where the Lonely Tree stood. In this, the first battle for the Bloc, the Palmach boys managed to drive them off. The Arabs left behind over a hundred dead and as many wounded. But there was no celebrating in Kfar Etzion – they had three dead to bury and mourn. And they didn't know if they could withstand another onslaught.

Josef trudged to the dining hall, through the mist that enveloped the village. The building stood silent, its windows blacked out. He sighed, recalling that this armed camp had once been a home; children had skipped along its paths, squealing with laughter. What was Leah doing? Had she heard about the battle? How much news reached them, there in the monastery? Was she sick with worry, or did she know they had won? She might have heard that the Bloc had sustained casualties. If so, she would be frantic.

His head throbbed, and his shoes, crusted with thick mud, were heavy. Tired, cold, and hungry, he plodded into the dimly lit hall. Its walls were riddled with bullet holes. Young women rushed about, serving a hot meal of soup and rice to the men who straggled in from their posts, sharing their descriptions of the battle. Josef sat apart, hearing, but not listening, preoccupied with his thoughts. Did they have enough ammunition to sustain them through even one more battle? And what about medical supplies? They had almost nothing with which to treat the wounded. Radio contact would soon be cut off as well. The batteries were so weak that radio messages were extremely faint.

He swallowed his food indifferently and replied to comments addressed to him, but his mind was elsewhere. He had a few hours to rest before he had to return to his post, but he did not think he could sleep. He mumbled the Grace after Meals, walked to the reading room, and checked that the windows were blacked out before he lit a small lantern. He took a volume of Talmud from one of the shelves and sat down, opening it to where he had left off studying two days before. The black letters danced before his exhausted eyes, and he could make no sense of them. He closed the book and rested his head upon it, the familiar smell of the leather comforting him. He felt ... afraid? No. Helpless. The way Isaac must have felt when his father led him to Mount Moriah and put the blade to his throat. Would not some miraculous intervention grant them their lives, like the angel who had stayed Abraham's hand? Josef dozed off, and when he woke, it was time for him to resume guard duty.

He made his way to the post and sat staring into the dark of the still early morning. Would it all prove to have been for nothing? He rubbed his eyes and slapped his face. He heard footsteps behind him and raised his rifle, but lowered it when he heard the password.

'If sometime toward dawn you see a column approaching on foot, don't shoot,' the Palmach commander instructed him. 'We just heard over the radio – reinforcements are on the way from Jerusalem. Since the road is impassable, they're coming on foot over the hills.'

Josef almost shouted with joy. Here was his miracle.

He peered into the dark, but even after the sky grew light, he saw no sign of them. After he was relieved at his post, he went to the radio room.

'They had to turn back,' the radio operator informed him. 'Thirty men left Jerusalem last night after midnight, but they ran into trouble. Searchlights from the Arab villages spotted them, so they turned back. They'll try again tonight after dark. This time they'll be driven to Har Tuv and come from the northwest.'

That night they received another radio message – the reinforcements had left Har Tuv. Thirty-eight men, each carrying a heavy pack of arms, ammunition, blood plasma, and gelignite. They should reach the Bloc by 2:00 or 3:00 that morning.

By the next evening there was still no sign of them, and the radio operator continued signaling Jerusalem. 'The reinforcements have not arrived. We heard shooting from the direction of Surif about 10 o'clock this morning.' At midnight, they radioed again. 'They still have not arrived. You must send a plane early tomorrow morning to search for them. We have heard no more shooting.'

Scraps of information began coming in. There had been a battle in the Judean Hills, with heavy Jewish casualties. On Saturday, a detachment left Har Tuv to search for the lost party, but encountered enemy fire and was forced to turn back, carrying one dead and a number of wounded. Josef went out with a search party from Kfar Etzion, but found no sign of them near the Bloc. A small plane was sent to search the area, but failed to find a trace of them.

The next day Josef listened while Aliza, the young woman who operated the radio, sent a terse message to Jerusalem. 'We have just received word that thirty-five bodies have been found on the path between the villages of Surif and Jaba.'

Later the kibbutzniks learned that the British Police Superintendent of Hebron had managed to persuade one of the local Arabs to lead him to the bodies and tell him what had happened. The column had been spotted near Surif, a few kilometers from the Bloc, and had been trapped on one of the hills. Surrounded by villagers, they had fought until their ammunition ran out.

British soldiers gathered the dead and loaded them onto trucks, to take them to Kfar Etzion. The Superintendent had received orders to take the bodies to Jerusalem, but informed his superiors that the bodies had been found naked and mutilated. In his opinion, it would be advisable to take them to the Bloc and thus avoid arousing hysteria in Jerusalem.

On Sunday morning the British commandant entered the kibbutz to inform the settlers of this decision. He told them that the thirty-five bodies would be brought to Kfar Etzion for burial that evening. Josef and a group of men silently picked up digging tools and made their way down to Wadi Abu Rish to begin carving a second common grave out of the hillside. At dusk three canvas-colored trucks with a military escort entered the village. A British officer approached a group of the settlers.

'Would you please have the women go inside,' he requested.

The men went to the backs of the trucks and stared at the sight of the naked, disfigured bodies, many of whose sexual organs had been mutilated, lying in the dark pool of their own blood. They backed off, in shock. Josef was the first to approach. He took the body closest to him and lifted it off the truck, cradling it gently in his arms, like a beloved child. He placed it upon a waiting stretcher, and another man helped him carefully wrap it in a sheet and carry it into Neveh Ovadia. He went back out to continue, but first approached the British officer. 'Could you please have your men turn off their headlights?'

The British complied, and the kibbutzniks worked silently in the dark. The British soldiers stood to one side, motionless and pale. A candle was lit by the head of each of the bodies, and members of the kibbutz would stand by them all through the long night, reading from the Book of Psalms. As the last of the bodies was carried to Neveh Ovadia, the British officer approached Josef. 'In what way may we be of help tomorrow?'

'The families have to come from Jerusalem. They will need an escort.'

The officer gave a silent nod, and they drove off.

Josef went to the shower. He peeled the blood-drenched clothes from his body and threw them into the trash bin. Then he stood for a long time under the shower, wasting precious water, and cried.

The next day a convoy from Jerusalem brought the mourners. Josef stood by the entrance to Neveh Ovadia and offered subdued condolences to the families. He was stunned to see Amos Amrani coming up the path, supporting his mother on his arm.

'Amos ...' The unspoken question quivered in Josef's voice.

'My brother, Ya'acov,' Amos replied.

'I'm sorry.' Josef's voice cracked. 'Please, come to my room ... the preparations are not yet ...'

The Burial Society was still cleansing the bodies, with Haganah men assisting in the final identification.

Josef led Amos and Rachel to his room, where they sat in silence. Josef hurried to the kitchen to bring them something to drink, and later accompanied them back to Neveh Ovadia. The shrouded bodies lay in the hall, a small wooden block with a name on it next to each one. An honor guard stood near the candles. Rachel found her son's body and knelt down beside it. She swayed as her lips moved in silent prayer. Amos stood beside her, pale and tense, and stooped to put his arms about her when she issued a long, low cry of pain.

'Ima, Ima.' He rocked her, and tears ran down his face.

Josef stood helplessly beside them and then heard the low drone of a plane overhead. He knew what this one had come to drop – stretchers. The village did not have enough for so many bodies.

Amos kept a tight grip on his mother's arm as they climbed down the rocky hill to the gravesite. Her face had grown rigid, stone-like, only her eyes revealing the pain. The bodies were laid in the grave and covered with planks of wood and stones. The British army had placed armed guards between the burial place and the foot of the cliffs, while settlers stood guard in the opposite direction. It was the first time they bore their arms openly, not bothering to hide them from the British.

The services were brief, and after one of the bereaved fathers said *Kaddish*, the mourners had to hurry to make the trip back before dark. Josef and some others would stay to cover the grave with earth, and he said goodbye to Amos and Rachel by the gravesite. Tears welled in his eyes. Amos offered his hand.

'Natan has been stationed in Jerusalem,' Josef said.

'Yes, I know.'

'If you should see him or Tonia, please tell them I am well.'

That night Josef plodded through the kitchen, dragging a huge rattling sack behind him. He sifted through the trash bins, picking out empty tin cans. He rinsed them out and tossed them into the bag. Then he made the rounds of all the guard posts, collecting empty shells and any other pieces of scrap metal that he found on the way. A few of the men were staying up nights, attempting to concoct homemade mines from scraps of metal. They had explosives, confiscated from the quarry, and detonators brought in from the city, but the rest of their materials were scavenged and their tools makeshift.

'Here you go.' He entered the bungalow where they were working and heaved the sack toward one of the young mine-builders.

'Thanks, Shulman. Want a cup of coffee? I was just taking a break to write home.'

'Don't let me interrupt you.'

'The interruption is more than welcome. Sometimes the Arabs are easier to deal with than our parents. Have a seat.'

Josef sat, glad of some conversation, an escape from his own thoughts and fears. The village was being destroyed. Ugly trenches encroached where grass and flowers had once grown. The buildings and furniture were taking a harsh beating from the enlisted men, who took little care with 'civilian' property. Just that afternoon he had stopped one of the soldiers and demanded that he show a little more consideration.

The young man spat out at him, 'I had to leave my studies to come here and guard you, and you have the nerve to complain!'

Josef turned away, wordless. Of course, the boy was on edge. They all were. And the soldiers lived under more difficult conditions than the settlers. They slept in patched tents, had no uniforms, and most of their clothing was inadequate for the cold. They stood long hours in outposts that offered no protection from the wind. Their mealtimes were irregular, as were their few hours of sleep. So Josef was not angry. But he was stung by the implication that the stakes in Kfar Etzion were personal. They were building a nation, not protecting anyone's personal possessions.

His thoughts returned to the present, to the young man preparing coffee for them.

'Your folks must be worried,' Josef said to the mine-maker.

'Yeah. I think it's harder on them than it is on us. Wait here, I'll go to my room and get the cookies my mother sent.'

Left alone, Josef sneaked a look at the letter the soldier had been writing:

I'm sure you have heard about the recent attack on Kfar Etzion. I have nothing to add to what was in the newspaper, except that they blew it up out of all proportion. And don't forget that in the end we beat the pants off them. Ignore their casualty reports. We estimate that they left at least one hundred dead behind them.

About your last letter – I don't understand what all the hysteria is about. How dare you – our parents – organize to demand that we be evacuated? While we are here fighting, you advocate our retreat? And why? Because I happen to be your son, and not someone else's? If I weren't stationed here, I am sure that you would NOT be lobbying for the total evacuation of the Etzion Bloc. You would probably have a lot to say about the need to defend every settlement, every frontier. Am I the only mother's son fighting in Eretz Israel? Is my blood more precious than that of those fighting in the Old City? Or any of the other isolated neighborhoods? Everyone has his task to do, and we are doing ours. Here.

Josef laid the unfinished letter back on the table. His gloom lifted. If this was the stuff they were made of, they could not lose.

CHAPTER TWENTY-SEVEN

Josef and three other men carried a stack of black and white ticked single-bed mattresses through the gate of Kfar Etzion. The clearing outside was already scattered with bedding, and they set the pile down and spread them out, filling in the gaps as best they could. Then they shaded their eyes and stared up at the sky, waiting for the Haganah's 'air force' – which consisted of nine single-engine aircraft – to parachute supplies.

One of them pointed up at a dot in the sky, shouting, 'Look, here it comes,' and they heard the drone of an engine.

The tiny airplane circled, and the kibbutzniks cheered as parachutes blossomed and packages sailed down. Josef clapped his hands and whistled – the first one was heading straight for the padded area near him. But it slammed into the thin mattress and seemed to explode, sending its contents flying in a wide radius.

Josef cursed as another carton crashed to the ground near his feet and he heard the loud crunch of breaking glass. '*Cus emakh*, not the medical supplies.'

The box had contained vials of medicine, but all of them were shattered, oozing thick red liquid. Tears filled his eyes as he picked up one of the infusion packs that had splattered on the ground. Friends were going to die without them.

One by one, the packages fell and split open, spilling their contents. Josef picked up a canvas sack and began gathering dented tins of food, but stopped to run after the precious newspapers that were blowing away. Others collected the remains of the ammunition.

'What a waste. We've got to have a landing strip,' Josef said to the men working near him, as they crawled about the hillside cleaning up the mess.

The kibbutz secretariat agreed with Josef and put in a strongly worded request; it didn't take long for them to receive authorization. Josef and two other men had already tramped about the area, looking for the most suitable stretch of road. They selected the one near the fork by the Lonely Tree. As soon as the authorization came, everyone in Kfar Etzion worked long days to widen it, clear it of rocks, and fill in the holes.

On a Sabbath soon after they finished, a Piper approached. Josef was at one of the guard posts when he heard it overhead. He shaded his eyes and watched, expecting parachutes; but the tiny aircraft circled, searching for a place to land. Josef leaped out of his post and ran to the runway, waving his arms, along with dozens of other kibbutzniks. Then they scrambled to get out of the way and Josef held his breath, praying as the plane descended, touched the ground, and bumped up and down, brakes squealing. When it screeched to a safe halt, he raced to see this wonder for himself, astounded by how flimsy it looked, an overgrown insect.

Restless quiet ensued in the Etzion Bloc. Weeks passed between the arrival of one convoy and another. Bad weather often prevented planes from landing. At least the cisterns were full, as rain fell steadily for days on end. Forced inactivity made the cold weather, lack of warm clothing, meager rations, long hours of guard duty, and the grayness of the days harder to bear. One morning they awoke to discover the village blanketed in white and romped about like children, pelting one another with snowballs.

But later that day, the Head of the Secretariat approached Josef. 'Our accounts are almost empty,' he said. 'There's no money coming in, and we can't afford to pay the Ratisbonne Monastery the costs of keeping the women and children in Jerusalem.'

'Have the nuns asked them to leave?'

'No, nothing like that. But our finances are becoming impossible.'

'I thought we were going to get paid, like soldiers,' Josef said.

'No, the bureaucrats didn't find a way to do that, since we're not officially enlisted.' The secretary kicked at the dirty snow. 'The Jewish Agency wants to solve the problem by evacuating all of the civilians. They're offering us the choice of joining existing kibbutzim or founding a new one somewhere on the coast, inside the Jewish State. They'll send more Haganah men here to try to hold onto the Bloc.'

'If we leave now, that's the end of the Community of Abraham,' Josef said. 'We'll wind up spread out among who knows how many other kibbutzim.'

'Probably. But what choice do we have, with no money coming in?'

'Get the paper-pushers to give us a salary. There has to be some way. If they're going to pay other men for being here, why can't they pay us? It's our home,' Josef said, but he spoke without conviction.

For the first time he held no strong opinion. He took a long walk to mull over this final cruel twist – they were to determine for themselves whether to stay or go. Soldiers weren't supposed to decide their own fate. They were supposed to receive orders and stay put until told to go elsewhere. In the end, he voted with the majority that rejected the proposal. They wanted to stay and defend their home.

More than a month went by without a convoy, and they were desperate for food, ammunition, and building materials.

'Anything new?' Josef stuck his head into the radio room.

'I'll say!' The beaming young female operator took off her headset and handed him a message. 'Are we getting a convoy!'

The message instructed them to be prepared early the next morning to unload 120 tons of supplies. These provisions would have to last for the next two months – until the termination of the British Mandate. Every available truck and bus in the Jerusalem area had been earmarked for the largest convoy ever assembled, in a last effort to re-supply the Bloc before the British left. The convoy would also bring 150 Haganah replacements and return to Jerusalem 100 university students and an airplane that had been damaged while landing. Kfar Etzion's bull and two mules would also have to go. The kibbutz no longer had feed for the animals.

'We're getting supplies tomorrow,' the Bloc commander informed the kibbutzniks gathered in the dining hall. 'I know it's the Sabbath, but you'll have to get up early and pray in your work clothes. We have to unload the supplies as fast as we can – get the trucks turned around and ready to go back. We don't want to give the Arabs too much time to put up blockades. We'll send a patrol out tonight to cut the Jerusalem–Hebron phone lines, but that won't stop the news from spreading, once they spot it.'

After prayers the next morning, Josef paced and kept looking at his watch. He finally climbed up to the roof of Neveh Ovadia to watch for the column of vehicles. It was hours late. He shouted with joy when it came into view. 'Look! Just look, there's no end to it!'

A small armored car led the convoy, followed by a blockbuster that would break through any piles of rocks they might encounter. It was trailed by eighteen trucks and buses, a command car, two smaller armored cars, and another nineteen trucks. Four additional armored cars brought up the rear. All the vehicles were iron-plated and mounted with machine guns. The column snaked up the feeder road, more than a kilometer in length. A small plane circled overhead. As the trucks reached the fork in the road, they were directed to one of several unloading areas, depending upon the kind of supplies they carried. They parked in a semi-circle, facing out, so they would be able to drive away the minute the goods had been unloaded.

'You didn't have any trouble in Bethlehem, did you?' Josef asked one of the drivers.

'Not a bit.' The driver smiled. 'The Arab guard took one look at us, raised the barrier, and ran like hell.'

Inside the kibbutz compound, men quickly unloaded the fuel, so the empty drums could be returned to the trucks. The radio operator began receiving urgent messages for them to hurry. The airplane's pilot reported that Arabs, hundreds and eventually thousands of them, were converging from the entire district and had already begun putting up roadblocks near Solomon's Pools.

220

The bull did not appreciate the urgency of the situation and refused to get into the truck. The drivers tapped their watches while Josef and two other men struggled with it. Precious minutes passed before the animal clomped up the ramp.

'Maybe you should wait, go back tomorrow,' someone suggested, and others nodded.

'Can't.' One of the drivers shook his head. 'They need the vehicles back in Jerusalem. Besides this is the biggest, best-armed convoy we've ever put together. A bunch of villagers aren't going to stop us.'

Josef watched the trucks pull out, mumbled a prayer, and set to work hauling the perishables into cold storage. The rest of the supplies would be left, under guard, to be stored away once the Sabbath was over. He worked effortlessly, seized with a new optimism.

Until the first of the cars returned.

'The whole convoy is trapped out there,' its driver jumped out and told Josef and the other men working with him. 'Almost every vehicle was hit, tires blown out.' He looked behind him at the five armored cars and five trucks moving back up the road. 'I think that's all that are coming. The rest are pinned down.'

'Are the men still in the vehicles?' Josef asked.

'Looked to me like most are. I saw some get out and run into that old building.'

'Nebi Daniel?'

'Yeah. The commander ordered the whole convoy to turn back, but we were the only ones who could get out.'

'Didn't the blockbuster make it through?' Josef asked.

'It smashed through six roadblocks, but the last one – enormous boulders – I don't know how they got them out onto the road. The driver lost control – blockbuster went straight into the ditch.'

'Are they under fire?'

'Like you've never seen. Constant. From everywhere. There are thousands of the bastards out there.'

Josef rushed to the already crowded radio room. About half the men on the convoy were trapped in their vehicles, many of them wounded. The others had taken up positions in Nebi Daniel. Negotiations for their extraction were already being held with the British and the Red Cross.

Josef trudged out to his guard post. Many of those trapped out on the road were close friends. He barked a loud, mocking laugh, remembering how invincible he had felt that morning, watching the convoy approach.

It wasn't until late the next afternoon that a British force, accompanied by Red Cross emissaries, came for the survivors and the thirteen dead. All of the vehicles were left on the road, as the Arabs' terms dictated.

The airlift from Tel Aviv was now their only contact with the rest of the country. The newspapers it brought were not encouraging.

Josef stood guard at night and tried to tend the trees in the orchards during the day. Though they were overrun with weeds, he hoped they would produce a bumper crop and help replenish the food supply. He had also taken upon himself some of the domestic chores – sweeping up the dining hall, trying to keep the synagogue clean.

The Passover holiday left him disheartened. He helped decorate the dining hall and maintained a façade of hearty optimism, but could not keep his mind off his family. Rina was in the Bloc, in Massuot Yitzchak, where she and her boyfriend Elon were stationed. Josef didn't know where Natan was, and the thought of Tonia and Leah celebrating the freedom festival in a dreary monastery left him melancholy.

One day in early May, Josef heard sharp repetitive blasts of shooting and shelling. He ran to the perimeter fence and saw the men who had been stationed in the two defense posts that overlooked the highway making a hurried retreat toward the kibbutz. A shell exploded a few dozen meters from Josef, showering him with earth. He fell flat on his face, arms over his head, feeling numb, and then ran his hands over his body and limbs. No shrapnel that he could feel. He lay paralyzed for a moment, until another shell burst into the ground behind him, sending more clumps of dirt flying toward him. Shells began to rain down all over the kibbutz compound, craters blossoming everywhere. Josef felt as if he were trapped in a fog, but became aware of men running and shouting all around him.

'Get to cover!' Someone kicked his leg.

He forced himself to his feet and fled to the shelter of the German Monastery. When the shelling stopped, he ventured out and saw that Neveh Ovadia, the dining hall, the kitchen, and several other buildings had all taken direct hits. He had no weapon, but started toward one of the guard posts.

Someone grabbed his arm. 'We're pulling back to second line positions.'

The Bloc commander stood nearby, surveying the situation. Josef overheard him say to one of the other officers, 'The bastards are taking a lot of casualties in the minefields and from our machine-gun fire, but I don't see how we can hold out.' He lowered his binoculars. 'Not without anti-tank weapons. And our defenses can't stand up to artillery.'

They watched anxiously as tanks and armored cars moved about the hillside, preparing to overrun the compound. The radio operator sent urgent messages to Tel Aviv, but they knew there was no way for reinforcements to reach them. The most they could hope for was an orderly surrender, under the auspices of the British or the Red Cross.

Then someone shouted, 'Look, I don't believe it. They're pulling back to the road.' They put down their weapons and watched this wonder. For no apparent reason, the Arab Legion was withdrawing.

As evening fell, the Arab armored vehicles drove off toward Jerusalem. The Bloc commander suspected a trap and sent cautious scouting parties to the abandoned outposts. They encountered no opposition and reoccupied them. Josef's hopes soared once again. God was with them. What had happened today could only be called a miracle.

But it was also a day of mourning. The bodies of twelve casualties were brought to Neveh Ovadia, and yet another burial party made the descent to Wadi Abu Rish.

There was relative quiet in the Bloc for the next week. The kibbutzniks worked long hours to repair the breaches in their defenses and continued manufacturing Molotov cocktails and mines. They knew the improvised mines would be useless against heavy armor, but each night sappers crept out into the dark to plant them on the hillsides.

The radio room and headquarters were moved from the damaged Neveh Ovadia to the German Monastery, where the cellar had been equipped as a shelter for the wounded. The small cisterns inside the compound were emptied of their store of precious water, so that they too might serve as shelters.

'They're discussing evacuation again,' the secretary told Josef. 'But we're not the only weak and isolated settlement. The bigwigs in Tel Aviv think that evacuating any of us would be bad for morale. So we're staying.'

CHAPTER TWENTY-EIGHT

Tonia felt miserable between the cold stone walls of the Ratisbonne Monastery, where she and Leah shared a small room with three other women. The babies in the neighboring rooms seemed to have conspired to ensure that at least one of them was always crying. The Arabs had cut off the road from Jerusalem to the coast, and there were no newspapers or mail. They had also cut the pipeline, and water was rationed – a few pints per person per day – though the monks had generously placed one of their own cisterns at the disposal of the women and children from the Etzion Bloc. Food was in short supply. Vegetables, eggs, and milk were unobtainable. The residents of Jerusalem existed on rice and tinned foods.

The Ratisbonne Monastery was not far from the Rehavia Gymnasium, and Tonia walked past her old school a few times. The door stood open, but she did not know if they were holding classes. Anyway, even if they were, she couldn't go back to school now, couldn't leave her mother alone all day. She would have to sort that out after all this was over. If she was still alive.

She went to the Rozmanns', but no one answered her knock. Holes gaped in the roofs of the buildings on either side, but the Rozmann house was intact. Only the garden had suffered the effects of the siege, the plants shriveled and brown. She went around to the back and peeked through the windows. The doors to the icebox and the kitchen cupboards stood open, and the house seemed to have been abandoned. One of the windows was unlocked, and Tonia slid it open and climbed in.

'Hello,' she called out. 'Mrs. Rozmann.'

She went to her room and knelt by the bed. The box with her white dress was still there. She pulled it out, opened it, and caressed the smooth silk. She remembered dreaming about having somewhere to wear that dress, but that seemed like a different girl in a different world. She folded it back into the box and set it by the window to take with her. She rummaged through the drawers in the kitchen until she found a scrap of paper and a pencil stub to scribble a note: *My mother and I are at the Ratisbonne Monastery, Tonia.* She left it on the kitchen table, picked up the box, and slipped back out.

One day at the end of April, Leah and Tonia were having a late afternoon nap when one of the women came to tell them they had a visitor. They got up, pulled on their coats and boots, and went out to the paved stone courtyard. It had once been lovely, with clean white paving stones and lush plants, but now looked desolate and neglected. Amos was sitting on a low stone wall and rose when he saw them approaching. His hair was long, he hadn't shaved, and the green jacket he wore was filthy.

'Hello, Amos.' Leah greeted him with a warm embrace.

'It's good to see you, Mrs. Shulman.' He stiffly returned her hug and looked down at himself. 'Sorry, you don't want to get too close.'

Tonia and Amos clasped hands, and it was the first time his touch had no magical effect upon her. She lived in a fog of fear – for her father, brother, and sister.

'How are you?' Amos asked Tonia.

'I suppose I shouldn't complain.' She relinquished his hand.

'Have you heard anything from your father?'

'We had a message last week. He's fine. Complaining about being bored.'

Amos turned to Leah. 'I saw Natan a few days ago. He said to tell you not to worry about him.'

'Thank you so much for coming to tell us that.' Leah put a hand on Amos's arm. 'I think I'll go finish my nap, leave you two young people. It was wonderful to see you, Amos, as always. Take care of yourself.'

'No, please, wait a minute, Mrs. Shulman. I wanted to talk to both of you. There's a convoy leaving for the coast in a few days. I think I could get both of you on it. You could go back to Tel Aviv.'

Fond thoughts of Uncle Shmuel's once-hated flat passed through Tonia's mind. Tel Aviv was not being bombed and shelled every day. There was food there. Water. Tonia looked at her mother, hoping she would leap at Amos's offer.

Leah, however, paled, shook her head, and refused. 'Oh no, we couldn't do that. I appreciate your concern for us, but we couldn't leave. We are with our friends here, and at least we are closer to Josef. We get messages. In Tel Aviv we wouldn't have any contact at all.'

'The Bloc has radio contact with Tel Aviv. The supply planes come from Tel Aviv,' Amos said. 'The food shortage in Jerusalem is going to get worse. So is the shelling.'

'But it wouldn't be ... Josef wouldn't approve of us leaving the others. Here, we are part of a community.'

'Ima, Abba would want you to do anything that kept you safe,' Tonia said softly.

'No. No,' Leah said. 'Thank you, Amos, but no.' She turned to go back to their room, or cell, as Tonia thought of it.

Amos turned to Tonia. 'I don't suppose you would consider going without your mother?'

'Of course not.'

Amos nodded wearily.

'You look exhausted,' Tonia said.

'So do you.'

'In my case, it's from doing nothing.'

He raised a hand, as if to brush a lock of her hair back from her face, but lowered it without touching her. 'I should go,' he said.

Aware that each time she saw Amos could be the last, Tonia grabbed his hand again. 'Be safe,' she said.

He smiled the way he had that first time she saw him. 'Haven't you figured out yet that I'm indestructible? That's what your brother says anyway.' He put his hands on her shoulders. 'I would give you a hug,' he said, 'but I know how I smell. You're the one who must take care. Stay inside the monastery. It's the safest place to be when shells start falling.'

'There's no place to go anyway.'

'I want you to have this.' He reached into his jacket pocket and took out a tiny brown paper bag, which he awkwardly thrust

227

at her. 'My grandfather used to make them – said they brought good luck. It will watch over you.'

He was gone before she had time to remove the delicate silver chain and charm from the bag.

CHAPTER TWENTY-NINE

The alarm sounded in the early morning hours, and Josef sat up abruptly in his bed. He had slept fully dressed, including boots. He grabbed his rifle, *tefillin*, and prayer shawl and ran to the makeshift shelter in the cellar of the German Monastery. It smelled of blood and sweat. Men with head and stomach wounds lay on cots moaning. There was no morphine to give them. The sounds of shooting and exploding shells were still distant, but growing closer. Josef paused near the doorway for a moment, feeling useless. He did not know how to care for the wounded men, and even if he had, there was no medicine. He overheard snatches of conversation, as other men brushed past. 'Coby and Ephraim are both dead ...' 'Dovi was trapped in the Russian Monastery, I don't think he got out, no one's seen him ...' 'We've pushed them back by Rock Hill ...' 'Some of their tanks are stuck, can't move.'

An officer half Josef's age strode in and thrust another rifle at him. 'Take this to the post to the left of the gate. Relieve the men there, so they can launch a counterattack.'

A few shells fell inside the kibbutz as Josef ran towards the post, but far enough from him that he paid no attention.

'You can go,' he said to the three boys in the small pit. They squinted and leaned toward him, so he repeated what he had said, this time shouting above the din of the battle. They nodded and hoisted themselves out. Josef handed the rifle to one of them, and they moved off in a crouch. They were so young. One of them was in shorts and sandals.

Josef lowered himself into the dugout post, feeling as useless as he had in the shelter. He watched as a parade of seven or eight armored cars crawled along the perimeter of the kibbutz, seeking a breach in its defenses. Josef raised his rifle and practiced taking aim at them. Then a figure on the other side of the fence appeared in his sights, struggling up the hill in a tattered undershirt, blood pouring from a head wound. When the man looked up, Josef recognized his friend Rafi. Josef leapt out of the dugout and ran toward the narrow opening at the side of the gate. He heard the shriek of a mortar shell and sprawled on the ground, sharp rocks cutting into his neck and arms. He lifted his head – was there nothing to hide behind, under, to use to cover his eyes? He could only remain as he was, exposed and praying. He heard the shell strike. Nothing tore into his body, and he got to his feet, brushing away bits of earth and gravel. He slipped out the gate and scrambled down the hill, moving on all fours when the loose earth gave way beneath his feet. He reached Rafi and half-carried his friend back to the post. He did not lower Rafi into the dugout, for fear he would not be able to lift him back out. Instead, he laid him at its edge and squatted at his side, sheltering behind the low wall of rocks. Josef tore off his own shirt and wrapped it around Rafi's head. He applied pressure to the wound, terrified that he might be doing more harm than good.

'You have to get to the shelter,' Josef said.

Rafi blinked, unable to speak.

Josef slung his rifle over his shoulder and clumsily picked Rafi up in his arms, staggering a few steps backwards and almost falling. He stumbled in and out of craters and blinked through the haze of smoke. When he reached the German Monastery, he laid Rafi on a bed and held a cup of water to his lips while he shouted for a doctor. Then he bent close to Rafi and said softly, 'Tell me.'

'In the Russian monastery … coming from everywhere … so many of them, everywhere you look … Yossi was blinded … I was trying to lead him. I told him to keep down. I told him. Bullets everywhere. I told him to keep down. Then he fell. I couldn't carry him. The Legion is everywhere. Tanks. Machine guns. I tried to lead him, but he just fell. He wouldn't get up. We're surrounded by them. Everywhere.'

Josef heard other men outside, screaming in pain, and ran to them. One had lost an arm, blood gushing from the stump. Another had been shot in the leg and was dragging himself over the rocky ground. Josef helped them into the shelter. Then, still bare-chested, he trudged across the compound to return to his post, eyes burning from the gunpowder that filled the air, oblivious to the shells falling around him. Back in the dugout, he fired a few shots at the armored cars, but he knew it was an empty gesture and a waste of precious ammunition. He sat there under the glaring sun for the rest of the day, without water, alone, bullets buzzing past and shells crashing down. Men ran past, shouting to one another. Josef remained at his post.

He felt detached from the battle raging around him. Wasn't it ridiculous, men not more than fifty meters apart, expelling exploding objects toward one another? Why on earth did human beings waste so much energy and ingenuity trying to kill their fellow man? He felt an urge to stand up, wave his arms, and shout, 'Stop! Stop! All of us want to live! We are all God's creatures. I don't want to take your life. What's the point of this nonsense? We can work something out.' He put his hands over his face, knowing that was a ridiculous idea, which would only get him killed. There was nothing a simple soldier could do about this mess. And why should he assume the simple Arab soldier on the other side of the fence had any interest in putting an end to the carnage? He leaned back, rifle between his knees, and watched the Legion's armored cars. One of them was trying to go over a boulder and seemed in danger of flipping over, but its tires rolled down and it straightened out.

Josef remembered one of his friends saying, 'Not everyone thinks like you, Shulman. Not everyone wants peace. There are cultures that happily send their sons off to war. Warn them not to come back alive. Send small children to kill.'

Josef sighed and closed his eyes. For the past few nights, he had been haunted by dreams of Leah's family, tumbling naked down a steep ramp, arms flailing, grasping for one another, eyes open wide in terror, falling straight into a gas van at Chelmno. Who had been driving that van? Who switched on the engine? Probably an eighteen-year-old German. Had he smoked a cigarette while he waited for Chava's screams to stop? Chatted with a companion? Complained about the headache all that wailing gave him? Josef opened his eyes and sat up straight, raising the

231

rifle to his shoulder. Yes, he would kill. Without enthusiasm, but he would kill.

Night fell and a young boy crept up behind him. 'I've come to relieve you.'

Josef knew he wouldn't sleep and staggered back to the German Monastery. Someone had lit a tiny kerosene lantern. Girls brought in trays of bread and sardines and pitchers of water, and Josef remembered that he had not eaten that day. He wolfed down a sandwich and drank a pitcher of water. Then he busied himself moving among the wounded, offering them water, holding their hands.

'Put this on.' One of the girls handed him a shirt, and he realized how cold he was.

He slapped two more pieces of bread together and chewed without tasting, before continuing to do whatever he could for the wounded.

'If reinforcements can get to us, we'll stay put,' a soldier who had come in for food quoted the Bloc commander. 'If that's impossible, we are going to have to surrender.'

'They've got all the major outposts. Cut the Bloc in two,' another soldier said. 'We're surrounded on three sides. The hills are crawling with them.'

'It will get worse tomorrow,' the highest-ranking officer in the room said. 'We have to move as many of the wounded as possible to Massuot Yitzchak. Tonight, while it's dark, before they cut off that flank too.'

'I'll go,' Josef volunteered. Rina was in Massuot Yitzchak, and he longed to see her.

An hour later Josef was laboring under the back end of a stretcher, one of a silent column of men picking their way over the rocky hills. They were passing over the slope beneath the airstrip, which had been occupied by Arabs. Josef thought he could hear them breathing on the hill above. One of the stretcher-bearers stumbled, sending a slide of small rocks crashing down the slope, and they froze. But no snipers responded to the noise, and they reached Massuot Yitzchak without incident.

It was another world, a paradise of silence. No sniping. No shelling. No screaming. Josef found Rina in the clinic, her face clean and hair combed. The expression on her face told him how awful he must look to her. Filthy, sweaty, face covered with grime. They embraced briefly after helping to get the wounded men into beds.

'I'll find someplace for you to get some sleep, Abba.'

'No, I have to get back to Kfar Etzion. I just wanted to see your face.'

'You know that's too dangerous.'

'If a whole column of us made it here, right under their noses, one man can make it back.'

Rina didn't argue with him. 'Are we going to be evacuated, Abba?'

'I think so. There's no choice. We can't hold out without reinforcements.' His voice was toneless.

'What will they do with us?' she asked.

'The Red Cross will negotiate our surrender,' he said and stroked her face. 'Don't worry. There will be an exchange of prisoners.'

Rina nodded, trying to look brave, and stood on her toes to kiss him goodbye. Then Josef made his way back over the rocky path to Kfar Etzion, silent in the dark.

The fires had spread while he was gone, and flames diffused the darkness. Everything was burning. He stomped at the smoking ground and then remembered that there was still water in the troughs. He tripped over shell craters to the cow barn, filled two pails, and began a desperate effort to extinguish the small fires spreading everywhere. But he soon slumped to the ground. It was pointless. Everything was ablaze. The stench of destruction was everywhere, and he choked on it. Bullets whizzed past him, and he could hear the guttural sounds of Arabic. They were so close. Was it yesterday that the kibbutz had been whole and peaceful?

He stumbled toward his own room. It was still intact, although the structures on either side of it were smoldering. He pushed open the door, struck a match, and groped about until he found writing paper and pen. Outside, he stooped to write by the light of the fires blazing about him, weeping as he hurried to put words to paper. By the time he had finished, he was dry-eyed. He stood and stretched, aware of his body, of the life pulsing through it. He went to a tool shed for a shovel and strode toward the front gate. Most of the shells were falling in that area, but he walked erect. He had a letter to deliver to his daughter. He counted paces from the fence and the flat boulder and dug furiously until he found the orange crate, exactly where Amrani had told him Tonia had buried it. He slipped the letter into it, re-buried it, and threw the shovel down. Then he staggered through the haze of smoke to the nearest trench, where he found five men who had been without water since the afternoon.

'I'll go to the main cistern,' Josef volunteered.

He stumbled over something in the dark – a body. He stooped down to slap the cold face, but there was no life in it. Josef gently moved the dead boy off the path, and then bent to lift the rifle strap and ammunition belt from around his neck. Yesterday we were arguing over each weapon, he thought; now there are more than enough to go around. He carried two pails of water back to the trench and waited there with the others for dawn to break.

With first light, one of the men nudged Josef and nodded at what they called Rock Hill. 'We still hold it,' he said. 'But it's all that's standing between us and the twenty armored vehicles they have on the airstrip.'

'They'll have to get past all the mines,' Josef said, clinging to a glimmer of hope. 'And there's an electric anti-tank mine buried in front of the gate. If it stops the first one, the others won't be able to get past.'

The shelling and sniping continued for hours. The defenders of Rock Hill were cut off, and Josef knew their ammunition could not last much longer. Shortly after noon, the firing from Rock Hill stopped, and Josef thought he could make out figures picking their way over the stones, in the direction of Massuot Yitzchak. With Rock Hill abandoned, the approach to the fence was unobstructed, and the tanks began grinding forward. The first one stopped in front of the gate, behind which the settlers had heaped furniture and farm implements.

One of the men removed Molotov cocktails from a sack and passed them to Josef and the others. Another soldier jumped into the trench with them, eyes on the tank.

'Why don't they set off the detonator?' Josef shouted.

'They did. Nothing happened,' the soldier replied dully.

'Fuck. *Cus ema shelahem*,' Josef cursed. 'Shell must have cut the wire.'

The tank turned its cannon on the kibbutz in what seemed like slow motion. It sat for an eternity before it fired a shell. The loud blast blew a hole in the gate, and the tank and other armored vehicles behind it started moving forward.

Josef and one of the soldiers climbed out of the dugout. The other men lit Molotov cocktails and handed them up. Josef had never thrown one before, and it felt strange in his hand, too big to hold properly. He was afraid of dropping it. He ran, pitched it forward, and returned for another. They continued heaving them and shouted with excitement when one of the advancing vehicles caught fire and retreated. A few minutes later, a second vehicle burst into flames, and they cheered.

'Look, two more tanks are pulling back,' a soldier called out.

The two tanks that had been closest to the fence did withdraw a short distance, but then launched a sudden swift advance. With one tremendous blow, they came crashing through the gate and the makeshift blockade behind it. They were inside the compound.

Josef and the others retreated to a second line of defense near the library of Neveh Ovadia, from which they continued firing at the vehicles that had entered the kibbutz. Arab foot soldiers followed the tanks and took up positions in the first structure inside the gate. Josef looked up at the hills. Thousands of Arabs were converging on them. Most were armed, though some carried nothing but large sacks in which to carry the booty away.

The shelling stopped, and there was relative quiet. Behind him, on the roof of the German Monastery, Josef saw the figure of a young woman. He recognized Aliza, the radio operator. She hoisted a white flag, and he knew it was all over. He felt no anger or despair, only a chilling numbness. He watched as Avraham, the Commander of Kfar Etzion, marched down the path toward the Arabs. A Legion soldier stepped out of the building they had occupied and trained his rifle on Avraham.

Avraham, his head bandaged, raised his hands and called out in Arabic, '*Halas!*' – It's all over.

He and the Arab exchanged a few words in Arabic, and the kibbutz defenders awaited the order to put down their arms. But the Arab raised his weapon and fired. Avraham's chest exploded, and he fell to the ground. Josef and the others shook off their shock and began firing at anything in front of them. Then they heard a loud command in Hebrew to cease firing.

Josef blindly made his way through the smoke to the center of the compound. Arabs with sacks were entering some of the buildings. The looting had already begun. He heard shots close to his right and turned to see an Arab fall to the ground. He had apparently been shot by the Arab standing over him, the result of a quarrel over Jewish property.

Josef could hear the Jewish soldiers in the southern and eastern trenches still firing. They had no idea what was happening, and Josef made his way to them.

'You can stop firing,' he shouted. 'We have surrendered.'

'What does Jerusalem say?'

'We have no radio contact. We've hoisted white flags over the water tower and the monastery. Their tanks are already inside. It's over. They've already started looting.'

'What are we supposed to do?'

'Destroy your weapons,' Josef replied.

He made his way to other outlying trenches and then back to the center of the village, where groups of dazed, grimy defenders were converging. Some of the men had already dismantled and disabled their rifles. Others clung jealously to them.

'Why have we surrendered?' a young woman cried, tears streaming down her face.

The shooting petered out. The defenders of Kfar Etzion gathered in the empty lot between the German Monastery and the school. A group of Arabs advanced upon them and ordered them to sit. Josef and the others obeyed. Then they were ordered to stand and put their hands over their heads. They obeyed again.

Arabs crowded around them. One of them raised a Tommy gun and aimed it at the defeated Jews, but another, apparently an officer, shouted something in Arabic and angrily grasped the barrel of the gun. Another Arab brandished a grenade, but was also restrained. Josef began mumbling prayers, weak-kneed, realizing that they had surrendered to a mob.

An Arab wearing a *kaffiyah* and a European suit stepped forward. He was carrying a camera and began taking pictures of the Jews. An armored vehicle pulled up by the school and trained its machine gun on them. The photographer finished and stood aside.

Then machine-gun fire shattered the silence.

Josef stood bewildered, staring at those who had fallen dead by his side. He had been hit twice in the arm but scarcely noticed the pain. In the mayhem, he slipped past a group of Arabs to the German Monastery and fled down to the cellar. Several other Jews had managed to reach the shelter, in which the wounded still lay, and found weapons there. The rattling of the machine guns above them stopped, and they heard single shots. Josef and the others exchanged glances. They knew what that was. The Arabs were finishing off the wounded. Two of the Jews in the cellar took up positions at the bottom of the stairs, prepared to stop anyone who tried to come down. Josef closed his eyes and whispered '*Sh'ma Israel*'.

One of the Arab Legion officers approached the doorway and tossed three grenades inside.

Josef Shulman died the instant the first grenade exploded. His body was later buried under heavy stones when the Legion's sappers dynamited the building.

Had he lived but one day longer, he would have heard David Ben Gurion declare the establishment of the independent State of Israel.

CHAPTER THIRTY

Exhausted after a long shift at the clinic in Massuot Yitzhak, Rina went outside for some air. She pulled the rubber band from her ponytail, raked her fingers through her hair, and gathered it back into the band. Bleary-eyed, she stood and watched a group of people piling up farm carts, tools, and boulders in front of the gate, preparing for the attack they knew was coming.

Her head throbbed from the constant thud of falling shells and crackle of sniper fire that came from the direction of Kfar Etzion. Billows of smoke rose over her former home. She walked toward higher ground, but the hills were blanketed in a thick haze, and she could see nothing.

Elon had gone out with some other boys to mine the road to the gate, and she saw him return, climbing over the makeshift barricade. She forced herself to wave and smile. As he came to join her, they heard a tremendous blast from the direction of Kfar Etzion, followed by the staccato rattle of automatic fire.

'What do you think that was?' Rina grabbed Elon's hand, hysteria rising in her throat.

'I don't know. Maybe a shell hit one of the buildings. Maybe that's us shooting at a tank,' Elon suggested and put his arm around her.

'Why did he have to go back there?' Rina cried. 'He could have stayed here. He didn't have to go back. He was right here.' She burst into tears, and Elon held her.

The gunshots became erratic, and then there was a long silence. 'They must have surrendered.' Rina raised her head. 'I hope to God they are surrendering. What's the point? It's over.'

'Don't say that. They were about to surrender before, and then the tanks just drove off.'

Rina gazed in the direction of Kfar Etzion. 'They're not going to–'

A long burst of machine-gun fire came from the direction of Kfar Etzion, followed by a series of single shots. Rina stood frozen, no longer able to think, to put together an optimistic scenario of what she had heard. Neither of them spoke. After a while, three tremendous blasts faded into a foreboding silence, and a thick black cloud rose into the sky.

'Is that smoke coming from Neveh Ovadiah or the monastery?' Rina whispered. She moved away from him and fell to her knees. She howled and beat her fists against the hard earth until her hands were bloody. Elon embraced her from behind, pinning her arms to her sides.

'Shh, shh,' he whispered and rocked her back and forth.

Eventually, she took a deep breath and sat back on her heels. 'It's all right, you can let go.' She ran her hands over her hair. 'Abba will be furious with me for sniveling like this when there are people in the clinic who need care.' She got back to her feet, wiped her hands on her trousers, and then wiped her eyes with the backs of her hands. 'I'm going back to work,' she said tonelessly.

'You should eat something.'

'I will.' Rina nodded and moved away, squaring her shoulders.

Half an hour later Elon came into the clinic and touched her elbow.

'Kfar Etzion did surrender,' he said. 'They heard it over the radio.'

She followed him back outside, and they climbed to the top of a hilltop where a group of enlisted men stood. The haze had cleared, and she could see dozens of trucks and carts rumbling out of the ruins of Kfar Etzion. Columns of smoke rose from most of the buildings.

'Did you see which way the trucks taking the prisoners went?' Rina asked one of the soldiers.

'No. We haven't seen any prisoners.'

By dusk snipers had begun shooting into Massuot Yitzhak, and Rina and the others awaited a radio message that their surrender had been negotiated in Jerusalem.

Rina had been ordered to get a few hours' sleep. She was lying on her cot when she heard the drone of a plane and explosions inside the compound. She rushed outside and saw people running in panic.

She stood blinking, and one of the soldiers running by grabbed her and dragged her down into a trench. 'Those were our bombs,' he said when it grew quiet. 'The pilot dropped them on us by mistake. And the arms they meant to parachute to us went straight to the Arabs. Not our day, I guess.'

Rina's body went icy cold, and she huddled against him. After a moment, she regained her composure and pulled away. The soldier took out a packet of cigarettes, and Rina glared at the flame of the match. 'I think the enemy already knows where we are,' the soldier said and took a deep drag.

'I'm going to find my boyfriend,' Rina said and climbed out of the trench.

Crouching, she scurried from one post to another until she found Elon.

'I can't sleep. I'm going to stay here with you,' she said, and he held up his arms to lift her down.

They waited in silence. Half an hour later, he handed her his rifle. 'Here. You watch. I'm going to the radio room to see if there is any news.'

He soon climbed back down into the post and told her there was none, but periodically went back to inquire about the progress of the negotiations. A little after midnight he returned from the radio room and put a hand on her shoulder. 'The ceasefire will go into effect at four o'clock this morning,' he said. 'The wounded and the women will be taken to Jerusalem. Turned over to our people.'

'What about you?' she asked, clinging to him.

'They are going to take the men to Hebron, as prisoners-of-war. It'll be all right,' he said and kissed her forehead. 'They have guarantees for our safety.' Rina remembered the sight of the Arabs poised on the hills around them and wondered what value those guarantees could have. Who would be capable of stopping that mob?

They sat in the trench, silent. Toward dawn, sniper fire roused them from a numb reverie. They could hear voices speaking Arabic within fifty yards of the fence and again saw the villagers gathered on the hillsides, rifles over their shoulders. There were no longer any armored vehicles in sight.

'The bloody Arab Legion must have pulled out,' Elon muttered. 'The British are evacuating Jerusalem. They're probably on their way there. We can't surrender to this rabble. Might as well commit suicide. I'd rather try to make it to Bilu or Jerusalem on foot.'

'That's crazy,' Rina whispered. 'Look at them. They're everywhere.'

'Do you see anyone who looks like an officer out there? Anyone capable of enforcing a ceasefire?'

Rina glanced back over her shoulder. 'Look,' she said and pointed at the guesthouse. Two flags had been hoisted on its roof, one of the Red Cross and one with a Red Shield of David.

An explosion drew their attention back to the hills. One of the Arabs had stepped on a mine. 'That's going to make them want revenge,' Elon said.

More Arabs were marching toward the kibbutz in columns, but stopped at a distance and did not raise their weapons. Rina and Elon remained in the post watching them for what seemed forever.

'Look, Elon!' Rina stood up to point, and Elon yanked her back down into the trench.

A Red Cross car snaked its way up the hill, but took the turn toward Ein Tsurim and Revadim. After a while, the latest news was relayed down the line of posts. Massuot Yitzchak would be the last to be evacuated. No one was to open fire, even if there were single shots from the other side. Nothing was to jeopardize the ceasefire.

A courier came up the line and informed Rina and Elon, 'In Ein Tsurim they are insisting that they will not hand over their arms to anyone but officers of the Arab Legion. If that isn't possible, they are going to continue fighting.'

A little after noon Rina heard shots fired from the direction of Ein Tsurim. Elon went to the radio room and came back to tell her, 'Those shots we heard were Arabs shooting at each other.'

'May they multiply,' Rina said.

Elon smiled and shook his head. 'The Legionnaires at Ein Tsurim had to fire on the mob to keep them from breaking into the compound. They're still waiting for the officers to finish at Revadim and go to Ein Tsurim.'

He had brought back two bottles of water and some bread and sardines. Rina drank half a bottle of water, but refused the food he thrust toward her.

'You have to eat,' Elon insisted, the tension showing in his tone of voice. 'You don't know when trucks are going to come up the road to take us away. Who knows when you'll next get anything to eat.' Rina choked down some of the dry bread. The smell of the sardines made her feel nauseated.

When they were informed that the surviving defenders of Revadim and Ein Tsurim had been carted off in trucks, Rina and Elon grew bolder and climbed up onto one of the hills. The mob was looting the two kibbutzim, uprooting all the trees, and burning every structure to the ground. The buildings collapsed one by one, sending up enormous showers of sparks.

'Why do they have to do that?' Rina asked in a small voice. 'Why destroy everything?'

At sundown, Massuot Yitzchak was still waiting its turn.

'It's the Sabbath,' Elon hoarsely reminded her. 'We're going to hold the evening prayers outside.'

Rina nodded. 'You go. I'm going back to the clinic.'

She found a new patient in the makeshift hospital – a survivor from Kfar Etzion who had managed to crawl in the dark over the rocky terrain to Massuot Yitzchak. The doctor gently took Rina aside and repeated to her what the man had told him.

'No prisoners were taken at Kfar Etzion,' he said.

'No.' She shook her head, her eyes wild. 'No. *He* escaped,' she said, pointing at the man on the bed. 'There must be others!'

'No. There's no one else.' The doctor led her to a bed and gave her a sedative.

She was still awake when she heard that units of the Arab Legion had arrived, and she stumbled outside. The Arab Legion's commanding officer had come, together with a kibbutznik from Revadim who spoke Arabic and translated what he said.

'He promises that we will be taken someplace safe. They will protect us. We've asked for permission to remove the Torah scrolls, and he has agreed.'

A group of men turned to go dig them up from where they had buried them the night before. A voice called out after them, 'It's already the Sabbath. It's forbidden to dig.'

One of the group turned back to respond, 'This is no ordinary Sabbath. We can't save ourselves and abandon the Torah here.'

Trucks and buses soon arrived, accompanied by an Arab doctor. A Jewish soldier returned from the radio room and told the settlers, 'Jerusalem says we should trust them, even without the Red Cross representative – he's already gone back to Jerusalem. We have been ordered to turn over our arms.'

Rina accompanied the Arab doctor to the clinic where he inspected the patients. Then the kibbutzniks helped load the forty or fifty wounded into two tiny buses. Afterwards Rina and the other women were ordered up into trucks. Elon helped Rina up, and she tried to hold back tears. What would they do with the men? Then the Torah scrolls were handed up to them. The men abandoned their positions, turned their weapons over, and got into the trucks. Elon turned and raised his hand to Rina, and she tried to smile.

The last to board Rina's truck was the radio operator, who told them she had made one last broadcast. It had ended: 'No one will remain here tonight. The Etzion Bloc no longer exists.'

The trucks turned onto the dirt road, both sides of which were lined with long columns of Arabs. As the prisoners passed, the Arabs raised their weapons and fired into the air. Finally, the trucks of captives reached the main road. The buses and trucks holding the wounded and women turned right, toward

Jerusalem, while the trucks carrying the men turned left toward Hebron. But when the truck Rina was in reached Bethlehem, it lurched to a stop. The women heard shouts in Arabic and English, and the truck began making a U-turn. Someone came to lift the back flap and shouted in English, 'The British have blocked the road. They are evacuating Jerusalem and refuse to let anyone through. You will have to go to Hebron.'

Rina forgot her grief for her father and worry for Elon and began to fear for herself. What would an Arab mob in Hebron do with a truckload of helpless Jewish women? The journey was slow and took close to an hour, the women tossed from side to side on the winding road. When they came to a stop in Hebron, Rina peeked out the back of the truck and saw that they were making their way through a mob to the gate of the police station.

'Look out there,' she said to the woman next to her.

Hundreds of Arabs brandished weapons and clamored for the Jews to be turned over to them. Legionnaires raised their weapons and threatened the crowd to stay back. The trucks entered the courtyard of the police station and stopped. An officer opened the back and ordered the Jewish women to get out. Rina climbed down, terrified. One of the Legionnaires approached her and said in English, 'Don't be afraid. We will protect you. It is the order of King Abdullah.'

She and the others hurried into the relative peace inside the building.

CHAPTER THIRTY-ONE

Leah waited for news of Josef and Rina. Radio contact with Kfar Etzion had been intermittent since the battle began and was often cut off for hours on end. The news that did get through was not good. Leah sat with the other women, Tonia at her side. Tonia was white, drained. She did not grasp at scraps of information the way her mother did. She knew that her father was going to die. She could feel it. Anger consumed her. Why did he have to stay there, throw his life away on a lost cause? It was suicide. A sin. Final and total abandonment. The pain in her chest grew as hysteria rose. She looked into her mother's face and forced herself to maintain control.

Early in the evening, they heard a news broadcast: 'Today at 1:00 p.m. the enemy took Kfar Etzion by storm. The defenders fought a courageous battle, fighting hand-to-hand until they were overwhelmed.'

A moment's silence was broken by the bitter sobs of the women in the room.

Leah clutched Tonia's arm. 'He's all right. I know he is. Some of the wounded were evacuated to Massuot Yitzchak during the night ... and there must have been other survivors. You know your father ... he always ...'

'Ima, Ima ...' Tonia put her arms around her and would have rocked her like a child, but Leah sat stiff and straight.

A group of women returned to the monastery sobbing. They had been up on the roof of a nearby building, where they could see the pillars of black smoke rising from the direction of Kfar Etzion.

'The rumors are true,' one of them said later. 'We have become a community of widows and orphans.'

After the surrender of the remaining Etzion Bloc settlements, the women in the monastery received a list of the wounded. Josef Shulman's name was not on it. Neither did it appear on the list of prisoners taken to Hebron.

'It's a mistake,' Leah insisted, her eyes and voice hard.

While the other women sat *shiva* for their husbands, Leah refused to join them. She waited for news of him, convinced he had escaped. He was hiding somewhere. Or there had been an error when they compiled the list of prisoners. Tonia admitted that such things could happen, but nurtured no such hopes of her own.

Rina's name *was* on the list of those taken prisoner, as was Elon's.

'The prisoners are all right,' a man from the Jewish Agency came to assure the women. 'When they took the prisoners to the police station in Hebron, it looked for a while like the mob might get hold of them, but the Legionnaires protected them. They did parade them through Rabat Amon in cages, part of a victory procession. That couldn't have been pleasant, but no one laid a finger on them. Now they are in a camp called Um el Jamal near the Iraqi border. We are already negotiating for their release.'

'Camp? What kind of a camp?' Leah clutched at his arm, terror in her eyes.

'A prison camp. I promise you, no one is mistreating them. The food may not be the best in the world, but the Red Cross visits them. You might even get letters.'

Two weeks after the destruction of Kfar Etzion, the radio announced that the Jewish Quarter of the Old City had surrendered.

Leah let out a whimper. 'Natan is still somewhere in Jerusalem,' she said to no one in particular.

The next day Amos appeared to pay them a condolence call, again looking filthy and exhausted.

'Mrs. Shulman,' he said, kissing Leah on both cheeks. 'I was so sorry to hear–' Out of the corner of his eye he saw Tonia frantically shaking her head and refrained from mentioning Josef. 'To hear about Kfar Etzion.'

Before he left, Tonia pulled him aside. 'Can you still get us on a convoy to Tel Aviv?'

'There are no convoys. The Arabs hold Latrun. Nothing gets past.'

'Oh.'

'Tonia, if there was any way I could ...'

'I know, Amos. I know. And if anyone could, it would be you. How are you?' Her eyes searched his face. Her hand rose and almost touched his cheek before she pulled it away.

Tonia could no longer bear the monastery. Every face she looked at was that of a widow or orphan. There was no privacy, little food, and nowhere to escape the despondency. The entire city wore a cloak of gloom. The British had pulled out of Jerusalem; the Schneller barracks and Allenby encampment stood empty. The debris left behind by an army floated in the wind.

The daily artillery assaults grew worse, planes droned overhead dropping incendiary bombs, and few people ventured outside. Tonia often ignored her mother's pleas and walked the streets, hoping to meet a familiar face. She daydreamed of meeting Amos, running away with him; but there was nowhere to go. The streets were empty. Only small boys skittered through the ruins, trying to hawk newspapers, mimeographed by candlelight, to the stores that remained open. A few frightened people drew their family's meager water ration from tanks mounted on horse-drawn carts.

Amos's cheeks were sunken. Since the British pulled out, he had not eaten a proper meal, nor slept for more than two or three consecutive hours. He had attached himself to an Irgun unit fighting in the Old City, but when it became obvious that they were about to surrender, he donned his *kaffiyah* and made his way out through the Arab-occupied Armenian Quarter. He walked to the Jaffa Gate and from there to his mother's flat.

'Is it bad?' Rachel asked him.

'The Arabs will hold all of the Old City by tomorrow,' he said.

She turned away and went to the kitchen. When she returned with a plate of soup for him, he was asleep.

248

He awoke in the middle of the night. An occasional shell exploded over the Jewish neighborhoods, and the sniper fire was distant. He dunked some dry bread into the cold and watery bowl of bean soup his mother had left on the table and gulped it down. Then he moved his bed away from the wall. It made a loud scraping sound, and Rachel's eyes flickered open. She watched as he shoved a pile of rags aside and removed the wooden slats that concealed the cache of weapons beneath the floor. Heavy sacks contained pistols, four Sten guns, stacks of ammunition, and a few grenades. He checked each one, slipped two pistols into the belt of his pants, and arranged the rest in two sacks. He paused to reconsider and returned one of the Stens and some ammunition to the hiding place beneath the floor. He tied the sacks containing the weapons and hoisted them over one shoulder. Satisfied that he could carry the load, he laid them on the bed and turned to his mother.

'Go back to sleep.' He kissed her forehead.

'You must eat something.'

'I did.'

She laid a leathery hand on his cheek for a long moment. 'You are a good son. A good man. Your father would be proud of you.'

He kissed her again and turned to leave.

'Wait.' She sat up and pushed her feet into the slippers by her bed. 'You have to eat.' She rose and placed a stack of pita breads in a cloth bag and slipped the long straps over his shoulder.

He delivered the weapons to an Irgun unit fighting in one of the border neighborhoods.

'Hey, Amrani,' someone called to him. 'Weren't you asking about a way to get someone to Tel Aviv?'

'Yeah. You got one?'

'You aren't going to believe this, but I hear they're building a new road.'

Amos got as many details as he could and rushed to the Ratisbonne Monastery.

'If there is a chance,' he asked Tonia, 'if there is a new road to the coast, will your mother go?'

'Yes,' Tonia replied, convinced that in her present frame of mind her mother would do as she was told. And if not, Tonia would drag her.

Tonia's stomach growled. The Jewish authorities had gone house-to-house confiscating food, in a desperate search for supplies. Everything was rationed – each of the city's hungry residents received 200 grams of bread per day and a weekly ration of dried beans, peas, and groats. Amos had brought the bag of Rachel's pita breads, and the scent of them was driving Tonia mad. She knew her mother would insist upon giving them to the children and pregnant women, just as Josef would have done.

'It may be possible,' Amos said. 'They're trying to make an alternate route into the city, one that doesn't have to pass under the guns at Latrun. They found an old goat track. So far, only jeeps have managed to get all the way over it, but they're paving it to make it passable to trucks.'

Tonia stared at his mouth, as if that might help her understand what he was telling her.

'They started leveling the road up from the coast.' He held his right hand slanted up. 'And managed to reach partway down from Jerusalem.' His left hand slanted down above it. 'But there is still a gap of almost five kilometers in between that is impassable. The engineers and bulldozers are working on it, but the city can't wait. There's no food.'

Tonia's stomach growled again, and they both grinned.

'So a few hundred people from Tel Aviv have volunteered to bring food to the city,' Amos said. 'They are going to climb up that five-kilometer stretch carrying sacks of supplies on their backs. And those volunteers are going to have to be taken back to Tel Aviv. If your mother will go, I don't see why a few hundred people can't become a few hundred and two.'

He paused for a moment and then went on.

'It won't be easy for your mother. She'll have to walk the five kilometers in the dark, downhill. But you won't be alone.'

'Are *you* coming?' Tonia asked.

'No. I meant you'll be with the other people from Tel Aviv.'

'Oh.' She tried to hide her disappointment. 'We'll go,' Tonia said. 'I'll throw her over my shoulder if I have to. Thank you, Amos. Thank you.' She touched his arm, but he shrugged off her gratitude.

'Be ready to leave tomorrow night,' he said and left.

He came to pick them up in a rusty old car that hardly looked capable of rolling over a cliff, much less transporting them to an unpaved goat path. Tonia and Leah each carried a tiny bundle of their most precious belongings. Tonia's included her English dictionary and the white dress, rolled up in a towel. The car rasped and rattled through the empty streets, to the outskirts of Jerusalem. Outside the city, Tonia nervously watched the dark countryside. Every tree the headlights picked up looked like an Arab irregular, waiting to ambush them. Amos turned off the main road, and it seemed to Tonia that he had driven into the woods. Her head nearly hit the roof of the car as they bumped along. At last he stopped.

'We'll walk the rest of the way.'

Amos took Leah's arm and led her over the rocky terrain. Tonia gaped at the sight to which he led them. A row of trucks had backed up to the crest of a *wadi*, waiting to receive the supplies being hauled up on mules, ox carts, and human backs. The volunteers from Tel Aviv were met part way by members of Jerusalem's Home Guard, who relieved them of their burdens, while they returned for the next load.

'Breakfast for your friends.' Amos nodded toward the trucks and smiled.

He went to speak with one of the men loading the trucks. 'You'll go back with the last group,' he told them when he returned. 'Meanwhile, why don't you sit here and rest.' He led them to a group of boulders, then peeled off his own sweater and went to help haul supplies.

Tonia sat and felt guilty, knowing that if Rina were here she would have pitched in to help alongside Amos. But didn't she have to stay with her mother? The members of the Home Guard were men in their forties and fifties. They huffed and puffed as they stumbled up the steep incline. Tonia saw one white-haired man struggling with a large crate and hurried down the slope to help him.

'What you're doing is wonderful,' she told him, as she took hold of one side of the crate.

'Each trip I carry enough food to keep one hundred Jews alive for another day,' he said.

Unable to abandon the task once she had joined in, she found herself in the line of porters, Amos at her side.

'Don't wear yourself out,' he warned her. 'You might have to carry your mother on your back. She doesn't look too well.'

'Oh, she'll be all right. She's a lot stronger than she looks.'

'So are you.'

Tonia stumbled on a rock, and he caught her arm. There was a fleeting instant, as she regained her balance, when she almost turned toward him, settled into his arms, and poured out her feelings for him. But she steadied herself, and they avoided each other's eyes. They walked side by side, and nothing was said.

When the path narrowed, he fell in step behind her, and she was aware of him watching her walk in the moonlight. She wore khaki pants and a work shirt. Her feet were encased in heavy high-laced boots. Her hair was pulled back and clamped with a clip. Her only ornament was the silver chain and charm that he had given her, and it was hidden under her shirt. She never ceased to wonder that he seemed to find her attractive. Weren't men supposed to like women all dressed up and smelling good, nails lacquered and face painted?

They reached the loading point, and Tonia hefted a large sack onto her shoulders.

'It's too heavy,' Amos protested. 'You'll hurt yourself.'

'I'm all right.'

She strained under the load, gritted her teeth, and forced one foot in front of the other. She could do as well as Rina. Amos walked behind her. When they reached the waiting trucks for the last time, Amos signaled for Leah to join them.

'You'll walk down with the others, to Kfar Bilu,' Amos told them. 'There are buses waiting to take the volunteers back to Tel Aviv.'

'Thank you, Amos.' Leah offered a delicate white hand. 'You are always so kind to us. It's like having another son.' Amos leaned forward to accept the kiss she planted on his cheek.

'Take care,' he said and turned to walk away.

Leah poked her daughter in the ribs, and Tonia cried out 'Amos!' and took a step forward.

He turned back. 'Yes?'

'I ... I just wanted to say goodbye. And thank you ... again.' She couldn't look into his eyes.

'All right. Goodbye.'

'Goodbye,' she whispered.

CHAPTER THIRTY-TWO

A few days after the fall of the Etzion Bloc, Natan Shulman found himself with some other Haganah enlistees in the ultra-orthodox Jewish neighborhood of Mea Shearim, near the Mandelbaum intersection. They lay down in one of the empty alleyways to sleep, heads on their packs, but in the middle of the night, shells began to rain down all around. Residents of the neighborhood ran out into the streets, barefooted and in their pajamas. The women, who were forbidden to go out in public with their own hair showing, had slapped their wigs crookedly on their heads. They pulled their bathrobes tight, looking around in a daze. Natan's comrades-in-arms tried to calm them and told them to go back inside.

About 4:30 am, the shelling ceased, and they heard the drone of Arab Legion armored cars. Within minutes Natan saw them snaking up the road toward them. His knees felt weak, and sweat poured from his body. He tried to choke back his fear. He thought of his father and of Amos, who was fighting with the Irgun somewhere in the city. He had no doubt that Amos would watch the enemy's approach with hard, cold eyes and steady hands. Natan took a few steps and felt light and queasy. A coward. He had lacked even the courage to face his mother's grief. After the news about Kfar Etzion was broadcast over the radio, he was granted leave to go see her and Tonia. He had stood outside the monastery, unable to force himself to go in, and fled back to the anonymity of his unit. For the antiquated rifle he carried Natan had only forty bullets, and he was not skilled at handling it. He watched the column of armor creep toward them, certain that he and the handful of frightened young boys at his side would be but a minor annoyance, dust in their eyes, to be brushed aside.

Tonia was the only one who had seen the truth. How had they been so foolish, thought they could win this fight? Why hadn't they listened to her?

He heard the evil scream of a shell and looked up to see its fiery trail coming straight toward him. Frozen, he managed to take only a few steps back before it exploded a dozen meters away. Its ear-shattering blast knocked him to the ground, and a shower of shrapnel cut through his uniform. He raised his head, spat dirt, wiped his eyes, and stared at the large jagged piece of metal protruding from the ground, centimeters away. He sat and pulled up his trouser legs. There were several wounds, but none of them deep. He got to his feet and stood numb and rigid, until a red-haired enlistee rushed past him shouting, 'Get under cover. Follow me!'

Natan obeyed. The boy led him into the cellar of a nearby building, where a handful of disoriented soldiers had congregated. Natan stared into space, vaguely conscious of the pain in his legs, while the others discussed the impending confrontation. He needed to urinate, but was afraid to go back outside.

'How many cars did you see out there?' someone asked.

'I counted thirteen.'

'Seventeen,' someone else corrected.

'Anybody got a spare cannon?' The red-haired boy said, but no one laughed.

'Our guys have got a machine gun upstairs in the Mandelbaum House,' a young boy said.

The Mandelbaum House was the abandoned home of a wealthy businessman that commanded the intersection that divided the Jewish and Arab occupied sections of Jerusalem. If the Legion continued up St. George Road, they would pass under its windows. Natan knew who 'our guys' were – a handful of Gadna teenagers, even younger and less experienced than he was. Apart from their one precious automatic weapon, they were armed with nothing but homemade Molotov cocktails.

The shelling ceased, and one of the boys suggested, 'We should be trying to find our way to headquarters, to be reassigned positions.'

The red-haired boy led them outside. As they wove their way through the winding cobblestone alleys of Mea Shearim, a heartening sight greeted them: the Haganah's own armored force, consisting of two stolen British armored cars and a scout car. The Star of David had been painted on their sides, and they were being paraded through the streets, in the hope that the sight would help calm the panicked residents. The group of soldiers to which Natan had attached himself fell in step behind the vehicles. A handsome young man leapt out of one of them, announced that he was the new CO, and stomped into the cellar of a nearby building, followed by the other men.

Natan waited outside. He felt unworthy - he stuttered when addressed by officers, handled his weapon clumsily, and choked with fear at the prospect of combat. Men who were their parents' only sons could request an exemption from combat duty, and the temptation to do so had been almost irresistible. He remembered the day he told Tonia that he had enlisted, blathering on about having to stand and fight. Now he managed to hang back among the stragglers. He was never singled out for special missions and never volunteered for them. He did his best to remain faceless. He did not want any of the men at his side now to know that he was the son of Josef Shulman.

He climbed up to the roof of one of the buildings and squinted, counting the Legion's vehicles, all too visible in the distance. Seventeen armored cars led a trail of trucks and half-tracks that transported the infantry. Their progress was slow, and Natan almost wished that they would hurry up, get it over with.

'Look at the bastards.' He heard a growl from the next rooftop. It was the handsome young CO. 'They've got all the time in the world. Trying to make us nervous. Well, let's hope they follow their British rulebook – move in the morning and consolidate in the afternoon. God knows we need the time.'

Natan stared at the column. He had heard that a small group of Irgun fighters had occupied the Police Training School in the field across Sheikh Jarrah Road. Those Irgunists and a pitiful makeshift barricade were all that stood between the Legion and Natan. Other men came back into the street and looked busy, but Natan had no idea what to do. No one barked any orders at him, so he remained on the rooftop, watching. The CO seemed to be everywhere at once, and Natan watched him enviously. He was so calm and commanding, his movements quick, but not nervous. He seemed to have renewed the confidence of the men about him. Even Natan felt a little better with him around.

At the first sharp curve in the Sheikh Jarrah Road the Legion vehicles encountered a roadblock of logs, stones, and barbed wire. One of the Arab officers alighted from his vehicle and appeared to be ordering his men to clear it away. Natan was staring right at him when a Legion shell fell short and killed both the officer and the soldier standing behind him. The column stood still for a while and then turned to move toward higher ground.

'What the hell are they doing?' asked a man who had come up beside Natan.

'Their plan got screwed up, so they don't know what to do,' someone else sneered in contempt.

'Improvisation isn't their strong suit. They have one golden rule – when in doubt, retreat.'

The CO shouted that he needed a runner to go back to the center of the city. 'They have a new Beza machine gun. Who's going to go get it?' Natan looked away. It wasn't a task that frightened him – it would probably be safer than staying here – but he didn't want the CO to become aware of his existence. He ducked into the stairwell and went back down to the street.

When darkness fell, Natan and the rest of his newly organized unit of thirty men huddled in the cellar that now served as headquarters. They shoved aside the old furniture and other assorted junk stored in it and sprawled on the damp floor. A few men left the cellar and came back with sandwiches and bottles of water to pass around.

'You, you, you ...' The CO jabbed his finger at one man after another. 'You're going to go out and mine the houses lining St. George Road. We'll let some vehicles pass before we set them off,' he explained. 'The wreckage of the buildings should make the road impassable, cut them in two.'

The 'volunteers' went out, and then the runner returned, accompanied by a wheezing man lugging a heavy machine gun. The soldiers greeted their arrival with cheers. By the eerie flicker of a candle, Natan looked around in dismay – this 'army' was exhausted, filthy, and tattered – and should have been in school.

The CO explained his tactics and the reasoning behind them. 'We are not strong enough to man a defense along the entire border of Mea Shearim, so we will concentrate our forces in the most likely points of attack. For the moment, we have to assume that they are going to continue hiding their infantry behind their armor. Either they know that we have no anti-tank weapons, or they are trying to avoid casualties.

'They could go north, across that open field toward the Police Training School. The Irgun has some men in there. I don't know how many. Or they could continue up Sheikh Jarrah, past the Mandelbaum House, into Mea Shearim. I believe they're going to come past Mandelbaum – that will take them right between Jewish and Arab Jerusalem, with only one flank exposed to our fire. That's what I would do, so that's my bet.'

He paused and looked around, but no one questioned him.

'So our heavy weapons are going to stay near Mandelbaum. I need volunteers to go north, to reinforce the Irgun.'

'What about the whole area in between Mandelbaum and the Police School?' someone ventured. 'You're leaving it wide open.'

'I'm holding the Beza back,' the CO responded. 'It won't go into position until they begin their advance and we know which way they're going.'

One machine gun against all those vehicles. Natan felt less afraid. The situation was so hopeless, there was no point in fretting over how to survive. None of them would.

The Legion's mortars began pounding Mea Shearim again long before dawn, and the civilians fled their beds. Natan lay on his back – body aching, the wounds in his legs throbbing, mind blank, bladder once again full – listening to the explosions and indifferent to their proximity. How long did he have to live? Was this the death his father had met, anonymous, rained down from the sky? He glanced around the cellar and wondered how hard it would be to hide in one of the buildings. No. No point in that. They would find every last Jew after the battle was over. Just like the Nazis, just like Tonia always said. Better die fighting than be hunted down like a rat.

The men about him rose and kicked one another awake. The air was heavy with the presence of more than thirty hot, un-washed men. The CO ordered them outside, but no one moved. Natan noted that many of them looked as frightened as he felt.

The CO went up to the roof. When he came back down, he sensed the collective fear. He drew his pistol and pointed the barrel at one of them. 'You have to the count of three to get out of here,' he growled. 'Or I shoot.'

They stumbled out into the dawn. The Arab armored cars were making slow progress into Sheikh Jarrah. The CO repeat-ed his orders. He told the man with the heavy machine gun to crawl with it as far as he could out into the field between them and the Police School, taking cover behind rocks. 'When you open fire, give them long bursts,' he ordered. 'Make them think you've got all the ammunition in the world.'

Natan crept, as ordered, out into the field and lay on his belly behind some rocks. Two of the Legion cars veered out of the column, turned down a dirt track, and cut into the field. They were no more than fifty meters from the Beza when it opened fire, and they halted. Moments later a bazooka rocket, fired from the positions near Mandelbaum, knocked the lead car off the Sheikh Jarrah Road. Three other cars moved up to aid it, and an Arab hoisted himself out of its turret. His legs had been destroyed by the blast. He slid down onto the road on bloody stumps and lay motionless.

The cannon on one of the Haganah's armored cars knocked out a second Arab car. Legion infantry swarmed out of the vehi-cles and rushed toward the Mandelbaum House. The Gadna teen-agers inside pitched Molotov cocktails from its upper windows, while the solitary machine gun tore into the Legionnaires. Natan watched them dying from where he lay.

Nausea overcame him, and his hands trembled. The fire of automatic weapons was all around them. He put his hands over his head and made no attempt to return fire. When he lifted his head and glanced over at the soldier lying nearest to him, he found himself staring at a large black hole in the face of a corpse. Another wave of nausea passed over him, and then he grew calm for a moment, accepting that he was going to die.

Had his father's death been neat, a single bullet wound? Would his mother ever know how he had died? He felt tears running down his face, and a sob escaped his throat. Then he regained his composure and looked back at the corpse. That is all there is, that is the worst that can happen.

The Legionnaires turned back and began to run. While his comrades whooped with unbelieving joy and relief, Natan lay motionless in the field. He had not fired his weapon. He picked it up and trained it on one of the fleeing Arabs. The man turned, and for an instant Natan could make out the lines of his face, the black mustache. He applied pressure to the trigger, but then released it. What did it matter? They were retreating. Let the poor bastard live for a few more hours, or days, or years. He kept his eyes on the man until he was out of sight. Natan knew that, if he survived, for the rest of his life, every time he saw an Arab, he would wonder if he was the one.

He remained in the field, his head throbbing in the sun, rationing the water in the only canteen he had. Most of the dead and wounded had been removed, but the stench of blood remained.

That night, after a brief afternoon nap in the cellar, he again lay in the field. He had been ordered to provide covering fire for a group of Haganah men who were crawling out onto the road, led by the CO. The Legion had left three armored cars behind, and the CO was determined to salvage them. They crept down the pavement to the closest of them and tied a rope to its front axle. One of the Haganah's own cars slipped down in the dark to pick up the rope and haul the crippled vehicle back to the intersection. They did the same with the second car. But when the CO and his comrades went back for the third vehicle, they were startled to see it moving silently off in the opposite direction. The Arab Legion's CO had had the same idea.

CHAPTER THIRTY-THREE

Sirens wailed in Jerusalem, signaling the beginning of the thirty-day ceasefire that a UN mediator had negotiated. Natan allowed himself to believe that some of them might survive after all. Only then did he begin to mourn his father's death and worry about what might be happening to Rina. He did not even know how his mother and Tonia were – they had been in Jerusalem during weeks of shelling worse than London's blitz. He also had to come to terms with the fact that all of them were now homeless. He had nowhere to go. His dirty khaki backpack contained everything he owned.

He entered the Ratisbonne Monastery. The women there offered their condolences for his father, assured him that Rina was safe in a prison camp in Jordan, and informed him that Leah and Tonia had left for Tel Aviv the day before.

'Tel Aviv?' His mouth dropped open. 'But there's no way ...'

'A friend got them onto some kind of convoy going down a new road.'

'What friend?'

'I don't recall his name. Tall dark fellow. Used to spend a lot of time in the Bloc.'

Natan fled the monastery and looked for a place to be alone. This last disappointment was too much. The meeting with his mother and sister that he had been dreading had become the most important thing in the world to him. He wanted his mother's arms around him, her soft hand on his brow, and longed for something, anything he could do to ease her pain. But what could he do? He felt useless. And angry. He knew he should be grateful to Amos for getting his mother and sister out of Jerusalem, but could not help resenting him. Amos to the rescue again. Making everyone else feel weak and inadequate.

With nowhere else to go, he made his way to Rachel Amrani's apartment. The building had suffered only minor shell damage and looked wonderfully familiar. Amos had shown him where Rachel hid a key. After his knock was not answered, he let himself in. He threw himself down on one of the mattresses on the floor and sobbed. When Rachel came home, she found him asleep there. She was seated on her cushion, embroidering, when he awoke. She had set a small dry pita bread, a few olives, and a glass of water on the table for him.

'I'm sorry for breaking in on you,' he stammered, his face turning red. 'Amos showed me where you keep the key and said ...'

'Of course.' She cut him off with a wave of her hand. She rose and brought him a basin of water to wash his face and hands.

The cool water reminded him how filthy he was. And the bread of how hungry. He stuffed large chunks of the pita into his mouth, barely chewing.

'Amos should be here soon with more food,' Rachel said.

'I have to get back to my unit,' he lied. He did not feel like having to thank Amos again. Thank you for helping my mother and sister, thank you for feeding me, thank you for being the man I'm not.

'You stay. There is no fighting now. Your unit can wait for you a few hours. You must be starving. You look bad. And you must change your clothes and wash. Amos will give you some of his clothes.'

He sat obediently. Rachel resumed her embroidery and left him to his thoughts. He lay back down and had almost dozed off again, when a young woman entered the flat.

'This is Elia,' Rachel said.

Elia nodded and held out a hand, and Natan took it shyly.

'Elia, go get him some clean clothes.'

'No, please,' he protested. 'I've already caused you enough ...'

'Sha!' Rachel dismissed him with an impatient wave.

Elia returned with some clothing and a plate of soup, which Natan gulped down.

'Fill the tub for him in there.' Rachel nodded toward the inner room.

Elia moved to obey, but Natan rose and insisted upon doing it for himself.

Elia took a large tin tub down from its hook on the wall in the other room and handed it to Natan. 'Here, set it on these blocks.'

Natan began drawing water from the cistern, while Elia lit the burner beneath the tub.

'You can use more,' Elia said, smiling at how little water he had taken. 'We have lots of water now, since they put in a new pipeline.'

'No, this is fine. Are you Rachel's daughter?'

'No.' She flushed and looked at her feet. 'I go with Meir.'

'Oh. I think he's the only one of Rachel's sons that I've never met.'

Elia brought him a clean rag to dry himself with and set the neatly folded pile of clothes on a stool. Then she left the room, pulling closed the blanket that covered the doorway. Natan undressed and sponged himself with the water, which quickly turned muddy. He finished washing and dressed, leaving his own clothing in a disreputable heap on the floor.

'Now you look like a human being,' Rachel said when he came out.

'I can't thank you enough.'

'I am sorry for the loss of your father. Amos thought very much of him.'

Natan did not respond. He knew that Rachel had lost a son in the column of reinforcements that had tried to reach the Etzion Bloc and that he should offer his own condolences, but he couldn't bear any more mention of death. He mumbled an incoherent reply, thanked the two women again, and fled.

The ceasefire held and two weeks later Natan boarded a bus to Tel Aviv. He stood outside Uncle Shmuel's building for a long while before climbing the stairs. Tonia opened the door and threw her arms around him.

'Thank God. Thank God. Ima, Natan's here!' She sniffed as she drew him in. 'Have you started smoking?'

He shrugged and set his backpack down in the hall. 'Too many hours of guard duty.'

Leah came to embrace her son. She was followed by Aunt Rivka, who gave him a peck on each cheek and hurried to the kitchen.

'I'm not hungry,' Natan said to her back, but Leah waved a hand at him.

'Leave her be. It's what makes her happy. I think she was glad to have us back. Likes having people to take care of.' Leah led him into the living room.

'How is Uncle Shmuel?'

'Grumpier. Seems he lost his job a few years ago, though they never said anything about that in their letters.'

'Why? What happened?'

'Factory had to shut down. He hasn't had the best of luck. Or as he puts it ...' Leah put a scowl on her face and lowered her voice in imitation of Shmuel's: 'If I started making shrouds, people would stop dying.'

Natan smiled, surprised to find his mother capable of humor. 'So what's he doing now?' He took shelter in small talk.

'He bought a horse. Keeps it in the stable up the street. Uses it to haul sand from the beach, sells it to the contractors putting up all the new buildings.'

Aunt Rivka came in with a tray. No one seemed to know what to say. Natan was not eager to speak of his experiences in combat and was grateful they did not ask.

'I heard they may be releasing the women prisoners from the Bloc,' Natan said.

'Yes, they say it will be soon, a week or two. We've had postcards from your sister. They are all right. Somewhere out in the middle of the desert, but safe. We had a panic when we heard that one of the guards there shot a man from Revadim. No one knows how that happened, but the Red Cross is there and promises that there have been no more cases of anyone being mistreated.'

'What do they do all day?'

'Rina's working in the kitchen. Some of the other women work, making some kind of objects out of metal. I don't know what. But they allow them to be together to study and for daily

265

exercise. She says between the exercise and the bad food, she's lost a lot of weight and has never looked better.'

'When are the men going to be released?'

'Seems that will take longer.' Leah sighed.

'I think I'm going to go downstairs for a cigarette. You feel like taking a walk, Tonia?'

'Sure.'

'Don't be too long.' Leah patted his arm. 'I'll help Aunt Rivka get you something to eat. Hungry or not, you're thin as a rail.'

Tonia followed her brother down the stairs.

'So, here we are, back on the living-room floor.' Natan lit a cigarette and took a drag. 'I didn't want to say anything about Abba ... when I went to look for you at the monastery, someone there told me that Ima didn't ... that she believes ...'

They started walking.

'I don't know what she believes,' Tonia said. 'She still says things sometimes. "I can't wait to tell Josef about that." "When your father comes home we can do so-and-so." But she's getting better. At first she sat around doing nothing all day. But you saw her now.'

'So am I supposed to pretend that I think–'

'No.' Tonia shook her head. 'I don't. I didn't sit *shiva* because I didn't want to upset her. Then she was so ... But now she knows ... I mean, I don't talk about him as if ...'

She stopped by a low garden wall, and they both hoisted themselves up on it, silent for a moment.

'You know, he didn't have to die.' Tonia spoke in a small, tight voice. 'The night before, he helped move the wounded to Massuot Yitzchak. He was there, with Rina. He could have stayed. But he went back.' She burst into tears, the first she had shed for her father.

Natan dropped his cigarette and put his arms around her, his own body racked with sobs.

People passed them on the street, keeping their eyes on the ground.

When Tonia and Natan grew quiet, Natan raised his head and wiped his eyes. He looked embarrassed as more people walked by.

'Don't worry,' Tonia said, her voice strong again. 'Crying in the street has become the national pastime. Do you know how many people have been killed? The whole city is plastered in black – one big mourning notice.'

'So what are you going to do now?' Natan asked.

'Wait for the war to be over. Try to stay alive. Look for a job. Look for a place to live. When do you have to go back?'

'Day after tomorrow. Do you think Rina will come here to live?'

Tonia shook her head. 'She wants to stay with people from the Bloc, wherever that will be. They're going to leave the monastery. There's no reason for them to wait there any more, since their home no longer exists. But they want to stay together. Have you heard anything about Amos?'

'No, but I was at his mother's last week. As far as she knew, he was all right then.'

Ten days later Leah and Tonia traveled to Jerusalem to bring Rina back home. Trucks pulled up to the Mandelbaum intersection, and the women from the Etzion Bloc climbed down. There was a long wait while the Jordanian guards turned them over to UN officials and the UN released them to the Jewish authorities. After what seemed hours, Tonia saw Rina walking toward them, wearing a plain brown dress and work shoes, her wild hair held to the crown of her head with a clip. She walked slowly, head high, an aristocrat in pauper's clothing. When had the rambunctious tomboy grown into such a lovely woman? Tonia felt overwhelmed by love for her annoying sister. The three Shulman women smiled and waved. When Rina passed through the checkpoint, they fell into one another's arms and sobbed until they were exhausted.

CHAPTER THIRTY-FOUR

October 1949, Tel Aviv

Truce negotiations at Lausanne had put a stop to the fighting, but Tonia knew it was temporary. What was it Amos had said? Peace is what happens for a while in between wars.

Tonia dragged herself up the stairs of yet another apartment building. It was a hot, muggy day, unusual for October. She stopped on the landing to catch her breath and wiped her brow with her sleeve. She was determined to find even a one-room flat for her and her mother, but during the last few months over 300,000 Jews had poured into a country with a population of 600,000. Homes vacated by Arabs who had fled were occupied, and tent villages sprang up all over the countryside.

Tonia and Leah seemed doomed to share a roof with Uncle Shmuel and Aunt Rivka forever. Even if she could find an available flat, they would not be able to afford it. Tonia earned little working at menial jobs, and Leah stayed home. She had accepted Josef's death, but spent long hours rereading his letters or running her fingertips over photographs.

Tonia sank down on the stairway, covered her face with her hands, and breathed deeply to force back tears. She was on her own, fighting a losing battle. Natan had another five months in the service, and all he talked about doing when he got out was studying at the university. He never mentioned sharing any of the responsibility for the support of their mother. Rina was consumed with helping to establish a new kibbutz, named for Ein Tsurim, but located on the coastal plain. Elon had been released from the Jordanian prison camp, and they had gone to the Rabbinate for a simple wedding ceremony.

Tonia looked up at the two remaining flights of stairs. What was the point? The flat advertised in this building must have been taken by now. She stood up, too tired to go on looking. Perhaps it was for the best. If they moved into a place of their own, Leah would be left alone for too many long hours, pouring cups of tea she forgot to drink. Better I should save my money for our tickets to America, Tonia thought with a sigh and descended the stairs to the street.

Outside she fished in her skirt pocket. She found a few coins and looked for a kiosk to buy a cold glass of soda water. She turned around and almost bumped into someone.

'Amos!' She caught her balance, and her hand went to her hair. What a mess she must look.

'Hello, Tonia.' As always, his eyes were steady on her face, as if waiting. Waiting for her to show him something that she could not.

'What are you doing in Tel Aviv?' she asked.

'Few days of rest and relaxation. Before I'm drafted.'

'Drafted? You? Haven't they heard the war is over?'

He laughed. 'So, what, you think they're disbanding the army? Don't you read the papers? The Knesset just passed a new law – two years of compulsory military service for both men and women. And my name's never been on anyone's official rosters. As far as they're concerned, I haven't served my country for a day.'

'I find it hard to imagine you in the army, learning how to march in step. Taking orders, God forbid.' She fought the impulse to touch him. 'What branch of the service are you going into?' she asked.

'The paratroops. And you?'

'Oh, well,' she mumbled, 'I have to take care of my mother.' She had obtained the exemption that religious girls could claim. She would apologize to no one, but knew that avoiding military service was not the best way to win friends in the young state. 'Parasites', they called the Yeshiva boys who declined to serve in the army.

'How's your mother?' Tonia asked.

'Fine. You know, I still owe you a cup of coffee and a movie. For now, you'll have to settle for the cup of coffee.' He took her elbow and led her up the street.

'So, what are you doing?' he asked, after they had seated themselves in a café.

'I have two fascinating jobs. I wash dishes in a workers' restaurant in the afternoon, and clean offices in the evening.'

'Why?'

'What do you mean, why? We still like to eat.'

'I mean, why are you doing those kinds of jobs? Can't the Religious Kibbutz Federation do better than that for you? Help you get some kind of office work, or teaching, or something?'

'I don't want to ask for their help,' she said and studied her cup.

'You don't want to feel like you owe them anything,' he said, a faint note of disapproval in his voice. 'Are you still living with your aunt and uncle?'

'Yes. I was looking for a flat back there where we met. But there aren't many available, and we can't afford the ones that are. Anyway, I suppose it's probably better for Ima where we are. More company. They're nice people. But you never have a moment's privacy, and Uncle Shmuel slouches around all evening, muttering, "Two thousand years the Jewish people have been waiting for a state of their own, and they have to go and get it during my lifetime".'

'Still planning to run off to America?'

'The moment I can.'

They sat in silence. Tonia watched him light a cigarette and mused how easy life could be. Let yourself fall in love with Amos Amrani. He would make all the decisions ever after, and she would be able to reach out and touch him whenever she pleased. She was nineteen years old. Girls her age married, had children. What beautiful children she and Amos would have, she thought, then flushed and looked away.

She stared out at the Mediterranean and felt him studying her profile. Let him look. Let him stop wanting her. She knew she looked older than her age. She used no cosmetics and still pulled her hair back into a ponytail. Her hands were rough and red, the nails short and stubby. He could have girls prettier than her. Why didn't he go ahead and marry one of them, let her stop thinking about him?

'How's your mother?' he asked.

'She's ... not so good. She says she knows Abba is dead, but sometimes I think she's still expecting him to turn up any minute. Thinks he's been hiding in a cave all this time, or was sent to the wrong prison by mistake ...' Tonia's voice cracked.

'She'll come around,' he said. 'I heard they're negotiating for the bodies.'

'Yes, I know.'

She smiled sadly at him, thinking the dead haunt every conversation in this country.

Amos puzzled her. He was always the same, unscathed. He had lost his father as a child, then a younger sister in the riots, and now, so recently, his brother Ya'acov. Not to mention countless friends. But there was no despair about him. Never a touch of self-pity. He seemed to meet each blow as if it were some kind of test. So like Abba, in his own way, she thought.

'Do you see much of my brother?' she asked.

'No, not much. Once in a while, when he's on leave, we do odd jobs together. Painting, making repairs. But that doesn't happen often.'

He seemed uncomfortable talking about Natan, and Tonia could guess why. Her brother had changed since the war, become irritable, petty.

Tonia looked at her watch. 'I have to be at work soon,' she said.

'I have a car around the block. I'll give you a lift.'

Tonia fell in step with him, shaking her head. It figured. The economy was at a standstill, unemployment was rampant, food was still being rationed, the government routinely confiscated vehicles – but Amos Amrani had a motor car. It proved to be another rusted-out jalopy, but the engine started when he turned the key, and soon they were parked outside the restaurant where a sink of greasy dishes awaited Tonia.

'Thank you for the ride.'

'If you're in Jerusalem ... I know someone who might need a secretary.'

'Thank you, Amos. I always seem to have so much to thank you for. And no way to return the favors. It was good to see you.

271

It's always good to see you. But I don't think that moving to Jerusalem would be a good idea for me. I have to go, I'm late.' She got out of the car and half-ran into the tiny restaurant.

Tonia finished at the restaurant and went to her second job, mopping floors. It was late when she dragged herself home. Her aunt was waiting up for her, the tea-kettle steaming.

'A friend of yours came by to visit your mother,' she said. 'Amos was his name.'

'That's nice,' Tonia said, too exhausted to display any interest.

'Look what he brought!' Rivka pointed at a large carton of foodstuffs. 'Such a nice young man.'

He must be making a fortune on the black market. She could imagine how enraged her father would have been by Jews getting rich selling food to other Jews, but Tonia passed no judgment. If anything, she envied him.

'You should have seen your Ima. The change that came over her. He even had her laughing. Flirting, if you ask me.'

Tonia nodded again. The skin on her hands had dried and cracked open in several places, and the pain was excruciating. The fact that in another twelve hours she had to return to the steaming pan of harsh, soapy water was of greater concern to her than her mother's affection for Amos.

'That's nice,' she mumbled again and took her tea to the living room where she and her mother shared the foldout bed. Leah's back was to her, her breathing even, but Tonia knew that she was only pretending to be asleep. Tonia bunched up a pillow on her side of the bed and climbed in, careful not to spill her tea.

'I know how much you like him, Ima.'

Leah did not turn over. 'You're a fool if you don't marry him.' Her voice was clear and forceful, a tone she had not used in months.

Neither of them spoke again. Tonia closed her eyes. Marry Amos. No more dishes. No more whistles from the workers who patronized the restaurant. He would take care of everything. All she would have to do was pop out mocha-colored babies. Amos would be there every night when she went to bed, every morning when she woke up.

No. She shook her head. Resourceful as Amos might be, there was no way he could protect her, himself, or their children from wars, border incidents, snipers, bombings. He would constantly be called to arms, and she would live in dread. Still … she could not imagine any other man caring for her the way Amos so obviously did. She understood why her mother thought she would be a fool to walk away from him. She turned and stared at the tattered photograph of 'her home'. It had accompanied her to the kibbutz, to the Ratisbonne Monastery, and then back to Tel Aviv.

No, she would not live the nightmare of her father's dreams. She would not bear beautiful children to see them orphaned. Or send them off to be maimed or killed. No, she would not marry Amos Amrani.

Three months later Tonia was still working at the same two low-paying jobs, unable to save a penny. One night she felt desperate enough to begin pilfering. She left the restaurant with tins of sardines in her pockets and stole some pens and pencils from one of the offices she cleaned. On her second night of criminal activity, she sank down into a chair in despair. Her thefts were so petty. Such a small price for which to lose her self-respect. Why couldn't there be something of value lying around for her to steal? The next day she returned the things she had pocketed to their places and took up her mop with a sigh.

As she worked, she tried to consider her situation logically. How did women get money? They usually either married it or inherited it. A few were famous actresses or singers. Fewer still ran their own businesses. She could run a business. She could certainly run a restaurant better than her boss, Mr. Greenblatt, did. All she needed was some scratch money.

She had a file of good, cheap recipes. All she would need was a few months' rent, a large rack of gas burners, simple furnishings, and a big icebox. Such a small sum, yet it might as well have been a million dollars. No bank would give her a loan. She knew one person who probably could and would – Amos. Several times, she made up her mind to go to Jerusalem and ask for his help. Even if he didn't have the money, she had no doubt he would find a way to get it. But she didn't want to take advantage of his feelings for her when she couldn't allow herself to respond to them. Besides, if he helped her set up a business, she would see him more often, her body melting every time he entered the room.

There must be some other way to get money. How about crime? She wouldn't have had any qualms about stealing from Mr. Greenblatt, but there was nothing worth taking in the grimy little restaurant. She shuddered each time she thought of her beady-eyed employer, who constantly managed to 'accidentally' brush up against her while she worked.

She glanced about the office, the last one she had to finish cleaning before she could go home. The husband and wife who shared it ran both a real estate agency and a matrimonial service. Tonia always smiled at the 'one-stop' nature of their business, where one could presumably acquire both a spouse and a flat.

She set down her mop and began looking through their files. Their business cards declared that they specialized in matches for 'the refined over-thirties'. There were not more than fifty men in the manila folders, few of them under forty, all Ashkenazim, most seeking a 'cultured' European woman younger than them-selves. Tonia studied some of the pictures. Ugh. There had to be easier ways than that. She rolled the drawer of the file cabinet shut, finished her cleaning, and walked home to save the bus fare.

CHAPTER THIRTY-FIVE

'We got a letter from Rina yesterday,' Leah said the next morning. She was sitting at the tiny table, spreading homemade apricot jam on a slice of bread. 'She's pregnant.'

'That's wonderful,' Tonia said and went to the kitchen for a plate and two slices of bread. She paused for a moment at the tiny window over the sink, staring sadly at the small patch of blue sea visible between the buildings. She was happy for her sister, but also felt left out. Rina and Natan were moving on with their lives. Tonia was stuck in hers, dreaming of an escape to America that seemed more and more like an impossible fantasy.

'How is she feeling?' Tonia asked as she rejoined her mother at the table.

'Fine. The morning sickness doesn't come until later.' Leah swallowed hard and turned to look straight at Tonia. She waited until her daughter was seated before continuing.

'She asked me if I would like to come and live with them on the kibbutz,' Leah said. 'They have a special arrangement for members' parents.'

'Do you want to?' Tonia asked, surprised by the thud she felt in her stomach, almost as if she had been kicked. Here it was – the freedom she thought she wanted from this responsibility; but it felt more like the threat of abandonment.

'I don't know.' Leah folded her hands in her lap, a good little girl, waiting for Tonia's reaction.

'Well, if you don't know, I don't know who does.' Tonia refused to make the decision. She heard the edge of anger in her own voice and, knowing it was unfair, forced a softer tone. 'I mean, you have to do whatever will make you happy. You might like the idea of living in a community, near your grandchildren, but Tel Aviv offers more ... opportunities. Jobs, I mean. And new people.' Until she said this, Tonia had never imagined her mother with another man. But the moment the words slipped out of her mouth, she looked at Leah with new eyes. She was a pretty woman. Slim, with beautiful eyes and long wavy hair. Beginning to gray, but that was why they made that stuff in bottles. How old was her mother? Forty-three. The answer shocked Tonia. She couldn't envision her mother loving anyone but her father, but didn't want her to spend another thirty, forty, or fifty years alone.

'You have to think about it, Ima.' Tonia pulled one of Leah's hands from her lap and held it in both of hers. 'You're a young woman. Half your life is still ahead of you, and you have to make one of your own. If you think you can do that at Ein Tsurim, fine. But don't go there and live on the edge of Rina's. I'm sure babysitting for grandchildren is a great pleasure and comfort, but it is not a life.'

Leah stared at her daughter and then shook her head. 'You never stop amazing me,' she said with a smile. 'I've also been offered a job, helping arrange schooling and activities for the children from Kfar Etzion. It's part-time, but I think I'm going to take it. And I'll look for something else, too. Once I've started working, maybe we can look for a flat of our own.'

That Friday night, Natan came for one of his infrequent visits. After dinner, while Leah was in the kitchen helping Rivka with the dishes, Tonia seated herself next to where he sat slouched behind a newspaper.

'You get out of the army in another two weeks, don't you?' Tonia asked him.

'Mmm.'

'And then you'll be going to the university?'

'Mmm.'

'What are you going to live on?'

'Untalented and useless as I may be, I think I can get some kind of job.' He rustled his newspaper. His tone was worse than impatient – he sounded as if he could barely tolerate having to talk to his sister.

'I just asked,' she said and snatched up her book.

But she soon glanced back at her big brother, unable to remain angry with him. He looked so unhappy.

'Natan.' She put a hand on his arm. 'What is it? What happened to you? Can't you tell me?'

He looked into her face for a moment, but quickly averted his gaze. 'Nothing happened to me. Why are you asking that?'

'You're different,' she said. 'Ever since the war.'

'Everything is different since the war.' He sighed. 'Haven't you noticed?'

Leah came into the living room, and Natan hid behind the newspaper again.

'Ima,' Tonia said, 'why don't we take one of our Sabbath walks on the beach? Like when we were little.'

'That would be nice. Will you come too, Natan?'

Unable to reply harshly to his mother's gentle plea, Natan folded the newspaper. 'All right.' He managed to force a smile, different from the boyish grin Tonia had always loved, but a peace offering nonetheless.

Down on the beach, Tonia and Natan each linked an arm in one of their mother's, but sadness crept over Tonia. How the family had changed. Abba gone, Ima sad and lonesome, Natan tense and sour. Rina seemed to have come through intact, but she was gone, part of another family unit. And when Natan married? There would be only Tonia and her mother. Tonia regretted having suggested the walk. Her legs ached. You can't go back, she admonished herself. You can never go back.

One late afternoon a few weeks later, Tonia stood over the rack of burners in the restaurant, stirring a steamy pot of bean soup for the next day's lunch. Mr. Greenblatt had promoted her to chief cook, with a raise in salary. She would now be able to save a little money each month; but even with her mother working, it would take years to put away enough to take herself and her mother to America and set up a business. She put a spoon into the pot, tasted, and nodded with approval. Then she looked at her watch. A friend of hers was getting married that evening, and Tonia had to go home and change before walking to the central station in time to catch the bus to Jerusalem.

The restaurant only served lunch, to factory workers in the area, and the rest of the staff had gone home for the day. Mr. Greenblatt emerged from the back room and asked if she wouldn't like to join him for a nice cup of tea before she left. Crumbs from the schnitzel he had eaten for lunch still clung to his beard. His black suit was covered with grease stains, and its vest strained over the expanse of his belly. A sickening sweet smell emanated from him.

'No, thank you. It's kind of you to offer, but I promised my mother I would be home soon.' She put the spoon down, placed the lid over the pot, and turned off the burner. 'Moishie promised to come back later, after the soup has had time to cool, and put it in the icebox,' she said.

She washed her hands and reached to pick her sweater off a hook on the wall. When she turned to go, she found that Mr. Greenblatt had taken a step to the side, placing himself between her and the door. His eyes were bright, and he ran his tongue over his lips. She stood and glared at him. She knew that he was afraid of her, but he seemed to be gathering his courage.

'I know how to be a very generous man,' he said, eyes darting from her to the walls.

She raised her right hand, palm toward him, like a traffic policeman. She felt like picking up the cast-iron frying pan and beating him over the head with it, but she needed to be out of jail and employed. She decided to pretend not to understand.

'I'm sure your wife is a lucky woman,' she said and looked at her watch. 'It's late. My mother will have the neighbors out looking for me.'

Counting on his fear of her, she took two rapid steps toward him, eyes narrowed, willing him to retreat. He did.

'Good night,' she said and pushed past him.

She slammed the door shut and leaned against the wall, tears rising, alone in a narrow alleyway lined with garbage cans. She had never felt so lonely. Helpless. If her father were still alive, no man would dare behave like that with her. Tomorrow she would have to come back here, face those leering eyes again. She couldn't. She would quit, find something else. No. Why should she? Give up her raise? Let him dread facing her. She wouldn't have to say anything; all she had to do was look at him as if he were a cockroach.

She straightened up and turned to stick her tongue out at the door. She walked home briskly and stomped up the three flights of stairs. Leah was alone in the flat, sitting in the living room, its shades drawn, lost in the graying darkness.

'Are you sure you don't want to come to the wedding with me, Ima?' Tonia asked, bending to kiss her mother's cheek.

'Yes, I'm sure.'

'Is something wrong?'

'We had a visitor today – Henia,' Leah said.

'Henia Friedman?'

Henia Friedman was another widow from Kfar Etzion. She lived in Givat Aliyah, along with most of the other widows and orphans, who had chosen to remain together as a community.

'Yes.' Leah stared into space, and Tonia waited for her to continue.

'The Jordanians have agreed ... Rabbi Goren and one of his assistants made the first trip today ... to Kfar Etzion ... to try and recover the bodies. It might take days and days to find them all. They'll have to dig out tons of rubble. All of the buildings and outposts.'

'Oh, Ima.' Tonia put her arms about her.

'Henia spoke to them after they came back. The Arabs destroyed everything, Tonia. Everything. Razed Neveh Ovadia to the ground, didn't leave one stone standing. All of the bungalows ... They didn't even spare the trees. All of them. Those thousands and thousands of little trees, ripped out of the ground. Why would they do a thing like that?' She looked at Tonia.

'I don't know, Ima.'

They sat together while the room grew darker.

'You go to your wedding.' Leah patted Tonia's arm.

'No, Ima, I don't want to leave you alone. Not tonight. They'll understand.'

'I'll be all right. I think I would prefer to be by myself. And Lord knows you get out little enough. I'm all right. I know. I've always known. I liked to pretend … my little daydream. But I know he's gone. And that he would have wanted us to go on living. So you go and have a good time.'

Tonia hesitated. She was reluctant to leave her mother, and she didn't know if Jewish law allowed her to attend a wedding. Perhaps under these circumstances there should be an additional period of mourning. In the end, she decided to go. The thought of spending the evening in the dark apartment was oppressive.

She opened one of the cartons in the living room to get her clothes and saw Mrs. Rozmann's white dress peeking out. She fingered the silk and was tempted to wear it, but no. It had waited this long – it could wait for a truly special occasion. She took out her black skirt and white blouse and went to shower. When she finished dressing, she kissed her mother and ran to the bus stop. The bus had begun to pull away, but the driver saw her waving and stopped to wait for her. There were still frequent attacks on the roads, but they reached the Jerusalem bus station without incident.

She walked the six blocks to the 'wedding hall' – a vacant lot hung with strings of colored lights and surrounded by tables. She arrived out of breath, just in time for the ceremony, and nodded shyly at a number of acquaintances. The tables held plates of homemade cakes, bowls of fruit, pitchers of orange juice, and bottles of wine and beer – a lavish banquet for the times. At the last wedding Tonia had attended, each guest received one glass of lemonade, one thin slice of sponge cake, and a napkin wrapped around four pieces of candy and tied with a ribbon. She stood there alone and almost regretted having come, reminded how poorly developed her social skills were.

Then one of Rina's friends came over and said, 'Why don't you join us at our table.' The boys at the table bragged and joked, and Tonia and the other girls laughed. Now I remember why I don't have a social life, Tonia thought. This isn't as much fun as it looks.

Two young men passed by, running a long extension cord out of the window of a nearby building, and a girl set a record player on one of the tables. A stack of records materialized, and couples began dancing 'slow' to the scratchy music.

That was when Tonia noticed Amos. He was wearing tight dark pants and a white, short-sleeved T-shirt. She watched as he moved among the crowd and greeted friends, seeming to know everyone. His step was jaunty, sure of himself. She felt slightly sick to her stomach, watching him plant kisses on the cheeks of two giggling girls. Then three Yemenite boys descended upon him and dragged him off to the side of the lot, out of Tonia's sight.

A few minutes later he reappeared, barefoot, wearing a long brown and white striped *galibiyah*, and with some kind of white cloth headdress wrapped around his head. Two other young men were dressed the same way. The crowd clapped and whistled and someone shut off the record player. Three more Yemenites turned empty tins upside down and tapped their hands on these improvised drums. Amos and the other two in *galibiyahs* began the alternately swaying and hopping movements of a Yemenite dance.

When they finished, to loud applause and more whistles, Amos pulled the *galibiyah* over his head and bent to retrieve his skullcap, which had fallen to the ground. He accepted the glass of *arak* a blonde girl held out to him, downed it in one draught, and wiped his mouth with the back of his hand.

The record player went back on, and Bing Crosby crooned. Tonia accepted a cup of wine from one of the boys at the table, but no longer felt any gaiety. Her head ached, and she wished she hadn't come. She turned her back to the dancers and sipped her wine. Then she felt someone standing behind her.

'Dance with me.' Amos's breath caressed her ear.

'I don't know how,' she said and felt herself flush as she turned to look up at him.

'Good. Neither do I.' He broke into his easy grin and held out his hand.

They faced one another awkwardly. He held her right hand high and hesitantly put his other hand on her waist. For a few moments she felt almost faint with the familiar desire to move close to him; then she found herself with her head on his shoulder, sobbing.

He led her away from the wedding party, to a bench hidden in dark shadows. He sat next to her, one arm around her, holding her close to his side. The warmth of his body was the first comfort she had felt in so long. She stopped crying and wiped her tears away with the back of her hand.

'What is it?' he asked.

'I don't know. Everything, I guess ... Right before I left to come here, my mother told me that they've started looking for the bodies in Kfar Etzion,' she said.

Her forehead was resting against his shoulder, and he stroked her hair. The luxury of allowing him to do so was almost painful.

'Yes. I heard. It may take a long time,' he said and ran his hand up and down her arm.

She turned her face up to him and let her mouth meet his. He ran his tongue between her lips, and she shivered. He kissed her, making her feel all the things he had never said.

It took every ounce of her resolve to pull away. 'Oh, I'm sorry. I am so sorry. That wasn't fair of me. You know how much I care for you. I don't want to ... You're the only one it will be hard to leave, except for my family. And I think it will be harder to leave you than them.'

'So don't,' he said, grasping her arms.

'I can't stay here. I can't. I can't stand it. I'm not like the rest of you. I can't.'

As if to punctuate her words, the staccato sound of automatic gunfire rattled in the distance. Jerusalem was divided, and Legionnaires on the battlements of the Old City walls occasionally fired random shots into the new city.

'I'm sorry, Amos, but I have to go home now.'

He let go of her and stretched his arm out in an 'after you' gesture. 'So go.'

She looked into his face, feeling miserable. The softness had gone from his eyes. I always told you, she wanted to cry.

'Amos–'

'Just go.'

She ran to the bus station and waited – alone and desolate, but no longer crying – for the bus back to Tel Aviv.

CHAPTER THIRTY-SIX

November 1950

Josef Shulman was buried in a common grave, together with his comrades, at the Mount Herzl military cemetery in Jerusalem. Over 50,000 people attended the funeral. While Tonia appreciated all the strangers who wanted to pay their last respects, their presence made it seem as if they were burying a national symbol, not her flesh-and-blood father. Tonia stood dry-eyed at the gravesite. On her way out of the cemetery, she saw Amos among the crowd. They exchanged nods.

One evening, a few weeks after the funeral, Tonia left home clutching a ring of keys. She no longer worked as a cleaner, but had kept a copy of the key to the office of the matrimonial service. She was dressed warmly, for the night was cold. She found an inconspicuous place on a bench from which she could watch the windows of the office building. She watched the new cleaner go in and waited for an hour while lights went on and off. When the cleaner left, Tonia rose and crossed the street. She was shallow-breathed and nervous as she climbed the stairs. Once she had fitted the key in the lock, let herself in, pulled the blind, and lit a small lamp, she grew calm and efficient.

She pulled a pad and pencil out of her purse and scanned each of the files in the drawer marked 'Matrimonial, Men'. It took almost three hours to browse through all of them. She selected four of the files, placed them on the desk, and leafed through each, writing down addresses and descriptions. Then she let herself out and walked the beachfront, wondering if she could go through with it.

She spent the next morning lurking, hoping to catch a glimpse of the men whose grainy photographs she had seen in the files. She did catch sight of two of them and disqualified both. Even desperate people have their limits. The first had either lied or gained seventy-five pounds since filling in the forms. The second came out of his apartment building and shuffled up the street for his morning paper, still in his purple and white striped pajamas and tattered bedroom slippers. He looked to Tonia as if he drooled a great deal in his sleep.

After her afternoon shift at Greenblatt's restaurant, she went to one of the two remaining addresses. Next to the front entrance of that building she found a mourning notice – that candidate had died. Tonia scratched the third name off her list.

That left one last possibility – Emil Balfour Greenberg. He was thirty-three, born in 1917, the year Lord Balfour wrote his famous letter to Haim Weizmann promising British support for the establishment of a Jewish National Home in Palestine. Tonia had hesitated before adding his name to the list. He was young enough to want children, though he had made no mention of raising a family in the section of his file titled 'What I seek in a wife'.

She surveyed his apartment building with approval. Stone front, two-story, a spacious and well-kept garden outside. Each apartment had its own terrace the size of Uncle Shmuel's living room. She lurked in the doorway of a building across the street and before long she saw him coming, looking roughly like the blurry photograph in his file. She scrutinized him with narrowed eyes. There was nothing repulsive about the man. He was tall and thin, with prematurely gray and thinning hair and thick spectacles. He was presentable, in a white shirt, tweed jacket, and dark slacks, and carried a large leather case. He was not an attractive man – his pink features were soft and bland – but he was not covered with warts or missing his front teeth. He walked up the street, his gait that of a much older man, and disappeared into his building.

Tonia walked to a nearby coffee shop where she sat and studied her notes on Emil Balfour Greenberg. He had lived with his mother, until her death six months ago. Now he lived alone and was looking for a wife. He owned the flat in which he lived, as well as three vacant lots and a motor car. He worked for a scholastic journal, *Relics*. He edited the sections pertaining to his field of expertise – comparative translations of Assyrian and Greek manuscripts. He was of Polish origin, but had been born in Palestine. He was exempt from military service due to his poor eyesight and a heart condition. He lived modestly. He had inherited enough money to live comfortably for the rest of his life without working.

In response to the question regarding what qualities he sought in a wife, he had written 'European, orderly, intelligent, good cook, cultured, of good family, modest, and not aggressive'. Under hobbies and personal interests, he had listed listening to classical music and collecting coins and stamps. He regularly attended the Philharmonic and the theater and read Russian novels. He abhorred popular music, folk dancing, and spicy food.

Tonia dipped into her meager savings and invested in a ticket to the next concert at the Philharmonic. She reread every Russian novel they had in the apartment and haunted Aunt Rivka in the kitchen, watching her prepare the heavy Polish dishes that Tonia herself disliked.

On the evening of the concert, she armed herself with a volume of Chekhov's plays, washed and ironed her black skirt and white blouse, pulled her thick dark hair back in a manner that she hoped was 'cultured', and set off. She spotted him in the audience and was relieved that he appeared to be alone – at least, he did not speak to the people seated on either side of him. When it was time for the intermission, Emil went out to the lobby to smoke his pipe, and Tonia followed him. She managed to bump into him and drop her book.

'Oh, excuse me,' she apologized. They both bent down, but she allowed him to reach it first.

'Not at all.' He handed it back to her, tapping the title with an approving smile.

'Oh my, you're Emil Greenberg, aren't you?' Tonia asked.

'Yes, I am.' His forefinger pushed his eyeglasses tighter against his face. 'Have we met?'

'Oh no. I've never had that pleasure until now. But just yesterday a friend of mine pointed out one of your articles to me. It had a picture of you, up in the corner by the title. That's how I recognized you. I don't know Greek or Assyrian myself,' she said, lowering her eyes, 'but my friend said that you're absolutely brilliant in your field. She said that this country needs more scholars like you, who know how to do serious research.'

'Thank you … I mean thank your friend,' he stuttered.

'Oh, the intermission seems to be over,' she said when the lights flickered. 'We'd better get back to our seats. It's been a true pleasure making your acquaintance.' She turned and went back into the concert hall, leaving him standing and gaping after her. She caught a glimpse of him a moment later, pleased to see that his face had broken into a broad smile.

During the second intermission, she sat in a corner of the lobby, far enough away from the crowd to be noticed, and kept her eyes glued to *The Cherry Orchard.* She sensed him approaching and then standing in front of her. He shifted from foot to foot and cleared his throat.

'Excuse me.' He looked as if he might faint with fright when she raised her eyes. 'Might I be so bold as to offer you a cup of tea?' He proffered a thermos and a thick paper cup.

'That would be a delight.' She smiled and closed the book.

He pulled a chair up next to hers and poured tea for her into the paper cup and for himself into the lid of the thermos. The tea was lukewarm and spiced with cloves, and Tonia wished she could spit it out.

'An old family recipe,' he confided when Tonia told him how delicious it was. 'My poor dearly departed mother used to make tea like this.'

'You must tell me exactly how to prepare it. I'm always looking for new recipes. I love to cook.'

After the concert, he insisted upon escorting her to her bus stop. She had counted on being driven home and wondered where his car was. Tonia had to buy tickets for two more concerts before Emil mustered the courage to invite her out for dinner. A week after their second dinner date she invited him for a home-cooked meal at Uncle Shmuel's.

He had undergone a metamorphosis since their first meeting. Tonia's constant flattery had banished his timidity. He had become the worldly scholar, eager to expound. He answered every question with a long lecture. At first, he had seemed dumbfounded to have a pretty young girl take an interest in him; now he seemed to regard it as only natural.

The day Emil was coming to dinner Natan turned up for one of his unexpected visits. He arrived in the late afternoon, said his hellos, and was soon snoring on the couch.

Tonia finished cooking and went to shower and dress. She would have to wear the same threadbare black skirt, but doubted Emil would notice if she opened the door wearing a hospital gown.

'Natan, wake up.' Tonia jostled her brother.

She looked down at him, lips pursed. It was going to be hard enough presenting Emil to her mother and aunt and uncle. She hadn't counted on Natan. Still, there might be some hope. Natan was so bent on having his own career at the university, he might appreciate Emil as a fellow intellect. Or at least as a useful contact.

'Why?' Natan mumbled.

'You have to get dressed. We're having company for dinner.'

'So what?'

'Please.'

Natan swung his feet to the floor. 'Who's coming?' He rubbed his eyes.

'No one you know.'

He regarded her with new interest, as she paused to study her face in the mirror.

'You mean a gentleman caller?' he teased.

'Yes, Natan.' She turned and stared him down. 'You won't like him. I know that. But please try to be nice.'

'I'm always nice.'

'Good evening.' Tonia opened the door to Emil and stepped aside.

'Good evening,' he replied.

She took his coat and led him into the living room to introduce him to her family.

He shook hands all around, nodding amiably. Leah did not manage to hide the shock on her face. 'Won't you please have a seat, Mr. Greenberg?' She recovered her manners.

'Thank you. And, please, call me Emil,' he said.

The one comfortable chair in the room creaked as he lowered himself into it, accentuating the silence in the room. Tonia's family seated themselves on the hard wooden chairs Tonia had arranged opposite the chair and couch. The room was so small that their knees nearly touched.

'Dinner will be ready in a minute,' Tonia said.

'I, uh, understand that you are quite a scholar,' Leah said, leaning away from Emil and the overpowering scent of pipe tobacco he exuded.

'Oh, well, when one's chosen specialty is as narrow as mine, it isn't all that surprising to be recognized as the best in your field.'

'What exactly is your specialty?'

He launched into a long discourse on the significance of some obscure texts, of which Leah understood not a word.

Tonia went into the kitchen. She soon returned to announce that dinner was ready and asked Natan to arrange the table and chairs. When the table was opened up, it took up most of the floor space. Chairs had to be shoved back and forth in order for everyone to reach their place. With their backs to Emil as they seated themselves, both Leah and Natan cast bewildered glances at Tonia.

During the meal, they were all content to let Emil talk about his work. They asked enough questions to keep him going, while they nodded their heads and enjoyed their food. The strain of maintaining geniality seemed to exhaust everyone except Emil, who smiled and expounded upon the discrepancies in various Assyrian New Testament texts.

'Do you mind if I smoke?' he asked Leah after the meal, taking his pipe from his pocket.

'Oh, well ... no ... I suppose we could open a window.'

'That's not necessary,' he said, filling the tiny, stuffy room with billows of smoke. 'My dearly departed mother always used to say that there was nothing like the smell of good pipe tobacco after a meal.'

'Would you like to go for a walk, Emil?' Tonia suggested in desperation.

'We wouldn't want to be unsociable,' he said with a tone of slight disapproval.

'Nonsense. We wouldn't dream of keeping you young people from a little healthy exercise.' Leah rushed to retrieve his coat.

Emil maneuvered his way around the room, knocking chairs about so that he could shake hands with each member of the family. He turned to Leah last, took her hand, and to Tonia's horror, bent to kiss it.

'It's been a most charming evening. I am a prisoner of gratitude for having had the privilege of visiting your home.'

Cheeks burning, Tonia led him down the stairs.

'Lovely family,' Emil mused, relighting his pipe.

'I'm so glad you've finally had the chance to get to know one another.' She forced brightness into her voice.

Emil disliked the beach – all that sand – so they walked in the opposite direction. Emil began relating the details of an argument he had had with one of the other editors. Tonia knew she needn't listen. A blank smile would suffice.

'Tonia.' He stopped on a quiet street. 'I know this will seem sudden to you, but I don't see any point in dragging things out. We are so obviously well suited to one another. I want you to marry me.'

Her mind went blank. This, of course, had been the object of her machinations, but she hadn't believed it would work. It had been far too easy and was happening much too soon.

'Yes, it is sudden. We hardly know one another.'

'Tonia, dear, I assure you, I know you better than you know yourself.'

She lowered her eyes to hide the anger and contempt she felt. She was ashamed of the way she intended to take advantage of Emil, but his arrogance helped ease her conscience. She would be using him, but what could his expectations of marriage be considered, if not exploitative? The survivors of this world do what is necessary, she reminded herself, not what is pleasant.

'Emil, you are so much older and wiser and know what's best. Still, shouldn't we wait until we know one another better? There are so many ... for instance, you realize that I am from an orthodox home. Our home would have to be kosher, and we would have to observe the Sabbath and holidays.'

'Of course, of course. My dear mother's kitchen was always kosher. And many of those folk customs are quite quaint.'

Tonia's heart sank. She plunged on, repeating the words she had rehearsed so many times as she lay in bed at night.

'There's another thing. There are men who want their wives to stay at home. But I ... I want to go on working. I plan to open my own business.'

'Business? What kind of business?'

'Oh, something small, to keep me occupied and out of your hair. I mean, you are busy with your research, and it's so important. I wouldn't want to become one of those bored housewives, with nothing to do all day but gossip about their husbands. Of course, I would never let my own occupation interfere with my obligations as your wife.' She pronounced the last two words as if they were a sacred trust.

'I suppose even a woman requires something more challenging than a pot of chicken soup has to offer,' he said slowly. He frowned at first, but then perked up. 'But that is something we can discuss in due course. As long as you realize that when a man takes a wife, he does so first and foremost so that she can tend to his needs.'

'Of course, Emil, of course. But I'm sure you realize that most wives invest the better part of their efforts in tending to their husbands' egos. Few men are above that sort of fawning, the way you are.'

'Well, as I said, it is something that we could discuss.'

'Oh please, Emil, it means so much to me. And with your help and guidance, I'm sure I could make a success of it. I don't see how I could be happy otherwise.' The last was said with a hard edge to her voice.

He lit his pipe and puffed on it, looking disconcerted by her tone – one she had never used with him before. His confidence seemed to desert him, and she imagined his suit crumpling in an empty heap on the sidewalk.

'Well, all right, I suppose it's not unreasonable for you to want to pursue other avenues of endeavor. As long as they don't interfere with your responsibilities at home. So let's go tell your family.'

'I think it would be better if I spoke to my mother alone.'

'As you wish.'

'There is one other thing. You've never mentioned children.'

'Children?' His jaw dropped open. 'Do you want to have children?' he asked.

'Well, no. But I thought that you might.'

'Oh, no, no, no, my dear. Children are a necessary evil for the survival of the species, but not necessary for all of us. I am content to leave the procreation of humankind to those who are suited to little else. I myself have never hoped for more than my work as a means of self-perpetuation.'

They shared a silent sigh of relief.

'So everything's settled?' Emil asked.

'I suppose so.'

He took a step toward her, his pink face looming close to hers, and she realized in dismay that he intended to kiss her. She stood rigid and closed her eyes as his thick spongy lips pressed against hers. His breath was heavy with tobacco and made her feel sick to her stomach. His eyeglasses cut into the bridge of her nose, but she almost welcomed the distraction of the pain. She counted – one thousand one, one thousand two, one thousand three. When she reached one thousand five he broke away from her. She longed to flee, but stood her ground. She knew that this was the least of what she must prepare for. The physical

292

obligations of marriage became real. His touch, the feel of his skin against hers was distasteful. But she reminded herself that the alternative was a lifetime in Israel, waiting for the next war to break out, waiting to dig more graves.

They said their goodnights at the entrance to the building. Tonia ascended half a flight and waited until she heard his footsteps fade away. Then she retraced her steps back downstairs and walked on the beach by herself. I owe myself one last chance to change my mind, she thought, as she pondered the anatomical technicalities of marriage. She had never quite been able to imagine herself doing 'that', even with Amos. Leah had never spoken to her about sex, beyond a short lecture on menstrual periods when she was twelve. No man but Amos, and now Emil, had ever touched her.

She bent to untie the laces of her shoes and kicked them off. She sank down onto the beach, digging her stockinged feet into the sand, knees bent and skirt gathered between them. She scooped up handfuls of sand and pitched them into the dark. I won't be the first woman in the history of the world to lie back and 'do her duty', she reminded herself. I can endure that, the same way I can endure his conversation and the sight of the gray hairs growing out of his ears and nose. I'll just think about something else. Two years. That is how long it should take. No more than two years. I'll only be twenty-two, young enough to start a new life.

Tonia put her shoes back on and rose. She squared her shoulders and headed back home. There was a single moment when her eyes stung with tears and 'Oh, Amos' almost escaped her lips.

Leah was waiting for her, sitting in the little hallway, doing some mending by the light of a tiny lamp.

'I thought you'd be asleep by now.'

'Well, I've had no shortage of food for thought this evening,' she said, studying her daughter's features.

'I didn't expect you to like him.'

'Whether I like him or not is not important. What's so puzzling is how obvious it is that *you* don't like him. Just what is it you want from him?'

'What is that supposed to mean?'

'Come now, Tonia, are you going to try and tell me it was romance that compelled you to bring him here? The man is a pompous ass! And chronological age notwithstanding, he would be too old even for *me*! Relics, indeed. He is one. Spoiled old maid of a man.'

'Ima!' Tonia was shocked. The steely-eyed woman facing her was a stranger. Even before Josef's death, Leah had never spoken her mind with such vehemence.

'That's right. I am your Ima. And now your Abba, too. I would hold my tongue if I thought you cared for him. But it's clear that you don't. I'll say what your father would say if he were here. What is the point in fawning over that old ...'

'I have agreed to marry him, Ima,' Tonia said, turning her back to Leah.

'Oh, Tonia,' Leah cried out, 'why? Why on earth would you throw yourself away like that?'

'Because, Ima, I'm tired. Tired of living off relatives, tired of working myself to exhaustion at dead-end jobs, tired of not having even four bare walls to call my own. Emil will give me a home, security ...'

'But, Tonia, there are so many nice young men. And what about Amos? What happened? I always thought you and he ...'

'That's nobody's business,' Tonia snapped. 'It's my life. I'm going to marry Emil. And you can stop trying to push Amos Amrani on me. He's an uneducated, unscrupulous–' She cut herself off and fled to the bathroom, where silent sobs escaped her. When she came out Leah pretended to be asleep; Tonia got into bed beside her and did the same.

CHAPTER THIRTY-SEVEN

On Tonia's last day of work before her wedding, Mr. Greenblatt called everyone together and opened a bottle of cooking wine. Tonia had not told him she would soon open her own restaurant and steal his three best workers. She raised her wine glass to them all, took a small sip, hung up her apron for the last time, and smiled as she strode through the front door of the restaurant and out into the sun.

She froze when she saw a familiar, beaten-up car parked across the street. Amos sat in it, staring straight at her, and her knees grew weak. She pretended not to notice him and marched up the street.

The car pulled up beside her, and the passenger door flew open. 'Get in,' he ordered.

She stopped, paralyzed and feeling sick.

'Get in the car,' he repeated.

She saw the rage in his eyes and obeyed. He drove off with a roar, and neither of them spoke. Tonia kept her eyes straight ahead, wishing this pointless encounter were over. When she did turn to look at him, she felt the familiar longing to move close, to seek the warmth and comfort of him – and faced the realization that now he would disappear from her life. Forever. Even his friendship would be lost to her. The tantalizing possibility of Amos would no longer flicker in the corners of her mind. She would never see him again. The magnitude of this loss stunned her.

Amos parked near the beach and got out. He slammed the door without looking at her, took a few steps, and turned to sit on a large boulder. His hands were shoved deep into his pockets, his shoulders hunched. The sun was still high in the sky. How could it be such a beautiful day? She got out of the car and reached back to gather her hair, keep it from whipping about her face in the warm breeze. Gulls cawed overhead, and Tonia stood still. She stared at Amos for a long while, as if burning his image into her brain might ease the pain. She didn't want to forget him, his eyes, his long legs, the way he smiled at her. She felt tears rising, but knew she had no right to them. She swallowed and looked out at the sunlight glinting off the sea. Nonsense. No need for such melodrama. They weren't meant for each other. She had to live her own life. He would be better off without her.

She slowly approached him. 'Amos?' Her voice was small, pleading. She felt as if she should be on her knees.

'Why?' It was more a cry than a question.

'Amos ...'

'I want to know why!'

'Must I account to you as well?'

'Yes. To me, most of all!'

'I think you know why,' she said.

He began to pace.

'If I thought ... if you could tell me you have real feelings for him ... and not for me ... but ... what is it? For money? You're selling yourself so that you can open a lousy little restaurant? Don't you think I would have found some way to get you the money?'

'I couldn't take money from you, Amos,' she said.

'God in heaven! "I couldn't take money from you, Amos",' he mimicked her. 'What the hell is that about, Tonia? You can't take money from me, but you can make yourself a whore to–'

'Amos!'

He raised a hand, and she thought he was going to strike her. She stood passively waiting, would have almost welcomed the blow. It would be easier if she could feel anger for him, rather than disgust for herself. But he lowered his hand.

'You could get a better price for yourself on the street. And with a great deal more integrity.'

She felt herself go cold. 'Goodbye, Amos.' She walked away.

'I hope – I truly hope – that you have the life you deserve,' Amos called after her.

Before the ceremony, Tonia found a suitable site for a small restaurant. She negotiated with the owner and presented the lease to Emil for his signature.

'I know I should have waited until after the wedding,' she apologized, 'but it's so hard to find property, and someone else was going to snap it up.'

After some gentle and not-so-gentle coaxing, Emil signed it.

'Now if I had a car ...' Tonia said, wondering what had happened to the blue Ford listed among his assets in the matchmaker's files.

'I own a car, as a matter of fact,' Emil said. 'It was my mother's. I don't drive myself, but I never sold it, thought I might learn. But I don't seem to have the proper temperament for dealing with machines. It's so much easier to call a taxi. I put it up for sale last week.'

'Oh no, Emil, don't sell it. I could learn to drive, and then I'd never have any trouble getting home to you on time.'

The next day Tonia brought him another document to sign – a contract with one of the city's driving schools. She had discovered that coddling words spoken in a voice with an edge to it could get Emil to agree to anything she wanted. Her demands, however, were few and specific. They all pertained to the restaurant. She found a diner in Petah Tikvah that was going out of business and rushed back to Emil with an agreement for the purchase of all their second-hand equipment.

'Look, Emil, it's a steal. A third of what it would cost new, and everything is in good condition.'

Emil sighed and squinted at the contract through his thick glasses, murmuring that he would have understood a fiancée who pressed him for clothes, jewelry, and silver tea services. But used stoves and iceboxes? He looked up at Tonia with a bewildered expression. She kept a careful record of every cent Emil spent for her. In her mind, it was all a loan, and she kept track of dates and compounded the interest upon it. She asked for nothing for the home. Nothing for herself.

297

They were married in a simple afternoon ceremony, at the small hall in the Rabbinate. Rina and Elon arrived early, lugging a heavy set of stainless steel cooking pots. Uncle Shmuel and Aunt Rivka slipped Tonia an envelope with cash in it. An uncle and aunt of Emil's gave them a teapot. Natan arrived late and told Tonia that Leah would not be coming – she wasn't feeling well. There were no other guests. Tonia didn't care. She wanted it over with and was indifferent to who did or didn't watch it happen. Mrs. Rozmann's white silk dress still lay untouched in its carton in Aunt Rivka's living room. Tonia was married to Emil wearing a simple white cotton shift and white patent leather pumps. Her hair was pulled back into a ponytail with a white ribbon around it, and she wore glossy pink lipstick for the first time in her life. A few yards of simple white netting served as a veil. The groom wore a dark brown suit. The color of dog shit, Tonia could not help thinking.

CHAPTER THIRTY-EIGHT

After the wedding, Emil ordered a taxi to take them to one of the new hotels on the beach. Tonia walked into the room and eyed the double bed as if it were a serpent-infested cesspool.

'Is this all right?' Emil asked behind her.

'Yes, it's a very nice room.'

'Would you like to use the bathroom first?'

The hotel management had left a packet of chocolate and a bottle of red wine on the table.

'How about if we have some wine?' Tonia asked.

'Certainly. Certainly.' He seized the corkscrew, seeming pleased to have a task to perform.

Emil looked almost as nervous as Tonia felt. She yanked the cord that opened the drapes and discovered a tiny balcony overlooking the Mediterranean. On it stood a small, round, glass-topped table and two chairs. She stepped outside, and Emil followed her with the wine bottle in one hand and the stems of two wine glasses between the fingers of the other.

'Maybe we can sit here to enjoy our wine and watch the sunset,' Tonia said. Her head throbbed with self-loathing. Emil did not deserve what she was doing to him. No one did. She had to find a way to get through this without revealing the revulsion she felt, without robbing him of his dignity. Perhaps they could at least be kind to one another. If she drank enough wine, and the room was dark enough, she could pretend she was somewhere else. He was someone else. He would think she was shy. That she didn't know anything. In fact, she really didn't know anything. She knew men had something dangling down there between their legs, but had never understood how that thing could be inserted into what she had between hers.

Tonia drank most of the bottle of wine, occasionally glancing over at her husband and giving him a tight smile. They spoke about the wedding ceremony, the gifts they had received, and his schedule for the coming week.

Emil cleared his throat. 'You look lovely.'

'Thank you.'

'I thought we would stay here just the one night. Go home tomorrow.'

Tonia nodded.

'I know you might want to make some changes to the apartment. My aunt told me women always want to make the home their own. So I have thought about a budget for that.'

He reached for the little notebook he always kept in his breast pocket, but Tonia touched his other hand. 'That's kind of you, but I think it's fine the way it is. I've already asked you to spend enough money. Anyway, I'll be so busy with the restaurant, I won't have time for shopping and decorating.'

'I see.' He looked both relieved and perplexed.

The sun was sinking fast. Tonia drained her last glass of wine and stood up. 'I guess I will go have a shower,' she said, matter-of-factly. Might as well get it over with.

Emil had given her a peck on the check after the ceremony and helped her in and out of the cab. Other than that, he had not yet touched his new bride.

She took her toothbrush and paste and the white cotton nightgown Aunt Rivka had given her into the bathroom and closed the door. She leaned against the sink and stared in the mirror for a long moment, feeling more alone than she had imagined possible. Then she scolded herself. No use feeling sorry for yourself. This is what you decided to do, this is what is necessary, the only way you will ever get away from here. You're not the first woman to marry out of financial necessity. All marriages used to be arranged, with dowries; love had nothing to do with it. They were business arrangements. And you'd better get used to being on your own, if you think you can make a new life in America.

She showered and pulled the nightgown over her head. To her horror, she saw in the mirror that her nipples and the dark triangle 'down there' showed through it. She picked up her panties to put them back on, but stopped. Either she or Emil would just have to take them off again. She closed her eyes in dread,

300

then opened them, turned off the bathroom light, and opened the door to peek out. Emil was in bed, shirtless, blanket up to his chest. His bedside light was on, and he was reading. He seemed not to have noticed that the door had opened.

Tonia took a quick step into the room, lifted the bedcovers, and slid under them. Emil turned toward her with a smile, placed a bookmark in his book, and set it on the table. Then he stood up, naked, and walked around the bed to use the bathroom. Tonia watched his progress in wordless fascination. When he came out, she had her first view of full-frontal male nudity, which was nothing like she had imagined. He got back into bed and reached to turn off the light.

'Don't be afraid,' he said.

'I'm not,' she answered, for a moment feeling a strange closeness to him, as they were about to go through this horrible ordeal together.

He took her right hand and placed it on himself, down there. He cupped his hand around hers, forcing her to grasp the soft lump of flesh and move her hand up and down. She almost gasped as the thing she was holding began to grow. Then she remembered the strange hardness she had felt brush against her while she was dancing with Amos at the wedding and the sniggering comments young boys were always making about it 'standing up'.

Think of this as a hands-on biology lesson, she told herself, and almost laughed aloud.

She was beginning to worry about just how big it was going to get when Emil let go of her hand and rose to his knees. In the dim light that seeped in from around the curtains, she saw him pull a tiny packet from under his pillow. He opened it with his teeth and removed something white, which he rolled down over his thing, which was now staring her straight in the face. Then he lifted one knee and placed it between her legs, and she waited to see what he was going to do next.

'Tonia, you must open your legs,' he said and pushed one of her thighs up with his hand. 'Like this,' he said. 'Both legs. Wrap them around my waist.'

She obeyed, thanking God the lights were off. She had never envisioned the process as this undignified. A picture of her parents involved in this ridiculous activity flashed through her mind, but she blinked it away. How many girls had Amos done this with? And Emil? He must have done this before. Who on earth with? Maybe he visited the prostitutes that she had heard worked by the beach at Tel Baruch.

When he first tried to enter her, she gasped in pain. He pulled back, reached under his pillow again, and took out a tube. He squeezed out whatever it held and spread it over himself, then squeezed more onto his fingers and touched her, rubbing it around, letting his finger slip inside her body.

He lay back on top of her and said, 'It will be better now, but it always hurts the first time.'

She gritted her teeth while he moved in and out of her. Then he made strange noises and collapsed on her, a weight so dead she feared she would suffocate. She was about to beg for air when he rolled over. After a moment, he rose up on one elbow, planted a kiss on her mouth, said thank you, and rolled over to go to sleep.

CHAPTER THIRTY-NINE

Marriage to Emil held no surprises. He was content, as long as she did not interfere with his routine. He wanted toast, a soft-boiled egg, and black coffee each morning; a bowl of soup and a chicken leg each noon. Clean socks in his drawer, starched shirts, and a woman to nod while she listened to him for an hour or so each evening.

He spent the morning hours in his study – a large, dark, dust-covered room lined with books. His enormous desk was always piled high with stacks of paper and folders. Tonia was forbidden to enter this sanctuary, let alone attempt to clean it. He emerged at twelve noon to eat. After the meal, he sat smoking his pipe and listening to classical music for precisely half an hour. Then he napped for an hour. During the late afternoon he was either busy at the offices of *Relics* or haunted the university library. He ate his supper in a nearby café with two old friends. When he returned home in the evening, he expected Tonia to greet him with a cup of tea with cloves and a slice of sponge cake, baked according to his mother's recipe. She found it amazing that two people could live under the same roof and have so little meaningful contact, but she was grateful for the great divide between them.

His sexual demands were modest, and Tonia gritted her teeth through them. By the time she finished showering afterward, Emil was asleep. Sometimes, late at night, she sat out on the spacious terrace, staring at the stars and weeping, remembering the sting of the words Amos had flung at her. But, damn him, who was he to judge her? Didn't he break every law he chose, do whatever suited him, to get what he wanted? A man simply had more options. As for Emil, he seemed to accept her reticence as a manifestation of female delicacy, of which he approved. He paid scant attention to how Tonia occupied herself, as long as she did what was expected of her.

She spent every free moment at the restaurant, which served breakfast and lunch to the workers in the neighborhood. She had named it 'Emil's', to her husband's puzzlement. It was clean, the prices reasonable, and she had made a half-hearted attempt at cheery decor. She got on well with her employees and trusted them enough to let them open in the morning and manage on their own for an hour at noon while she rushed home to put Emil's lunch on the table. She returned to help clear up, tally the till, and take the proceeds to the bank.

Emil's would never make her wealthy, but she was soon taking in a decent profit. A few months after opening, she handed Emil the first of a series of checks.

'What's this? Another bill?' he asked.

'It's money. From the restaurant. I can start paying you back now.'

'I don't understand.'

'I'm making enough money to start paying you back.'

'What do you mean?'

'I've kept a record of everything you've invested in Emil's. Every penny. I'm going to pay it back with the same interest you'd have gotten if you'd left the money in the bank.'

He looked up at her with a bewildered expression. 'But, Tonia, you are my wife. How can you owe me money?'

'Business is business,' she replied. 'It's better this way. Because of income tax and things like that. We should keep our accounts separate.'

Every few months Tonia handed Emil another check, though she did not turn all her profits over to him. She opened an account in her maiden name into which she made regular deposits. She also spent some money on herself – two almost-new dresses from a second-hand shop, a pair of shoes, a thick warm bathrobe, a handbag, and a lot of books, all of them in English.

She also bought modest gifts for her family, though she seldom saw any of them. Rina could not tear herself away from the kibbutz, Natan was obsessed with his studies, and Leah had all but disowned her for marrying Emil. She was cold and distant when Tonia stopped by and never invited them over. The main beneficiary of Tonia's largesse was Rina's baby girl, Oranit. Tonia sent her boxes of toys, books, and clothing. Knowing Rina, she realized that most of it probably ended up community property, but she couldn't resist buying something every time she passed a children's store.

'Ima?' Tonia entered her uncle's flat.

'In here,' Leah answered, and Tonia found her seated at the table with sheets of figures spread out in front of her.

Tonia paused in the doorway, captivated by her mother. Though the hair pulled back on the crown of her head was graying, she still looked slim and youthful, radiant with enthusiasm. She loved her job and had helped organize a summer camp and other activities for the children of Kfar Etzion. Though the orphans no longer lived together as a community, they remained a cohesive group. They gathered whenever possible and shared a closeness of experience no outsider could understand. Tonia had accompanied her mother on one of her recent outings with the children. On the way back to Tel Aviv, they climbed up a hilltop near Beit Guvrin. From there they had a clear view across the new border and could see the top of the Lonely Tree, still standing solitary at the crossroads of what had once been their home. Tonia blinked back tears with the rest of them. Only Leah had remained dry-eyed.

Tonia nodded at the papers and bills on the table. 'What's all this?'

Leah looked up at Tonia. 'Trying to work out some activities for the children for the Succoth vacation. But staying within the budget won't be easy.' She rubbed her eyes. 'So how is the blissful Mrs. Greenberg?'

'If you're going to start in, I'll leave. You know, mothers aren't supposed to like their sons-in-law.'

'Ah, but the daughters are supposed to like them,' she said, her voice hard. Then she looked at Tonia and softened. 'I'm sorry, but I can't help it. To me, marriage will always be a sacred trust. You – and the business arrangement you call a marriage, to a man to whom you are at best indifferent – defile it. You are an insult to the life I shared with your father. I cannot begin to imagine how you cope with the marriage bed. Perhaps you are waiting for the frog to turn into a prince.'

'Ima!'

'Maybe it's wrong of me to speak this way.' Leah sighed. 'What's done is done. But you could have had so much more. You and Amos could have made each other happy. Your father would have dragged you kicking and screaming from under that bridal canopy.'

Tonia smiled a sad smile, acknowledging the truth of her mother's words.

'Well, each generation to its own failings,' Tonia said. She didn't add, 'And where is Abba now?'

Tonia tried turning to Natan. He seemed to have mellowed, and Tonia assumed time was healing the wounds left by whatever horrors he had witnessed during the war. But regarding Emil, he was as harsh as Leah was.

'Natan, why are you so angry with me?' she asked him during one of her rare visits to Jerusalem.

'I'm not angry. But I'll never understand the things you do.'

'Is it that you can't forgive me for hurting Amos?'

'No, it's not Amos,' he retorted. 'Don't waste your energy feeling sorry for him. He's recovered quite nicely, thank you. You should see the blondes on his arm.'

CHAPTER FORTY

Tonia waited until Emil returned from the café and joined her for a cup of tea. She had rehearsed it so many ways, but ended up gripping the arms of her chair, knuckles white, staring straight ahead, and blurting out, 'I want a divorce.'

'What did you say, dear?' He looked up from his newspaper.

'I said I want a divorce.'

'A divorce? You mean to stop being married?'

'Yes, Emil.' She sighed.

'Is this a joke?'

'No, it's not a joke,' she said, beginning to feeling more impatient than guilty. 'I want a divorce. I'm going to go to America. If you won't give me a divorce, I'll go anyway, without one. But I won't live with you any more. I'm moving out tonight.'

'You can't be serious.'

'I'm sorry, but I'm very serious.'

'But ... but ... we've been happy together. Never quarreled. Not a single time. I bring my paycheck home. Never hit you. Never look at other women. I don't understand.'

'I'm not happy at all, but it's not your fault.' She softened. 'Our getting married was a mistake. We were never suited to one another. I am sorry. I've put the restaurant on the market. I'll leave as soon as I can.'

'I bought you that restaurant!' His eyes narrowed.

'And I've paid you back every cent you put into it. With interest. I've kept records,' she said. 'I won't make any financial demands of you. A divorce won't cost you a cent. But the restaurant is mine.'

'But you can't just leave!'

She rose and set the car keys on the table. One suitcase containing all that she was taking stood by the door.

'I am sorry, Emil. I hope we can do this like two civilized human beings. Goodbye.'

She rapped on Uncle Shmuel's door. Leah opened it and stared at the suitcase that stood next to Tonia.

'Come in.'

'I've asked Emil for a divorce,' Tonia said, expecting applause.

Leah said nothing. She went into the kitchen to put the teakettle on. 'And?' She turned back to Tonia, who had followed her.

'And what?'

'And once you have your divorce, what will you do?'

'Go to America. I've already applied for a visa.'

'I see.'

'Ima, can't you be on my side for once? Try to understand? Stop blaming me for everything?'

'I understand you, Tonia. Too well. I suppose you had it all planned from the beginning. My God, you can't use a person like that. And suppose you had gotten pregnant?'

'Should I look for a hotel?' Tonia was tired and in no mood to quarrel.

'No, no. You will always be welcome here. There is one thing you should know – Amos sometimes sleeps here and will continue to do so for the next two or three months, until he finishes up a job he's working on in Tel Aviv.'

'Amos?'

'Yes. He opened his own business quite a while ago. Repairs and remodeling. He often hires Natan to help him, and sometimes when Amos is in Tel Aviv he stays here.'

'Can't he afford a hotel?' she asked, jealous of her mother's affection for Amos.

'Yes, he can afford a hotel,' Leah snapped. 'He's doing quite well.'

'How is he?' Tonia asked, voice soft and eyes lowered.

'Fine.'

'Married?'

'No.'

'Does he ever ask about me?'

'No. We make a particular point of not mentioning your name. I doubt that he would continue coming here if I did.'

The next day Tonia bought a folding cot and put it in the storeroom of the restaurant. She wanted to be able to sleep there whenever Amos was going to be at her mother's.

A week later Amos and Natan spent the night at Uncle Shmuel's. After dinner, with painful nonchalance, Leah remarked, 'Tonia was here last week. She and Emil are divorcing. She plans to go to America.'

The next day, while they were standing side by side whitewashing a wall, Natan asked Amos if he would like to see Tonia.

'No, I would not like to see Tonia.'

Tonia stood quaking in the Rabbinical Court, terrified that Emil might change his mind and refuse her the divorce, but the whole thing took less than an hour. The decree was granted, and they walked to the door, which he held open for her. Apart from a few outbursts for which he later apologized, Emil had behaved admirably during the entire process. They had no financial involvements to disentangle, she had not asked for alimony, and there were no children. It was simpler than dissolving a business partnership.

'Tonia, would you join me for a cup of tea?' Emil asked.

'All right,' she said, her voice hesitant. What could he want now? But why not? She walked with him to a nearby café, feeling benign now that she was free of him.

'Why did you marry me, Tonia?'

It would have been a great relief to blurt out the truth, which he seemed to suspect, but that seemed cruel.

'I thought it might work out. I was never happy here in Israel, always wanted to go to America – ever since I was a little girl. But I thought that maybe with a husband like you, a home, security, I might feel safe and be able to make a life here.'

'Yet you never asked me to go to America with you.'

She was horrified at the thought, and her jaw dropped open. 'Why? Would you have come with me?'

'No.' He shook his head.

'No. I knew you wouldn't. Your work is here, and it's much too important for you to leave. I'm sorry for it all, Emil. For having made such a mess of things.'

They parted cordially, and Tonia realized that her mother was right – she was getting off far too easily. She had done a terrible thing and there must be a price to pay. But she shook off her gloomy thoughts and walked down to the beach. She might have to pay later, but right now, today, this moment, she intended to savor her freedom. She kicked off her sandals and threw them up in the air with an uncharacteristic whoop of joy. Then she pranced along the water's edge. No more listening to Emil slurp his soup with his napkin tucked into his collar. No more lectures on Assyrian grammar and script. Best of all, no more listening to him gargle for ten minutes – a sure sign that he would require the use of her body.

She was twenty-two, financially independent, and grateful to be alive for the first time she could remember in years.

It didn't take Tonia long to find a buyer for the restaurant. Natan took her out to dinner that night to celebrate the sale and to try to talk her out of leaving.

'Can't you see that Abba was right? We're here, we won, against all odds. How can you not see that as a manifestation of God's will? Besides, you can't go. It's forbidden. Settling Eretz Israel is the most important of the commandments.'

'Well, Natan, since God's will apparently also included the burning of six million Jews, maybe I don't care so much about what God wants.'

'Don't you think that's a rather easy way out? People make machine guns and build gas chambers. You can't lay those things at God's door. If you must blame God for something, blame him for tuberculosis and polio, for floods and famines and tidal waves. If you need a neat excuse for leading a selfish, meaningless life, at least be logical. And why do you always have to be such a pessimist?'

'Now you sound like Abba. I am not a pessimist. I'm the only optimist in the family. The one who believes there can be such a thing as a country that doesn't want to torture and kill Jews. Where different kinds of people can live together. Maybe the Germans are too German and the Poles too Polish, but in America they take in people from all over the world.'

'Sure, after they wiped out the Indians, they took in a whole lot of people from Africa. Even provided free transportation.'

'You'd do better, Natan, if you tried to make me feel guilty about breaking up the family. I'm more vulnerable on that point. But you can save your breath. That wouldn't work either. I'm going.'

CHAPTER FORTY-ONE

March 1953, Grand Rapids, Michigan

Tonia stepped off the Greyhound bus at the Grand Rapids station. She carried one small suitcase, which she had refused to allow the driver to stow in the luggage compartment. Every cent she had – apart from the $300 she had sewn into her brassiere – was hidden in its lining. She shivered and blinked sleep from her eyes. She set down her bag and glanced at the driver, thinking she might say goodbye to him. This day, the first of her new life, should not begin without some kind of human contact, however impersonal. But he was having words with a hefty woman who had marched out of the office carrying a clipboard, and the one passenger who had spoken to Tonia, a young black woman, seemed to have evaporated.

She slipped her hand into the pocket of the thick black woolen coat she had bought at the Salvation Army store in Brooklyn and touched her list of things to do. Then she looked at her watch – nine o'clock in the morning. She had the whole day to accomplish the first item – find a room to rent.

The sun was shining, but the March wind blew cold, and she took her black and white knit hat and gloves out of her other pocket and pulled them on. She forced herself to smile as she walked away from the station, past grimy buildings of red-brown brick.

Everything will be all right, she repeated over and over. She had spent a few weeks with third cousins in Brooklyn, preparing herself for this new beginning. She was now armed with the two most basic essentials for life in America: a valid driving license and fluent English.

She trudged up the gray, slush-covered street and came to a coffee shop with a torn and faded sign in the window declaring 'Come on in, the Coffee's Hot!' Frankie Laine blared from the radio singing 'I Believe' as she pushed the door open and sat on one of the green vinyl stools at the counter.

'What can I getcha, doll?' asked a frazzled, forty-something waitress from beneath a cloud of brass-colored hair that her hairnet could not contain.

'Just a cup of black coffee, please,' Tonia replied, wondering how noticeable her accent was.

Tonia eyed the grease stains on the waitress's faded pink uniform. She had expected New York to be dirty. But the Midwest? Didn't it teem with well-scrubbed children who played tag in swaying fields of corn and went home to sleep in four-poster beds in houses surrounded by white picket fences? Automobile industry or not, a state that called itself the Water Wonderland ought to be clean. She had read in a book at the New York Public Library that no matter where you stood in Michigan, you were never more than five miles from a body of water. She couldn't quite imagine life without cisterns, surrounded by unlimited supplies of sweet water. A picture in that same book of a doe and fawn drinking from the Manistee River amidst the red-orange-yellow blaze of autumn leaves had helped make up her mind. Michigan was where she would start her new life. Tonia had been at the library frowning at a map of Michigan when one of the young librarians passed by.

'Hi, I'm from Michigan. Anything I can help you find on that map?'

Tonia sat back and studied the cheerful, blonde, blue-eyed girl, who looked like she should be wearing a baseball cap.

'Did your family go on picnics and make homemade ice cream?' Tonia asked.

'Well, sure, sometimes ...'

Tonia smiled at the girl's puzzled look, realizing how ridiculous her question must have sounded. 'What I meant to ask was – is Michigan a nice place to live? Safe. Quiet. Nice place to bring up a family?'

'It doesn't get much quieter than where I come from.' The librarian grinned. 'That's why I came to New York.'

'Are there really a lot of deer like that?' Tonia nodded at the book that lay open to the picture of the doe and fawn.

'School's closed on Opening Day.'

Tonia had no idea what that meant, but the girl pulled up a chair and pointed out Grand Rapids, her hometown.

'It's real nice. Especially East Grand Rapids. Has a little lake, Reeds Lake, right in town. Before he got sick, my Dad used to keep a sunfish docked there – took it out on weekends. The nice thing about Grand Rapids is that it's big enough to have hospitals and lots of stores and all, but still not a big city, you know what I mean?'

'Do you happen to know if there are any Jews in Grand Rapids?' Tonia asked.

'Sure. My parents have some Jewish friends. I couldn't tell you how many there are, but I know they just finished building a brand new synagogue over on East Fulton Street. Temple Emanuel.'

So Tonia had boarded the bus for Grand Rapids.

The coffee was bitter, and Tonia's stomach was churning, but she drained the cup of its warmth. Her body ached, and she found herself fighting tears. No. I will not think about my family. Not now. I can do this. I am strong. I am determined. I am not penniless, and I know the language. I'm better off than most immigrants who wash up here, and they don't seem to do too badly. Life was so haphazard, she mused, offering a weak smile to the waitress as she refilled Tonia's coffee cup. If she hadn't met that girl at the library, she might have ended up in St. Louis or Minneapolis. Anywhere in America's heartland would have done.

The librarian had taken Tonia downstairs and shown her the Grand Rapids telephone directory, which had a street map in the front of it. On it, she pointed out three neighborhoods where she thought Tonia could find a cheap rental. After the girl left, Tonia looked around to make sure she wasn't being observed and then hunched over the phone book and ripped the map out with one quick movement, half-expecting the guard to rush over and arrest her. She now took that flimsy map from her pocket and stared at the maze of streets, their names so bland she found them exotic. Did people really live somewhere called Cherry Blossom Lane?

314

She left the exact change, no tip, and fled the coffee shop. She still had two apples in her bag for breakfast, but decided to hoard them a while longer. She walked in what she guessed was the general direction of one of the neighborhoods she had marked on her map, but the blocks were long and the wind harsh. When she came to a gas station, she stopped and approached the attendant, a pimply high school-aged boy who was polishing the windshield of a shiny black Packard.

'Excuse me, please. Is this the right direction to get to there?' She pointed at her map.

'Yeah,' he answered.

The boy walked around to the other side of the car, and she followed him. He glanced at her, and she again wondered about her accent and the way she was dressed. She knew that not all Americans were blonde-haired and blue-eyed, but this one was, and she became conscious of her own dark hair and eyes. Did she look Jewish, she wondered. Could these Gentiles tell? Did they care?

'But you can't walk there,' the boy said. 'Too far. You'd better catch a cab. You ought to be able to find one back down by the bus station.'

'How far is it?'

'Dunno. Couple of miles. Five, maybe.'

'There's no bus?'

'Nope.'

The car door opened, and the driver got out. He was a tall, pleasant-looking, gray-haired man in a three-piece suit under an expensive-looking overcoat. He exuded money and good manners.

'Where do you have to go, Miss?'

She pointed at the map.

'I can give you a lift. I'm going in that general direction.'

'Check your oil, Mr. Whalen?' the boy asked.

'No thanks, Buck.'

The man circumvented the long front end of his car and opened the door for Tonia. She hesitated before she got in, allowing him to put her precious suitcase in the back seat. Since

Buck knew his name, she decided that Mr. Whalen was not likely to slit her throat and toss her remains in a ditch.

He paid Buck and got behind the wheel.

'I'm Bill Whalen,' he said and offered a hand.

'My name is Tonia. Tonia Shulman.' She wiped her hand on
her coat before shaking his.

CHAPTER FORTY-TWO

Mr. Whalen started the engine, and Tonia settled back and noticed how badly her back and arms ached. Her body soaked up the warmth of the heater. Her new penny loafers were wet, and she shoved her toes close to the blower on the floor. This was more like it. Life in America. The front seat was cavernous, the white upholstery plush.

When he stopped for a traffic light next to a Sew 'n' Save shop, Tonia ogled the neatly arranged bolts of cloth. She remembered going with Leah to buy fabric at a hole-in-the-wall shop in Mea Shearim in Jerusalem. It was so tiny, only one customer could go in at a time, and the queue of women stood out on the sidewalk. The bolts of fabric had been stacked on top of one another, ceiling high, behind the counter. The proprietor, an ancient man with a long white beard, had climbed up onto one of the stacks in order to reach down the blue corduroy that Leah wanted to see.

Mr. Whalen drove out of the downtown area and entered a residential neighborhood, orderly rows of houses with well-kept front yards scattered with bicycles and toys. This was a place for children to grow up, like in the movies. Screen doors banging, mothers calling out for them to come home to dinner.

'Did you just get into town?' Mr. Whalen asked.

'Yes.'

'Visiting relatives?'

'No.'

She sneaked looks at him out of the corner of her eye. Was there the slightest chance that he might be Jewish?

'What address did you want to go to?'

'Oh, you can let me off anywhere in the neighborhood.'

He pulled over to the curb and turned to regard her with a fatherly expression. 'Do you have somewhere to go?'

'I'm looking for a room to rent. A girl I met in the library in New York suggested this neighborhood.'

'I see. Are you a student at one of the colleges?'

'No.'

He seemed perplexed. 'Look, I don't mean to pry, but if I can, I'd like to help you out. I know some of my wife's friends would be thrilled to find a live-in mother's helper. It wouldn't pay all that much, but it would be a roof over your head and meals.'

Tonia shook her head. 'No, no thank you, but it's nice of you to offer.'

'What brings you to Grand Rapids, then?'

'I want to live here.' She squirmed in her seat. 'Make a new life here. I'm going to start my own business. I have money. In the bank, I mean, not here with me,' she added hastily.

'So you picked a city off the map, got on a bus, and here you are?'

'Yes.'

He shook his head and smiled.

'And you don't know anybody in town?'

'No.'

'Not a soul?'

'No.'

'How old are you?'

'Twenty-two.'

'Well, that's something at least. You look about fourteen. Where are you from?'

'I came here from New York.'

'I mean, where were you born?'

So much for wondering if her accent was noticeable. She hesitated before answering, but then grew angry with herself. She wasn't going to apologize to anyone for who she was. 'Israel. I was born in Poland. But I grew up in Palestine. Israel now.'

An expression passed over his face that she couldn't read. His features seemed to turn to cement, and for a moment she was afraid. He looked straight ahead, drumming his fingers on the steering wheel. Then he turned back to her. 'I'd have to call my wife and ask, but we could probably put you up for a few

318

days while you look. And I'd be happy to show you around the city, help you get settled.'

This unexpected kindness made her feel like crying, but she turned him down, saying she wouldn't want to impose on them and that she was sure she would find a room of her own.

'Well, at least let me show you around, welcome you to our city. I'm just out for a drive. You might as well come along for the ride, get your bearings.'

Tonia didn't believe he was out for a drive, not dressed in a business suit, but she gratefully accepted his offer. She wondered if all Americans were so kind. God had been generous with this part of the earth, graced it with topsoil that allowed it to feed much of the world's population. Did that create a generosity of spirit in the people who lived here?

'That's my house, there on the left,' he said, as they passed a large white colonial on Lake Drive in East Grand Rapids.

Tonia renewed her promise to herself that within five years she would own her own house. A few minutes later Mr. Whalen pointed out a new strip mall in the final stages of construction.

'If you want to open a little shop, my advice would be to stay away from downtown and think about one of those new centers,' he said nodding at it. 'Lots of folks are skeptical about them, but if you ask me, they're the thing of the future. Get all your shopping down in one place, where you've got a roof over the sidewalk, and plenty of parking. Time will come when no one will bother going downtown any more. And you can rent space in them a whole lot cheaper than downtown.'

Tonia listened carefully. This man looked successful at whatever it was he did.

'What kind of business did you have in mind?' he asked.

'I haven't decided. Something that doesn't require too much equipment or inventory. And I don't want to hire a lot of help right away. I think something to do with food, but not a restaurant. Maybe a bakery. I would start out selling a few kinds of special breads and my mother's strudel. I thought I'd bake them fresh every day and sell the leftovers the next day at half price.'

He nodded his approval. 'Sounds reasonable. But I'd give some thought to selling individual portions, so that people can walk in and eat on the premises. You know, you're out shopping, tired, and that bakery smell gets to you, but what are you going to do with a whole cake? So give them a place to take a load off and have a cup of coffee. That's more work, but if your cake is good enough, they might end up taking a whole one home to the family. And you want the local businesses to start sending someone over to you for pastries for their coffee break.'

'I hadn't thought of that.'

'Think about the Plaza, the one we just passed. A few of the stores there have already opened, and they haven't rented to any of the food chains yet. Buy a couple of cute little tables and chairs and a coffee pot, and you'll get walk-in trade. Shoppers are always looking for an excuse to sit down. And there are quite a few office buildings in that area.'

'So you don't think it's a stupid idea?'

'Why no. People always want to eat. It's the fancy restaurants with enormous overheads that get into trouble. Long as you keep your costs low, you can't go too wrong. Start out like you said, with a few things, and if folks don't go for them, switch to something else. Keep yourself flexible. Don't sink money into equipment that's geared to making one thing.'

'What about advertising?'

'I wouldn't put a whole lot of money into that. Your product is its own best advertising. Once you have your location, scout the neighborhood, send the office workers some free samples along with flyers. In a small community the grapevine is the best advertising there is.'

He drove her back to the modest neighborhood off Lake Drive where she intended to look for a room. He stopped by a corner grocery and left her in the car while he went in and bought a copy of the Grand Rapids Press. He handed it to her, together with his business card.

'Well, I wish you luck, Tonia. If I can be of any help, you give me a call. And I mean that.'

320

'I will,' she promised. 'I don't know how to thank you. You have been so kind.'

'Nothing to thank me for. You wouldn't let me do anything but drive you around and run my mouth off.'

'It's been very helpful. I don't know how to say it, but the day looks different than it did before I met you. Friendlier. I'm not so scared any more.'

She smiled and waved as he drove off. America was already being good to her. But when she picked up her suitcase and looked around, some of the lonely, heavy feeling returned.

CHAPTER FORTY-THREE

No one was home behind the first two doors on which Tonia knocked. The room at the third had already been taken. At the fourth, a young woman flung the door open.

'Hello, I'm here about the room,' Tonia said.

The girl wore a pink and white checked poodle skirt and pink sweater set. Her black and white saddle shoes had pink shoelaces, and her curly blonde hair was pushed back off her forehead by a pink headband, studded with rhinestones. She gave Tonia and her bulky black wool coat a cool once-over and stood back to let her enter.

'It's upstairs,' she said and turned to mount the stairs behind her.

'Maybe I should take my shoes off,' Tonia said, looking for a doormat to clean her feet on.

'Okay.' The girl shrugged and continued up the stairs.

Tonia slipped her feet out of her loafers. She would have liked to leave her suitcase in the entryway by her shoes, but all her money was still in it, so she lugged it up the stairs with her.

'That's it in there.' The girl nodded at an open door.

The small room had a slanting ceiling and a dormer window. Flowered wallpaper peeled from its walls and the beige carpeting showed its age. Its furnishings consisted of single bed, nightstand, desk, and dresser.

'How much is it?' Tonia asked.

'Twenty-three dollars a month, two months in advance, plus utilities.'

'I'll take it,' Tonia said. When the girl didn't answer, she added, 'If that's all right with you, I mean.'

'Are you a student?'

'No.'

'Then you want it for the summer too?'

'Yes.'

'Well, I guess that's all right, then. You'll be sharing the house with me and two other roommates, Sally and Kerri. I'm Julie.'

'My name's Tonia.' She moved to offer her hand, but Julie had already turned to go back downstairs.

'We're students at Calvin College, but we all stay for the summer,' Julie said over her shoulder.

'Do you want me to meet them, before you decide?'

'No. They'll agree. The room's been empty for almost a month.' Julie stopped halfway down the stairs and looked back up at Tonia. 'The girl who had it before had to go home, and there aren't many people looking in March. Do you want to go get your stuff, then?'

Tonia stood at the top of the stairs and held up the suitcase. 'This is all I have.'

Julie shook her head almost imperceptibly, but kept her voice cheerful. 'So you're ready to move in right now?'

'I guess so.'

'Okay. I'll go get your key.' She started back down the stairs. 'I have to go to class now, but I'll show you around when I get back this evening. The bathroom is right next door. There's another one down here.'

'Do you want me to give you the rent?' Tonia shouted after her.

'We can do that after I get home.'

Julie came back to hand Tonia the key and skipped down the stairs. Tonia set her suitcase by the bed and ran her hand over the bumpy white bedspread. After the front door banged, she subjected the blue-tiled bathroom to a closer inspection. It also had a slanting ceiling, but looked enormous to Tonia. She stared at the bathtub and opened the faucet. Water gushed out. Yes, everything was going to be all right.

Then she went back to her room to unpack. She removed the thick wads of bills from her suitcase and stuffed them into her bra before she went downstairs to look around. A web of cracks marred the yellow linoleum that covered the kitchen floor. Stairs led down to a damp-smelling basement, but she didn't venture down there. The living room held two love seats and two easy-boy rockers, each covered in different upholstery. A large console television set with a rabbit-ears antenna dominated the room.

Tonia walked to the corner grocery and bought the makings for coffee and sandwiches. Then she settled down at the desk in her room with her lunch and the newspaper Mr. Whalen had bought. She ignored the news about Josef Stalin's death and the ceasefire in Korea. The classifieds and advertising sections were far more pertinent to her needs, and she began a serious study of Automobiles for Sale. She knew that it would be difficult to live, let alone run a business, without a car.

She began dialing numbers and on the tenth call spoke to a man who was selling his Rambler. He lived only seven blocks away, and Tonia said she would be right over. When she knocked on the door, a hairy-chested, shirtless man with a substantial midsection stepped out onto the porch.

'You the Tonia that called?'

'Yes.'

He held out a key. Nodding at the red and black car in the drive he said, 'Go ahead and take 'er for a little spin.'

She stared at him. 'You mean me, drive it?'

'You wanna see how it runs, don'tcha?'

'Alone?'

'I'm kinda busy right now.'

'Don't you want to come with me?' She had only driven the car she had taken lessons on.

He looked her up and down again. 'Nah. Go ahead.' He tossed her the key and went back inside, where a television was blaring.

She slipped behind the wheel and backed out of the drive. She took her map from her pocket and surprised herself by managing to find the gas station where she had met Mr. Whalen. Buck was still there, leaning back on two legs of a chair and blowing big pink balloons of bubble gum.

'Hello again. Do you know a lot about cars?' she asked him.

'You bet.' He pushed the blue baseball cap back on his head and sat down on all four legs of the chair.

'For three dollars would you look this car over and tell me if you would buy it and for how much?'

'Getting a car already? Cool. Sure, lady, I can take a look at it.'

He popped the hood and poked around, kicked the tires, and lay down on a little wheeled board to slide underneath it. Without a word of warning, he got behind the wheel and drove off, shouting 'Watch the store' to Tonia. She wondered how many years she was going to get for grand theft auto, but he soon appeared around the corner and screeched to a halt.

'Not bad for an old jalopy. It will get you around town. Wouldn't take it on any trips to California,' he said. 'What're they asking for it?'

'Five hundred dollars.'

'Offer four hundred and fifty.'

She drove it back, again considering it no small miracle that she found her way, and offered the shirtless man four hundred and twenty dollars. He accepted, and she found herself the owner of an automobile. She spent the next few hours driving around the city, committing its main streets to memory. After getting lost several times she found the Plaza strip mall, parked, and walked up and down its wide sidewalk. The contractor had managed to leave five tall trees growing out of evenly spaced circular beds cut in the concrete and had built a small fountain next to each. Tonia glanced into the few stores that had opened. She drove through the nearby streets and decided to take Mr. Whalen's advice. First thing in the morning, she would come back and look into renting one of the vacant spaces. She had noticed one that had a tree and fountain outside its door.

By the time she got home, it was early evening. Her three roommates were in the kitchen sharing an enormous pizza. Julie introduced her to Kerri and Sally.

Sally sat near the window looking out at the drive and said, 'You got a car. Wow.'

'Yes. I just bought it.'

'You don't waste any time,' Kerri said. 'Want some pizza?'

'Thanks, but I'd better not. I'm on a diet.'

Tonia glanced at the pepperoni and pork sausage smothered in cheese. She knew she was going to end up eating things that were not kosher, but that was too much, too soon. 'But is it all right if I sit down?'

'Sure. Have something to drink. Where are you from?' Sally asked, pushing a bottle of diet Coke toward her. 'There's glasses up there in the left cupboard.'

'I'm from Israel.'

'Where is that, out East somewhere?' Kerri asked.

'No. It's in the Middle East.'

'Gee. So how'd you get here?' Sally asked.

'Well, I saved up some money, and I had to wait a while for a visa, and here I am.'

'All by yourself?'

'Yes.'

'Gee. That's really cool. My parents had a cow when I asked to go to California by myself. You sure you don't want some pizza?'

'No thanks.'

Tonia asked them about their studies and their families. When they finished eating, she moved with them into the living room. Tonia stared at the TV and wondered if Victor were somebody's name, and, if so, what RCA stood for. The Dinah Shore show was ending, and the girls began arguing whether they should watch *Burns and Allen* or Groucho Marx's *You Bet Your Life*.

Tonia excused herself, went up to her room, took her first luxurious bath, checked on her wad of fifty-dollar bills, and went to sleep.

Less than two months of sixteen-hour days later Tonia was close to opening her bakery. She had rented a space in the Plaza. The electricians were still working, but had promised to be done in a few days. She had gotten the store she wanted, the one with the tree and fountain outside. It was near the space where a Crowley's department store would open soon. She reasoned that the people coming out of the supermarket at the other end of the shopping center would be hurrying home with their defrosting meat and melting ice cream. Women with shoes and sweaters in their shopping bags would be more inclined to sit down for coffee.

She had purchased a second-hand commercial oven, a mixer, a refrigerator, utensils, and baking pans, and had hired an agreeable workman to install a wide countertop. Its sides were painted white, and its top a beautiful deep blue that matched the covers of the four stools. A glass display case would stand at one end. The workman also put up shelves behind the counter, for the coffee machine and cash register, and partitioned off the back third of the store to serve as a storage space and work area, with a large sink, counter, and cabinet. Then Tonia found wholesalers and stocked her storeroom with staples and canned fruit, wishing it were summer so she could go to the farmers' market for fresh cherries and berries. She had followed Mr. Whalen's advice and prepared a list of local businesses to which she would send free samples, neatly boxed and ribboned. The choice of a name gave her some difficulty. She considered 'Well-Bread' but discarded it. 'Tonia's' would sound too foreign and 'Shulman's' too Jewish. She settled on 'The Pastry Shop', imagining droves of exhausted women saying to one another, 'Oh, let's stop in at the pastry shop before we go home'.

By experimenting with strips of strudel dough wrapped around fruit she learned to create individual servings and tested the results on Julie-Kerri-Sally, who declared them out of this world. She planned to keep one of the windows partway open and let a small fan propel the aroma of baking bread and pastry outside.

When it came time to purchase the last furnishings, she decided to opt for tasteful simplicity and let the shop be its own decor. She painted her own sign with simple letters, blue on white, along with a price list to put in the window. She bought four round white tables and sets of chairs with comfortable cushions and selected high-quality plastic plates and cups, some dark blue and some pale yellow. The last touch was simple glass vases for cut flowers. Then she went to Sew 'n' Save for blue and white checked fabric and used a machine borrowed from one of her roommates to run up ruffled curtains, dark blue covers for the chair cushions, and napkins. She drew up a handbill, had three hundred copies run off, and spent her evenings trudging through the neighborhood stuffing them into mailboxes.

Tonia went through the motions of agonizing about opening on the Sabbath, but there was never any real doubt that she would. Being Jewish was going to have to come second. The Passover holiday had fallen in the midst of her preparations, and Tonia had done her best to 'forget' about it. She had not sought contact with the Jewish community, though she had looked in the phone book and seen that Grand Rapids had two synagogues, one Reform and one Conservative. On the day before Passover she started feeling guilty and knew that she could not completely ignore such an important holiday. She gave her room a thorough cleaning and went to the supermarket for kosher-for-Passover *matzah* and Mogen David wine. On Passover Eve, she went to her room, poured a glass of wine, and began reading the *Haggadah*. She didn't get far before she lay back on her bed and began to weep silent tears, imagining Josef looking down at her with an appalled expression on his face.

But where are you, Abba, and where am I?

CHAPTER FORTY-FOUR

In the damp and gloomy basement of the house Tonia discovered a battered, but working, chest freezer and filled it with ready-to-bake strudels and turnovers. She bought cute cardboard boxes and shiny red ribbon to package her free samples and thumb-tacked ads for a delivery boy to trees and bulletin boards. Two days before her grand opening she propped the door of the shop open with a chair and mopped the floor. She was exhausted, more from the worry than the hard work. What if the oven stopped working? What if she burned everything? What if no one came? What if people came but hated her pastries? What if the health inspector came back and shut her down? What if her calculations were off and she lost all her money? What if something went wrong with the pilot light and the place burned to the ground? What if, what if.

A deep voice boomed behind her. 'You must be awful ticked off at that floor.'

Startled, she turned and saw a large high-school-aged boy in a red baseball cap.

'Hi, I'm Mike.' He stuck out one hand and removed the hat with the other, revealing a head of frizzy red-gold hair trying to resign itself to a buzz cut.

He was big and boxy. Square-shaped head and jaw, black rectangular eyeglasses, thick chest, no waist, and enormous hands. He wore a black and off-white varsity jacket embossed with purple and gold letters. He must play American football, Tonia thought. That strange game where they knock each other down and jump in a big pile. Soccer she could understand – at least you could see where the ball was, and it did not seem likely to result in anyone's death.

'Hello, I'm Tonia.' She wiped her hand on her apron before taking his.

He pumped it and smiled. Even his teeth were big and square. 'I saw the ads you put up for a delivery boy.'

'It would be temporary. A few hours. To deliver free sample boxes of pastries and bread to some of the office buildings around here. Maybe twenty boxes a day, next Monday, Tuesday, and Wednesday morning.'

'I got a bike with a basket and a rack on the back,' he said. 'Or I could use my Dad's pick-up, you wanna pay for the gas.'

'I think the bicycle will do.'

'You need any other help, washing dishes or anything, I'll take it.'

'I don't think so.'

Mike raised his eyebrows. 'You got anyone?'

'No. Can't afford to. I'm going to have to manage by myself.'

'You say so.'

'Don't you go to school?' Tonia asked.

'Graduated in January.'

'Would a dollar ten an hour be all right?'

'Sure.'

He left his name and phone number and on his way out said, 'See you Monday morning at eight, Tony.'

The shops at the Plaza would be open from 9:00 in the morning until 7:00 at night, six days a week. That was sixty hours a week, about 3,000 hours a year, allowing for holidays. She calculated that if she netted $1.80 an hour, she would pocket $5,400 a year. Long hours at an adding machine belonging to one of her roommates led her to the conclusion that she would have to gross $4 an hour in order to net $1.80. If that happened, she would have no trouble saving the $600 or $700 she would need for a down payment on a house.

She rose at three in the morning on the day she was opening. She soaked in the tub, shampooed her hair twice, and brushed it 200 strokes. The evening before she had manicured her nails and polished her new penny loafers. She was in the shop by five, in pressed blue slacks, button-down blue and white striped shirt, and spotless white apron. She was bursting with energy, checking trays of pastries in the oven.

330

At 7:30 the kickstand of Mike's bike squeaked, and he knocked on the glass door. He was in shorts and T-shirt, and Tonia found it hard not to stare at the size of his thighs.

'Hey, Tony.'

'Hi, Mike. Good morning. You're here early.' She shut the door behind him. 'There's coffee in the pot. Help yourself. I'll have the first boxes of samples ready for you in a few minutes.'

He nodded and followed her behind the counter. She held up the box she had just finished putting together, which was larger than the rest. 'I'd like you to deliver this one first,' she said. 'It's special, and I want it to get there while the strudel is still warm.'

Mike poured himself a cup of black coffee and sat at one of the tables. She arranged an entire strudel, two loaves of bread, and as many turnovers as she could fit in the box. Before tying it up with a ribbon, she slipped in a handwritten note: 'You were of great help and encouragement when it was sorely needed. People like you make this country a place where other people want to live.' She didn't sign the note, somehow thinking that more personal.

'Oh, I'm sorry.' She glanced over at Mike. 'I meant to tell you – help yourself to pastries. Whatever you want.'

He rose and went to the counter for an apple turnover and took a bite. 'Good stuff,' he said with his full mouth open, holding his other hand under it to catch the crumbs. 'Still hot though.'

'Okay, here, this one's ready to go.' She set the box on the table next to Mike. 'It goes to Mr. Bill Whalen at the first address.' She handed him a handwritten list of twenty businesses, but gestured for him to remain seated when he started to rise. 'No hurry. Finish your coffee. I don't even know what time they open.' She glanced at her watch.

Mike helped himself to a second cup of coffee and an apricot turnover and then pedaled off with the box in the basket on his handlebars. Tonia finished packing the rest and stacked them at one end of the counter. She cleared the mess she had made, turned the sign on the door to Open, and waited for customers. None came.

CHAPTER FORTY-FIVE

The hour between 9:00 and 10:00 that morning was one of the longest of Tonia's life. A lot of people wandered along the sidewalk of the Plaza, but none of them seemed to be tired, hungry, or thirsty.

Mike returned and leaned his bike against the front window. 'Back and ready for more.' He clapped his hands as he came through the door. 'After I get done stuffing my face again. I got to have another one of those thingies with the apricots. That is good stuff.' He strode toward the coffee pot. Then he looked at Tonia and at the empty tables. 'Don't worry, Tony. It's early,' he said. 'They're going to love the stuff you bake. It's delicious.'

'What did Mr. Whalen say?' Tonia asked.

He shrugged. 'I left the box with his secretary. Why, was I supposed to give it to him personally?'

'No, that's fine.'

Mike sat down at one of the tables with his cup of coffee and a plate of three turnovers, one each of peach, blueberry, and apricot.

Tonia stood at the counter kneading bread dough with a determined smile on her face. Two women paused outside the window to read the price list. One of them commented on how delicious whatever was baking smelled, but they walked on.

Mike cleared his dishes away and picked up a stack of boxes. 'They'll probably stop in on their way back, after they knock themselves out shopping. See you.'

Tonia began calculating how many weeks she could afford to stay open before she would be forced to declare bankruptcy. She was starting to feel desperate, when the shop was mobbed. All four tables were taken, and pairs of women took their plates and cups outside to sit on the edge of the fountain. Two of the businesses that had received free samples sent gofers with large orders. One of them requested a standing order that would be picked up daily, Monday to Friday. Yes, Tonia wrote back on the note for Mike to return to them, she would be happy to bill them every two weeks.

A woman came up to the counter holding her empty plate. 'How on earth do you get it so light and flaky?'

'I'll show you,' Tonia said.

Tonia cleared and cleaned the table where the woman and her friend had been sitting and went to the back room for a mound of strudel dough. A small audience gathered as she worked the dough, stretching it paper-thin over the tabletop. When she finished, they clapped and most of them asked for strudel rolls to take home.

She was relieved when there was a short lull, giving her time to wash dishes, clear tables, and slide more trays into the ovens. During lunchtime, she was busy again, dealing out turnovers and slicing strudel. The bread was less successful, until one customer asked if he could taste it. Tonia smiled, cut a few slices of each kind, spread them with butter, and passed them out as free samples. The bread nearly sold out, and this caused a new type of panic to grip her.

She couldn't keep up with everything at once – watch the oven, clean tables, serve coffee and cold drinks, wash dishes, and run the cash register. And if she couldn't get back to the house to get more ready-to-bake goods out of the freezer, she would soon have to close the door. Mike had finished his deliveries, but she glanced up and saw him outside, leaning against the tree and watching her with a knowing smile on his face. A few minutes later, he came in.

'Still think you're going to manage on your own?' he asked.

'You still want a job?'

'What are you paying?'

'I don't know. How much do you want?'

'A dollar an hour to start and some leftovers every day, if you've got them. If you still want me after two weeks, make it a dollar ten an hour.'

'You've got it,' she said, feeling very American.

She wrote down her address, gave him the keys to her car and the house, and told him what to bring back.

'Fast, please, I'm almost out of everything.'

At seven that evening she raced to the supermarket at the other end of the walkway. They had closed, but she persuaded the manager to let her in. She had sold everything in the store, and after his last trip to the house, Mike told her the freezer was nearly empty. She rushed back and found Mike slumped at one of the tables, having a cup of coffee.

'Man, that was some day,' he said.

'Yes, it was.' She owed him $13.20, but took a twenty out of the register and handed it to him. 'I don't know how to thank you. You saved my life. Sorry there are no leftovers.' They both grinned.

She poured herself a cup of coffee and sat down with Mike. The shop was a shambles, but Mike had cleared off the tables and washed the first batch of dishes, which were drying on the dish rack. She realized that she would not sleep that night. She needed to have 50 strudels, 300 turnovers, and 30 loaves of bread ready by 9:00 the next morning. The shop also required a thorough cleaning.

'Mike, didn't you say that your father has a pick-up truck?'

'Yeah.'

'Do you think you could borrow it this evening?' she asked.

'Sure.'

'And do you have a couple of friends, as strong as you are?'

She hired them to move the freezer from the basement of her house to the shop. It belonged to the landlord, and she was stealing it, but she didn't see how she would manage otherwise. She doubted that anyone would notice. None of her roommates used it, and the landlord had probably forgotten it existed. One of these days when she had the time, she would call him up and offer to buy it.

By the time Mike and his friends came back with the freezer, she had cleaned up the mess and set to work making a new one, baking. The thought of stretching dough for fifty strudels nearly reduced her to tears. The euphoria had drained away. Yes, she would make a modest success of this business, but it was going to be hard work. At midnight, she granted herself a coffee break, sat at one of the tables, and put her head down. When she woke it was 3:30, and bread dough was oozing over the tops of bowls.

She punched it down, switched on the oven, and began patting it into loaves. She was halfway through the mountain of strudel dough when she glanced at her watch and saw that it was almost 8:30. Tears came to her eyes; she was so tired.

She slumped into a chair, defeated. That was it. She wouldn't open today. She could put a sign in the window, family illness or some other excuse.

No, she scolded herself. There wasn't that much left to do. Mike would arrive soon. She wouldn't send out more samples today; that could wait until tomorrow. Mike could deliver the large standing order and then wait on customers, while she finished baking. If today was going to be like yesterday, she had until 10:00 before customers started coming in.

She stood up and squared her shoulders, mopped the floor again, rubbed the front window with newspaper until it shone, arranged the tables and chairs, picked the wilted flowers out of the bouquets in the vases, and ran a cloth over the door handle. She noticed that there were only two clean aprons and three clean dishtowels left. When was she ever going to have time to do laundry? When would she ever be able to go home again?

At five to nine, she grabbed her bag and raced down the walkway to the washroom. She splashed water on her face and pinched her cheeks. She had large circles under her eyes, but otherwise did not look too bad. She combed her hair and put on lipstick.

'Thank God, you're here on time.' She almost threw her arms around Mike when she came back and found him standing by the locked door. 'Does this shirt look as bad as it feels?' she asked and turned around.

'You been here all night?' he asked.

'Yes. And I'm not done. You're going to have to wait on customers. Forget delivering free samples today, there's just that one order that has to go. I'll have it ready soon, but you don't have to take it for a while.'

He poured coffee and watched Tonia pack the order in a box and make out a bill.

'I'll get those dishes,' he said when he finished his coffee. Then he took the mop to the floor in the back. Tonia smiled and wondered what guardian angel had sent him to her. He was so big that he looked clumsy, but he worked quickly and efficiently. Something good must come of playing football.

'Do you want to slice bread, like yesterday?' he asked.

'Yes, I suppose. But wait until people start coming in, and just a few slices of each to begin with.'

That evening, at the end of another hectic day, she locked the door and sat with her back to the window, counting her money. In two days she had taken in over a thousand dollars. When would she ever get to the bank?

'I would stay to help you tonight if I could,' Mike said. 'But I can't. I gotta go out with my folks.'

'I wouldn't dream of asking you to. You've been such a godsend.'

She handed him twenty-five dollars. 'Starting tomorrow I'm going to pay you what we agreed. Business may taper off, but if it doesn't and this becomes a permanent arrangement, it will have to be official, with income tax and all.'

'Sure.'

'I do want you to know how much I've appreciated all your help.'

He pocketed the money and nodded goodnight. She watched out the window as a long-legged girl in cut-off blue jeans rose from the edge of the fountain and kissed him. She had long straight brown hair and was prettier than Tonia would have guessed Mike's girlfriend would be. Way to go Mike, Tonia thought to herself with a tired smile. She didn't have quite as much to do as she had the night before. During the afternoon, while Mike took care of customers, she had managed to prepare and freeze a large stock of goods for the next day. She finished a little after midnight, gathered up the dirty laundry, and drove home.

Tonia tossed the laundry into the machine, took a long hot shower and washed her hair, ate two peanut butter sandwiches and made two more for her lunch the next day, transferred the laundry to the dryer, set the alarm for 5:00 am, and fell into bed.

She awoke refreshed and hurried back to the shop. She breezed in humming, switched on the oven, turned on the coffee machine, and folded the clean laundry. Then she spread a slice of bread with butter and sat down with a cup of coffee, luxuriously idle. Mike arrived and joined her, placing a plate of turnovers on the table between them. She realized she had eaten nothing but bread and pastry for two days and should send him out to get her a salad, if she didn't want scurvy to set in.

She surveyed her little empire with pride. It wouldn't be that hard, she thought. One just had to want a thing badly enough. Tonia pictured Leah in the shop, in a starched apron, chatting with the customers, charming them with her Polish accent.

She was taking plates from the rack and stacking them when a voice boomed behind her. 'Best damn cake I ever had.' Mr. Whalen was on the other side of the counter, holding a single yellow rose.

CHAPTER FORTY-SIX

Tonia poured two cups of coffee and went around the counter to sit at one of the tables with Mr. Whalen. She saw Mike frown and cast a sidelong glance their way.

'So how are things going?' Mr. Whalen asked, stirring sugar into his coffee.

'It's been busy,' she said, holding up the creamer. He put his hand over his cup, and she poured some into her own. 'I took all your advice, about giving out samples and everything. Does the place look all right to you?'

'Couldn't have done as well myself.'

Three women came in, and Tonia glanced up at them.

'Don't let me keep you,' he said. 'I wanted to see how you're getting along, but I know you're busy. Just box me up a few of those cakes and one of those rolled-up apple things to take home.'

Tonia sipped her coffee. 'Mike will take care of the customers. I can take a little break – I am the boss, after all.' She smiled, but wondered why he kept staring at her hands.

'Oh.' He patted his breast pocket. 'Almost forgot. Our secretaries want to put in a regular morning order. They take their break around 10:30.' He took out a folded piece of paper, handed it to her, and seemed to have run out of things to say.

Tonia searched for a topic to chat about with this man. What would Mike say? How about those Tigers? Or was it Lions this time of year? She unfolded the paper and read the order.

'Thanks for this.' She held it up. 'You've already been so much help.'

'Wish I could do more.' He looked embarrassed. 'And that's not help. Everyone loved the stuff you sent over.'

She rose and wiped her hands on her apron. 'Let me go wrap up the things you wanted to take home. Can I get you more coffee?'

'No, no. Drink way too much as it is.'

She was conscious of him watching her as she worked behind the counter. She finished and brought the box to his table.

'Sorry I couldn't sit and talk longer,' she said.

'Of course, of course,' he said. 'You've got a business to run.' He pulled out his wallet. 'What do I owe you?'

'My treat.' Tonia gestured for him to put his money away.

He hesitated, but put the wallet back in his pocket. 'My office isn't too far from here. I'll stop in from time to time.'

'That would be lovely.' Tonia smiled, but feared she might have created a 'situation' with this man. Did he imagine she wanted more from him than his advice? She had wanted to show her appreciation, but could he have misinterpreted the gift box and her note?

Mr. Whalen left, and Mike went to clear his empty cup away and wipe the tabletop. 'Your friend's a big tipper,' he said and handed Tonia a fifty-dollar bill.

Tonia pocketed it with a worried sigh.

Her life settled into a difficult routine. She struck a deal with the Plaza's night watchman – he would let himself in to switch on the coffee maker and preheat the oven, in exchange for coffee and a turnover during his mid-morning break. This allowed her to sleep for another half hour. She was in the shop by 6:30 and remained there until 8:00 or 8:30 at night. There was a slight decrease in off-the-street business, but more and more offices were putting in standing orders, so she began taking in the same amount of money with less effort.

Waiting on customers was the hardest part for her. She smiled and provided good service, but nothing more – her 'shoot the breeze' skills were pathetic. She envied the way Mike chatted about the weather, last night's news, and events at the local high school. He called, 'You have a nice day now,' after each of them and even sounded like he meant it. He teased Mrs. Angelino about how Frank Sinatra was going to be available as soon as his divorce from Ava Gardner was final. He listened to Mrs. Van Camp worry about whether there would be enough polio vaccine this summer. He assured Mrs. Reese that her new silk dress with its 'low and behold' neckline was not too daring and that wool flannel slacks were appropriate attire for women.

They showed him their purchases – cashmere sweaters, hoop earrings, and dolls with removable internal organs. Tonia realized that Mike was her most valuable asset. He could have sold them mud pies with a little powdered sugar sprinkled on top. She began to leave him out front, while she baked and washed dishes.

'I'm giving you a raise,' she told him. 'A dollar twenty an hour.'

One night she came back to the shop after midnight, worried she had forgotten to put the last batch of turnovers in the freezer. She heard rustling that she thought was rats, until she switched on the light. Mike and the girl with the long legs were scrambling up off a blanket they had spread on the floor, both in a state of serious undress.

'Oh!' Tonia turned and fled out the back door to the parking lot.

Mike followed her a few moments later, blushing, barefoot, and buttoning his shirt. 'Ton ... I mean, Miz Shulman ... I'm awful sorry. We had no right being here.'

Tonia was too embarrassed to answer.

'I know it wasn't right. You've been real fair with me. It was nice working for you. I'll just get my stuff.'

'What are you talking about?'

'You're going to fire me, aren't you?'

'What are you, crazy? Why on earth would I fire you?' she almost shouted. 'I'm not angry, Mike,' she said more softly and put a hand on his forearm. 'Just embarrassed. It's none of my business.' What I am, she thought, is jealous. Her own bed was pitifully unrumpled each morning.

She changed to a matter-of-fact tone of voice and asked, 'Did I leave a sheet of turnovers out?'

'Yeah, but I wrapped 'em up and stuck 'em in the freezer.'

'Well, then, that's all I wanted to know. I'm sorry that I embarrassed you and your friend. I'll see you tomorrow.'

The incident forced her to face how empty her own life had become. She went home each evening after closing up, showered, and collapsed into bed to read for a few minutes before falling asleep. On rare occasions, she went downstairs to watch a TV movie with Julie-Kerri-Sally. She slept through most of her Sundays, but as the weather got warmer, she began driving over to Lake Michigan to walk the beach or stroll through the shops in Saugatuck. Everywhere she went she was surrounded by couples holding hands. She had no social life. Some Friday evenings she took the long way home and drove past Temple Emanuel. She parked and watched the Jews coming out of services there, wishing one another Good Shabbes. She knew that she should join their community. That would be the natural thing to do. Hope to meet a nice Jewish boy. She couldn't explain to herself why she always drove away. She had no friends. The only people she talked to were Mike and Mr. Whalen, who had made a habit of stopping by for coffee every Monday morning, and, to her great relief, was never inappropriate. But each conversation with him was an effort. She found herself watching the news on Sunday evenings, in search of topics she might discuss with him.

She did have a slowly swelling bank account. If the bakery continued to do well, within a year she would have enough money to make a down payment on a house. She lay in bed at night planning the furnishings she would buy, imagining a beautifully set table. The notion of who might sit down at that table to share a meal with her was becoming more elusive. Amos haunted her in the dark. She couldn't imagine feeling again the way she had about him. But Amos was lost to her. Probably married to one of his blondes by now.

It was already her second summer in Michigan, and Mike insisted that she spend the late afternoon and evening of the

Fourth of July with his family, having a picnic and watching the fireworks.

'It's kind of your parents to invite me, but I was going to go house-hunting that day.'

'Won't be no one home to hunt. Anyway, if you're gonna be an American, you gotta celebrate Independence Day. My brother Pete will be there, but don't think we're trying to fix you up or anything. He's got a girl. Not that you'd be interested in a jerk like him.'

So she found herself standing in a field by a stream, helping Mike unfold and spread out three blue and green plaid blankets.

'Here,' Mike's mother, Mrs. Knoft, said and handed him a white plastic tablecloth. 'Spread this over that blanket under the tree. Set the cooler next to it, nice and level, and then you can get out the lemonade and set it right on top, use it for a table.' She was a small woman with watery blue eyes, tight blonde curls, and buck teeth. She wore green plaid pedal pushers and a white shirt that had a collar and short sleeves made of the same fabric as her pants. The black plastic frames of her eyeglasses were studded with rhinestones. 'Tony, you just sit yourself down on one of those other blankets. You're our guest. Pete,' she addressed Mike's older brother, 'get the napkins and cups out of that brown paper bag.'

Pete was small and delicate and bore no resemblance to big boxy Mike. Tonia wondered if one of them had been adopted. Tonia did as commanded and sat watching the Knofts' scruffy gray terrier snap at butterflies.

Mrs. Knoft set out plastic plates and platters of fried chicken, potato salad, coleslaw, and frosted brownies. 'All right, I guess we're ready for grace.' She looked at her husband.

Mr. Knoft was a healthy-looking blond man, as silent as his wife was talkative. He mumbled a lengthy grace to 'Our great and only Lord Jesus', filled his plate, wolfed down his food, and hid behind a newspaper. Tonia paled when she noticed the headlines on its inside pages. Tensions along Israel's border with Egypt had heightened. Mines, sniping, burning fields. The Israel

342

Defense Forces had launched reprisals, some of which had escalated into full-scale battles. Why didn't her mother have a telephone? How could a country that had won a war against five armies be incapable of installing simple phone lines? She forced the picture of Natan and Amos in uniform out of her mind. Tonia tried to get away with smiling and nodding at whatever Mrs. Knoft, Mike, and Pete said. The Knofts, however, made valiant attempts to draw her into the conversation.

When Mike asked his brother where his girlfriend was, Pete replied that she was spending the day at her parents' cottage, on a lake in the Irish Hills. Then Pete turned to Tonia to ask, 'Did you do much water-skiing when you were a kid?'

Tonia almost burst out laughing. Should she tell them about washing once a week using a cup of trucked-in water?

'No. We didn't have that in Israel,' she said.

'So what did you do on your vacations?' Mrs. Knoft asked.

Tonia paused, thinking. She couldn't remember anything that would qualify as a vacation. 'My father used to take us on hikes,' she said. 'He'd choose a chapter of the Scriptures, and we'd walk to those places, see where the story happened.'

'Doesn't that sound fascinating.' Mrs. Knoft turned away, busying herself clearing up.

After each scrap of stilted conversation, Tonia felt her throat constrict. These were nice people; why was it so hard to find anything to say to them?

'Mike ...' Mrs. Knoft made conspiratorial signals to her son, 'could you get the ... you know ... from the car?'

The 'you know' turned out to be a large decorated birthday cake covered with candles.

'Surprise!' Mike set the cake down in front of his father.

'Ain't my birthday.'

'Well, it is too, dear. Day after tomorrow. We wanted to celebrate it when we're all together.'

Mr. Knoft rolled his eyes, blew out the candles, and cut the cake. Mike and Pete presented him with a new power drill. Then he opened the gift from his wife.

'What the hell is this? An electric bath mat? You trying to kill me?'

'Don't be silly, dear, it's for Spike. It's just the best thing. It's called a Woofwarmer. You plug it in, and it gets nice and warm for him, like a heating pad. It'll keep him off the furniture. I saw it in a magazine and ordered it, all the way from California.'

'Ain't that swell,' Mr. Knoft said and tossed it aside. 'You should have given it to the dog for his birthday.' Then he turned to Tonia. 'Looks like you people are really going at it over there.' He nodded at the newspaper.

'Yes, it seems so,' Tonia replied and moved to get up. 'I think I left my chapstick in the car,' she said. 'I'm going to go see.'

'You don't have to go talking to her about wars,' Tonia heard Mike say as she moved away. 'Her father was killed in the first war they had over there.'

'Well, that's sad.' Mrs. Knoft sniffed and then added with a wave of her hand – which Tonia couldn't see but could hear in the tone of her voice – 'But those people are used to it.'

Tonia tried to keep her stride and pretend she hadn't heard, but she couldn't help turning her head. Her eyes met Mike's for a fleeting instant before he looked down.

'Ma ...' was all he managed to say.

Later Tonia and Mike went for a walk along the stream.

'She didn't mean anything by it,' Mike said.

'I know,' Tonia replied. But she didn't. She would have liked to ask Mrs. Knoft who 'those people' were. Jews? Israelis? Anyone who wasn't American? And how did anyone get used to having their father killed? All she said to Mike was, 'Let's talk about something else.'

'Okay. There's something I been wanting to ask you ever since I started working for you. What do you do for fun?' he asked.

'Fun?'

'Yeah, fun. Having a good time. Ever hear of it? Doing something you enjoy.'

'I don't know if I can explain it – your life has been so different from mine. All I want to do is make a life some place I can feel safe. That's what I will enjoy, and the bakery is the way I can get it. So I guess that's fun for me.'

'You're burying yourself in that place.'

'Hard work will get me a real house, with a yard and trees.'

'You could spend the next twenty, thirty years paying off a house like that. That's one hell of a lot of popovers. What do you need a house so bad for? What's wrong with renting a nice apartment? No mortgage, no upkeep. You could drive a swell car, take trips, buy clothes. What are you going to do all alone in a big empty house?'

'My family will come eventually,' Tonia said.

Somewhere inside she knew that they never would, but she still had to have that house.

CHAPTER FORTY-SEVEN

In November Tonia registered with three realtors and spent her Sundays and some late evenings viewing properties. They showed her several houses that she could have afforded, but none of them felt right.

Her life changed little. Julie-Kerri-Sally became Julie-Mary Gay-Chrissie. She continued to put in long hours at the bakery and to be without friends, other than Mike who took her out for a drink every other Thursday night. On one of these occasions he asked, 'for personal reasons', to borrow $400. The next day when they were closing up, she pressed a wad of bills into his palm. He flushed and started to say something, but Tonia squeezed his hand shut around the money.

'It's okay,' she said and turned away. 'I don't need an explanation. Did you switch off the oven?'

A week later, he tossed the money onto the counter next to the register and shoved his hands into his pockets. 'I guess me and Lynnie are getting married.'

'Congratulations.' Tonia tried to sound elated, though Mike looked far from it. 'I'm so happy for you.'

'Thing is, I got to give you my notice.'

'Oh.'

'My Dad's getting me in at Steelcase,' he said. 'Gotta make more money.'

Tonia paled. Now she wouldn't have even him.

'Well, it's still wonderful news.' She gave him an awkward hug. 'I'm sad to be losing you, but I knew you wouldn't stay here forever.' She pulled away and sighed. 'I never could have managed without you.'

'Well, I'd say you got things going pretty good now.'

'Yes.' She looked around, pleased.

'There's this girl I graduated with. Kerrie Beth Schumacher. She's looking for a job. Real nice girl. Dependable and all.'

'Do you think she's going to want to make deliveries on her bicycle?' Tonia asked.

'Sure. I told her about everything I do here. Long as you don't need any more freezers moved around, she's got no problem with any of it.'

'All right. Tell her to come see me. But I bet she won't be as much fun as you.'

He grinned and shook his head. 'That'd be a safe bet. Kerrie Beth's Dutch Reform.'

'What's that?'

'You been in Grand Rapids all this time and don't know what Dutch Reform is?'

Tonia shrugged.

'It's a religion. They don't drink or play cards. I don't think they're even allowed to drink Coke or coffee. Too stimulating.' He hesitated before continuing. 'And you know why they won't make love standing up?'

Tonia's face went blank.

'Neighbors might see them and think they're dancing.'

Her expression stayed frozen another moment before she grinned. 'That's a joke, isn't it? Because they're not allowed to dance.'

'Yes, Tony, that was a joke.' He shook his head in mock despair with her. Then he punched her in the arm. 'I'm going to miss you.'

At Mike and Lynnie's wedding Tonia saw a young man with nice eyes, the first to catch her attention in all the time she'd been in America. She grabbed Mike's arm and asked who he was.

'Over there by the bar? In the blue jacket? That's my cousin Jack. But forget it, Tonia. Jack's queer.'

'I don't see anything strange about him.'

'Not strange queer. Queer queer.'

Her expression did not change.

'Likes guys,' he said slowly.

'Oh.'

She went home alone again. She lay on her bed and imagined she could feel herself shriveling up.

Tonia found her house in the fall of 1954. She barely listened to the realtor. She cared not in the least that it had a remodeled kitchen, new shingles on the roof, and double-glazed windows. He could have told her there were three varieties of snakes in the basement; she still would have bought it. It reminded her too much of the house in her picture. It was a two-storied Colonial of light gray brick, one side of it covered with ivy. It had good solid lines. Gracious, but unpretentious. No Greek columns. No circular gravel drive, fishpond, or fountain. A chimney and woodpile at one side proclaimed the existence of a fireplace. A flowering hedge surrounded the yard, affording privacy.

The front door opened into a small white-tiled hallway with a coat closet and antique boot box. Thick red carpeting covered the stairs that led to the second floor. To the left was the spacious living room, carpeted in beige and brown shag. The matching wallpaper had bright accents of red, and a red velvet cushion covered the seat in the bay window. That window had been made for Leah. Tonia could imagine her mother perched there, reading a book or looking out on the garden.

To the right were a half-bath, kitchen, and dining alcove, paneled in wood and brick face and accented with tasteful touches of brass. At the back of the house, tucked behind the stairs, was a room so perfect Tonia gasped when she stepped into it. The back wall was glass from floor to ceiling and looked out over a flower garden and the enormous willow tree that shaded a picnic table and hammock in the backyard. Bookshelves and built-in cabinets covered the walls on each side of the room, and the wall facing the window housed the fireplace.

A circular wooden table surrounded by four leather chairs stood on one side of the room. A plush couch, easy chair, and two upholstered footstools graced the other. They were covered in a bright, flowery fabric – red, blue, green, orange, and yellow on white. Tonia would never have chosen anything quite so flamboyant, but thought it was perfect. Before she had seen the rest of the house, Tonia agreed to pay their asking price. Her one condition was that the sale include the furnishings of that room, even the painting of the beach scene that hung over its doorway.

She sauntered through the rest of the house as if she already owned it. Upstairs were three bedrooms and two more bathrooms. A tiny efficiency apartment nestled over the two-car garage. The finished basement held a new washer and dryer set, also included in the sale. Tonia had no doubt that this was the one. This was the home where her family would join her.

Her mind raced ahead. Once they came, she would open a second bakery and then a third, for Leah and Rina to run. Grand Rapids had several small colleges where Natan could teach. They would attend services at Temple Emanuel together.

The realtor called the owners and Tonia wrote a check for the down payment.

On a snowy afternoon in January, Tonia left Kerrie Beth in charge of the shop and took possession of her new home. The realtor met her at the door and handed her the keys and two gifts from his agency – a bottle of red wine and a wide snow shovel with a red ribbon tied around its handle. When Tonia was finally alone in the house, she lay down on the living-room carpet and fanned her arms and legs the way she had seen children make angels in the snow. It was so soft. So luxurious. She got up and swirled her way out to the perfect room at the back, singing 'On the Street Where You Live'. She flopped down on the couch and hugged herself, wishing she had a corkscrew for the wine. Then she hopped up the stairs to her rendition of 'Wouldn't It Be Lovely' and danced her way around each of the bedrooms. She had done it. She had really done it. Her own private bathtub. A glistening tiled shower. A willow tree; she owned a house with a willow tree.

On her way back to the bakery, she stopped to buy bubble bath. When she got there, she called the furniture store to arrange for them to deliver the queen-sized bed she had ordered for the master bedroom. Her next call was to Michigan Bell. When they asked her what day next week she would like her phone installed, her mouth fell open.

'Ima,' she wanted to shout. 'Look at this country. Life doesn't have to be impossible. Next week. They're coming next week!' People in Israel waited years for a telephone.

Mike helped her move her things that Sunday. She had few belongings and didn't really need him, but it was nice not to be alone. She hung her few skirts and blouses in the enormous walk-in closet and liked the way it looked, almost empty, waiting to fill up, to accommodate her new life.

Every night when she came home from work, she floated through the house, unable to believe it was hers. And every night she took a bath.

CHAPTER FORTY-EIGHT

The rest of that winter and early spring passed in a blur. Tonia made a nodding acquaintance with her neighbors. She got a library card and swallowed two or three books a week. She learned to appreciate the noise the television made. When she could leave the shop before dark, she went for long walks and watched the sailboats that began to venture onto Reeds Lake. She kept herself busy with projects for the house – planning the garden, stocking her kitchen with shiny pans and gadgets she never used, sewing curtains for the bedrooms.

Loneliness caved in upon her.

She tried hard to convince herself that she loved Sunday mornings. She waved and smiled at whatever neighbor happened to be in their yard when she stepped outside to pick the *Grand Rapids Press* off the front porch. Then she padded into her beautiful little glass-walled room carrying a turquoise mug of steaming coffee. She worked the Jumble puzzle and seldom read more than the headlines. She often glanced at her watch to discover that she had let the entire morning waste away, while she sat and stared out the window, daydreaming.

Tonia ran the same scenarios through her mind, over and over. The way she would fix up the little apartment over the garage for her mother or Natan, whichever of them wanted it. Driving around together to find the best location for the new bakery Leah would manage. Serving her family their first meal in America, on her shiny new dining table. Tonia could spend hours fretting over the menu. Chicken or beef? Maybe steaks on the grill? Or would soup and salad be more appealing after the long trip? She would have to go to Detroit for kosher meat. She clipped local travel articles out of the paper and planned the places she would take them – Saugatuck, the lighthouse at Ludington, Sleeper State Park. Maybe they would even rent a cottage on Higgins Lake. Drive across the state to Dearborn and spend a day at Greenfield Village.

The letters she received from her mother were short and blunt – Tonia's house sounded lovely, but it was time she realized that a house was not a home. Any family news, such as Rina being pregnant again, was added in a by-the-way tone of voice, as if Leah hardly expected it to be of any interest to Tonia.

The warmer the weather got, the more unbearable being alone in her house became.

Sometimes, during the slow afternoon hours, Tonia left Kerrie Beth in charge of the bakery and slipped out to stroll down the sidewalk, past the other shops. Bright flowered drapes covered the last tiny storefront at the end of the mall before the super-market, and Tonia had more than once paused to stare at the sign on its door – Dr. Julia Meyers, Individual, Couples, and Family Therapy. One day the door opened and a gray-haired woman in a navy blue suit came out. Tonia recognized her – she came into the bakery for coffee and pastry almost every morning. She always sat alone and always smoked two cigarettes, lighting the second off the butt of the first. Except for the cigarettes, she re-minded Tonia of Leah. Hair swept up and back. Same soft eyes. Same kind smile.

'Hello.' The woman glanced up at Tonia. 'Nice day today.' She turned back to fit her key into the lock.

'Hi,' Tonia said.

The woman locked the door and turned to move away.

'Excuse me ...' Tonia said to her back.

'Yes, dear?'

'Are you Dr. Meyers?'

'Yes, I am. Were you looking for me?'

'Not really. I was just taking a walk, but ... I've noticed your sign before.'

'Do you have time now?' Dr. Meyers asked. 'Or do you need to get back to your bake shop?'

'I guess I could ...'

'Why don't you come in then?' Dr. Meyers unlocked the door again and switched on the light. 'Please.' She held the door and motioned for Tonia to follow her in, nodding at a love seat and two armchairs arranged around a small round table.

Tonia seated herself on the love seat. She felt ridiculous. What was she going to say to this woman?

Dr. Meyers strode to the desk at the back of the room, picked up a box of tissues, and came back to set it in the center of the table. 'Crying is not mandatory,' she said with a smile, 'but I've found it pays to keep them handy.' Then she seated herself in one of the armchairs across from Tonia.

Tonia grinned and sat back in her chair.

'You have a sense of humor.' Dr. Meyers nodded and smiled again. 'I love your accent. Where are you from?'

'Israel. I hope you don't mind if I ask ... are you Jewish?'

'Do you need me to be?'

Tonia jiggled her right leg and studied her fingernails. 'Not really. I was just asking.'

'Why don't we leave me out of this? For now, anyway. I promise to answer your question – if you need to know – but first let's see if we can figure out what brought you here.'

'You do talk, don't you?' Tonia raised her gaze.

Dr. Meyers shook her head, looking amused. 'I have been known to string together a coherent sentence.'

Tonia blundered on. 'I mean, you say what you think. Express an opinion. You don't just sit there going "Mmm ..." and repeating everything I say and asking me how that makes me feel.' Tonia leaned forward. 'The truth is, all I need is someone to talk to. Like a friend. If I had any friends, I wouldn't be sitting here. But I guess I'm willing to pay someone like you to pretend to be my friend. By the way, how much does this cost?'

Dr. Meyers stared at the wall over Tonia's head for a very long time. Then she sighed. 'I suppose I could use a new friend myself,' she said at last. 'I think I can let you have this first session for a cup of coffee and a slice of that killer strudel you sling.' She lowered her eyes to Tonia's face. 'We'll see about what happens after that. You say you have no friends?'

To her own mortification, Tonia burst into tears. Dr. Meyers leaned forward, pushed the tissues across the table, and waited. Sobs convulsed Tonia and then she slumped back, exhausted.

'How about answering a question for me?' Dr. Meyers said. 'What is the one thing that is disturbing you the most? One thing. Think about it for a few minutes while I make us some tea.'

When she came back with the tea, Tonia said, 'I don't like myself. I used to, but I don't any more.'

'Why not?'

'I hate my life. The way I'm always alone.' Tonia looked away, avoiding Dr. Meyer's eyes. 'After I bought my house I was so excited about how easy it was to get a telephone installed. I mean, in Israel the waiting list is about three years long. But I was so smart, I came here and got my shiny new telephone.' She looked back to face the doctor. 'But it never rings. Never. In Israel, we used to have to go to one of the shops and stand in line to use their phone. So I came to America where all I have to do is pick up the receiver, and there's my very own dial tone. But I don't have anyone to call. I have this beautiful house, but only one person besides me and the realtor has ever been inside it. I can't stand to imagine someone else seeing how I live, how pathetic I am.'

Dr. Meyers looked puzzled. 'This is the reason you don't like yourself? Because you have become lonely?'

'Not just that ... before I came here, I did a terrible thing.'

Dr. Meyers raised her eyebrows and waited.

'I wanted to come here so badly, I got a man to marry me so I could use his money to open a restaurant. As soon as I had saved enough, I paid him back and divorced him.'

'I see. And he was devastated by the divorce?'

Tonia let a burst of air through her lips, like a horse. 'Hardly. He wouldn't admit it, but I think he was sort of relieved to be rid of me.'

Dr. Meyers shook her head. 'So why does this make you dislike yourself?'

'I didn't mean it was terrible on his account. Oh, I knew, it was a terrible thing to do. Everyone made sure of that. "You

354

can't use people like that, Tonia.'" She leaned forward, mimicking a nagging old woman. 'But all he wanted me for was to cook and clean. And for you know what. If you ask me, he was using me as much as I was using him.' She sat back.

Dr. Meyers sat and waited.

'But there was someone else,' Tonia said in a softer tone of voice. 'Amos. He did love me. Really cared about me. Whenever anyone in my family needed anything, it was Amos to the rescue.'

'And you think you hurt Amos?'

'No ... that isn't it. To tell you the truth, I don't think I was any great loss, even if he did love me. He's better off without me. I mean, look at me. I might as well be a hermit. What kind of wife would I be?'

'I'm sorry, Tonia, I don't understand. So what was this terrible thing you did?'

'I hate myself for what I did to *me*. I'm the one that I hurt!' Tonia looked at the floor. When she spoke again, it was almost a whisper. 'There will never be anyone else like Amos. Not ever. I'm the one I did the terrible thing to. He would have been a Share-a-Leg husband,' she said almost to herself.

'Now you've lost me.'

'I used to have this dream when I was little.' Tonia looked back up at the doctor. 'There was this crippled boy in my class at school. Dov Sharon was his name. One of his legs was way shorter than the other, so he limped and all the kids made fun of him, but I liked him and I felt bad for him. In this dream, I was sitting by a lily pond and a Good Fairy, you know, like in *The Wizard of Oz*, appeared and said she could grant me three wishes. I told her I only wanted one – she should make Dov Sharon's leg better. But she shook her head and said she didn't have that kind of power. She couldn't take life away, or bring it back, or cure sick people. But she could arrange a bicycle or clothes.'

Dr. Meyers smiled. 'That's some dream. Go on.'

'I begged her. Please, please, please. That's all I want. Just fix his leg. Can't you roll all three wishes together? She said she'd have to go ask her boss and she would come back tomorrow. The next day she said there was something she could do for Dov. She could take his crippled leg away – but only if she could give it to someone else. And she could only give it to a person who agreed to accept it. I could have her cure Dov, if I was willing to be a cripple instead of him. Then we could take turns with the leg. You know, pass it back and forth. But if he refused to take it back, I would be stuck with it forever.'

'That's some test of trust.' Dr. Meyers shook her head. 'So what did you do?'

'Woke up. But ever since then, every couple I see, I look at them and wonder if they are a Share-a-Leg couple.'

'Do you know many?'

'I don't think there are many in the world. My parents were.'

'And this Amos fellow, you think he would have made a Share-a-Leg husband?'

'For sure.'

'Is he married?'

'No.'

Dr. Meyers thought for a while, lips pursed, while Tonia waited for her to say something. Then she leaned forward and stared into Tonia's face. 'Okay. You're not paying me, so I'm not your therapist. So I'm going to talk to you like a friend. Like a mother. I'll say what I'd want someone to say to you if you were my daughter. What the hell are you doing here, moaning and pissing to me? Go back and get him.'

'That's not possible. He would never forgive me. Never. He'd never take me back. Not Amos.'

'Then he doesn't sound like much of a Share-a-Leg husband to me.'

'You don't understand. I was the one who broke the trust. Anyway, I thought people like you always tell their patients they can never go back. To get on with it. Move forward. Forget the past.'

Dr. Meyers shrugged and sighed. 'There are all kinds of ways to get to where you belong. Forward. Back. Sideways. Trick is knowing where you want to go. One you've figured that out, getting there is usually the easy part.'

Tonia frowned and pinched her mouth and nose together, like a rabbit. 'Yes, I suppose that's true,' she said. 'That's what's wrong with me. I don't know where I want to be. I don't belong anywhere.' She began to cry again, face in her hands.

'You seem to be making a go of it here.' Dr. Meyers ignored her sniffling. 'Why would you want to leave, after all your hard work?'

'I don't want to leave, but I miss my family. And I told you, I don't have any friends. I'm all alone.'

'So find some nice Jewish boy and create a family of your own. Go out and make some friends. Stop feeling sorry for yourself.'

Tonia raised her head. 'If I was paying you, would I get more sympathy?'

Dr. Meyers smiled. 'Why do you think you are so lonely? Why aren't you dating? Going out, having fun?'

'I feel so different from everyone here. My life has been nothing like theirs.'

'You may find that some people are fascinated by that.'

'I don't want to be fascinating. I want to be able to talk to someone without having to explain every little thing. A kibbutz? You lived on a kibbutz? What was that like? Did they really take all your money? Jerusalem? You mean there's a real city called Jerusalem, like in the Bible, with people living in it?'

'What's wrong with people asking questions when they meet someone from another country? If you met someone from Tibet, wouldn't you want to ask all about it? You only have to answer the questions once, and as you get to know these new people, you accumulate common experiences. We don't spend our lives comparing notes on our childhoods. What was on TV last night is more like it.'

Tonia pouted. It sounded so simple. She had often scolded herself with similar words. But stating the obvious didn't seem to help.

'Why don't you tell me a little bit about your childhood?'

Tonia told her about living with Aunt Rivka and Uncle Shmuel, moving to the kibbutz, and dreaming of coming to America. She ended by trying to describe the sting of that Fourth of July picnic, Mike's mother saying 'Oh, those people are used to it' when told that Tonia's father had been killed in the war.

Dr. Meyers sighed. 'There is no shortage of idiots in this world, and you're much too smart to let one thoughtless remark like that get to you, keep you from seeking out other people. But you feel isolated by what you've been through. There are experiences that are so overwhelming, so intense, they create a special bond. No one who was not there will ever understand. You and your family lived through one of those times. But that's no reason you can't become close to other people in a different way. Do any of us understand everything about the people we love? Don't the blind manage to connect with people who can see? We all have huge gaps of understanding with one another. Men and women have a great big built-in one. As do good-looking people and ugly people. Can a tall man imagine what it's like to go through life short? Stop expecting people to understand. Settle for kindness. That's all we have to offer one another.'

Tonia clenched the wadded tissue in her fist. 'I don't think I'll ever feel like I belong here.'

Dr. Meyers chewed on her top lip, thinking. 'Listen to that word, "belong". It doesn't sound like much of a choice. *That book belongs on that shelf. He belongs in jail.* If each of us *belonged* in some specific place, we'd have no free will about where to live.'

Tonia pressed her fingers to her lips for a moment before she spoke. 'You remind me of a teacher we had in high school. He talked sort of like that. According to him, everything is either a fact or a value. He'd say, "Most people don't waste time and energy treating facts as if they were values – trying to decide if they want the sun to come up in the morning, or how much two plus two should be this week. But they do wear themselves out acting as if values were facts. Like trying to find evidence to prove that there is a God. People believe in God because they have chosen to. Period. There isn't any proof."'

'Ah yes, taking the famous leap.'

'Yeah, he used that phrase for other things, besides religion. His favorite example was if you ask some guy why he married his wife, he'll say something like, "Because she's so pretty and smart and I love her red hair". But that's never the last word, not like two and two are four, because you can ask him, "But what about that beautiful woman over there? Why not her?" You can always find somebody smarter and someone with better hair. And in the end all he can say is, "Just because I did".'

'Sounds like a great teacher.'

Tonia smiled. 'Once he climbed up on the table in the middle of class, threw his arms out and shouted, "Embrace the choices you make. That's the secret to happiness."'

'You haven't followed that advice, have you? At least not regarding your choice to leave Israel.'

'No. I thought the hard part was going to be opening the shop and buying a house, but that's been easy. I never expected to feel like such an outsider around all you people who grew up here.'

'I can't see that you have made any effort to feel differently. To make friends and try to fit in. Not even with the Jewish community. You're the one who's kept yourself an outsider. Almost as if you don't want to belong. You know, Tonia, we identify with what we are, but sometimes even more strongly with what we are *not*. Why don't you try being a little less aware of what you are not?'

'Right now what I'm most aware of is not being in my shop.' Tonia stood up and held out her hand. 'This was generous of you. I don't know how to thank you.'

Dr. Meyers rose and took her hand. 'Do one thing for me. Figure out *who* you want to be. Maybe then you'll know *where* you want to be it.'

CHAPTER FORTY-NINE

One evening at the end of October 1956, Mike came into the bakery before closing and plopped the *Grand Rapids Press* down on the counter. 'I bet you haven't heard, have you? There's a war on over there – in Israel.' He pronounced it 'Iz-reel'.

Tonia grabbed the newspaper and read the scanty details it provided. She locked up, leaving the shop in a shambles, and drove home to begin pestering the local radio station. They knew no more than the newspaper had printed. She tried to get through to one of the television networks in Chicago, but couldn't get past impatient secretaries.

She had been warning her mother for months, begging her to come. Nasser had signed an elaborate arms deal with Czechoslovakia. Egypt alone now had four times as many tanks as the Jewish state, and two hundred warplanes to Israel's fifty. Each time the papers reported another border incursion, Tonia wrote a hysterical letter. Leah's replies were always the same: Tonia should be living among her own people where she belonged.

After an hour dialing the international operator, Tonia got through to the only one of Leah's neighbors in Tel Aviv who had a phone. He went to call Leah.

'Tonia, calm down, we're all fine.'

'Where's Natan?'

'In Jerusalem waiting for orders.'

'Oh, Ima, I'm so worried.'

'Believe me, you would be a lot less so if you were here with us. Things always seem worse from far away.'

'Has Elon been called up?'

'He's with a tank battalion, somewhere in the south.'

'And what about Amos?'

There was a short pause before Leah answered. 'As far as I know, he's up north, keeping an eye on the Syrians.'

'Ima, you listen to me. These aren't Arab irregulars. These are real armies. And you know how they've been stockpiling weapons. I can send you all tickets tomorrow.'

'Run away like you, Tonia? Turn my back on everything your father gave his life for? Don't you dare suggest such a thing to me again! Not ever!'

The line went dead.

Tonia couldn't sit still so she went out for a walk. She felt as if she was going to throw up, and her back and ribcage ached from the tension. But she preferred moving about to sitting alone in front of the television. She was lost in images of falling bombs and rockets when she heard someone call out her name.

Mr. Whalen and a woman Tonia assumed was his wife were getting out of a car. He was in a suit and she in a filmy pink dress, apparently on their way to a cocktail party.

'Alice, this is Tonia. Tonia, my wife Alice.' The two women shook hands.

Alice Whalen was a well-preserved and expensively maintained woman in her fifties. She told Tonia how much she enjoyed the pastries Bill brought home.

'I've been thinking about you all day,' Mr. Whalen said. 'Ever since I heard what's going on over there. Have you been able to contact your family?'

'Yes, I spoke with my mother about an hour ago.'

'It must be awful hard living over there,' Alice said. 'Bill's told me about your father. It's so sad, what happened to him. You can't help but wonder how different things might have been for your family, if he hadn't taken you to a desolate and dangerous place like Palestine.'

'Oh, things would have been quite different,' Tonia heard herself saying. 'If my father hadn't taken us to that desolate place, we would have been forced into a cattle car with a hundred other Jews, ridden three days without food or water, and then been stripped, gassed, and gone up in smoke. Like my grandparents and all my aunts and uncles and cousins. That's what would have happened to us, if not for my father.'

The Whalens stared at her in stunned silence.

'I'm sorry,' Tonia mumbled. 'I don't know what made me say that. I know you were trying to be ...'

'It's all right,' Alice said, and continued after a long pause, 'Bill, why don't you go on in without me? I'll be there in a minute. I think I'll walk a little ways with Tonia. Get some fresh air before I go in there with all those smokers.' She took Tonia's arm and led her away.

'I am sorry,' Tonia apologized again. 'I guess I'm just on edge.'

'Of course you are. You didn't offend me, dear,' Alice said. 'You know, that first day you got off the bus in Grand Rapids, Bill came home and told me about you. That you had come from over there. He has so much admiration for what your people have accomplished, after all they suffered. He thought you ... that you might have survived one of those camps. He so wanted to help you, if he could. You see, Bill was over there in the war. He volunteered, but he was too old to fight, so he served as a communications officer. But he went into Bergen-Belsen with Eisenhower. He's never forgotten the things he saw.'

So the mystery of Mr. Whalen's incredible kindness was solved. Tonia did not appreciate it any less, but felt unsettled. She was his adopted pet Jew, the cynical side of her sneered. But she knew that was unfair. He was a good man who felt helpless in an evil world.

'He was very kind,' Tonia said. 'It meant a lot to me. Especially that first day, when I got off the bus, all alone.'

'He wanted to do more. But he worried that you might ...' She stopped walking and turned to look at Tonia. 'Well, you know, that you might think he had other intentions.'

'Oh no,' Tonia lied. 'I never thought that.'

The fighting was over in a week. Another phone call to her mother assured Tonia that Natan, Elon, and Amos were unharmed.

She could hardly believe the reports on the news. The Jewish state had survived another full-scale war. Her relief and joy was tinged with frustration. Now it would take them even longer to come to their senses.

It began to be difficult for her to get up in the morning and drag herself to the shop. She thought of going back to see Dr. Meyers, but what would be the point? She was a nice lady, but couldn't tell Tonia anything she didn't know. There was no place on earth she truly wanted to be.

CHAPTER FIFTY

A month had passed since the end of the Sinai Campaign.

Amos Amrani sat in a parked rental car, a dozen yards up the street from Tonia's house in Grand Rapids, Michigan, waiting for her to come home. He had spent the past three days watching her, as he sat chain-smoking in the car. Her Rambler turned up the street, and he glanced at his watch. She was predictable. She arrived home between 8:00 and 8:30 each evening, after a long day of work.

She pulled into the driveway and got out to open the garage door. She wore a flared gray skirt and matching sweater, dark-tinted nylon stockings, and low-heeled pumps. She had her hair pulled back in a tight bun. She was still slender, but her gait had lost its girlishness. She drove the car into the garage and reappeared when she yanked on the rope to pull the garage door shut.

She lived in a big house in a nice neighborhood, like she had always said she would, but he had seen no sign of a social life. No sign of a man. She had never mentioned one in her letters home, which Leah left lying around where Amos was bound to see them.

He lit another cigarette and watched the pattern of lights going on and off in the house. He could imagine her nightly routine. A light dinner in front of the blue haze of the television, a half-hour of wandering about straightening up an already overly tidy house, and an hour of reading in bed, before the upstairs light went out.

He again tried to talk himself into driving straight to the airport and leaving. It made no sense. She was no longer the charming girl of fifteen who had captured his imagination. She was twenty-six years old, had callously married a man she cared nothing for, and just as callously divorced him. She had run out on her people, and he doubted that she lived as a Jew. Exile could not be more total than Grand Rapids, and it was an exile of her own choosing. Tonia had denied her own feelings and spat upon his. She was ruthless, calculating. She used people.

Rachel had been vehemently opposed. 'She's not for you,' was all his mother had to say. 'She's not for you.'

There were so many reasons for him not to be here. There had been other women who would have made more suitable wives and some whose bodies he had desired. But Tonia Shulman was the only one he had ever wanted both in bed and across the breakfast table.

The light went on in the upstairs bedroom window. He imagined her applying face cream, checking doors, another cup of tea on the bed stand, double-checking doors, turning the bed down just so. And then? What did she think about when she lay there alone in the dark?

His mind went blank. Her bedroom light went out, and he reached for the ignition. What was he doing here? She would not come back with him, and why should he want her to? He must have been out of his mind to come here. He still felt the anger of the day Natan had come to him, hanging his head and shuffling his feet, to tell him that his sister was going to marry that decrepit old lecher with his pop eyes and fish-belly skin. Over the years, he had thought about her less and less. He had been busy running his business, and there was always someone warm and soft, eager to share his bed.

Then the war broke out. Amos hadn't fired a shot. A generation of men younger than him was being blown to bits this time. Amos sat out the Sinai Campaign in an isolated outpost on the Syrian border, with far too many silent hours spent remembering. He sat in his dugout feeling old. He was thirty-one, far past the time to marry and have children.

A radio message informed him that his younger brother Meir had been killed in Sinai. The bodies in the wreckage of his tank had been burned beyond recognition, but the army had retrieved their dog tags. Amos disobeyed orders, abandoned his post, and stumbled about the hills crying until he fell to his knees and rocked back and forth. And at that moment the one person in the world he wanted by his side, her arms around him, was Tonia.

That was when he decided to go get her. He wanted life, not old grudges. A wife he could love. Children. He wanted to live.

So she had made a mistake. A lot of mistakes. Hadn't she paid? She had never lied to him, never led him to believe that she would behave any differently. She must be sorry by now. What kind of a life did she have over there? According to her letters to her mother, all she did was work.

'What's done is done,' Rachel had pronounced. 'You can't turn back time. I know you, Amos. In your heart, you will never forgive her. And she wouldn't come with you anyway. She has her life there. She cared more about having things than she did about you. She won't come back here. And you shouldn't want her to.'

He shivered in the cold November air. Perhaps his mother was right. But one thought haunted him. What if he went home and married one of the nice Yemenite girls Rachel was always inviting over, and then Tonia came back, came to him?

He stubbed out his cigarette, turned the key in the ignition, and headed back toward his motel. He would think about it one more night. Tomorrow he would decide.

CHAPTER FIFTY-ONE

The next day Tonia left the shop earlier than usual. Kerrie Beth may not have been as entertaining as Mike, but she was no less reliable and Tonia trusted her to close up. The flowerbeds in Tonia's front yard were overrun with weeds, and she wanted to get home while there was still enough light to work outside. The garden would soon be covered with snow, but she still felt compelled to take care of it. She pulled on a tattered old pair of trousers and a sweatshirt and went out to kneel in the dirt.

She had been working for about half an hour and was sweating in the chilly air, dirt smeared across her face, when she heard a familiar voice behind her speak in Hebrew.

'Don't you ever do anything but dig around in the ground?'

She froze, then slowly turned and rose. Soft lines creased the sides of his face, but he was the same young boy who had been starring in her dreams for years. She let out a whimper and took a step forward.

Amos pulled her toward him, and she buried her face in his neck. She was shaking, her heart pounding. The scent of him, the warmth of his arms around her brought the first sense of well-being she had known in years. She clung to him so tightly she was afraid she might crush his ribcage. She lifted her mouth to his ear and managed to say his name in a hoarse whisper.

He ran his hands over her back and through her hair before he gently gripped her shoulders and pushed her away so he could look into her face. Then he bent to kiss her. She hadn't showered, her hair was uncombed, and she wished she had brushed her teeth, but she soon forgot about all that. Her body melted into his. She had come home. This was where she belonged, in his arms. Her place wasn't in Israel or in America. It was wherever Amos Amrani was. In an instant, she relinquished her childhood dreams. Amos would not live anywhere but Israel, so Israel it would be. No enormous, well-lit supermarkets. No clean public restrooms. No milkman. No hot baths every day. But she would be Amos Amrani's wife. The woman Amos Amrani loved and shared his life with. The mother of Amos Amrani's lovely children. Dr. Meyers had been right. Tonia at last felt sure of who she wanted to be. The rest was easy.

They kissed for a long time, and Tonia leaned away to take his hand. 'Come inside.'

He nodded. 'Nice house.'

Tonia turned and searched his face. Was he being sarcastic?

'You did everything you said you would,' he said.

She realized that he had no way of knowing where her thoughts were racing – and that she had no reason to assume he had come for her. That he wanted to marry her. But what else could Amos Amrani be doing in Grand Rapids, Michigan?

'Yes, I did,' she said. 'But I didn't realize how empty my wonderful house would be without you. I was so excited the day I got the key to it, but ever since I've felt so lonely.'

'Any Bedouin can tell you – you don't comprehend the reality of the desert until you reach a mirage.'

She opened the front door and led him to the glass room. Her heart began thumping harder. The queen-size bed was a staircase away.

'This is my favorite place,' she said and turned to face him. Then she couldn't help throwing her arms around him. 'Oh God, Amos, you have no–'

His mouth found hers again, and they moved toward the couch.

She pulled back to look at him. What had brought him here? What had happened after all this time? What had made him able to forgive her? If he had forgiven her.

'Is your mother all right?' she asked.

'Yes. That is, her health is good. But we've had another funeral. My brother Meir.'

'Oh,' Tonia cried out. Poor Rachel. The third child she had lost to violence. How could she bear it? Tonia felt ashamed of the part of her mind that couldn't help regarding Meir's death as a kind of guarantee for Amos. Rachel couldn't lose another child. It was unthinkable. Amos would always be safe. His family had sacrificed far more than their share.

Tonia took his hand. 'I'm so sorry, Amos. I wish there was something I could do for her. For you. I can't imagine that kind of grief. She's such an amazing woman. Was he killed in the war?' she asked.

'Yes. His tank took a direct hit. At least they didn't suffer. A lot of guys were trapped alive in burning tanks, but Meir and his crew never knew what hit them.'

Tonia squeezed his hand, and they sat in silence for a moment.

'I'm going to get something to drink,' she said and rose. 'Are you hungry?'

'No, but coffee would be good.'

He was standing by the window staring out at her back yard when she returned with a tray – coffee, Coca-Cola, and a bowl of fruit.

She set it on the table, and they seated themselves in the leather chairs.

'It is a nice house,' he said, leaning back and stretching, lacing his fingers across the back of his neck. 'You've done well for yourself.'

Tonia watched his face. This must have been so hard for him, coming here. He had taken the first step. She had to do the rest. She took a sip of coffee and then leveled her gaze at Amos over the brim of her cup.

'Amos, will you please take me back to Israel and marry me?'

She watched him relax and his beautiful smile slowly spread across his face. It was all right. He did want her. She said a silent thank you to God and promised to go back to keeping kosher and observing the Sabbath. Anything, so long as she could have Amos. Tonia set down her cup and leaned back to let out a long breath. Her body felt limp. She longed to shower and drag him to the bed upstairs.

He lowered his arms and leaned toward her. 'How long will it take you to sell everything?' he asked.

'I don't know.' She glanced around her perfect room and felt a sharp pang. Then she looked back into Amos's dark eyes. Her mother was right. A house was nothing but empty walls. She wanted Amos. She wanted her mother. And her brother and sister. She returned his smile.

'Amos.' She paused and looked down at her hands. 'I didn't think you would ever forgive me. Didn't think you would ever speak to me again.'

'Neither did I.'

'So what happened?'

He cupped his hands and stared at them before answering. 'People we love are taken from us. Like that.' He flicked the fingers of one hand. 'There's nothing you can do. They're just gone. You always thought you'd have another chance, see them again, talk to them again. And then they're gone. So the ones God leaves here with us – we don't have to push them away. Even if they made some mistakes ... did some things ... When someone dies ... it makes you think differently about what's important. What's forgivable and what isn't.' He looked up at her. 'You hurt me. But you hurt yourself more.'

'Don't go away.' She reached out to grasp his hand. 'Stay here tonight.'

'I have a motel room.'

'Stay here tonight. Please.'

He reached for his cigarettes. 'Do you have an ashtray?'

She rose and brought him a small glass bowl, and he lit a cigarette.

'I'll go back to my motel,' he said. 'We've waited all this time. I think we should have a proper wedding. Maybe you can't wear a bright white dress, but we *can* have a real wedding night.'

Her mouth fell open. 'Amos, it could take weeks, months, for me to sell the house and business. You want to wait all that time?'

'Yes, I think we should. Start our life together the way it's supposed to be.'

'Okay.' She pouted. 'But stay here tonight. Please. I can make the couch up for you. It's real comfortable. I don't want to spend another night alone in this big house.'

He nodded his consent. 'I want you to know,' he said, 'that you won't have a hard life. Everything has changed. It's not at all like you remember. There's no more rationing, lots of new shops. You'll see. I have a house in Jerusalem, in Old Katamon, and my own business. I'm not rich, but you won't have to work.'

'I don't mind working, and I'd live anywhere with you.' She couldn't help wondering if that was true. A lot of people in Israel still lived in tents. But the sentiment matched her frame of mind.

'I have to check out of my motel room.'

'I'll come with you.'

They stayed up late, discussing whether he could leave his business long enough to stay in Grand Rapids with her while she sold everything and packed. It was after midnight when he stretched and said they should get some sleep.

'Does my mother know you're here?' she asked.

'No.'

'Does anyone?'

'My mother.'

'What did she say?' Tonia asked.

He rubbed the end of his nose. 'You know she always liked you.'

Tonia brought sheets and blankets, reluctantly said goodnight, and went upstairs. She showered and put on her best nightgown and perfume, hoping he might change his mind and climb the stairs after her. He didn't.

She woke at 3:00 am, drenched in sweat, and sat up in bed. Amos? Panic seized her. Had it been a dream? Was he really downstairs on the couch, or would she look for him in the morning and discover she was still alone? She got out of bed and looked out the front window. Was that his car parked out on the street? She couldn't be sure, hadn't paid any attention to what

371

kind of car he was driving. It had to be true. The memory was so real. How could she have made up something like that?

She had to know. She would never be able to fall back asleep. She put on her bathrobe and crept down the stairs.

CHAPTER FIFTY-TWO

Tonia put her head through the doorway into the glass room. There he lay on the sofa, softly snoring, moonbeams casting a gentle light over him. Amos. He really had come for her. She let out a long sigh of relief, causing him to stir.

'Tonia?'

She moved to the couch and knelt at his side, laid her head on his chest. 'I know I shouldn't have come down here. I just ... I was so scared. I woke up and couldn't believe it. I panicked, got afraid it was all a dream. I had to make sure you were here. I'm sorry, for waking you up. Go back to sleep.' She stroked his hair.

He turned on his side and pulled her onto the couch, her back to him. He tucked the blanket around her and kissed her neck.

'Amos.'

'What?'

'We have to stay here anyway while we make all the arrangements. Why shouldn't we have this time together? Like a honeymoon. Who cares if it's before the wedding?'

He didn't reply, and she thought he had fallen asleep until he moved slightly.

'You know what it's going to be like when we get back to Israel,' she continued. 'Your family, my family, you'll have to work all the time. Bombs will go off. War will break out. We'll never have time like this together again.'

There was no response for a long while; then he turned her toward him and kissed her. He pulled her nightgown over her head and began making love to her. She happily surrendered, let him turn and twist her any way he pleased. He touched her in places and ways that would not have occurred to her, but she willed her startled body to relax. This is Amos; he can do anything he wants. At first she murmured things like 'I love you, don't ever leave me, I want you forever,' but gradually her words grew less coherent. She longed for him to speak back to her, but he said nothing. He did lift his upper body several times, so he could look into her face and smile. They fell into each other's arms, exhausted, but after a short while he gently lowered her to the floor and began all over again on the carpet

Afterwards she propped herself on an elbow and ran her fingertips over his face and torso, amazed by what one human being could do for another. Now Tonia knew what her mother had meant when she said about her marriage to Josef, 'Our bodies were good to one another.'

'I want you to teach me how to please you,' Tonia said, looking dreamily up at the ceiling. 'I love your body. Your back. Your legs. Your hands. I remember the first time I saw you – that day I got off the bus in Kfar Etzion. Your beautiful back.' She sighed.

When she looked down at him, his features were stone. He said nothing, but she read the accusation in his face. So why had she robbed them of the simple joy of loving one another while they were young? Why had she given him cause for so much anger and resentment? She hadn't gotten off so easily after all. There would be a price to pay.

She sighed again, this time sadly. 'You'd better get that out of your system. I do not intend to spend the rest of my life doing penance. If you can't forgive me for marrying Emil, then you shouldn't have come here.'

'And since you've been here? Has there been anyone else?'

'No. And what if there has?'

'As a golden ring in the snout of a swine, so is a fair woman who lacks discretion.'

'And what about you, holy-of-holies, Mr. Amrani? I suppose you've been in a monastery all this time.'

'That is not a question a modest woman asks.'

His mood seemed to have suddenly changed again. He pulled her to him and she relaxed in his arms.

The first thing she did upon waking early the next morning – after breathing Amos in, stretching, and smiling – was go to the kitchen and dial Mike's number.

'Good morning. I'm sorry for calling at this hour, but I wanted to get you before you left for work.'

'Hey Tony, that's okay. I was up.'

'I'm going back to Israel,' she said in a rush. 'So I have to sell everything. But before I close up, I was thinking you and Lynnie might want–'

'Whoa, what happened? Is your family all right?' Mike asked.

'Yes, they're fine.'

'So why are you going back there all of a sudden?'

'I'm, um, getting married.'

'Married? Where'd you dig up somebody to marry?'

'He's from Israel. Someone I've known a long time. I, uh, just ran into him, and we decided. But, listen, about the bakery – it's been making pretty good money. I'd let you have the fridge and ovens and stuff for what I could sell them for, and that isn't much. You could pay me later. I'm not trying to talk you into it or anything. Makes no difference to me. I just thought you might like to have the option.'

The other end of the line was silent.

'Listen, I've got to go. You talk it over with Lynnie. If you want it, it's yours. I'd rather give it to you than close it down, after all that work.'

'It's a good offer. We'll have to think about it. And congratulations to you. I was getting worried you'd never find a sucker willing to get hitched to you. But I hope you are going to watch out for them damn A-rabs.'

After she got off the phone with Mike, she called Kerrie Beth at home.

'I can't get into the shop this morning,' Tonia said. 'Do you think you could open?'

'I can get there on time to open. That's no problem, but I don't know if I can manage all by myself.'

'Oh, sure you can. But if you feel swamped, that's okay, just close up. Put a sign on the door about sickness in the family or something. The only thing that really matters is the standing orders. If you could get those ready and deliver them, that'd be great. I'd hate to lose those customers. If you have to, just close up while you're gone.'

'Sure, I guess I could do that alone.'

Tonia thanked her and sat drinking coffee until it was late enough to call the realtor who had sold her the house. Then, after a breakfast of scrambled eggs and toast, she drove Amos over to Lake Michigan.

'Just look at it, Amos. An ocean of sweet water!' It was a gray November day, but they walked on the beach, arms around each other. Despite the cold, she took him to the House of Flavors ice cream store, which she considered one of America's greatest contributions to western civilization.

Then they drove back to Grand Rapids and walked through the zoo at John Ball Park. After a quick tour of downtown, stopping to watch the diehard fishermen in waders in the Grand River, Tonia stopped by the park at Reed's Lake and started to feel weepy. Everything was so much more beautiful with Amos at her side. Why couldn't she have both? Why couldn't they stay here? She watched him skip a few stones on the water and wondered if she would ever regret this decision. No. There was no better life she could have than one spent with this man. She put her arms around him from behind. This was one choice she *would* embrace. She was going to be the best wife in the world. He would never see anything but a smile on her face. No complaining. No quarrelling or nagging.

'We could get married here, you know,' she said.

'We will be married in Jerusalem, by my uncle, and my mother will be there, and your mother will be there, and you will go to the *mikveh* before the ceremony.'

Tonia bristled. Who did he think he was, bossing her around like a little girl? She might be willing to go to the *mikveh*, the ritual bath required by Jewish law, but she wasn't going to do it because *he* ordered her to. She bit her tongue and said nothing, but they walked back to the car in silence, Tonia's mood spoiled.

The next morning the front bell rang, and she found Mike on the doorstep.

'We'll take it,' he said. 'Here's the first payment.' He handed her a check for $30.

'That's great.' Tonia gave him a hug and a kiss on the cheek.

'And congrats to you,' he said and held out the bottle of Bailey's Irish Cream he was clutching in his other hand.

'Thanks. Come in and meet my fiancé.' He followed her into the kitchen.

'Amos Amrani, this is Mike Knoft.' They shook hands, and Amos looked Mike up and down.

'I'm so pleased that you and Lynnie are going to take over the bakery,' Tonia said.

'Well, I'll tell you, it's nothing we would ever have thought of ourselves, but now that we're doing it, it seems about perfect. I hate working for a boss – there aren't many of them like you around. Lynnie can help out, and we'll keep Kerrie Beth on.' He paused and clapped his hands together. 'So, you're going back over there to Iz-reel.'

'Yes, as soon as I can sell the house. Or at least arrange for a realtor to take care of the sale.' She turned to pick a sheet of paper off the countertop. 'Here, I've written down what I think the appliances would sell for and what the stock of flour and sugar and all that are worth. And there's the address you can send the money to whenever you have it.'

He looked it over and shook his head. 'This is nothing. You sure you aren't stiffing yourself?'

'It's all second-hand.' Tonia shrugged. 'Would you like to join us for coffee?'

She tried to maintain her smile, but couldn't ignore the sad fact that after four years in this city she had no one but this young boy to say goodbye to. And not much to say to him. She glanced at Amos and wondered why in hell he wanted to marry her. She had made such a mess of her life.

'No, thanks. I still got a job to go to.'

377

'If Lynnie has any time today, you might want to send her over to start working together with Kerrie Beth. I've pretty much abandoned the poor girl.'

'I'll do that. It was a pleasure meetin' you, Mr. Amrani.' Mike turned to leave.

'There are a lot of arrangements we'll have to make,' Tonia said to his back. 'Go down to City Hall and sign the municipal taxes over to your name. Change the lease. And the utilities. I have to give Lynnie the recipes, show her how to make everything. And we need to go over the inventory together, check that list, and divide up the cash in the register. As far as I'm concerned, you can take over tomorrow, but we have to draw a line between me being the owner and you.' She wondered if this had been such a good idea. What made her think Mike would know how to run a business? But she shrugged off her concern. That was his problem. She was going to have more than enough of her own.

CHAPTER FIFTY-THREE

The security checks at the El Al counter in New York were
a nightmare, take-off was delayed by two hours, and the in-flight
service was appalling, but Amos was happy – he felt at home. He
flirted with the stewardesses, kicked off his shoes, and settled
back with yesterday's *Maariv*, one of Israel's Hebrew newspapers. Tonia felt as if she had awakened from a bad dream, only
to discover it was real. What have I done? The Middle East? I'm
going back to the Middle East? I gave up my house, my yard.
Peace and quiet. She felt like screaming for them to stop and let
her off.

Amos was soon asleep, and she stared at him – the man she
had made herself dependent upon. He had not shaved well that
morning, and the top three buttons of his shirt were open. He
had grown up a street urchin. He made frequent spelling mistakes, and she did not believe he had ever read a book cover to
cover. He was nothing like the elegant husband of her childhood
fantasies. He would never remember her birthday or their an-
niversary. He would probably never take her out to a restaurant.
He had been at her house for a month and a half and had not
once offered to make *her* a cup of coffee. But she did not believe
any of that would ever change the love she felt for him. For years
she had resisted it. Now it felt as natural as breathing. Now she
was determined to enjoy it. Embrace it.

She closed her eyes, but couldn't sleep. Poor Amos. She
looked at him again. It had been a grand romantic gesture, coming after her, but wasn't he already regretting it? He stirred in
his sleep, and she, the dutiful wife, tried to tuck a pillow between him and the side of the aircraft. He opened one eye and
smiled, and she snuggled up to him.

No one was waiting for them at the airport in Tel Aviv. She
had begged Amos not to tell their families which flight they
would be on. She wanted time to get her bearings and brace
herself. Amos stacked their luggage on a pushcart and wheeled

it through customs. Outside, they piled into a taxi for Jerusalem with five other passengers. Tonia relaxed. It was a beautiful day, and the countryside looked lovely to her, familiar, though changed. More buildings, more paved roads, more lighting. Almost a normal country, if you ignored all the military vehicles barreling down the roads and uniformed soldiers hitchhiking.

They arrived at the taxi stand in Jerusalem, and while Amos unloaded their luggage and hailed another cab, she stood aside hugging herself, taking deep breaths of the cool, clean air. Jerusalem's air. Abba had been right. There *was* something magical about it. She felt dizzy, as she often had lately.

'Are you feeling all right?' Amos asked when he turned back and took her arm.

'Yes. Fine.'

They climbed into the private taxi that would take them home. Tonia stared out the window, hypnotized. She had forgotten how beautiful Jerusalem was, with its buildings of hewn stone. The streets were clear of rubble, most of the shell damage had been repaired, the gardens were green, and trees had been planted.

'Amos, could we drive around for a bit? See the city?'

'Sure.' He seemed pleased with the request.

The driver took them past the Mahane Yehuda market, then wove around toward the Mandelbaum Gate, where the city was divided between Israel and Jordan. The border area, called the City Line, was ugly, marred by wall works, barbed wire, and the scars of snipers' bullets on the buildings.

'Is it safe to drive here?' she asked Amos.

'Safe as it ever was,' he said with a shrug. 'That hasn't changed. Every so often, a Jordanian soldier takes a potshot at someone, we protest to the ceasefire commission, the Jordanians claim it was the isolated act of a lunatic whom they have already locked up, and things are quiet until the next lunatic in line takes aim. But,' he said, 'if you're going to live in this city, you go about your business as if it was safe. And basically it is. The Abu Tor neighborhood is divided by no more than a coil of barbed wire, and Arab and Jewish housewives stand on either side of it, selling each other things and gossiping.'

'How far is your house from the border with Jordan?'

'Five or six blocks.'

The taxi driver cut through Mamilla to Rehavia. Tonia had to admit that the stone homes with their arched doors and windows had a lot more charm than American split-levels and ranch houses. Gray-haired women sat outside on benches, knitting. Younger ones pushed baby carriages. A normal life, perhaps, Tonia thought. She almost asked to drive past the Rozmanns and the Gymnasium, but decided to leave that for another day. They drove to the Old Katamon neighborhood, and she gasped when the taxi stopped and Amos said, 'Here we are.'

His house was on a broad, tree-lined street, and it was enormous. The thick Jerusalem stone was set off by black shutters and grillwork. A low wall of stone surrounded the garden area in front, and a huge tree shaded the windows.

'Oh, Amos, it's a beautiful building. How many apartments are there in it?'

'I have the whole house,' he said, smiling.

'You're kidding. The whole thing? It's all ours?' She leapt out of the cab and through the gate into the dirt yard, whirling around. 'I can't believe it! Amos, it's beautiful. It's really all ours?' She ran back to hug him. She wasn't about to ask him how he had come by it, assuming she would rather not know.

Amos carried their suitcases into the front hall, where the floor was inlaid with mosaic tiles. Tonia peeked through the three doorways that led into large, high-ceilinged rooms that were almost bare of furnishings. The walls were newly whitewashed, and the floors shone. Tonia looked around, her eyes wide as a child's.

'I don't know what to say, Amos. It's so lovely.'

She threw her arms around him again, but his response was restrained. Tonia turned to see what he was looking at over her shoulder – his mother was standing in one of the doorways behind them.

'Oh hello, Rachel, I didn't know you were here.' Tonia smiled shyly. 'It's so good to see you again.' She offered a hand and then leaned forward as if to embrace the little woman, unsure the gesture would be welcomed. Rachel stood straight and her face betrayed no emotion.

'I am surprised to see you also. Welcome. Did you have a good trip?' she asked Amos.

'Yes, Ima.' He bent to kiss her cheek.

Another woman, Tonia's age or younger, hovered behind Rachel. Two small children clung to her skirts.

'Tonia, this is Elia, my brother Meir's widow. And her children, Shlomi and Dvora.'

Tonia pressed Elia's hand and patted both children on the head. Elia looked her up and down with barely concealed animosity. She was darker-skinned than the Amranis, with black almond eyes. Her head was covered with a scarf, and she wore a long embroidered dress. Her features were delicate and Tonia thought her beautiful. Too beautiful.

'Tea is ready. Sit,' Rachel commanded them.

They went into the kitchen and Rachel served strong mint tea, together with cakes and pieces of fried dough. Amos ate quickly, then leaned back and lit a cigarette. 'It's good to be home.'

'Maybe you want to rest?' Rachel asked Tonia, but Tonia felt no warmth in her voice.

'Yes, I think I would,' Tonia said, anxious for them all to go home so she could have Amos to herself.

'Come.' Rachel led her up the stairs, and Amos followed. Rachel opened the door on a spotless room, furnished with a single bed and a small wardrobe.

'It's all ready for you.'

Tonia opened her mouth, then closed it. No point in making a fuss. She would move into the master bedroom with Amos as soon as Rachel and the others left. Rachel turned to leave the room with Amos behind her.

'Amos,' Tonia said and he came back.

'If I fall asleep in here,' she whispered, 'come wake me up after your mother goes home.'

'Goes home?'

'Yes, once we're alone in the house.'

'Tonia, she is home. She lives here.' He said it as if it were the most natural thing in the world, but there was an edge of challenge in his voice.

CHAPTER FIFTY-FOUR

Tonia's mouth dropped open, and her eyes narrowed. 'And Elia? You don't mean that she …'

'She has no one else. Her parents are old and live in a single room. She came to stay with us after Meir was called up. You wouldn't have had me throw her out after he was killed, would you?'

'And it never occurred to you to tell me that all these people would be living with us?'

'It never occurred to me that you would think I would leave my mother in that cold old flat, when I have this enormous house. If *your* mother wanted to live with us, I wouldn't mind. And Elia … Elia slipped my mind.'

'I see. A woman and two small children just slipped your mind.'

'And Aunt Nechama has always lived with us.'

'Aunt Nechama! There's someone *else*?' Tonia glared at Amos, and he avoided her eyes. 'Is that it? Are you sure? We could make the rounds of a few orphanages. How about all of your old neighbors? There's probably room in the cellar for a few of them.'

His face hardened as he set his jaw. 'Why don't you get some rest? I have to get to the office. I've been away too long.'

She hadn't expected him to go off and leave her alone so soon. She threw herself down on the bed and cried into the pillow. What had she done? Once again living with relatives, and not even her own. She would never forgive him. Embrace her choice. She should give his balls a good embrace.

She spent the rest of the day in her room, listening for his return. Rachel's footsteps approached the door a few times, followed by tiny knocks, but Tonia didn't answer. She couldn't. Tonia wouldn't hurt Rachel for the world, and how would she explain her red swollen eyes? Rachel – who had raised seven children in two rooms and taken in her sister-in-law – would never understand how Tonia felt. More hours passed before Amos's heavy, sure tread approached the door. He knocked loudly, but Tonia didn't answer. She rolled over in bed, feigning sleep like a stubborn child. He came in and stood over her.

'I know you're not asleep.'

She pulled the covers up higher.

'All right. I'm sorry. I should have told you. I figured we'd work it out. I can't turn them out into the street.'

'Don't be so melodramatic.' She sat up and hugged her knees. 'We could sell this house and buy three flats. Or divide it up to give everyone some privacy.'

'That's not the way we do things. Families stay together. Elia's children need more than a roof over their heads. They have no father, so they need me around, whether you like it or not. Meir would have done the same for my children. And why should my mother end her days all alone in an empty flat?'

'Oh, Amos.' She put her arms about his neck, craving him. 'I know you think I'm a spoiled brat. I just wanted everything to be perfect for us. I don't need a big house any more. I'd rather live in one room and have you all to myself.'

He sighed. 'I should have thought you had enough privacy in Grand Rapids to last you a lifetime. Why don't you try to concentrate on the advantages? You won't have to do all the housework and cooking by yourself. Our children will have their grandmother around.'

'All right. I'll try,' Tonia said evenly. This was going to be some choice to get her arms around. But she did like Rachel. And she didn't like to cook. She plastered a smile on her face.

'Ima ironed one of your dresses for you. I'm going to take you out for dinner. Just the two of us. Our coming-home celebration. Tomorrow morning I'll put you in a cab to Tel Aviv to see your mother. But before you leave, we'll go to the Rabbinate to register to get married. And Rina has invited us to her kibbutz for the Sabbath. Natan will be there too.'

Tonia couldn't decide if it was a comfort or an annoyance to have someone organize her life for her. She kept the smile on her face and nodded to everything he said.

'Out to dinner' turned out to be one of the little places near the Mahane Yehuda market that served grilled meats and salads to people crammed around tiny Formica top tables. Their conversation was constantly interrupted by people stopping to welcome Amos back, and Amos glanced apologetically at Tonia when one of the men who worked for him pulled up a chair and took out a wad of invoices to show him. Tonia burst out laughing and put her hand on Amos's knee under the table.

'I didn't know it was going to be like this,' Amos said when the man had left.

'I did,' Tonia said. 'It's all right. At least you gave me my time in Grand Rapids.'

And Amos made it up to her when he slipped into her room that night, after everyone else had gone to bed.

The next morning Tonia knocked on the door of her mother's flat.

'Oh, Tonia, Tonia, my baby.' Leah pulled her inside and hugged her. 'Didn't Amos come with you?'

'He had to work.'

'It's so good to have you back home. You have no idea how much I missed you, how I worried about you. Come into the kitchen. I'll make tea.'

The flat was small, but palatial compared to any other living arrangement Leah had ever enjoyed. A living room, a tiny bedroom, a kitchen, and a sun porch – all to herself.

'How did you ever find this place?'

'It belongs to Amos's company. I rent it from him. He sometimes sleeps here on the couch when he has to stay over in Tel Aviv. But I'm planning to move to Jerusalem soon. My work for the Religious Kibbutz Federation often takes me there, and I'd rather be closer to you and Natan. So, tell me everything. It must have been astounding to have him turn up like that.'

Tonia was at first reluctant to discuss her emotions with her mother. Because Leah had disapproved of Emil, she had all but shut Tonia out of her life. Then she had disapproved of Tonia going to Grand Rapids and barely written a letter to her. Now, just because she thought Amos was God's gift, they were supposed to be best friends? Didn't she know that doors that had been slammed shut so often could get stuck that way? But Tonia could not maintain her reserve. She desperately wanted her mother back and soon told her everything.

'And are you happy now?' Leah asked.

'Yes, I am. I really do love him. I made up my mind the instant I turned around and saw him standing there in my yard in Grand Rapids. I want him and will do everything I can to make him happy. To make our marriage work. I know how wonderful he is, how everyone depends on him. He's the most attractive man I've ever seen. But then we got here, and out of the blue I find out he's got a whole tribe of people camped in the house. I mean, his mother, all right, that I can understand, and you know how much I like her. But an aunt *and* a sister-in-law *and* her two kids?'

'Yes, I know. That won't be easy. Didn't Amos tell you about them?'

'No, not a word. And I had planned the dinners I would make for him – the way I would set the table ...'

'And polishing the silverware is your idea of doing everything you can to make a marriage work?' Leah turned disapproving again.

'I should have known you'd be on his side.'

'I didn't know there were sides. I do think it was unfair of him not to tell you. But you have to realize that candlelight dinners are not what make a marriage work. Learning to put up with difficult situations and keep your mouth shut is. Marriage is give and take.'

'I'll say. The women give and the men take.'

'Oh, honestly, Tonia,' Leah said in exasperation. 'Do you have any idea how many girls would love to trade places with you? Girls younger than you, prettier than you, who haven't been married and divorced? You turned your back on a man who loved you. What do you think that was like for him? But he took you back. Went halfway around the world to get you. Not to mention everything he's done for your family. If you don't think Amos Amrani does a tremendous amount of giving, then it's time you opened your eyes.'

Tonia looked at the floor, ashamed. 'I know,' she said, then raised her eyes and smiled. 'I know. So, you finally got the son-in-law you always wanted.'

'I got the son-in-law I think can make you happy. I'll say one thing – I doubt the two of you will ever be bored together.'

'How's Natan?'

'Fine. Finishing his MA. Then he intends to go on for his doctorate.'

'Girlfriend?'

'Not that I know of. He seems to keep pretty much to himself. Been like that ever since the war. He won't talk about it with anyone, but it's almost like he's angry. Especially with Amos.'

'Has it ever occurred to you that the way you idolize Amos might have something to do with that?'

Leah looked startled and then flushed. 'Perhaps there is something to that,' she murmured.

'Ima, why did Abba hate Amos?'

'Oh, part of it was the excuse he used – politics. But Josef would have disliked anyone who expressed an interest in you. No one would have been good enough for his princess.'

'But he seemed to hate him the first moment he saw him – that day Natan brought him to tea. Before Amos had a chance to express an interest in anyone.'

Leah laughed. 'You should have seen the two of you. The way you kept looking and not looking at each other. Only a fool wouldn't have noticed, and your father was no fool. Men are often possessive of their daughters like that.'

'But he liked Elon.'

'That was different.'

'Why?'

'Surely, Tonia,' Leah said and sighed, 'you must have known. You were always his favorite. He didn't even try to hide it.'

When Tonia returned to Amos's home late that afternoon he was still at work. She joined Rachel and Elia in the kitchen, where the radio blared Arabic music.

'Would you mind if I turned it down just a little?' Tonia asked.

Rachel nodded her assent, and Tonia lowered the volume. Elia rose and switched it off with an angry twist.

'How is your mother?' Rachel asked.

'She seems very happy. The apartment Amos rents to her is lovely. She may move to Jerusalem soon.'

'That will be nice for you.'

'You have beautiful children.' Tonia held out an olive branch to Elia.

Elia muttered something in return, but Tonia didn't understand her guttural Hebrew.

'Have some *malawah*,' Rachel said and nudged a plate of fried puff pastry in Tonia's direction.

'No thanks. I had lunch with my mother. And I should start getting dinner.'

'It's made,' Elia said.

'Oh, then I'll set the table,' Tonia said.

Rachel and Elia exchanged glances, as if she had made a strange suggestion. 'No need to do that yet,' Rachel said.

Tonia sat with them for a few minutes, feeling as though she had crashed a party that she didn't want to be at. She excused herself and went upstairs. The moment she walked out of the kitchen, the radio went back on.

CHAPTER FIFTY-FIVE

When Tonia was called to the evening meal she understood why her offer to set the table had been met with such strange looks. Today's supper – and tomorrow's lunch, and tomorrow's supper, and the next day's – consisted of thick spicy Yemenite soup and a pile of pita bread. Elia 'set' the table, plunking down a stack of plastic bowls and a handful of spoons. Then she served the meal, carrying out a large battered aluminum pot and ladling out the soup. Amos ate hurriedly and then lit his inevitable cigarette, using his soup bowl as an ashtray.

Tonia forced some soup down, then excused herself and went back upstairs. So much for *Good Housekeeping*'s hints for being creative with leftovers – you just pour them back into the pot for the next meal. 'Make each meal a romantic adventure', my eye, she thought. After a while, Amos knocked on the door. He sat on the bed next to her and took her hand.

'How are you?' he asked.

'All right.' She forced a smile and curled up so that her head was in his lap.

'Do you want to go to Rina's for the Sabbath?'

'Yes, that would be nice.'

The next morning she lay in bed, unable to think of a compelling reason to get out of it. Aunt Nechama did the shopping and kept the floors spotless. Elia did the laundry and some of the cooking, when she wasn't busy with her children. Rachel did the rest of the cooking. The three of them spent most of their time in the kitchen, laughing and quarreling. When Tonia entered the room, they greeted her politely and grew silent.

Tonia dragged herself out of bed and showered. The radio was blaring again, but Elia switched it off when Tonia entered the room. Tonia sat at the table, and Rachel set a cup of coffee down in front of her.

'I could have gotten that for myself,' she said, flushed. 'Can I help you with something?'

'Not now. Later you can peel some vegetables if you want.'

Tonia took her coffee outside. The bare yard held only a few straggly patches of cooking greens. Tonia sighed, remembering her lush green garden in Grand Rapids. Then she stood up and paced the yard, marking off sections in the dirt. She returned her coffee cup to the kitchen, changed into blue jeans, and took a long walk downtown to Amos's office.

'Can I borrow the keys to your van for a while?' she asked him. 'For about two hours.'

'Okay, but I need it back before two.'

'No problem.'

She drove to a nursery on the outskirts of the city and bought gardening tools, a hose, fertilizer, shrubs, and flower seeds. She unloaded everything at home, returned the van to Amos, and walked home whistling. If you can't beat them, find another game to play, she said to herself.

When Amos got home that night she was out in the yard, muttering curses as she struggled with a stubborn weed. Her face was smudged with dirt, and she had stuck a large clip in her hair to hold it back. She looked up and caught him watching her. The look on his face melted her heart.

'Hi.'

'Hi.' He walked over and put his arms around her.

'I'm all dirty and sweaty,' she protested, but he buried his face in her neck. 'Come and see the beautiful garden I'm making.'

'So you're still a peasant at heart.'

She wanted to show him where she was going to put every kind of flower, but he pleaded exhaustion and went inside. Half an hour later Rachel came out to call her to dinner.

'Rachel, let me show you.' Tonia took the little woman's arm. 'I'm going to put some wisteria here by the wall. It will climb right over it and has those gorgeous little flowers. Then, over here, a big flowerbed. The taller varieties farther back and the little delicate ones along the edge here. I'll move the parsley and coriander around to the back – put in a real spice garden and a vegetable patch. This whole area here will be grass.'

'Grass. Ach. It's nothing but a waste of water. Come in. The soup's getting cold.'

'I don't need the car tonight if you feel like going to see your brother,' Amos said at dinner.

'Won't you come with me?'

'I have a lot of paperwork to do. Anyway, you two haven't seen each other for four years. You should have a lot of catching up to do.'

Natan had taken to smoking a pipe, and he stabbed the table with it whenever he wanted to emphasize a point. When she asked how he was, he replied, 'I got both my degrees with honors. I've already published two articles, one of which I will expand upon for my doctoral thesis. My advisor is quite enthusiastic about it. And I'm teaching a seminar this term.'

Tonia didn't know what to say. Who are you and what have you done with my sweet big brother? she wondered. He sounded just like Emil. 'Do you see Rina often?'

'As often as I can, but it isn't easy to get away. And if you don't have a particular interest in milking cows or growing cotton, a visit there can get pretty tedious.'

Tonia sat and listened to him, sadly remembering the pale young boy with the big eyes who always wanted to take care of everyone. What had happened to him? Tonia had thought he and Amos were still good friends, but Leah told her Natan only worked with Amos when he really needed the money. As soon as he got a student job, he stopped.

'Do you see much of Amos?' she asked.

'No time,' he said, fiddling with some papers on his desk.

She soon made her excuses and left her brother to his research. By the time she got home, Amos had gone to bed. Tonia climbed between her cold sheets, lonely and miserable.

On Friday, Amos and Tonia drove to Tel Aviv to pick Leah up on their way to Ein Tsurim. Leah had insisted upon taking a bus part of the way and was waiting for them at an intersection on the outskirts of the city. It started to rain before they got there, and she stood on the corner with her cardboard suitcase, holding her skirt in the wind.

'You should have let us pick you up at home,' Amos admonished her.

'Nonsense. No harm done. Well, Tonia, how are you surviving your first week back in this godforsaken country?'

'Barely.'

Rina's new kibbutz was in the south of the coastal plain, in an expanse of fields that spread toward purple hills on the horizon. There were no Arab villages in the area, and the roads were safe. Amos pulled into the parking lot, and they walked to Rina and Elon's tiny two-room dwelling. Rina saw them coming up the path and burst out the door. Tonia had forgotten how energetic her sister was.

'Oh, Tonia.' She embraced her sister. 'I'm so glad to have you back. I've missed you so much.'

'You look wonderful, Rina.'

'No, I don't. I look old and fat. But that's all right. The rest of us have to make people like you look even better. You're the one who looks wonderful. Wait till you see the girls. Oranit has been so excited about meeting her rich aunt from America. Hello, Ima. Amos. I guess I have you to thank for bringing her back to us. Elon will be right back. He went to the kitchen for a few things. We can sit here under the tree. Let me take your bags, Ima. You'll sleep on our couch. Tonia, you and Amos and Natan will have our neighbors' apartment. They went to Jerusalem for the weekend. Where is Natan, anyway?'

'He preferred coming by bus – said he was going to be busy with his students until the last minute. But he should be here soon.'

'Amos, can you help me set up this table? Or do you think it's too cold to sit outside? It did drizzle a bit this morning. Oh, well, let's not give in. Look, here comes Natan.'

They all greeted him, and he held out a hand to Amos. 'Good to see you, Amrani. You never look any worse for wear. I suppose it's the physical work. All that fresh air. It's academics like me, rotting away in our libraries, who show the effects of time.'

'Any time you want a job on a crew, all you have to do is ask,' Amos said dryly.

Natan's smile was tight, and he took out his pipe. 'How is business?'

'Can't complain.'

The short, awkward silence was broken by Rina and Leah serving tea. Rina bombarded Tonia with questions about her life in America and graciously accepted the gifts Tonia had brought. How strange, Tonia thought, that it is Rina who is welcoming me back so effusively, without a trace of censure.

Tonia was surprised by how at home she felt at the kibbutz. The familiar melodies of the evening prayer service brought tears to her eyes. She could almost hear her father's voice booming out from the men's section. She spotted a few familiar faces in the dining hall and chatted with old acquaintances. Rina's two little girls were a delight. Elon was a member of the secretariat and entertained them with tales of kibbutz intrigue. And while she couldn't very well make avid love to Amos with her stuffy brother in the next room, she at least had him next to her in bed all night long for the first time since they had left Grand Rapids.

When they awoke the next morning she found Natan already up, sitting in an armchair reading one of his journals.

'We thought you were still asleep,' Tonia said, coming out of the bedroom.

'I can't afford to sleep in. There's never enough time.' He sighed.

Amos came into the living room and glanced over Natan's shoulder.

'Nothing you'd be interested in,' Natan said.

'No, not me. Doesn't have any pictures in it,' Amos said coldly and left for the morning prayer service.

'Natan.'

'Yes, Tonia?'

'Don't you ever – I mean *ever* – look down your nose at Amos,' she said and walked out.

Tonia and Amos were married two weeks later, in the dirt yard of their home. Only their immediate families attended – Natan, Leah, Rina and Elon and their daughters – and about three hundred Yemenites. Tonia finally had an occasion to wear Mrs. Rozmann's beautiful white dress, and the look on Amos's face when he saw her in it had been worth waiting for.

That night Tonia gleefully supervised as another single bed was moved into her room and shoved up against hers.

She continued to keep busy in the garden, though her labors met with scant encouragement. Amos muttered vague comments. Elia snorted in disgust and did nothing to prevent her children from trampling through the flowerbeds. Aunt Nechama thought the fertilizer was laundry powder and soaked a load of wash in it.

Rachel shook her head in consternation. 'But Tonia, there's nothing to eat in it,' she said.

One night Tonia climbed the stairs to find that one of their single beds had been moved out into the hallway. Amos was in the room, lying on the remaining bed, reading a newspaper.

'What's that bed doing out there in the hall?' Tonia asked.

'You, uh, got your menstrual period this morning, didn't you?'

'So?'

'So you know we're forbidden to cohabit until it's been over for a week, and you've been to the *mikveh*.'

'I know that,' she said impatiently. 'What's that got to do with the bed out in the hall?'

'That's how it is with us. The woman doesn't sleep in the same room with the man.'

'Do you mean to tell me that you expect me to *sleep* out there?'

He looked sheepish.

'Well, you can forget that.'

'Tonia, that's the way the Yemenites do.'

'Fine. You're the Yemenite. You go sleep out in the hall.'

CHAPTER FIFTY-SIX

Tonia soon grew bored with gardening and began eyeing the house. Amos's business seemed to be doing well, and Tonia thought he would one day be a wealthy man. He never complained about the things she bought – china to replace the plastic plates, shiny stainless steel pots instead of the battered aluminum ones, thick white tablecloths, good wines, a hi-fi set. But neither did he voice any appreciation of them. He seemed indifferent to material comforts. He watched her shop with an amused smile and continued to wear the same white T-shirts, eat the same simple food, and drive the same old jalopy.

He did have a few specific extravagances of his own. Over the loud protests of all three Yemenite women in the house, he hired a young girl to come in and clean once a week, declaring that his mother had done all the heavy housework she was ever going to do. As far as Tonia could see, the girl spent as much time in the kitchen drinking tea and eating sticky cakes with Rachel as she did cleaning. Amos also spent enormous amounts of money on Elia's children. He had never owned a toy as a child, but their room looked like a store. And though Tonia remained indifferent to fashion, he encouraged her to buy clothes for herself. He loved to see her well dressed, and she did her best to oblige.

Tonia gave up trying to infiltrate the kitchen. She went to her mother's or to a restaurant when she couldn't face another pot of soup with turkey necks or chicken feet in it.

'Amos, are you rich?' she asked one evening.

'I do all right.'

'I mean, do we have money to spend?'

'Most of it's tied up in the business. If cash got tight, there are things that could be sold. Why?'

'I want to buy furniture.'

'What for?'

'What do you mean, what for? Chairs, you know, those things people sit on.'

'We have chairs.'

'I had something post-Russian revolution in mind. And a table that doesn't need a wad of newspaper under the leg. And a nice living room set. And curtains and rugs would make such a difference.'

'How much money are you talking about?'

'I don't know. A few thousand dollars.'

'Are you out of your mind? Who spends that kind of money on furniture? You can get perfectly good stuff at the flea market in Jaffa.'

'Never mind. I'll use my own money. It's not tied up in anything.'

'We agreed that your money would stay in the bank.'

'You agreed. I think that's silly.'

'I am your husband, and I will support you. If you can't live without furniture, buy furniture. I'll find the money.'

The day they delivered Tonia's new living-room couches, Elia's daughter spilled a glass of chocolate milk on one of them. While Tonia was mopping it up, the little girl began coloring on the new coffee table.

'Elia, please ask Dvora to put something under her paper.'

'You mean you bought furniture we aren't allowed to use?'

'Well obviously you can use it, but there's such a thing as being careful.'

'You know how kids are.' Elia shrugged and left the room.

Later that night Tonia went to their room where Amos lay in bed reading a newspaper and complained to him about Elia. His response was, 'Well, maybe it wasn't such a smart idea to buy a lot of expensive furniture while there are small children around.'

She made a great effort, literally biting her tongue, but finally exploded. 'All right, Amos. I give up. I can't go into my own kitchen without feeling like there's a secret password I don't know. I worked so hard to make a lovely garden, and you all complain that I'm not raising field crops. And no one but me gives a damn how the house looks.'

397

Amos put his newspaper aside and stared at her. She could see he had no patience for this, but was also making an effort.

'I don't see anything wrong with the house,' he said and sat up, swinging his legs over the side of the bed. 'Come here.' He held out an arm to her.

She pouted for another moment before she slipped into his embrace, feeling as if she might cry.

'I know you gave up your dream house,' Amos said.

'Stop trying to make me feel like a spoiled brat. Just because I want a nice home doesn't make me selfish and materialistic.'

'You know that's not what I think about you. But I do think you sometimes forget what's important. We live in a country where you really need your family.'

Two weeks later, Tonia's doctor told her she was pregnant. She walked home slowly, marveling at this news, hands drawn to her flat stomach. A baby. A whole new person. A tiny Amos. No, she wanted a daughter. A sweet little mocha-colored girl with enormous eyes who would grow into her best friend. She waited another two weeks to tell Amos, hoping for the perfect moment. But he was spending more and more time at work, coming up the stairs after she was already asleep, and she was beginning to wonder when she would find any moment alone with him, let alone a perfect one. On one of the few evenings he was home in time for dinner, she literally dragged him outside for a walk.

All he said was, 'It's about time.' But he was beaming. She clasped his hand, feeling relaxed and happy. Now he was stuck. He would never leave her. She had Amos forever.

Tonia gave birth to a tiny dark-skinned girl and was stunned when the midwife laid her daughter across her chest. She could not stop staring, studying fingers, toes, ears. For the first time in years, she found herself wondering about God. Where had this amazing creature come from? What a brilliant way to bind a man and woman together. The miracle of procreation went a long way toward making up for some of the other really bad ideas God had had.

Amos had not been there; he had been at a building site all that day, with no way to contact him. When he came to the hospital that evening, he cooed at the baby and started calling her Sarit without bothering to consult his wife. Tonia bristled for a moment, but held her tongue.

Elia, Shlomi, Dvora, Rachel, and Aunt Nechama were all out in the yard to welcome Tonia and Sarit home. Elia took a step forward and put her arms out to offer an awkward embrace.

'She's beautiful.' She took Sarit from Tonia and showed her off to the rest of the family, as if she were her own.

When Elia turned to hand the baby back to Tonia their eyes met. 'Thank you, Elia,' Tonia said. 'I'm so lucky to have you here to help me.'

One day while Sarit was sleeping and Tonia and Rachel were working in the kitchen, Tonia asked her mother-in-law, 'Do you think the husband should make all the decisions?'

'Ach! Did I have a husband to make decisions for me?'

Tonia went back to drying dishes and had her back to Rachel when she asked, 'You didn't want Amos to marry me, did you?'

'No.'

'Why not? I always thought you liked me.'

'You are very different from one another.'

'And now?'

'Is it my business? What's done is done. I did always like you.'

'But you think he'd be better off with a nice Yemenite girl.'

'Who knows? He wanted you. Now he's got you, to quarrel with all he wants.'

One evening Tonia found Amos huddled in the kitchen with one of his uncles.

'What was all that about?' she asked after the uncle had left.

'He has a match for Elia. A widower with two children of his own. He lives on a *moshav* near Netanya.'

'So far away?' Tonia was taken aback by how sorry she was at the thought of Elia leaving. Dvora and Shlomi adored Sarit and kept her occupied for hours. Elia lavished concern upon her and possessed an encyclopedic knowledge of every childhood disease ever thought of and a remedy for each of them. Tonia had gained a grudging respect for the medicines the three Yemenite women brewed up in the kitchen.

'We're paying for the wedding,' Amos said, watching Tonia's face for objection. 'And her dowry.'

Tonia nodded and reached out to squeeze his hand. 'Good,' she said and smiled. 'I have figured out that you were right – family is more important than new chairs. Though I still don't see any reason we can't have both.' She stuck her tongue out.

Four months later, Elia was married and gone. The house seemed empty.

'Ima, why are men so wrapped up in themselves?' Tonia asked Leah over a cup of tea.

'What has poor Amos done this time?'

'Oh, he's just like Abba. Never home. Always something dreadfully important to do. If it's not work, it's some thrice-removed cousin, or some friend from the army that he has to help out with something. I'm always at the bottom of the list. Same as you always were. I've never understood, Ima. Why did you put up with it?'

'Did it appear to you that I had much of a choice?'

'I never heard you complain.'

'Well, I didn't marry Josef in order to spend my life quarrelling with him, and I would have lost either way. I never could have bent his will to mine, but suppose I had gotten my way, had him home. Could you imagine him standing behind the counter in some shop? Working in a bank?'

'Yes, I see what you mean. But, still, how did you keep from being resentful?'

'Oh, I was at times,' Leah conceded with a faraway look. 'I was never blind to his faults. He could be impossible, closed-minded, tyrannical ...' She smiled sadly. 'But, Tonia, some men are like that. They have such a strong need to prove themselves. Constantly. It isn't something they can choose to do or not to do. They aren't at peace otherwise. What you have to keep asking yourself is – would you love him as much if he were any other way? The simple truth is, no matter how angry and abandoned I sometimes felt, I was always glad to find him on the doorstep and take him into my bed. You have to live a long time and watch and listen to a lot of friends and neighbors before you realize how great a gift that is. You start noticing how many women treat their husbands like children, because they long ago ceased to exist in their minds as men.'

'Are you going to sit there and tell me that sex is all that counts?'

'No, certainly not all. But without it, none of the rest matters. It's the glue that holds everything else together. Didn't living with Emil teach you that much?'

Tonia soon discovered that she was pregnant again. The day their son was born Amos was at the hospital, pacing the waiting-room floor. He again named the baby without consulting Tonia – Josef, but they would call him Seffi. Tonia sighed and smiled when he told her. She was pleased with his choice, but it seemed that all her children would be named after people who had met violent deaths.

Soon after Tonia came home from the hospital with the new baby, Aunt Nechama had a stroke while picking over the apples at one of the stalls at the Mahane Yehuda market. The vendor called for an ambulance, but she died before they reached the hospital. Tonia began to glance at Rachel, appalled at the thought that something could happen to her. Tonia had gotten used to and come to depend upon the extended family she had so resented.

In July of 1961, Tonia gave birth to non-identical twins – a boy and a girl. Amos named the boy Coby, short for Ya'acov, after his brother who had been killed trying to reach Kfar Etzion during the siege. He tried to name the girl after Aunt Nechama, but this time Tonia objected.

'Amos, I want one child who is not named after someone who has died.'

'What do you want to name her?'

'I was thinking of Nurit,' she said. It was the name of one of Israel's red wild flowers. 'It would be the same first initial,' she said.

'All right,' Amos agreed.

CHAPTER FIFTY-SEVEN

May 1967

'Honestly, Amos, I don't see why we have to drag the children to a stupid military parade. Armaments are a necessary evil, not something we should be parading through the streets.'

'All of their friends will be there. And you could show a little appreciation for the hardware that's keeping us alive.'

Tonia could hardly argue with that. Just last week the air force had downed six Syrian planes.

'Well, I still think it's juvenile, not to mention a waste of our taxes, to stand around in the hot sun watching a bunch of tanks drive by.'

'Don't worry. There won't be any. The ceasefire agreement doesn't allow us to bring tanks into Jerusalem. Or planes. Or heavy artillery.'

'Great. So what are we going to see in this big deal parade, pop guns?'

'A lot of soldiers whose mothers took great care ironing their uniforms. And small arms. It's the morale-building aspect of the thing. Your father would have loved it. He would have watched and wept. You Europeans get so emotional about the concept of an armed Jew.'

'I suppose in Yemen the Chief-of-Staff was a Jew. Anyway, I don't see why we can't just have a nice picnic.'

'We will. While we watch the parade.'

Tonia and Rachel packed a basket lunch. They drove to the campus of the Hebrew University at Givat Ram where President Shazar, Prime Minister Eshkol, Chief-of-Staff Itzhak Rabin, and the District Commander of the Central Command stood on the reviewing stand. The crowd was in a festive mood, and the children, most of them dressed in blue and white, waved flags.

Amos spread a blanket on the grass, Tonia set out the food, and they all ate hungrily. Then Amos lay back and lit a cigarette, and Tonia rested her head on his stomach.

'Won't you ever get fat?' she asked and reached back to tap her knuckles against his abdominal muscles.

'Not as long as you insist on helping with the cooking.'

'Pooh to you too. Do you have to smoke?'

'Yes.'

She rolled over, would have liked to kiss him, but even after eleven years of marriage and four children, she was shy in front of his mother.

'Hey, Amrani,' one of his army friends said and plopped down next to him. 'I got a call-up order. For next week.'

'Bloody hell. I'd better not get one. I have to get four crews together next week. Did Elisha get one?'

'Don't know. Haven't seen him around.'

Tonia's spirits drooped. His prolonged absences for army reserve duty led to anxious waiting and resentment.

'Cheer up. Tonia will be glad to get rid of you for a few days.'

'Yeah, right.' Tonia sat up and grinned, brushing blades of grass from her sleeve. 'So long as he takes the four kids with him.'

Amos sat up and pinned his skullcap back on his head. He made a quick survey of his children. Sarit sat under a tree reading. Seffi had joined a soccer game. The twins were doing their best to ruin a lot of public gardening. Rachel sat near Sarit, embroidering. Amos switched on the transistor radio and turned to the Voice of Cairo, which blared guttural Arabic and martial music.

'What are they saying?' Tonia asked.

'Nasser's not real fond of Jews,' Amos answered and switched it off.

The next morning when she awoke Amos had already left for work. She lay in bed and refused to begin the day. When she did go downstairs, she found Rachel sitting next to the radio wearing a grim expression. Large numbers of Egyptian troops had moved into the Sinai Peninsula. Tonia dialed Amos at work.

'Have you been listening to the news?' she asked.

'Yes.'

'So what do you think is going to happen?'

'I don't know. Lot of people think Nasser's just showing off. Rattling sabers for internal consumption. He'll claim we were massing troops, and he forced us to back down.'

'Do you believe that?'

'I believe Jews are too damn smart for their own good,' Amos said. 'Always reading between the lines. When Hitler published *Mein Kampf*, all those smart German Jews were sure he didn't mean it. I think we should take Nasser at his word, until he gives us reason to do otherwise.'

She hung up and stayed close to the radio for the rest of the day. She couldn't stop thinking about the numbers. Three tanks for every one of ours. More than twice as many planes. Rumors claimed Egypt had over 100 missiles.

The next day Nasser ordered UN observers out of Sinai. Jordan put its army on alert. The Voice of Israel began reading out meaningless phrases – code names for the reserve units being called up. Amos's unit was not among them.

Tonia had hoped to lure her husband to bed early that night, but some army friends dropped in. She didn't feel like taking part in the conversation, but after she brought out soda water and snacks, she lingered in the hallway eavesdropping.

'I think we should all report tomorrow,' one of them said. 'The hell with waiting to be called up.'

'No,' Amos said. 'We can't stop living every time Nasser says "Boo". Screw up the whole economy every time he decides to move a few units around.'

'And if he does close the Straits to our shipping?'

'He hasn't done that yet, has he?'

'Do you think we'll make a pre-emptive strike?'

'Of course. What would you do if you were the Prime Minister?' Amos asked. 'What choice do we have? If you have to fight a war, make sure you fight it in the other guy's back yard. Especially if your country is the size of a postage stamp.'

'What about the UN? They say not even the Americans will sanction a first strike.'

'So we'll get condemned in the General Assembly,' Amos said. 'Unfortunately, that's not the worst thing that could happen to us. Someone in the Pentagon must have both a map and a brain – can see how easy it would be to cut the country in two, to isolate Jerusalem, how well within artillery range all our population centers are. Only a madman would seriously expect us to sit here and wait for them to attack.'

'But this could be a two- or three-front war. We can't fight them all at once.'

'First you go after Egypt,' someone said. 'Throw everything you've got at Nasser. He's got the biggest army, and once he's beaten, the others will turn tail. Anyway, he's got to be cut down to size.'

'No.' Amos shook his head. 'If we have to fight a war, we might as well get some good out of it. Don't forget, the minute we get a clear upper hand, they'll start hollering for a ceasefire, and Johnson will lean so hard he'll flatten us. We might not have enough time to finish off Nasser. And even if we take Sinai from them, we'll just have to turn around and give it back, like we did in '56.'

'So?'

'So, Jordan is another story. If Hussein is stupid enough to give us a crack at him, we push his artillery across the river – away from Jerusalem and Tel Aviv – and we take back the Old City.'

'Why stop there, Amrani?' one of the others scoffed. 'I hear Amman is nice this time of year.'

They all agreed to agree that war was unlikely. Nasser would find an excuse for backing down, without losing face. Tonia smiled tolerantly. They all spoke with such authority; one might think the Joint Chiefs of Staff were meeting in her living room. She wondered if their confidence was more than skin deep. Didn't they ever consider the possibility that Israel might lose? She went upstairs to bed, but couldn't sleep. King Hussein's soldiers were poised to attack, only a few hundred yards from where her children slept. She listened for sounds of the guests' leave-taking, for Amos's step on the stairs. She wanted his arms around her, making her feel safe.

She knew he would probably be called up the next day. He would rush home, change into his faded old uniform, lace up his red boots, kiss her on the cheek, and leave her to wait for a phone call, a postcard. No, you're too old! she wanted to shout. Forty-two years old and the father of four children. There are younger men. Why must you go again? True, two years ago he had been retrained as a medic; but he was still attached to a unit of paratroops and would be with them on the front line, wherever they fought.

She was still awake, feeling sick to her stomach, when he climbed the stairs. She didn't speak as he undressed silently in the dark, but when he climbed into bed, she laid her cheek on his chest.

'Amos, I'm so frightened.'

'I know. Everyone is. Let's just hope it all blows over.' He kissed her forehead and was soon asleep.

The following days were a nightmare of waiting. Like everyone else in the country, Tonia left the radio on, day and night, and was never far from it. The Secretary-General of the UN, U Thant, made a trip to Egypt, but Nasser repeated that he wasn't bluffing; he wanted the UN troops out. They withdrew that afternoon. Egyptian paratroops took up the positions they abandoned. The entire Egyptian army was mobilized. The Palestinians in the Gaza Strip shelled and made incursions over the southern border, sniping, burning fields, and planting mines.

Israel's Prime Minister, Levi Eshkol, spoke in the Knesset. 'I want to make it perfectly clear to the Arab states that our intentions are peaceful. We have no desire to undermine their security, their regimes, or their legal rights ...'

'Why doesn't he get down on his knees and beg?' Amos switched the radio off in disgust.

Then Nasser, speaking before his troops in Birgafgefa, proclaimed: 'Our forces reached Sharm el-Sheikh yesterday. The Straits of Tiran are Egyptian territorial waters. Not one more Israeli ship shall pass through them. Neither will we permit the passage of strategic materials on non-Israeli ships. The Jews threaten us with war? All I have to say to them is – Welcome! Come ahead. We are ready for war.'

Tonia heard a translation of his speech on the late morning news and sank into a chair in despair. Not even she could expect Israel to allow the closure of the Straits of Tiran. All that evening she couldn't take her eyes off her husband. *Please, God, don't let anything happen to him. I'll never complain again. I'll cover my hair and say morning prayers every day.*

The Egyptian and Syrian armies massed on Israel's southern and northern borders. Tonia had no illusions about their fate if they lost. She, like Amos, took the Arabs at their word. Not one Jew would be left alive, they promised. No other country was offering help to Israel. The world was preparing itself to mourn the demise of the Jewish state.

More and more reservists were being called up, but Amos was still at home. He worked sixteen hours a day, trying to put things in order before he would have to go. Little construction was being done. Most of his crews and their vehicles had already been mobilized.

Egypt mined the Straits, and the radio said that the streets of Cairo were filled with jubilant crowds calling for war. Nasser gave another speech: 'We will completely annihilate Israel. This will be total war.'

Amos returned early from work to listen to a speech Eshkol was scheduled to give at 6:00 in the evening, hoping it would be a declaration of war. He found Tonia pale and tense, deep circles under her eyes. She could not go about her daily business the way Rachel did. She didn't care if the house was clean or dirty or what she wore or ate.

'I can't stand this any more,' she said. 'I almost wish war would just go ahead and break out already.'

'I know.'

Eshkol began speaking and Amos turned up the radio. The Prime Minister offered a lengthy explanation of why Israel had not yet taken any action toward ensuring that the Straits would remain open. In the middle of the speech he lost his place in the text and stammered for a moment before he found it again.

'The hell with you, you bumbling old fool,' Amos shouted at the radio. 'Why don't you at least form a unity government with Begin? Why don't you appoint a Minister of Defense who knows what he's doing? Why don't you do something, anything, besides sitting there acting like you're afraid of them?'

That day King Hussein flew to Cairo to sign a mutual defense pact with Nasser.

CHAPTER FIFTY-EIGHT

Amos told Tonia he was fed up with waiting for the radio announcer to read out his call-up code and put on his faded uniform.

'Don't worry. I'm an old man, a medic, not a hero,' he said and kissed Tonia. She found no comfort in this assurance.

She tried her best not to cry as she followed him out to the company van. The army would conscript it anyway, so Amos was going to drive it to his unit's assembly point.

'Stop looking like that,' he admonished her. 'I'll be back before you've had time to miss me.'

The children were at school when he left. Tonia knew they would accept his absence as natural. They were used to Amos, and all their friends' fathers, 'going to the army' several times a year. Only Rachel shared Tonia's gloom. After her son left, she sat in silence for several hours on the little wooden bench that Amos had built in the garden. Tonia approached her carrying two cups of tea. They switched on the transistor radio and listened together. Tonia snorted as the commentators analyzed the effect Eshkol's speech had had on public morale.

'Good Lord, the poor man lost his place on the page. That's all. What's such a big deal? Why don't they shut up about it?' She switched the radio off.

Rachel rose and took the teacups into the kitchen, followed by her daughter-in-law. She tied a white apron about her waist and began scooping cups of flour into a bowl.

'What are you doing?' Tonia asked. The refrigerator was full of food, and the tins in the pantry were filled with cookies.

'For the soldiers.'

Tonia took her own apron off its hook, and the two women worked in silence, baking small round cakes and puff pastries and putting together sandwiches.

The children came home from school and Tonia forbade them to leave the yard. Toward evening, Rachel and Tonia loaded the food they had prepared into Seffi's wagon and started down the street, in the direction of the City Line.

'You stay home!' Tonia admonished her children, who were trailing behind them.

'Let them come,' Rachel said with such finality that Tonia obeyed.

Whenever an army vehicle stopped near them they handed cakes and sandwiches up to the smiling young faces. They were not the only people in the street dispensing food, cold drinks, and hot coffee to the grateful soldiers. Tonia wondered if Amos was enjoying similar hospitality. Word spread in the streets that Rabin had given permission for families to visit soldiers where they were stationed, but Tonia had no idea where to look for Amos. She eavesdropped on the soldiers' conversations as they repeated the same arguments, speculations, and anxieties. A few of them handed her scraps of paper with phone numbers and asked her to call their wives or parents for them.

It was dark when they got home. Rachel cleared the kitchen and began preparing supper. Tonia made the phone calls for the soldiers. Then she went around to the side of the house and descended the stairs to the bomb shelter Amos had built. Sixteen clay water jars, like those Rachel had had in her old apartment, lined one wall. Tonia lifted the lid of each of them. She and Amos had recently changed the water in all of them, and she blessed her husband's paranoia. A set of metal shelves held medicines, bandages, canned food, a kerosene lamp and supply of kerosene, candles and matches, a primus burner, a few pots and pans, and plastic cups and plates. In another corner was the pile of mattresses and blankets from Rachel's old apartment. Next to them stood a strange black plastic barrel, fitted with a toilet seat. She could think of nothing essential that her husband had overlooked.

She covered her head with a scarf and called the children to help her. They dragged the mattresses out to the yard to beat the dust out of them, while Tonia took a pail of soapsuds down to the shelter and scrubbed every surface. She took all of the eating utensils to the kitchen to wash and dry them. Everything was back in place by the time Rachel called them to supper.

'Listen to me,' Tonia told her children, 'if you hear any kind of siren, or shooting, or planes overhead, or any loud noise, you go right down to the shelter. If you're at school, you stay in the shelter there. If you hear a siren on your way home, run straight home and into the shelter. No stopping to look for me or get a book. No stopping for anything.'

They nodded. Yeah, yeah. They had heard it all at school.

After supper, Tonia and Rachel took the radio outside.

'Will there be a war, Rachel?'

'Yes.'

The next day was Friday. Rachel made the soup for the evening meal, sent Tonia out to shop, and commenced baking for the soldiers again. Tonia returned with her purchases and helped Rachel in the kitchen. They spoke little. Tonia tried to strike a bargain with fate. Amos could not die in this war. Rachel had already lost two sons and a daughter, and Tonia had lost her father. It wasn't fair, she almost cried, verging on hysteria. She wanted her husband back. What gave anyone the right to send him off to be shot at?

The children returned from school and told her that they had been asked to go back in the afternoon and help the Civil Defense authorities fill sandbags. Tonia would have protested, but Rachel interrupted her. 'Let them go.'

Rachel and Tonia spent the afternoon in the street, handing out food. They met Leah on their way home.

'I was on my way to your house,' she said. 'If it's all right with you, I thought this is a Sabbath we should spend together.'

'Of course, Ima.' Tonia threw her arms around her.

'Natan called this morning. He's still in Jerusalem. Have you heard from Amos?'

'No. But he's only been gone since yesterday morning.'

'Elon has been sent up north.' Leah inquired about Rachel's other sons, to whom Tonia had barely given a thought.

'Benjamin works in a laboratory at Hadassah hospital, so he won't be called. Haim is still in Elyakhin. His eyesight is poor, and he's in the Civil Defense.'

Leah nodded and took Rachel's hand in hers. 'I hope you don't mind me barging in on you.'

'It's good to be together when there are troubles.'

The house was untidy, but none of the three women cared. They sat in the kitchen, drinking tea and listening to the last news broadcast before the Sabbath.

'Rachel,' Tonia said, 'I'm sorry, but I'm going to leave the radio on over the Sabbath. I'll put it upstairs in one of the empty bedrooms and turn the volume down low, but I can't bear not to know anything.'

Rachel nodded. Tonia took the radio upstairs and came back down with a scarf to cover her hair while she lit the candles. They were all sitting in the living room when the front door opened and Amos came in. The children made a mad rush for him. He was in his faded green uniform, covered with dust, his hair unruly, with two days of stubble on his face. He carried a large automatic rifle, which he set down in the corner before bending to embrace his children.

'Have you been good?' he asked each one, and each nodded.

He kissed his mother's cheek, greeted Leah with a wide smile and hug, and then turned to Tonia. She put her arms around his neck, pressed herself to him, and said nothing. He smelled of the army – the musty, heavy smell of khaki uniforms and dirty socks that have spent days on feet in tightly laced boots. He pulled her close for a moment, then gently took her arms from about his neck.

'I have until tomorrow night,' he said, as if this were an eternity. 'I want to go to synagogue services. I'm late.'

He splashed some water over his face, ran a comb through his hair, and trod out, still wearing his dirty uniform. Tonia went upstairs to change. She chose a simple black dress that Rachel had made, its bodice embroidered with silver and white threads.

She brushed her hair, regretting that she had been too apathetic to wash it before the Sabbath. She changed the sheets on the bed and tidied the room. Then she sat at her dressing table and applied make-up. The men must have rushed through the service, for Amos was soon home.

'I'm going to shower before *Kiddush*,' he said and disappeared upstairs.

Tonia followed him into the bathroom and scrubbed his back for him, admiring his body. His face showed signs of age, and his hair was graying, but his body bore no trace of the passing years. She handed him a large white towel. He wrapped it around him, and, still wet, carried her to the bed and quickly made love to her. 'We'll do it right later,' he whispered in her ear and rose to dress.

When they went back downstairs Leah and Rachel were setting the table, conspiring to conceal the fact that they had been waiting for them.

'Oh my, what a difference.' Leah smiled at Amos in his clean white shirt.

Stubble still covered his face, for shaving was forbidden on the Sabbath. He reached into his pocket and handed each of his children a hard candy before reciting the blessing over the wine. He ate three helpings of soup and finished two glasses of *arak*. They were all tired and went to bed early.

Amos undressed and lay on the bed on his stomach. Tonia changed into a summer nightgown and sat beside him, one leg tucked under her, running her fingertips over his shoulder blades and taut back muscles.

'Do you remember the first time you saw me?' she asked.

'Stop it, Tonia!' He turned over and sat up. 'I am not going to die!'

She put her head on his shoulder and sobbed. 'I can't help it. I'm so scared.'

'I know. But you've always said that I'm a survivor. Besides, I'm a medic. Attached to a back-up unit. It will be all right.'

'But there's always another war to survive! God, why did we ever come back here? Won't they ever leave us alone? I'm sorry, Amos, I can't send you off with a brave smile, like a good Israeli wife is supposed to. I don't have all that ideological baggage. For me there is nothing – nothing in this world that would justify losing you. I'd rather run away.'

'Would you really?'

'Yes. Dammit, yes! Life is too hard here. The Jews got along without a state for two thousand years. What makes having a Jewish tax collector and a Jewish trash man worth all those young lives?'

'Try looking at it this way,' he said, lying back down and yawning. 'There were eight years between the first and second wars. And eleven between the second and this one. At that rate, by the time the next one comes around, I'll be busy helping little old ladies, like you, into the shelters. So this is my last war, and I have no intention of getting myself killed in it.'

'Are you so certain there will be a war?'

'Yes.'

'Do you still love me, Amos?'

'Why do you ask such stupid questions?'

'Why is it so hard for you to say it?'

'Why do you need to hear it?'

'You're impossible.'

He kissed her, and they made love again. Then he rolled away and began snoring. She sat for hours, watching him in the moonlight, before she plunged into exhausted sleep.

When she awoke the next morning, Amos had taken Seffi and gone to the synagogue. Leah and Rachel were in the kitchen making salads. Tonia sat at the table, and Rachel set a cup of coffee down in front of her. After she finished it, Tonia went back upstairs to dress and then made a detour into the back bedroom to listen to the radio. She hurried back down, pale and shaken, and found Amos in the kitchen, leafing through the Friday newspaper.

415

'*Shabbat Shalom*, my dear wife,' he greeted her with a broad smile, then saw the look on her face. 'What's wrong?'

'Hussein signed a treaty with Iraq. Two divisions of the Iraqi army have been ordered over the border into Jordan.'

'Yeah, I heard. I wouldn't worry too much about Hussein. You know what the Arabs are like. They make a lot of noise about unity, right before slitting one another's throats. But Hussein's too smart to give us the chance to take the Old City back. Nasser's the one we have to worry about.'

They ate lunch and went out for a walk, though Tonia refused to stray far from the shelter. Then Amos played backgammon with the children and wrestled with them on the floor before they all lay down for a nap. In the late afternoon, Rachel set out fruits, cakes, and nuts. They sang Sabbath songs and attempted normal conversation.

Too soon, the sun was setting. Amos changed back into his uniform and mumbled the evening prayers. He hurried through the *havdalah* ceremony that ushered out the Sabbath, gave Tonia a perfunctory kiss on the cheek, ruffled the children's hair, retrieved his rifle, and hurried away.

Thirty-six hours later, the Six Days War began.

CHAPTER FIFTY-NINE

Amos's company, the 55th Paratroops, was taken to Lod Airport on Sunday night, June 4th. They lounged about on the floor waiting. They had all heard rumors that the Israel Air Force was about to make a pre-emptive strike against Egyptian air bases, to be followed by an armored assault in Sinai. Early the next morning Amos's commanding officer strode to where the men lay sprawled on the floor of the airport terminal, waiting for their orders to board the planes.

'Change in plans,' the CO informed them. 'We are going to divert one battalion to Jerusalem, to aid in the city's defense.'

Many of the troops began to grumble. They didn't believe that Jordan's King Hussein would attack and didn't want to sit out the war on its quiet eastern front. When the CO asked for volunteers to return to Jerusalem, no one spoke up. They cast lots, and Amos's battalion was selected. He heaved a secret sigh of relief, having been paralyzed with fear during the long wait at the airport. Amos was always afraid before combat, as he assumed all sane men to be, but this time was different. He suffered not the fear of combat, but the fear of death. He had never contemplated his own mortality – never imagined his mother's grief, his children orphaned, Tonia's sense of abandonment. Would she remarry? He broke into a sweat. He wanted to grow old, to father more children, to hold his grandchildren in his arms. Even the prospect of making the jump terrified him. What if the parachute didn't open? Amos got to his feet. He and some of his comrades started toward the mountain of haversacks to retrieve theirs.

'No time for that,' one of the officers shouted. 'Just get on the buses. We'll re-equip you in Jerusalem.'

They pulled into Jerusalem's Beit Hakerem neighborhood at about 2:00 that afternoon. They carried only their personal arms and an insufficient quantity of ammunition. The CO told them to wait there while he went to the city's military storehouses.

While Amos and his comrades sat in the stifling bus, families from the neighborhood came out with pots of coffee and offered them the use of their telephones and bathrooms. Amos climbed down to stretch his aching body and spotted Natan getting off one of the other buses.

'Hey, Shulman, what the hell are you doing here?'

'Amos? I just finished a medic's course. No one knew what to do with me, so here I am. Too bad about the change of plans. You must be disappointed to be out of action.'

'Are you nuts? They've had their chance to blow my brains out. I'll gladly sit this one out. One of these good citizens just offered me coffee and a phone call. Come on, I want to try and get Tonia.'

They entered the flat, which was crowded with soldiers, and nodded their thanks to the elderly couple by the door. Amos got in line for the phone, and Natan brought him a cup of coffee. It was almost Amos's turn when they were called back down to the street where the CO awaited them. Everyone else filed out, but Amos reached for the phone. As he dialed his own number, he heard one of the other men shout, 'Hey, we're going to see some action after all. The Jordanians attacked Government House! We'll knock their teeth out.' Amos's knees went weak as Tonia picked up the phone.

'Tonia?'

'Amos! Where are you?'

'Not far away. I can't say on the phone – but it's not so far from where you went to high school.'

'Oh, Amos, are you all right?'

'Fine. Just bored. Being hauled around in buses. They can't make up their minds what to do with us, so we're having a long field trip. How are you and the children?'

'We're fine, except they're mad at me for making them stay in the shelter. It's fantastic luck that I was here to answer the phone. I just came up to get some books for them.'

'That's good. Keep them down there. You and Ima too. Natan's here with me.'

'Natan? That's good. You can look after one another.'

'Tonia?'

'Yes, Amos?'

'I love you.' He hung up the phone and rushed out of the apartment. On his way out, he paused to stuff some money into the mailbox.

'We'll be defending the city from the Mandelbaum Gate to Givat Hamivtar. North of us is the 10th armored division, south of us the Jerusalem Brigade,' the CO began to brief them out in the street. 'Our primary objective is to get through to Mount Scopus. In order to do so, we have to take Sheikh Jarrah and the Police School. Be ready to head towards the Rockefeller Museum and the Old City, but only if you receive orders to do so. No one, I repeat no one, is to go near the Old City without specific orders.'

A more detailed briefing would come later. The time of attack had not yet been fixed. They climbed back into their buses for the ride to the Schneller base, while their CO conferred with the District Commander.

It was after midnight when Amos and Natan emerged from Schneller in full battle dress and began walking toward the front. Tanks rolled down the street beside them, their engines off. Columns of paratroopers marched on either side of the tanks. The night was clear, windless, the sky bright with stars.

'How're you feeling?' Amos asked Natan in a hoarse whisper.

'Okay. You?'

'Scared shitless,' Amos replied. 'Getting old, I guess.'

Shells began to fall around them, exploding into the silent night, filling the air with residue that stung their eyes and skin. The orderly columns scattered, shrapnel ripped into men, and cries of 'Medic!' pierced the air. In the chaos, Amos and Natan located the makeshift clearing station and began evacuating wounded. The other soldiers resumed their forward march, appearing apathetic to the falling shells.

Amos's eyes burned so badly he could hardly see, and the smell of blood nauseated him. He bent down to lift a man onto a stretcher and had to turn aside to vomit before he regained control of himself. He and Natan carried the man back to the station and then moved forward again, dodging the shingling tiles that came hurtling down from the rooftops.

'Wait a minute.' Amos put a hand on Natan's arm, while he stopped and gasped for breath.

'You okay?'

'Yeah. Yeah. Okay, let's go.'

Then they were told to stay put. The order to launch an attack had not yet come.

'So what, we just came out here to give their artillery some target practice?' Amos demanded. He strode back to where Georgy, the radio operator, was crouched. 'What gives?'

'They're still arguing,' Georgy replied.

'*Cus emakh*,' Amos cursed as a shell exploded nearby. He pulled Georgy with him, closer to the wall behind them.

'There are only three hours of darkness left anyway,' Georgy said. 'I heard someone say that if we wait for daylight, they can give us some air support.'

'Air support, my ass,' Amos grumbled. 'No one's going to drop bombs this close to the Old City. There's a church, mosque, or synagogue about every three inches. And look how close we are to the Jordanians. They'd aim for the Legion, but end up blowing us to bits.'

Georgy shrugged and cringed as more shells fell around them. 'They're also waiting to see if the tanks can make it through to Ramallah without our help,' he shouted.

'So we get to sit here in this shit.' Amos lit a cigarette, and Georgy raised an eyebrow.

'Report me,' Amos said. 'I'd like to be put in a room with one of the idiots who sent us out here before they made up their minds what the hell they're doing. I can tell you what they're going to decide. We're going in at night.'

Georgy reached for Amos's cigarette and took a drag. 'Fifty liras says you're wrong.'

'That would be stealing money,' Amos slapped him on the shoulder. 'They can't wait,' he said. 'Haven't you learned? It always comes down to time. The army has to run forward like hell before the politicians cave in and agree to a ceasefire. Do you really think they'll pass up this opportunity Hussein has given us to get the Old City back?'

A few minutes later, the radio crackled. Georgy frowned and listened. When he looked up, he shook his head and put out a hand for Amos to shake. 'Two am,' he said. 'We're going in at two am.'

Amos stared ahead at their immediate objective – the high, white rectangular building of the Jordanian Police Training School. Three hundred meters from it was another fortified position known as Ammunition Hill, but they had been told to expect the greatest resistance to come from the school building itself. It was spotlighted by a large projector shining from the roof of Beit Hahistadrut in Jewish Jerusalem.

Their briefing had been hurried, but clear: 'Our artillery will start pounding both the school and Ammunition Hill. Under that artillery cover, our tanks will move into position and work over their machine-gun positions, in and around the school building. We'll give them another barrage of artillery while the sappers go forward and put down mines to break up the thick coils of barbed wire. Then A Company will breach the fencing and take up positions in the field in front of the school. From there a communications trench leads into Ammunition Hill. B Company will take the school building and the outbuildings between it and Ammunition Hill. C Company will complete the assault on Ammunition Hill, while D Company provides backup and moves on Sheikh Jarrah. Meanwhile, an engineering unit will widen the breaches in the fences, making them passable for our tanks.'

It proved to be a major failure of Israeli intelligence. They had no idea how formidable a target Ammunition Hill would be. The Jordanians had strongly fortified it since 1949, and Israel's aerial photographs had failed to reveal a well-camouflaged network of trenches and reinforced bunkers. Natan and Amos were walking toward forty such machine-gun positions, all with thick concrete walls that could withstand even a direct hit by a shell. These positions protected all approaches to the hill, while providing covering fire for one another. Each contained large stockpiles of ammunition. Central Jordanian positions higher up on the hill dominated all of the trenches. In the center of the hill stood a fortified command bunker and ammunition store.

CHAPTER SIXTY

At 2:00 am the big Israeli guns began blasting the Jordanians. Then the shelling stopped and a company of paratroops made a stealthy advance toward the outer barbed wire fence. They managed to cut the first coil and lay a mine under the second before a Jordanian machine gunner spotted them and opened fire. There were more cries of 'Medic!', and Amos's colleagues ran with stretchers.

Amos lingered behind at the clearing station and observed the progress of the battle as he busied himself giving the wounded water and morphine, inserting the needles of infusion packs, and applying compresses. Natan had gone to extricate more wounded, and Amos felt alone as his lips moved in silent prayer. His knees buckled when his company's second-in-command spotted him and ordered him forward.

'Come on, Amrani.' He slapped his back. 'They need you up there.'

Bile filled Amos's throat.

'You all right?' the officer asked.

'Yeah. Right behind you.'

'Come on.' The officer nodded.

They crouched down and scrambled forward, shells falling around them and bullets whizzing by. The paratroops had broken through three fences, but then encountered a fourth that didn't appear on their maps. More men had been torn apart while attempting to breach it.

'There's the bastard,' shouted a soldier near Amos. He had spotted the flash of the Jordanian machine gun and charged forward, emptying the clip of his Uzi.

Two Jordanian soldiers slumped over dead, and the paratroops in front of Amos jumped onto their bodies with a sickening crunch as they leapt into the trench.

A medic behind Amos was struggling to get a wounded man onto a stretcher. Amos seized the opportunity to turn back from the trench and help him. The soldier had a gaping stomach wound, and Amos knew he wouldn't make it. He lifted his end of the stretcher, and they stumbled back through the haze to the clearing station. By the time they got there, the soldier on the stretcher was dead. Amos's eyes filled with tears. It was all such a waste. Why were they always shooting at one another?

'Come on, we don't have enough stretchers.' Another medic touched his arm. They raced back up the street and returned to the battlefield, straining under the weight of a stack of stretchers. Wounded lay everywhere.

Amos was terrified of entering the trenches and attempted to append himself to another unit preparing to move toward Sheikh Jarrah.

Lior, one of Amos's officers, spotted him. 'Amrani, I don't have to threaten you, do I?'

'No.' Amos followed him, shamefaced, to enter the trenches of Ammunition Hill. He tightened the strap of his helmet, checked the grenades on his belt, clutched his Uzi, and prepared to advance.

The Jordanians had no avenue of retreat and fought savagely, lobbing grenades and spewing machine-gun fire, and the paratroops advanced by inches. Lior entered the trench first, followed by Moshe Cohen, Sammy Leibowitz, and Ido Singer. Amos was behind Ido.

The trench was narrow, and with the heavy pack on his back Amos felt suffocated. He could barely move, let alone turn around. He could see only the helmets of the men in front of him and a bit of the trench on either side.

Lior advanced a few meters, approaching the entrance to the first bunker in the trench. When he was within a meter, two grenades flew out of the bunker, hit the opposite wall of the trench, and landed near his feet. Lior grabbed one up and stepped forward to toss it back into the bunker, where it went off. Then he turned to scoop up the other, but before he could throw it back, it exploded in his hand. Lior's body absorbed most of the blast, shielding the men behind him. He fell face down in the trench, a lifeless blood-drenched rag doll. Moshe Cohen hesitated, but Sammy pounded a fist on his shoulder.

'Go on, crawl over him. We've got to keep moving forward,' Sammy shouted, but Moshe still didn't move.

'Get going,' Sammy shouted again. 'But watch it. The next bunker is probably only a few meters ahead. And hit this one with another grenade on your way past.'

Amos peered around Sammy and Ido to watch. Moshe was on his hands and knees, carefully moving over what remained of Lior's body, clutching his Uzi. He was covered with Lior's blood. Moshe passed the opening of the bunker and twisted his neck to look back.

'Grenade!' Sammy shouted. 'Toss a grenade!'

As he shouted, the bunker spat the flash of a machine gun, and Moshe crumpled to the ground. Sammy stood up, cursing and trampling over Lior's body as he moved forward, firing constantly. Then he pitched two grenades into the bunker. But Moshe Cohen was dead. Soaked with sweat, Sammy dragged his body into the entrance to the bunker so they wouldn't have to climb over it. Ido followed Sammy forward.

The smell of blood made Amos want to vomit. The sun was rising, and the Jordanian covering fire from the hill above grew more intense. Amos dreaded having to put his weight on the remains of Lior's body. And what was the point? He didn't see any way for them to progress forward. The Jordanians in the bunkers had them pinned down.

How many orphans was this useless stony hill going to create? He sucked in deep breaths and calmed himself. Your children are sleeping within walking distance of this useless stony hill. Losing their father is far from the worst thing that could happen to them. He held out his hands, relieved to see he had stopped shaking. All right. Let's go. Let's get it over with. He crawled forward, silently apologizing. When he looked down, he saw that Lior's face was gone.

Sammy was ahead of Ido and Amos, still a few meters from the next bunker. He turned around and said, 'I'm going up there.'

He nodded at the rim of the trench opposite the bunker. 'From up there I'll be able to fire directly into the bunker and cover you. From the time I start firing, count to three. I'll stop so you can move forward and pitch a grenade.'

Ido nodded, and Amos watched as Sammy hiked himself out of the trench and took a few steps forward. He crouched, moving like a crab, firing constantly. When he stopped, Ido rushed to the opening and threw the grenade in. Amos moved up, close behind Ido.

'Next!' Sammy shouted down to them and advanced toward the next bunker.

But as Ido threw a grenade into the next bunker, Sammy was hit by fire from above and fell dead at the edge of the trench. Bullets continued to tear into his body, and Amos reached up to pull him down into the trench.

'Leave him.' Ido put a hand on Amos's arm. 'Better he should stay up there than we have to walk over him.'

Amos nodded and looked helplessly at Sammy.

'Okay, I guess it's my turn,' Ido muttered, moving past Sammy and putting his hands on the edge of the trench.

Ido pulled himself up and assumed Sammy's crouching position. Amos moved like a robot, through air heavy with smoke and the stench of death, and they took out the next two bunkers.

Amos looked up, surprised to see Ido still alive. Amos began to move forward again, but his backpack caught on the end of an iron rod that jutted out of the side of the trench. At least the trench was wider here, so he could turn and try to free himself. When he did, he saw movement out of the corner of his eye. Then he heard the blast, felt something tear into his back and legs, and fell forward, still clutching his Uzi. He looked at his left hand. All that remained of the last two fingers were bloody stumps. The first thought in his mind was that he should look for his fingers. Couldn't they sometimes re-attach them? Then Ido fell into the trench ahead of him, his body riddled with bullets.

Amos pulled himself to a sitting position and turned to look behind him. He was alone in the trench. There must have been a Jordanian left alive in the bunker behind him that they had thought was clear. Amos leaned against the trench, pulled his knees up to his chest, and tried to think clearly. He attempted to get free of his backpack, but couldn't. He sat still, drenched in his own and his friends' blood. He again sensed movement. A Jordanian soldier was edging out of the bunker. Amos forced his right hand to lift his Uzi and fired. The Jordanian disappeared back into the bunker.

'Amos, hold on, we're coming!' He heard Natan's voice behind him.

'Stay back!' Amos shouted. 'Don't go past that bunker. There's at least one of them still alive in there. But he must be out of grenades, or I'd be dead.' Amos hung his head, exhausted from the effort of speaking.

Natan inched toward the bunker, back pressed to the wall of the trench, and threw a grenade in. Then he crept to where Amos sat and struggled to help him out of his pack.

'Glad to be rid of that damn thing,' Amos murmured.

'That damn thing probably saved your life. You carrying rocks in there?'

Natan took out a knife and cut the shirt from Ido's body to make a compress for the gaping wound in Amos's lower back. Shots came from the bunker behind them. The Jordanian had stuck his machine gun out, firing blind, but neither of them was hit.

'Goddamn, who the hell is in there, Superman?' Amos said and tilted his head back. 'That's the second grenade–'

'Don't talk,' Natan said. 'Just sit here and keep your back pressed against the wall. As much pressure as you can. We'll have to carry you out, but we can't do that until we clean out that bunker.'

Natan shouted to a soldier a few meters behind the bunker. 'Watch it. There's at least one of them in there. I'm going up to cover you.'

Amos tried to grab at his sleeve. 'You won't last a second up there,' he whispered. 'Listen, Natan, I've had it. I know that. Don't die for nothing.'

Natan ignored him and hoisted himself out of the trench. The other soldier moved forward to pitch a grenade into the bunker, and Natan jumped back down to safety. He crawled into the bunker and fired shots into each of the four bodies there. Then Natan and the other paratrooper tried to pick Amos up by the arms and legs, but he convulsed with pain and bled profusely. Natan removed his own pack and turned around.

'Okay, Amos, listen, I'm going to carry you piggy back, but backwards, with your back pressed against mine. You've got to get to your feet, put your back against mine, and reach your arms around me, to hold on. First let him get on the other side of us.' He motioned to the other soldier, who squeezed past them. 'He'll get your feet, while I lean forward, get my balance. Once we get the right angle, I'll be able to take you out of here.'

They slowly made their way out. More paratroopers were moving into the trench. The thin ones took off their packs and stood on them in order to let Amos by. Once they came to the narrower part of the trench, there was no way past anyone, and the soldiers coming in had to retrace their steps. Amos moaned and lost consciousness.

'Come on, Amrani, come on, you're not going to die,' Natan yelled over his shoulder.

They got him back to the clearing station, and Natan dragged a doctor over to him.

'Will he make it?'

'I'm sorry son, I don't know. He's in real bad shape, but we'll do our best.'

428

For Tonia, the war began on June 5th at 8:00 am, when sirens sounded all over the country. The children had just walked out the front gate on their way to school, but she called them back and herded them down into the shelter. She grabbed the transistor radio, and she and Rachel joined the children. The Voice of Israel said little – only that fighting had broken out in Sinai.

'Put on one of the Arab stations,' she urged Rachel. They listened stone-faced to the Arab newscaster for a few minutes.

'What did he say?' Tonia asked.

'That Jordan has taken Mount Scopus.' Rachel shrugged.

King Hussein delivered a speech announcing that his country was at war. Tonia switched back to the Voice of Israel, but all they heard there was a dry voice reading out more call-up codes.

'I didn't know there was anyone left to call up,' Tonia muttered.

The children chafed at being kept in the shelter, and Tonia climbed the stairs to get some toys and books. She wandered into the garden and peeked out the front gate. It was a beautiful day. The streets were empty, except for an ambulance that turned the corner. Its loudspeaker asked for blood donors, and she strode out into the street and flagged them down to give a pint of hers. Then she went to the children's rooms to gather up the things they wanted and returned to the shelter. It was stifling. The children begged to be allowed to play in the garden, but she refused. Rachel brewed tea on the primus burner and opened a tin of biscuits. Tonia was considering letting the children up for some air when the shelling started.

'Is Abba in a shelter?' Sarit asked.

'I don't know. I hope so.' Tonia put out her hand to rub Sarit's back.

'Heck no,' Seffi protested. 'Abba's not hiding in any shelter. He's out there breaking their bones!'

'Can he get killed?' Nurit asked in a small voice.

'We must pray very hard to God to look after him.'

'Didn't you pray to God to look after Sabba Josef?'

A troubled discussion of war and death left Tonia drained.

'I'll go heat up some soup and bring it down here,' she said to Rachel.

This time when she glanced out into the street the mayor's green car was passing. Teddy Kollek stuck his head out the window and waved to her as he drove by. Tonia assumed he was inspecting the damage thus far done to his city.

While Tonia and Rachel were giving the children lunch sounds of battle came from the direction of Government House, but the radio told them nothing. Later in the afternoon Tonia again ventured up for more toys and books for the children. She lingered in the house, savoring the fresh air, and decided that she would have to start letting the children up, for at least a few minutes.

The phone rang, and her heart stopped when she picked it up and heard Amos's voice. She wept with relief that he was in Jerusalem, but apparently far from the shooting she could hear. It was not until he muttered a choked 'I love you', that she heard the terror in his voice. The arrogant confidence was gone. Her own terror echoed back to her from the phone. She hung up, laid her head down on the table, and wept. What made men think a piece of land was worth slaughtering one another? She straightened up, washed her face, and returned to the shelter.

'Abba just phoned,' she said. 'He's all right, and he's here in Jerusalem.'

A chorus of 'Why didn't you let us talk to him?' assailed her.

'He only had a moment. And he insisted that I keep you all safe in the shelter.'

After the children fell asleep on the mattresses, Tonia and Rachel took turns going up to shower. The shelling had petered out, and the shooting sounded farther away. They slept fitfully, and the next morning they lay on the mattresses long after they awoke. Tonia allowed the children into the garden for fifteen-minute intervals.

When Rachel switched on the Voice of Israel, they were stunned to hear the Chief Rabbi of the army, Rabbi Goren, announce that he was broadcasting from the Western Wall in the Old City. They could hear shouts of joy in the background. Tonia switched off the radio in disgust. Who cared anything about a pile of moldy old stones when people were dying? The news had mentioned heavy fighting the previous day, in both the north and south of the city. Where was Amos?

During and after lunch they heard a great deal of shooting. The evening news told them what it had been. The Arab half of the Abu Tor neighborhood, only a few hundred meters from them, had been taken. After hearing this, Tonia decided to let the children out of the shelter, but still forbade them to leave the yard. They had learned to recognize the shriek of a shell before it hit and promised to run for the shelter if they heard one coming. Tonia wandered the rooms of the house, touching Amos's things.

A filthy young soldier came to the front gate. 'Are you Tonia Amrani?' he asked.

'Yes.' She paled. She had dreaded this scene so many times. 'Oh God, not Amos!'

'He was wounded. Yesterday. Your brother Natan was with him and said to tell you that Amos is probably at Hadassah hospital in Ein Kerem.'

'How badly wounded is he?'

'I'm sorry. I don't know. Natan asked me to give you that message. That's all I know.'

She stood rooted to the ground.

'Are you all right?'

'Yes. Yes. Thank you for coming.' She turned and fled into the house.

'Rachel,' she called as she flipped through the phone book and then dialed. 'Rachel! Amos has been wounded. He's at Hadassah.' She gasped, and began sobbing, as if saying it was what made it true. 'Damn!' She slammed the phone down. None of the cab companies she tried answered their phone. Their taxis

431

had probably all been appropriated for military use. She ran out into the street, but it was empty.

'Come,' she said to Rachel. 'We'll go out to one of the busier streets and flag somebody down.'

'Wait, Tonia, the children.'

Tonia paced while Rachel herded them back down to the shelter and got one of the neighbors' teenage daughters to stay with them. The third car she stopped agreed to take them to the hospital, the driver refusing the money she offered him. It seemed an eternity before she found a nurse who could confirm that Amos was there.

'Yes, it is serious. A grenade exploded right next to him. Dr. Avneri operated on him yesterday, right after he was brought in, and he's operating again now. It may be quite a while before we know anything.'

'His back and legs, you said? Is that all?' Tonia asked in a whisper, remembering the nightmares of being blinded that Amos had lately admitted to having.

The nurse went to her station and flipped through a chart. 'He took a few pieces of shrapnel in his back, and some in his right leg, which may leave him with a slight limp. And he lost two fingers on his left hand,' the nurse said matter-of-factly.

'Thank you for telling me,' Tonia whispered.

'Is anyone here with you?'

'My mother-in-law.'

'There are some comfortable chairs down the hall. And a coffee machine next to them. The pay phone is around the corner. I have tokens if you need them. I'm afraid there isn't anything you can do but wait.'

'Thank you.' Tonia turned back to Rachel, who had re-mained stone-like, listening to the nurse.

Tonia went to the pay phone and dialed Leah's number. She told her mother what had happened and asked her to go stay with the children. Then she shuffled back to where Rachel sat and took one of Rachel's hands in both of hers. Don't let him die. Please don't let him die. She couldn't live without Amos. No one

432

to make her feel safe. Not ever again. Not anywhere. She let go of Rachel's hand and rose to pace the hallway. Scattered pictures of her husband cluttered her mind, but she willed them away. No. Nothing resembling a farewell. Not now. Not yet. Not one moment sooner than I have to. When I know, when they come to tell me, then I'll begin to mourn. Right now he's still alive. He's alive.

Some time later, Leah arrived. 'The children are fine,' she assured Tonia. 'That neighbor girl is staying with them. I wanted to be here with you. Have you heard anything yet?'

'No,' Tonia answered, and repeated what the nurse had told them.

Tonia's thoughts drifted back to the Ratisbonne Monastery, to the certainty with which she had sensed her father's death. She didn't feel it now – that cold clamminess. What she felt now was a calculated dread. Maybe he would be all right, she allowed herself to hope. Her mind was blank, her senses dull. Cups of coffee and cold drinks were brought to her, but she didn't touch them. Leah left her to herself. Rachel sat alone, reading Psalms. Tonia focused on her for a moment, realizing how much pain the tiny woman had already endured. Why do we bother? Life is such a struggle. People suffer so much, only to rot in the end. Can unconscious people think? Was Amos thinking of her? Of the children? Or was he already gone, beyond reach? She squeezed her eyes shut and attempted to will some form of contact, some sense of him. There was only cold darkness, and she began to weep.

'Mrs. Amrani?' A nurse touched her shoulder.

Tonia nodded.

'Your husband is in the recovery room. We have to keep a close watch on him for the next forty-eight hours, but right now his condition is stable enough for the doctors to think he has a good chance of pulling through.'

Tonia stared at the nurse. 'He didn't die,' she whispered.

'No.' The nurse smiled. 'He didn't die.'

Leah came over and hugged her. 'Thank God.'

433

'When can we see him?' Rachel asked.

'You could look in on him now, if you want, just for a moment,' the nurse answered. 'It will be a while before the anesthesia wears off, and then he'll have to rest, but you could have a short visit then.'

Tonia declined to enter the room. 'He wouldn't want me to see him now. Not like that,' she said in a hoarse whisper. 'You go.' She nodded to Rachel, and Rachel turned to follow the nurse.

'I'm going to go get you something from the cafeteria,' Leah said. 'You ought to be able to eat something now. I'll be right back. You sit down and try to relax.'

'Praise God,' Rachel said to Tonia when she returned from Amos's room. 'I'll go home now to stay with the children. I'll come back later.'

'Thank you, Rachel.' Tonia kissed her leathery cheek. 'What would I do without you? I love you so much.'

'Would you prefer to be alone?' Leah asked when she returned and handed Tonia a sandwich and a paper cup of juice.

'No. Stay.' Tonia set the food on the chair next to her and looked at her mother. Leah was pale and her hands seemed to be shaking. 'What's wrong?'

'The radio – in the cafeteria ...' Leah sat down and clasped her hands.

'What? What is it, Ima?'

Leah rubbed her hands over her thighs and seemed to collect herself. 'A force of the Jerusalem Brigade fought its way south, all the way to the Etzion Bloc. They just rode in, encountered no resistance at all. The Legionnaires had abandoned their camp. Our soldiers walked in and took it back.'

'What?' Tonia blinked.

'Kfar Etzion. It's ours again.'

Tonia closed her eyes. It was the first time in months she had thought of her father. Roaring with laughter, burning with ambition, slapping backs, hunched over his books. So alive. And

434

then dying. A grenade tearing his flesh apart, the roof of the monastery crushing his body.

She imagined Amos standing on a bloody hillside, charging into enemy fire, cut apart, falling, pieces of jagged metal slicing into his beautiful body. What made men do it? It was insane. Thank you, God, for letting my husband live, but why must you claim so many others? What is the purpose of all this killing? What makes it matter so much where Jews live and where Arabs live? She slumped back in her chair, opened her eyes, and took her mother's hand.

'They never had a chance. Not a chance,' Leah murmured.

'No.' Tonia knew she was talking about the defenders of Kfar Etzion, so many years ago.

'It's different now. Now we have a real army, hospitals. He would have been so proud.'

The two women sat through a long silence. Then Natan came striding down the corridor, still wearing his filthy uniform, his shoulder bandaged. He gazed about, looking bewildered, until he saw his mother and sister.

Tonia rushed to him and threw her arms around his neck. 'Oh God, it's good to see you. We've been worried sick. No one knew for sure where you'd been sent after Ammunition Hill.' She pulled back to look into his eyes. 'Some other men from your unit came and told us what you did,' she said. 'The way you saved his life.'

'How is he?' His eyes searched Tonia's.

'He just got out of surgery. They think he'll be all right.'

Natan sighed with relief.

'What happened to you?' She looked at his arm.

'Nothing. Just a scratch.'

'Have you been discharged?'

'No, but our CO gave me a couple of hours to come and see about Amos. Have you heard about the Etzion Bloc?'

Tonia nodded.

'And that we retook the Old City?'

435

'Yes,' she said wearily. 'But neither one of them is worth one hair of your or Amos's heads.'

'Still.' He grinned his old boyish grin. 'If you're going to fight a war, you might just as well win it.'

A nurse approached. 'Mrs. Amrani? Your husband is awake if you'd like to see him for just a few minutes.'

Tonia pushed the door open. 'Amos?'

His eyes blinked open. He looked awful, worse than she had imagined, full of tubes and needles. He lay limp, almost lifeless. She knew part of him hated having her there.

'Well.' She forced a bright smile onto her face and strode to his bedside. 'This is absolutely the last war I let you go off to.'

CHAPTER SIXTY-TWO

Dr. Zucker came in to remove the last of Amos's bandages, and Tonia paced in the corridor until a hand touched her shoulder.

'I'm very pleased with your husband,' Dr. Zucker said. 'If only all my patients healed so nicely.'

'They're not all as stubborn as he is.' Tonia smiled and hugged the doctor.

She sat on the edge of Amos's bed and reached for his mangled left hand. Amos pulled it away, and she stared at him.

'Amos, you stupid man,' she said, 'don't you know that nothing – nothing – could make any part of your body unattractive to me?'

He looked out the window. 'I can't touch you with this,' he said.

'Yes you can.' She reached for his hand again, and he let her take it. The pinkie finger was missing, as was the top of the ring finger above the second joint. 'Hah, look, you still don't get out of wearing your wedding ring. Might exempt you from doing dishes though.' She shook her head with a smile and caressed his hand in both of hers, being careful of the injured fingers

He stared into her eyes and then pulled her to him to kiss her in a way he hadn't for years, the way he had kissed her on the front lawn in Grand Rapids. Her body responded as it had then, and she was oblivious to the curious stares of the nurses and visitors who passed by in the corridor.

She pulled back and placed her hands on either side of his face. 'I am so glad that I have never loved any man but you. Now,' she said in a lighter tone and softly slapped his shoulder, 'let me see what they've done to your back.'

He leaned forward, and his hospital gown fell to the sides. Tonia swallowed a gasp. His beautiful back. Amos's beautiful back. She ran her fingertips over the ugly red gashes that marred his flesh. One of them extended almost around to his stomach. Tonia couldn't imagine how horrible his wounds must have been when they brought him in. She squeezed her eyes shut to drive that image from her mind. He was alive. That was all that mattered. She still had him. He would be too old to fight by the time some idiot started the next war.

'I'm going to have a limp,' Amos said.

'I know.' Tonia nodded. 'Good. That'll make it easier for me to keep up with you.'

Amos was moved from the hospital to a rehabilitation center near Tel Aviv. Two weeks later Tonia drove there to bring him home. A pretty young nurse pushed him out to the sidewalk in a wheelchair.

'All day, every day, all she's done is nag, nag, nag at me to get up and do gymnastics,' Amos said to Tonia, nodding at the nurse. 'Now she insists on bringing me out to the car like a cripple.'

'Rules.' The nurse smiled and shrugged.

Tonia watched as he lifted himself out of the chair and winced when she saw the pain on his face. He stared out the window on the way home, nodding as she chattered. Her throat constricted. He almost felt like a stranger. Amos always put his left hand on her knee when she drove, but that day his arms remained crossed.

The children had tacked balloons and a colorful 'Welcome' sign to the front door. They rushed out to greet him and the old Amos reappeared, laughing and teasing. That night he initiated lovemaking and the last of her fears faded.

A week later, he came into the kitchen where Tonia sat reading the morning paper and picked up the keys to his new truck, which had an automatic transmission. 'I think it's time to see if I can still drive. Feel like going for a ride?'

'Don't you want to eat something first?' Tonia asked.

'No.'

Tonia tried not to look at the way Amos held his left leg stiffly to the side as they got into the truck. He drove aimlessly around the pockmarked streets of Jerusalem, weaving past the crews repairing the war damage. Tonia sat smiling at her husband's profile, grateful to have him back, unable to imagine desiring another man.

'Why is it so difficult for you to talk about your feelings for me?' she asked.

He groaned. 'Don't the wounded get any slack?'

'What is so hard? Once – in all these years – you've said you love me. One time. And it took a war to drag that out of you. Why can't you talk about how you feel about me?'

He thought for a long while. 'I don't know if "feel" is the word I would use. I don't "feel" about you. You just are. How do you feel about your right arm? I suppose I could live without mine, but I wouldn't want to. If you cut it off, the pain might eventually stop. I might get a prosthetic and be able to open doors, but I would always know my right arm was gone.'

She thought about this reply, and decided it would have to do. For good or bad, Amos was never going to change. She put her hand on his thigh, and squeezed. It was a beautiful day, and the city was alive with activity – barbed-wire barriers coming down, building repairs, pedestrians streaming toward the Old City.

'I may be a gimp, but I guess I'm not a public menace,' Amos said, as he turned south on the Hebron Road.

'Where are we going?'

'Don't you think it's time you went to get your grandmother's candlesticks?'

'Oh,' she said, with neither enthusiasm nor reluctance.

She turned her head and watched the streets flash by as they sped through Talpiot. When they approached Bethlehem, a cheerful-looking IDF soldier waved them past a raised barrier, and they wound their way to the Etzion Bloc.

The road was narrow, convoluted, and full of holes. The Israelis had not had time to remove all of the 'dragon's teeth' – jags of concrete that the Jordanians had planted in the ground to obstruct the passage of tanks. The wayside was littered with damaged vehicles, but the rolling hills were as they had been almost twenty years ago, when she had last traveled this road, going in the opposite direction.

'What on earth is Israel going to do with all these Arabs?' She stared at a village in the distance.

'Would you rather they were all armed, with their own regular army, on the other side of the border?'

'They're going to be the excuse for the next war,' she said.

They came to a makeshift sign that pointed the way to Kfar Etzion. Amos slowed down as they passed the Lonely Tree at the fork in the road, but Tonia didn't ask him to stop. Neither of them spoke as they drove through what had been the gate. The area seemed deserted, except for a young man in a disheveled army uniform sitting on the ground nearby.

When they got out of the car, Tonia looked around, tears in her eyes. Three walls of one of the bungalows remained standing. Other than that, the destruction had been total. The Arabs had even dynamited the cisterns. Only eight or ten scraggly fir trees stood on the hilltop. Twenty thousand fruit trees and over a hundred thousand forest saplings had been uprooted. The Legion had razed all of the kibbutz buildings and put up Quonset huts for their own use.

'I think Neveh Ovadiah would have been right about here.' She took a few paces and kicked at the rubble. 'Oh, look, Amos, yes, this is where it was.'

A small section of its floor showed through the ruins. Using it to orient herself, she found the remains of the German Monastery. She stared at it, and Amos took her hand.

'This is where they found his body,' she said.

'I know.'

'I was almost glad they had the Bloc,' she said. 'So that Ima would never have to see this spot again.'

Amos limped back to the truck and took a shovel out of the back. 'Come on,' he said.

'Wait, just a minute.' Tonia was squinting at the young soldier sitting by the gate. 'Eran?'

She started walking toward him, now certain she recognized the little boy from Kfar Etzion who had come wandering to her guard post late one night, looking for his Ima and Abba.

When she drew close, she saw that he was crying. Large silent tears streaked his face.

'Eran?' she said again, more gently, and sat down on the ground next to him. 'I'm Tonia. Josef Shulman's daughter. My mother, Leah, used to take care of you.'

'I know. I remember you.' He nodded and wiped his eyes.

'Were you one of the soldiers who took the Bloc?'

'No.' He shook his head. 'I was in the Old City. I got my first leave today. I had to come here ... couldn't remember ...' His voice trailed off.

'It's difficult, I know.' Tonia's voice broke. She put an arm around him, and he allowed her to pull him close to her.

'It makes it even worse that they just ran away!' Eran said. 'I've talked to the guys who took the Bloc. It was empty! They walked right in. The Arab Legion was sitting here with warehouses full of arms and ammunition, but they ran away, didn't put up any kind of a fight!'

Tonia looked out at the hills. She didn't care what the Legion had or hadn't done. It didn't matter to her that they hadn't cared about holding on to this particular hill. At least no more young men had had to die trying to reclaim it.

'My father ...' Eran went on. 'I don't really remember him. He's just a picture in the album. He died here, fighting with his bare hands ...' He began crying again.

Tonia rocked him back and forth, trying to recall his father's face, the sleepy-eyed man who had opened the door to take Eran from her arms.

'Your father was a wonderful man,' she said. 'He loved you very much.' She fished a tissue from her pocket and handed it to him. Then she kissed his forehead and rose. 'Goodbye, Eran. I'm sure we'll meet again.'

The tree from which Tonia had paced off her hiding place had been torn from the ground, but the large, square boulder on which Amos had sat watching her was still there. Before he started digging, Amos paused and looked at her.

'I'm not sure we'll find anything,' he said. 'Before I left the Bloc for the last time I told your father where you had buried

441

those things. I thought he might want me take them to you and Leah in Jerusalem. If he did dig them up, your grandmother's candlesticks are probably in some Arab house in Hebron.'

She nodded, and he began wielding the shovel. An hour later, he was still digging.

'Sorry,' he said and sat down next to her to rest. 'I guess we're not going to find anything.'

'It doesn't matter,' she said. She grasped his damaged left hand in hers. 'They're only things. We might as well go home.'

'Let me have one last try. A little farther over this way.'

'I'll take a turn.' She rose and took the shovel from him. She dug for a long time, welcoming the physical exertion. Then the shovel thudded against something hard. 'Amos, I think there's something here.'

She handed him the shovel and stood aside while he removed the earth around the orange crate. The sack inside of it was moldy, but intact. She laid it on the ground and squatted. Her grandmother's candlesticks, black with tarnish, protruded from it. She reached inside for the small bag of jewelry and coins, but her fingers touched something else. She drew a folded sheet of stiff, yellowed paper from the sack and carefully opened it, laying it on the sack. The writing on it was faded, barely legible.

'Oh God, it's a letter. From my father,' she said hoarsely. She fell back to sit on the ground and burst into tears.

Amos dropped to his knees and put his arms around her, but she calmed herself, pulled away, and wiped her eyes.

'You read it to me.' She nodded at the letter. 'Please.'

He picked it up and read.

My Beloved Tonia,

Our situation seems hopeless, and I am afraid that this is where I may find my death, today or tomorrow.

What words can I say to you, child? How can I possibly tell you how I love you? How can I ask you to forgive me for leaving you fatherless in this world?

442

I can only pray that one day you will understand why I chose the path that I did. Why there could be no other.

I know your feelings. Your eyes accuse me. But you don't know how well I understand you. You had the right to expect an easier life – though God willed you for better things than ease. Few generations are privileged to take part in a miracle.

You think me mad, but someday you will understand that the world exists only by the grace of its madmen. That the true beauty of the world, of life, lies beyond what the cynics call reality. Had God in his infinite mercy not blessed Man with the illusion that he is more than an animal, he would be but a beast. Illusions have always given shape to the material.

So I cherish an illusion.

I am a stateless Jew, welcome in no land. The country of my birth is buried in the ashes of my family and my people. My new home is in flames and surrounded by those who wish only for our destruction. But before I die, I declare myself a free man, inheritor of nationhood.

The world that has trampled us into the dust will one day wonder at – and no doubt resent – our strength. The strength into which our mad illusions will forge themselves.

Would you, with the Gentiles, believe that we are too weak, too unworthy, to seize for ourselves a common destiny?

I know your fears. I share them. But this war will decide the fate of our nation for generations to come. How insignificant are our own petty fears and aspirations. You ask, 'But why us? Why should we be singled out to fight this battle?' Blind fate. The same blind fate that left us peacefully tending our orchards while our brothers died screaming for breath in the gas chambers.

My blood will seal your claim on this land. That is the inheritance I will to you and Rina and Natan and your children and your children's children.

My deepest love, your father

Josef Shulman

AUTHOR'S NOTE

The characters described in this book are fictional and in no way resemble actual personalities. There was no family in Kfar Etzion with adolescent children. However, the historical events described as taking place in Kfar Etzion are, to the best of my ability, accurately portrayed.

Immediately following the liberation of the Etzion Bloc in 1967 most of the children of the first settlers – now aged 18–24 – visited Kfar Etzion. They petitioned the government of Israel for the right to resettle their former home and were granted permission to do so. On September 27th, 1967, a convoy led by an armored car took them to the cemetery on Mount Herzl to visit the graves of their fathers. Then it continued south to the Etzion Bloc.

THE AUTHOR

Yael Politis grew up in Dearborn, Michigan and moved
to Israel in 1973. She graduated from the University of
Wisconsin, Madison and studied towards an MA at the Hebrew
University of Jerusalem.

She has held a number of positions, often to do with her talent
for writing and her knowledge of English and Hebrew. She has
translated a number of books and stories from Hebrew into
English.

The Lonely Tree, which won a YouWriteOn Book of the Year
award in 2009, is her debut novel.

More details are available from
www.hollandparkpress.co.uk/politis
and
http://yaelpolitis.wordpress.com

.

Holland Park Press is a unique publishing initiative. It gives contemporary Dutch writers the opportunity to be published in Dutch and English. We also publish new works written in English and translations of classic Dutch novels.

To
* Find out more
* Learn more about Yael Politis
* Discover other interesting books
* Practice your writing skills
* Read our unique Anglo-Dutch magazine
* Take part in discussions
* Or just make a comment

Visit

www.hollandparkpress.co.uk